MW01539020

Surviving in Africa

Marie Pierce Weber

authorHOUSE®

AuthorHouse™
1663 Liberty Drive
Bloomington, IN 47403
www.authorhouse.com
Phone: 1-800-839-8640

First published by AuthorHouse 8/31/2009

ISBN: 978-1-4389-9441-3 (sc)
ISBN: 978-1-4389-9442-0 (hc)

Library of Congress Control Number: 2009906012

Printed in the United States of America
Bloomington, Indiana

This book is printed on acid-free paper.

To my husband, Jack... always supportive!

To Mike Alft, “A friend in need – is a friend indeed!”

To the ‘Generous Souls’ who helped me along the way!

"Friend: One who knows all about you – and loves you just the same."   Elbert Hubbard

For my loyal ‘horse’ friends:

“There is something about the outside of a horse that is good for the inside of a man.” Anon

In Memory of Robert R. Rugel ~ Gentleman and Friend

Contents

1

Hope

Paula had been waiting outside the Douala Hotel since eight o'clock. The day had the usual morning mist, a result of the three hundred inches of rain (or more) on Mount Cameroon each year. Paula had never been good at waiting... it was a flaw in her character. After five minutes, she began to fret: what if I don't find them, then what? They can't save my life over and over and then just walk out of it! We didn't even say goodbye! How could they think that I would go home without saying anything to them? I was the one who asked them to meet me here! I wonder if they feel as bewildered as I do.

Tamubu had said to me, "I will be there for you as long as you need me." We had agreed on the beach before I left that: 'this can't be the end.' And he had agreed with me, knowing that I wanted to discuss our future. If only I hadn't forgotten it was a Leap Year, which made eleven days March 4th, not March 5th. If only they hadn't left right away... after Albert had told them, "Missy Paula went home to the States.' They don't know that I'm here now... only a few hours late. If only my messages hadn't gone astray... if only, if only... a defeatist's mantra.

I hate this horrible feeling of emptiness and disappointment, although I have the one hope: the carriage driver '...who drove them off...' yesterday morning according to the hotel manager, who then added: 'Ben is usually here most mornings, but he doesn't bring the carriage out in the rain.'

Paula's apprehension increased as she looked at the dark

lowering sky. She'd been waiting for the carriage for half an hour. What will I do if the carriage doesn't come today? They'll get so far ahead of me on their trek to Kenya that I'll never be able to catch up with them... even if I do find out which way they went.

Paula didn't analyze her need to be with Tamubu again, she just knew that this couldn't be the end; she had to find a way. If I have to–I'll just go to Kenya. But the thought didn't solve her problem. It could take three or four months for them to trek to Kenya... besides, how could I tell his parents that their first-born son, who was lost to them when he was ten, was alive... but they'd have to wait several months for him show up? No, I simply must find Tamubu now!

Her relief was intense, when she heard the clip-clop of shod hooves crossing the paving stones that surrounded the hotel.

Turning to the sound, she saw an elegant landaulet driven by a man in full livery: bright red jacket with gold epaulets, gold braid and brass buttons. He was magnificent in a shiny black top hat, black gloves and black trousers with a matching red stripe down the side. Beside him sat a diminutive boy in a darker red jacket with a sky-blue collar and sky-blue pants with a dark red stripe down the side. He wore, at a jaunty angle, a pillbox hat of red and sky-blue trimmed in gold braid.

The big Belgian horse had shiny black hooves, and was decked out in black patent leather harness inlaid with ivory conchos and bright brass fittings. The carriage was a glossy black with yellow spoked wheels, pinstriped in red and black. There was a large gold crest on the small door above the step. One almost expected to see the Queen sitting on the tufted red leather seats waving subtly to the crowds. The carriage stopped under the trees that surrounded the park-like circle in front of the hotel.

Paula hastened across to the driver and said, in French, "Good morning," giving him a charming smile. "My name is Paula Thornton. Mr. Pandi, at the hotel, tells me that you drove two of his guests when they left yesterday, Mr. Thomas Caulfield and his brother, Mr. Jon Caulfield. I was supposed to meet them here at the hotel yesterday, but I arrived late, and my messages had gone astray. Can you tell me where they have gone?"

Ben looked down at the pretty lady, who was stroking the flanks of his horse, and to his surprise, Goldy was responding to her touch. She was dressed for safari and was wearing a peculiar belt, with an empty holster for a gun and an empty sheath for a hunting knife–very odd. Then Ben noticed the red nylon cord around her neck, under her collar, and into her chest pocket. Thomas Caulfield, known as Tamubu, the Medicine Man of the Great Zuri Watu, had amused his son, Gomojo, with a story about a special whistle that could tell you which way to go in the forest, help you make a fire for your meal, and then help you eat it too. Gomojo had laughed a long time at such a foolish story.

The carriage driver said, "Miss, would you mind showing us what is attached to the cord around your neck and tucked into your shirt pocket?" He glanced at his son and gave him an almost imperceptible shake of his head.

Paula was astonished, but she needed to win this man's cooperation and said, "No, not at all." She lifted the flap and pulled out the red-barreled *5in1*.

"Would you be kind enough to demonstrate it for my son?"

Paula moved to the other side of the driver's seat next to Gomojo and lightly blew on the whistle for the young boy, whose eyes opened wide in anticipation. Then she showed him the compass where the needle pointed north. He watched the needle remain stationary, as she rotated the barrel until the needle touched the 'N'. She pointed to the 'E' and then to the rising sun and said, "Est." The small boy bobbed his head, smiled and said, "Oui." Then she unscrewed the compass head and took out a wooden match, which she struck on the metal rim of the carriage wheel. Replacing the compass head, she pulled the fork and spoon out of their slots in the red barrel and mimed eating.

The little boy laughed until tears ran from his eyes. His father looked at Paula and said, "It is our greatest of pleasures to meet you. Gomojo was told about your special whistle. He could not believe the story was true."

Paula was ready to cry herself, so great was her emotion that either Tamubu or Jon had shared a story about her *5in1* with this young lad.

"So, you do know where they have gone."

"Yes, we drove them east into the mountains, where the Medicine Man and his brother left for the Wahutu Village to get Kybo, who was visiting his cousin."

"Would you please drive me there now?"

"I can drive you there–but I would not leave you all alone in such a desolate place."

Feeling desperate, Paula reasoned with him: "If you gave them directions, you can give me directions. I am accustomed to traveling in the forest."

Gomojo tugged on his father's sleeve. Ben leaned down while Gomojo whispered in his ear. Ben smiled as he looked at Paula and said, "Gomojo would like to know if you are the Safi-Mitiriki?" (White Tree Goddess)

Paula smiled, feeling self-conscious, "I guess I am. That was Tamubu's name for me, when he first saw me, days before we met."

Gomojo tugged again on his father's sleeve. Ben again leaned over to hear what his shy son had to say. He turned to Paula with a broad smile. "Gomojo has offered to guide you to the Wahutu Village... if I can do without his services for a day or two."

Paula was stunned. This boy could not be more than seven years old and he was small for even that. "Gomojo, if your father can spare you, I would be pleased to have your help–of course I will pay you to guide me."

Ben beamed down on Paula. This woman truly was a Mitiriki, for only a goddess would have been so gracious about his tiny son's offer. This son, his only son, whom he loved above all things, had a congenital disorder that had inhibited his growth. While he looked to be about seven years old, he was actually twenty-five years old. He was so shy that he never talked to people. Ben was astonished that he had offered to guide Miss Thornton to the Wahutu village. Gomojo was not strong, he could not handle the team, but he was wiry and agile, smart and kind and loved the deep forest. It was where he spent his free time.

The Medicine Man of the Great Zuri Watu and his brother had, by their man-to-man demeanor with Gomojo, given him confidence in himself. Helping Miss Thornton could be a new beginning for him.

Ben looked kindly at Paula and said, "The Medicine Man of the Great Zuri Watu has already paid, many times over, for whatever help we can give you. He has given my mother respite from the constant pain of her knees. Whatever we can do for you, will be nothing compared to all he has done for us. Do you need help with your belongings?" Ben hoped she had packed lightly.

"No. I just have the one pack. I'll be back in a few minutes." Paula went into the hotel and spoke to Mr. Pandi about storing her suitcase. Mr. Pandi was quite pleased that Miss Thornton was going to meet her friends after all. He had felt that his reputation for impeccable service to his guests, and attention to every detail, had been sullied by the undelivered messages.

Ben opened the little door for Paula to board the carriage, saying, "We have to stop at home, so Gomojo can change his clothes and prepare a pack for the forest. I hope you don't mind. It won't take long." He then climbed into the driver's seat beside his son, picked up the reins and put Goldy into a smart trot–but the stalwart Belgian needed no urging–for this was the direction of home.

The village was southeast of Douala off the road to Edea. Paula showed Gomojo how to follow the direction of their travel, using the *5in1* compass and the map that Captain Jones had given her yesterday, when she'd gone back to the *Wind Drift to use the* marine radio to contact the *Just Cause.* Today, Paula left a message to be delivered to the *Wind Drift* and Captain Jones, telling him she was on her way to find Tamubu and Jon. She handed the message to Mr. Pandi, so she knew it would not get lost. She also gave him a letter for either Thomas or Jon Caulfield, should they come back to the hotel again.

While Gomojo changed and put a few things in a shoulder bag, Tirini, Ben's wife, made a basket lunch for them. Ben changed the patent leather harness for the plain leather working harness. Goldy would work up a sweat in the foothills, which he rarely did in town.

Ben had a spacious lot at the edge of the native village. In addition to the hut and vegetable garden, there was a small thatched-roof stable for two horses, with a lean-to for the carriage. Near the paddock, where another Belgian grazed, there was a forge under a high tin roof with a dray in a lean-to behind it.

Harnessed again, Goldy showed his reluctance to leave home for a second time in the same day with a shortened and hesitant stride. After Ben turned him onto the road leading away from Douala, Goldy became, once again, enthusiastic in his work. Ben leaned towards Gomojo and said something to him. Gomojo flushed, but turned to face Paula saying, "Goldy likes the country roads better than the city streets."

Paula agreed with Gomojo by saying, "I'll bet he likes to get going and keep going, instead of having to stop and start all the time."

Gomojo replied, "Yes, that is true." He further surprised his father by adding, "Your French is very good. Do you speak it often?"

Paula knew her French was rusty, but was pleased by the kindness and replied, "Not as often as I would like."

Gomojo sat smiling, while Ben marveled at the sudden change in his son. Tirini had been so excited by Gomojo's offer to guide the lady that she said she would clean the fancy harness for him, which was Gomojo's job each evening.

BEN HAD WORKED ALL his adult life as Coachman for the Comtesse DuVries, until the Comtesse became bed-ridden with disease.

When the Comtesse reduced her staff, she allowed his mother, to retire to the seaside cottage, which Maybella loved so dearly, as caretaker. She gave Ben the draft horses and carriage, so he would have a way to earn a living.

When the Comtesse DuVries died, her son sold the African Estate, with all furnishings, through lawyers and estate dealers. But, he was obliged to come for the funeral as his mother, the Comtesse, wished to be buried in the grassy lea next to the seaside cottage, not in the family vaults in France.

The seaside cottage had been wrongly included in the Count's estate; for it was her property, bought with her money. She had used her money to build the Cotswold style cottage on the property. In her will she left the cottage and the cemetery property to Ben and his family as caretakers, in perpetuity, with her attorney as advisor. She also endowed the cemetery with a small income for perpetual care.

Her contrivance annoyed her son, who was a snob of the first order, but he was unable to find anyone who would testify that his mother was in her dotage and didn't know what she was doing. She knew! How well she knew.

Ben missed the dignified and serene Comtesse. She had been a part of their lives for more than thirty years. Each week he went to the cottage with supplies for his mother, and always took flowers to put in the marble vase between the wings of the marble angel, who sat atop the marble headstone reading a book about horses.

Ben felt a tugging on his sleeve. Gomojo pointed to a wide area at the side of the road, where a rivulet of spring water gushed out of the mountainside under a big old sepele tree. Ben had been so engrossed in his reminiscent thoughts that he hadn't even noticed arriving at the trailhead to the Wahutu village.

Goldy had managed to keep up a brisk pace with a load several hundred pounds lighter than it had been yesterday, for his full brother Sunny, who took the Medicine Man and Jon to the trailhead.

Gomojo went to pull grass for Goldy while Ben put Paula's lunch on a tray, which he served in the carriage. He and

Gomojo sat on the ground under the tree, near the head of the tethered horse.

After her meal, Paula went to sit with Ben, who began to give her directions, when Gomojo said, "There is a faster way, father. In less than an hour's walk, there is a trail that goes over the hillside and leads directly to the Wahutu Village."

"Why didn't you mention this trail to the Medicine Man and his brother?"

"I did not want to gainsay you, father."

"Thank you for your respect, my son. I shall leave Miss Thornton's safety in your capable hands. When do you expect to reach the village?"

"We will be there before dusk, father."

"When do you expect to return to the trailhead?"

"I will be back at the trailhead tomorrow at noon. I will not stay to visit as you will need my help."

Gomojo rose, as did Ben and Paula. After brief good-byes and many thanks, Paula followed Gomojo into the forest.

Ben gave Goldy a good drink before he replaced the bit. He then checked the harness: following each shaft back, checking the saddle, bellyband-girth and breeching before he picked the horse's hooves. All the time Ben was thinking about the startling change in his son. He had talked more today than any other day of his life. What had wrought such a change? It was an enigma.

The Wahutu Village

GOMOJO MOVED DOWN THE trail almost as fast as Tamubu did. Paula's ankle began to throb and ache. As much as it galled her, she said to him, "You walk very fast; much too fast for a woman to keep up with you."

Gomojo turned to her, smiled and said, "Forgive me; I'm usually alone when I'm in the forest. Do you need to rest?"

"No, I just need to slow down a bit."

"The trail is easy to see here. You lead and I will follow. Then I will know the speed to travel when I lead again." Paula took the lead and a few minutes later Gomojo said, "You have a sore ankle. You should have told me. There is a spring not far ahead where you can soak it. It is beginning to swell."

Paula was surprised by his keen observation and replied, "Yes, a short soak would be good; and then I'll bandage it for support."

Gomojo led her to the spring, perplexed that a woman with a bad ankle would choose to go on a long trek, with the Medicine Man of the Great Zuri Watu, his aide, Kybo and his brother, Jon. After the cooling soak and the application of Tamubu's homeopathic paste, an Ace bandage, and a few aspirin, Paula managed to keep up without comment.

The trail through the forest was well-used and easy to travel–akin to walking in a wide green tunnel that was lit by sporadic shafts of sunlight. The trail over the hillside was narrow but shaded by trees; it was built with walking in mind, and for rain run-off in the hairpin turns. Gomojo was a considerate leader; he stopped often, but not for long.

He came across a fallen branch and trimmed off the foliage

to make a walking stick for her. It was just what she needed, for it gave her sore ankle support, and allowed her to push her way up the often-steep hill.

As the day lengthened, the forest thinned and the village appeared below nestled on a wide flat plateau. Soon, warriors came from the village to greet them. Whatever it was Gomojo said to them, it was magic. In a trice, a native had taken her backpack to carry, while two others made a litter, from a kitamba and their spears, to carry her to the village.

A WHITE WOMAN ARRIVING on a litter caused a stir in the village. This must be someone very important for the warriors to carry her thus. By the time Paula and Gomojo reached the center of the village and the lanai, where the Elders were gathered, a crowd was following them.

Gomojo went up to the covered platform and spoke to the Elders seated there. Chief Kuteka arose and signaled the men to bring Paula to the lanai. A hush overcame the crowd. This woman must be a very special person: the Chief has risen and the Elders have asked her to sit with them.

Gomojo said to Paula in French, "I told the Elders that you were held in great esteem by the Medicine Man of the Great Zuri Watu and that he referred to you as a Safi-Mitiriki. I will translate for you."

Paula was perplexed by the deference, and said to Gomojo. "I just want to find Tamubu, Jon and Kybo, so I can join them. Will you tell them that?"

"Yes, but the day is gone. You need rest. We must first be proper guests. It would be considered rude not to follow tradition. We must introduce ourselves and drink a bit of palm wine. Then the women will take you to wash and change and rest. Later, we will partake of food and drink. Then the Elders will question you and I will translate for you and for them. An important guest must be treated with respect. Your visit, because it is unusual, will become a story to be told for generations. No courtesy can be omitted or the story will lose its importance."

Paula thought: I wonder if my visit to these people will

become a story like 'Emula', Tamubu's legendary story about the little clubfoot girl. With that thought, her anxiety evaporated–what will be... will be. She listened as Gomojo chatted with the Elders. She was offered palm wine or lemon-water, and chose the water.

When the greetings were finished, and they arose to leave, Paula turned to Gomojo and said, "I'm concerned that Tamubu and Jon will get so far ahead of me that I'll never be able to catch up to them–or become hopelessly lost trying."

Gomojo smiled broadly with a twinkle in his eyes, as he glanced at the woman waiting to escort Paula to her rest. Paula was perplexed by his reaction to her comment. "You must be patient," he replied. "Runners have already been dispatched to catch up with the Medicine Man and his party. He will be told you are here."

Paula was stunned. When did that happen? Then she remembered that one man from the escort party had gone on ahead. Had Gomojo told him of her quest?

Paula followed the waiting woman to a tidy hut where there was hot water in a leather basin and soap sticks and small towels–real towels. A good wash would feel wonderful. Paula rummaged in her pack and brought out clean clothes. As soon as she took off her soiled clothes, her hostess gathered them up and took them away. The loss of her clothes concerned her not at all, for she looked forward to becoming a part of a legend. They wouldn't steal the clothes of a legend, would they?

When her ablutions were finished, the woman pointed to a pallet covered with a gorgeous leopard skin and gestured for her to lie down and rest. It was not a bad idea. The five-hour walk had been the most continuous exercise she had had in weeks and, in truth, she did feel tired. It was only moments before she was asleep.

The drums roused Paula from her slumber. She saw her hostess standing at the opening to the hut and noticed that the long African dusk was almost gone. The woman beckoned with her hand for Paula to follow her back to the lanai, which now contained a long table with fat candles guttering down the center. The woman led her to a place at the table and departed. The village resembled the Ndezi village. There were cooking pots in front of most of the huts, but the fires had gone to embers indicating that the meal had been removed from the pots and eaten. This surprised her... did I sleep through dinner?

There came a voice at her shoulder. "The Elders have delayed their dinner hour so you could rest; you must thank them for their consideration when they arrive. I will translate for you. But be aware, the Elders are wily. It is possible that they understand some French, so you must be careful in what you say. They are easily offended."

Paula asked Gomojo, "It looks like everyone else has had their meal, is that so?"

"Yes. After the Elders arrive, the village people will gather around the outside of the lanai to listen to your talk with the Elders. It is a tradition with guests of distinction–for the villagers to hear your story as you speak it to the Elders is a special treat."

Paula wondered how she had become so important. Then she remembered that Gomojo had told them she was a Safi-Mitiriki, a tree goddess, which had been Tamubu's pet name for her. It made her think: I have a great responsibility here. I must live up to my pet name and the people's expectations. I will be the radio, movies and TV of the village, their 'Gone with the Wind', their 'Old Man and the Sea'.

The drums interrupted her thoughts. Gomojo arose and Paula followed his example. He smiled at her thinking. She does not have to work at being regal–it is a natural part of her demeanor. The Elders arrived with two young men bearing torches to light their path. They were dressed in their finest red kitambas; the edges of which were decorated with intricate brass-wired-bead-work in complex patterns inlaid with ivory. Their headdresses were as ornate as any she had ever seen, with brass wire woven for the base of the feathers and interspersed with the teeth and claws of large carnivores.

Paula was glad she had added a brightly colored scarf to dress up her khaki shirt, and had worn her birthstone aquamarine earrings and ring. The scarab bracelets came from Egypt and were reported to have been favorites of Queen Cleopatra. It was only at the last moment that she had tucked these few items in the hidden compartment of her backpack thinking: if I need them, I'll have them... if not, the extra six ounces won't make much of a difference.

ONCE SEATED, THE ELDERS began their meal without preamble. Paula followed Gomojo's lead, eating when he ate, drinking when he drank. She did not want to offend or lose stature with poor table manners. At first, she was a little tense, but the palm wine soon relaxed her and she began to enjoy this most unusual experience–that of becoming a legend!

There was little talk during the meal, except when asked if she wanted more stew; or if the meal was to her liking; or had she had palm wine before? Once finished, the table and low three-legged stools were removed and a brazier was placed in the center of the lanai. Women appeared with armfuls of animal skins and placed them in a circle around the brazier. During the set change, which took only moments, the diners washed their hands as they had done before the meal, in teak bowls of minted lemon water.

GOMOJO LED HER TO a place where they sat, with their backs to the hut attached to the lanai. The Elders arranged themselves in a semi-circle opposite. This gave the best view of her to the villagers, who came and sat on the ground around the open lanai.

The Chief spoke: It was a greeting, which Paula understood. Then he continued.

Gomojo translated, "The Chief has asked what brought you to Africa?"

Paula replied, "I came with a group to study plants." When translated, this clearly pleased the Elders.

"What kind of plants do you study?"

"Plants that heal the body." This too, seemed to gratify them.

"Why are you not with your group?"

"I became separated from them by a huge ocean wave, called a tsunami." The 'oohs' and 'aahs' from Elders and villagers alike, assured Paula that this indeed was going to be a great legend.

"How were you saved from such a disaster?"

"I was alone aboard a sailboat that was being carried by a huge ship, called a tanker. When the wave struck, the empty tanker rose on the crest of the wave, a heeled over on her anchors, and the sailboat was tossed from the deck of the tanker into the trough behind the wave and carried far out to sea by the massive ebb tide. Days later, the sailboat was deposited by the unusual high tides into a land-locked cove north of Douala. I was unable to sail away, back to my group."

After Gomojo translated, there was a long silence. Paula feared they did not understand about the huge wave, or the deep-sea seismic disturbances that changed the tides–so her explanation had made no sense to them.

Then the Chief spoke: "It is clear that the gods look after you. Those that the gods protect are not to be questioned by mere Elders. We hope we have not offended you with our ignorance. Our people would be honored to hear your story, if you would share it with us."

Gomojo added, "Tell your story in short sentences if you can. I will translate each sentence when you finish. I will hold my walinka up while I am translating. I will drop it to my lap when I am finished. Will that work for you?"

"Yes, but what story do they want to hear?"

"Just what they asked–how you came to be in Africa–here in their village."

Paula asked, "Do they have coffee? The palm wine has made me sleepy."

Gomojo translated her request and a flurry of activity ensued.

While the coffee was being prepared, Paula said to the Elders through Gomojo, "I would be pleased to share my story with the noble Wahutu people; for Kybo, to whom I owe a debt, has a cousin married into this tribe."

Smiles appeared on the faces she could see and a few people patted a lovely young woman on the shoulders and back–this must be Nishani–whom she had not yet met.

The coffee arrived, with powdered coconut (used for sweetener) and coconut milk and a four-inch long vanilla bean, used for stirring, which imparted a hint of flavor, making the coffee a taste treat. Paula said, 'Uhmm' to show the woman she liked it. The audience smiled at her pleasure. Sitting the hardened gourd-cup down, she began:

"Several days after I was stranded in the cove, I went ashore to gather plant specimens, and was captured by six natives.

"These natives, the Ndezi, took me seven days inland through the mountains.

"I was to be a trophy wife for their Chief." A great uptake of breath let Paula know that this had shocked them.

"The day after we reached the Ndezi Village, the traders Max Mason and Jon Caulfield arrived.

"The traders were sent to tell me of my fate, but once they heard my story, Max Mason tried to obtain my release from Bolbonga, the Ndezi Chief.

"He was unable to dissuade the Chief from his intent.

"After the trading, Max and Jon were escorted back to their camp. I never talked to them again.

"That evening, I was forced into ritual combat with the Chief's first wife–for status in his household.

"I managed to best Kira with a surprise gymnastic move, but I knew my well-being was still in great peril.

"In the small hours of the night, I escaped through the smoke hole in the roof of my prison, into the trees.

"I fled for days through the trees leaving no trail for the Ndezi to follow." Cheers and warbling followed the translation, and Paula smiled at her audience.

"Tamubu, the Medicine Man of the Great Zuri Watu, first saw me as I came through the trees. It made him think of me as a Safi-Mitiriki.

"Tamubu later told me that the Ndezi stopped searching

for me, because they felt they were tracking a Bahariki who had great powers during the full moon, and they feared reprisal.

"I wished I had known that sooner! Traveling through the trees was slow, difficult and great work." The audience smiled and some tittered.

"Tamubu was intrigued by my traveling in the trees. He followed me to the foothills below the high savanna, where I strolled into an area of lion dens.

"Rounding a curve in the trail, I came face-to-face with a huge female lion, crouched and ready for the attack. I had no weapons, but a knife.

"I knew I could never win a fight with this huge beast, but I also knew I shouldn't run. Terror helped to hold me immobile.

"I reached into my shirt pocket for my whistle, for wild animals often fear strange loud noises... when a pistol was fired. The lioness ran off into the bush.

"At the report, I threw myself into some thorny scrub until Tamubu appeared, and helped me to my feet, saying, 'Do you always throw yourself into the lion's mouth? How have you been able to survive doing that?'"

Paula was pleased by the laughter. If she knew one thing and only one thing about the natives, it was that they liked to laugh and loved a pun, or a phrase with a double meaning.

"Only later, did I learn that the female lion I saw had two accomplices stalking me in the scrub, right where I threw myself at the pistol report."

Again, the laughter pleased her.

"He told me to go quickly and climb a nearby oak tree.

"I no sooner gained the lofty branches when the angry lioness returned with her two young hunting companions.

"My friend was caught. He was flanked on three sides by hungry carnivores.

"Suddenly, he gave a fierce battle cry and attacked the once again crouched lioness with his spear.

"His action startled the huge beast out of her killing crouch, which was just the few seconds he needed to use his

spear to pole-vault to the top of a huge bolder, where he leapt for the limbs of the oak tree."

Paula saw the rapt expressions on the sea of faces. She was glad she had included the details of the lion confrontation, for her listeners.

"Seeing her dinner escaping, the huge lion was atop the boulder in two bounds.

"She sprang to the tree to snag Tamubu with her terrible claws, just as I leaned down, grabbed his wrist and yanked him out of her reach."

Again, sudden high warbling and cheers erupted from the listeners; even the Elders forgot their dignity for a moment, and smiled, showing teeth.

"Seated in the upper branches of the old oak tree, Tamubu and I became acquainted.

*"Later, after the lions had gone off to hunt other non-tree-climbing meals, (*another little titter came from the listeners*) Tamubu took me to a high ledge, attainable only by climbing a dead tree.*

"There, we made camp. There, I asked him for his help to get back to the cove. There, he agreed to help me.

"We traveled back to the cove for two weeks. During that time we encountered an enraged and nasty bull ape on a narrow mountain trail.

"I stepped back at his sudden appearance in front of me, and twisted my ankle between some rocks.

"Later, while hobbling along on crutches, I stepped through matted foliage, and fell down a steep cliff.

"I was unconscious when Tamubu found me and took me to a native traveling hut, where he cared for me.

"As I lay recuperating, Jon Caulfield, one of the traders who had come to the Ndezi village, found me resting under the roof overhang of the traveling hut.

"Jon had given up his trading venture to search for me, after he heard I had escaped from the Ndezi.

"He feared I did not have the ability to survive all alone in the wilds of Africa.

"The beach, where the yacht was anchored, was only a day's hike from the traveling hut.

"But it took us two days to reach it, for I was unable to walk on the hills.

"Jon had brought five men with him, and between them, they carried me back to the cove.

"We arrived in the late afternoon to find the cove empty–the yacht gone.

"The next day, while Tamubu was out gathering, he came across a Fulani lad who had injured his foot, and it was now badly infected.

"The injured boy and his three friends were out on their manhood trials. The injured boy could not accept help from his tribe or family, without disgrace, so Tamubu and I cared for him.

"His friends stayed with us too; and worked at gathering wood and collecting food to repay us for his care.

"Then, my parents arrived from America on a beautiful motor yacht, which made six more of us on the beach.

"At dinner, one evening, there were seventeen of us... almost enough people to start our own village." The Wahutu laughed happily at the irony.

"All we lacked were women who knew how to build huts." This sent them into gales of laughter; even the elders needed long moments to compose themselves.

"My parents had learned that the sailing yacht was found and taken from the cove where I had been marooned.

"Knowing me well, they knew I would do my best to return to the yacht.

"They came to Africa to be there for me when I returned to the empty cove.

"Two days later, Captain Jones, the skipper of the Wind Drift, took us to Douala; except for Kybo who stayed behind with Tamubu and Jon to tend to the injured boy, for he was not yet well.

"Before I left, Tamubu and I agreed to meet again in Douala in eleven days, on March 5th. I had forgotten about Leap Year, so eleven days was March 4th.

"My parents and Jon's men disembarked in Douala to fly home.

"Captain Jones took me to Port-Gentil, where I resigned from the plant-finding Expedition.

"The next day, we went up river to Lambaréné to visit Dr. Albert Schweitzer, taking four missionaries with us, who were to study with the venerable teacher.

"On my return to Port-Gentil, I stayed in a Guest House.

"Captain Jones had business to finish before he could return to Douala.

"When I had not arrived at the hotel, or sent a message in eleven days, Jon radioed the Expedition yacht in Port-Gentil.

"Albert told Jon I had gone home, back to the States.

"I had sent two messages, one for Jon and one for Tamubu, but both went missing. I would have been better off with drums!" More delighted laughter.

"I had not gone back to America. I was on my way to meet them; but I arrived a half-day after they were gone.

"Ben and Gomojo brought me here to the village of the Wahutu, where Jon and Tamubu came to fetch Kybo, and start their long journey to Kenya.

"I am grateful to the Wahutu and the Elders for your help and your hospitality. Shukrani."

A MOMENT LATER, THERE was great native cheering and the high-pitched warbling, which was their way of clapping.

Gomojo said, "You did very well, they were quite pleased."

Later, in a light cotton nightshirt under the soft blanket, Paula snuggled atop the leopard skin, drifting off just as her senses noted that the hut had a pleasant odor of vanilla... a scent she had not noticed earlier.

3

A Messenger

BONOMO, THE WAHUTU SCOUT, stayed with Tamubu, Jon and Kybo, until they reached the end of the Wahutu hunting lands, which made the miles seem like a walk in the park. Before Bonomo left them he said, "Travelers are usually welcome in most villages; but tribesmen need the approval of the drums to cross neighboring lands. Beware, there are marauders that come up the river at night after the hippos climb the riverbanks to feed. They raid the villages, taking older children to sell as slaves. You must beware of these foul pillagers. They have no humanity at all."

Manutu had already warned Tamubu about traveling near the rivers. He had also said, "The drums will tell of your passage, so be prepared for supplicants asking you to come and help their loved ones. This is the most difficult part of traveling for a healer–when you have to refuse people needing help–so go in quiet, or you will never complete your journey." Remembering Manutu's admonitions Tamubu had asked for a scout to lead them, and for the Wahutu drums to remain silent.

The trail was unusual, wide and open, probably made by the pygmy elephants that inhabited the area. While the pygmy elephant is only about six and a half feet at the shoulder, with small tusks, they are known to be quite aggressive. The side trails too, were wide if a little overgrown, indicating they were probably not paths to the river. They came to a small grassy clearing, which was a salt lick–judging by the deep narrow grooves below the grassy area. Here they ate a late lunch and had a short rest.

Later, the trail closed in, which indicated the pygmy elephants had not yet feasted on the new growth, and might soon return. These narrow trails were haunts for carnivores as they gave the prey almost no warning.

In the dimness of late dusk, they found an open space that had been used for camping before, as the area was almost completely surrounded by a thorn boma. Spring water had formed a large puddle, but when examined for spoor showed no traces of carnivores drinking, just the small creatures of the rainforest.

"It's this place or the trees. What do you think? Jon? Kybo?"

"Yes, Kigozi, it will do." Kybo replied. "I will go and fetch some wood." Jon looked around, keeping an eye out for comfort, saying, "A fire might keep the animals away, but what about the creepy-crawlies?"

Tamubu laughed, "I can see that you are going to be a great bother to me on this trip. It is not too late for you to return to Douala and fly home."

Jon was not at all put off and replied, "I was just thinking we might find a place where I could set up my string hammock and still not burn down the forest."

Tamubu looked around. Jon was right. All the growth here was new, and would not support a hammock... and the ground was a bit stony.

He said, "Clear a space big enough for the three of us to sleep. Place the rocks in a circle around the edge of the cleared space. We will set a ring of fires just beyond the rocks. That will keep out the creepy-crawlies."

Jon jumped up saying, "Spot on!" and went about the task enthusiastically.

When Kybo returned to see Jon at his labors, he raised his eyebrow and asked, "Do you want me to find some thick leaves for pallets?"

Without even looking up from his search for the smallest stone, Jon replied, "That would be super, Kybo!" Tamubu caught Kybo's look and just shook his head and smiled. Kybo had become used to Jon's little quirks while they were on the trail searching for Miss Thornton; and while he would never admit it, Kybo too, liked a bit of comfort on the trail.

Sitting on a thick pallet of leaves after dinner, Jon watched Tamubu prepare the food they would eat tomorrow, at the noonday rest. Kybo had gone out to find small branches and twigs for the circle of fires before it was totally dark. Jon's mood was pensive as he thought: Maybe I have not given this trek proper consideration. I had pictured myself the center of attention in a native village each night, sleeping safely in a hut, out of the rain, and away from foraging animals... the way it had been with Max. His forest camps had tents with soft cots and sentries, as did the base camps. A native village is close enough to comfort to suffice, but this–roughing it–for three months... maybe more... and there's always the unexpected... I don't know; this could get to be a dreadful bore!

Tamubu picked up on his thoughts, as Jon was transmitting clearly, as he used to do when he was a small boy, and unsure of himself or his surroundings.

Unbidden, a picture of Paula preparing pallets on rocky cliffs and in the clefts of boulders on the ground, with never a word about the creepy-crawlies, came to mind. She had enjoyed the trekking back to the beach. Her only complaint had been sleeping in the dank and airless traveling huts the natives built along the trail. Outside with the creepy-crawlies was fine with her. Tamubu had steeled himself not to ponder Paula's unknown reasons for not returning to Douala, but all the self-control in the world did not dictate to the heart–and he was truly heartsick.

Tamubu arose with a cup of broth laced with kimmea, (an herb that relieves anxiety) and went to sit beside Jon. "Here, drink this. We will be fine here tonight. I don't think it will rain, but we can set up the radio tent if you like."

Jon jumped up, "I forgot we had that–Kybo was carrying it. Neato, I'll set up the radio tent!" In a flash, Jon had sorted through the gear and had the tent out. In a few minutes, the small tent covered half of the pallet space–no matter, Tamubu would sleep in the trees nearby. It was what he did on the trail–and he liked it that way.

Kybo returned with his kitamba slung over his shoulder, filled with sticks, to see the little tent covering most of the prepared sleeping space. Kybo glanced at Tamubu, who shook his head slightly, before he smiled back at Kybo's knowing resignation.

The Wahutu scouts found the remnants of the camp the next day. The returning scout, Bonomo, had met and joined with the messengers to show them the trails taken, which enabled them to travel faster. When the messengers traveled with urgency, nights were always spent in the trees, wrapped in their kitambas. They rarely lit cooking fires, eating a prepared trail mix of dried meat, dried fruits, ground grains and nuts, which they mixed with water to make a cold gruel. It was not uncommon for them to travel for days eating nothing more.

Tamubu, Jon and Kybo were not traveling for speed, so they took the time for a hot breakfast of oatmeal, with bananas and coffee. Jon loved coffee. When he found Kybo could make coffee as good as Motozo's, he had bought a thermos so none of it went to waste.

Late in the afternoon, they came to the Nyong River. The plan was to follow the almost due east course of the river to Sembe where they could renew their supplies. Following a river meant daytime travel only and little hacking through vegetation. But the trail would be fraught with critters, especially crocodiles and snakes. The carnivores would stalk the prey animals that came to drink in the mornings and evenings; but most of the animals would shy away from a group of men, their feared enemies.

At a rest stop on a high path beside the rain-swollen river, Jon became engrossed watching the hippos frolicking in the river below–yawning with their huge gaping maws to display their long, sharp, stump–like tushes. Tamubu took the opportunity to slip away to *roam*. He did not intend to be gone long. He had the feeling they were being followed and wanted to make sure they were not being stalked for a nighttime attack.

You could not have surprised him more, when he came upon the small party of Wahutu scouts, who were following their trail. He shadowed them until the leader said. "We should find them soon. These tracks are very fresh. Let's pick up the pace."

Tamubu immediately returned and found Jon and Kybo still absorbed in watching one of nature's most engrossing spectacles–mating hippos.

Tamubu stood behind them, like he'd always been there, when Jon said, "Where did you go?" Caught! Jon was becoming watchful.

Tamubu replied, "Am I going to have to inform you of every excursion into the bushes for privacy?"

"Oh." Jon muttered, somewhat chagrined. Then he said brightly, "I wish Paula was here with her camera. This is quite a show!" I left my camera with Max, wanting to travel as lightly as possible. I should have bought another when we were in Douala, but I didn't think of it."

The day was lengthening but no one wanted to leave the wild splashing and plunging below. It was like watching sounding whales... fascinating. A half hour later, the show began to change. After wild leaping and splashing, a bull would let out an awesome bellow and submerge to reappear down river. He would let out another roar and dive again to show up elsewhere. In the meantime, the serviced cows moved upstream to the shallower water, rejoining the other cows with calves. Yet the bull still bellowed, and raced around looking for enemies–mostly other mature bulls.

Tamubu said, "The male hippo is the most dangerous animal in Africa, killing more people than any other beast. Bulls will kill for the pure joy of it, sometimes killing his own offspring when remating with the cow. See those steep wide gullies over there on the other side of the river? They are hippo grooves; formed when they come out of the water at night to feed on grasslands, which are sometimes several miles away.

Hippos look slow and clumsy, but they are quite fast on land and can run a man down."

"Kigozi, I think people come, Kybo said. Let us move into the brush."

Tamubu knew it was the Wahutu, and replied, "They are making too much noise to have bad intentions Kybo, don't you think?"

Kybo replied, "Maybe so, but I'd rather be in the bushes when they get here." Jon wasn't going to debate the point. He was already headed toward the greenery.

A few moments later, the Wahutu appeared. Seeing fresh tracks going into the brush, Pimio called: "We have a message for the Medicine Man of the Great Zuri Watu."

Tamubu stepped from behind the tree. "Bonomo, we left you yesterday morning. What are you doing here?"

"Gubu and Pimio have an important message for you. I came back to show them the way–to make sure you received your message."

Gubu stepped forward and said, "The lady you call Safi-Mitiriki is now a guest in our village. What are your wishes?"

Tamubu was stunned. His chest grew tight with emotion. He took a deep breath. He could not believe his ears. Jon and Kybo had grins, ear to ear, but did not want to be rude and interfere with the delivery of the message. When he had control of his voice, Tamubu said, "Please continue."

"The lady arrived with Gomojo in the evening of the day you left. Gomojo said you would want to know this information right away, so the Chief bade us catch up to you. What would you have us do?"

Tamubu's mind was spinning. How had she enticed Gomojo to lead her to the Wahutu village? Where had she been if she had not gone home to the States? Why had she not left a message for him, or for Jon?

Tamubu said to Jon, "I must return to the Wahutu village. What will you do?"

Jon said, "I won't speak for Kybo, but I go where you go."

Tamubu and Jon looked at Kybo who said, "If we make a camp at the top of this slope tonight, away from the hippos and drinking carnivores, I could stay there with all the gear, for a few days. Traveling lightly, you could be back in the Wahutu village in a day, and back here in two or three days, not long. But it is for you to decide, Kigozi."

Tamubu liked Kybo's plan; it was the fastest way to return to the Wahutu village. "Yes, Kybo, that's what we'll do." He turned to the Wahutu scouts and said, "We will find a good place to camp tonight and leave at first light." The scouts agreed.

They found a good campsite about half a mile from the river, high on a bluff overlooking a dry rift. In a heavy rain, the rift would carry the water away from the bluff. It was a good camping spot. The large trees gave shade and safety from carnivores except, of course, the leopard. A man might go higher in a tree than a leopard with its greater weight, but man moved like a sloth in comparison. There were always perils in the deep rainforest, and the agile-like-a-squirrel leopard was really the least of them.

Once settled, Tamubu made a stew for dinner, using vegetables he had gathered while walking. A little dried meat, boiled to give flavor, onions, elephant ear, sweet potatoes and a large squash. He made biscuits from farina, ground coconut and bananas, which he baked on flat rocks covered by coconut shells. He needed to keep busy. Manutu had taught him patience in all things, but the training had not covered controlling his heart's desire.

First light saw them on the trail. Tamubu set a challenging pace, but Jon was fit and determined to keep up. At the lunch stop, Tamubu combined the trail mix with a green powder and rolled it in a pancake, saying it would help them breathe deeper. No nap was taken, just a rest while they chewed and drank. Light, even at noon, was valuable for speed, and the tunnel-like trails made by the pygmy elephants gave good cover from the brutal sun. At this pace, they would arrive back at the Wahutu village before the long dusk ended.

The next morning, Gomojo brought Nishani to Paula's hut for

an introduction. He stayed to translate while Paula served Nishani a cup of tea with cookies. Nishani, like many native women, was shy; but Paula was so relaxed and friendly that soon Nishani was talking of her three small children and of seeing Kybo again. The visit ended when Gomojo said he must leave for the trailhead. Paula felt lonely when Nishani was gone. Left to her own amusement, she walked about the village. Wherever she went, the women welcomed her and, in sign language, tried to explain what they were doing.

Paula then spent the remainder of the morning bringing her diary up-to-date. She had been so busy with her correspondence that she had made no entries since leaving the Guest House in Port-Gentil. She finished just as lunch was served to her in the little hut: fruit, thin pancakes and a gelatinous mass that tasted like boiled leaves and coconut. After a long and restful nap, Paula went out, and again wandered around the village. She was always greeted with smiles, and welcomed with gestures and simple words, some of which she understood. Even the men were tolerant and used pantomime to explain what they were doing.

She watched them carving wood and making weapons; the women weaving cloth, making bead work appliqué and other lovely hand crafts. She watched the small children playing with unique toys, and was amused by the antics of the young boys. One boy stood on his hands, feet wavering in the air. Another boy tried to copy him, but always fell over backwards. Paula signed to him that she would show him how to gain his balance. But the boy was shy and shook his head. The other boy, who had done the handstand, pointed his finger and made fun of him. He was acting the bully and his ridicule annoyed Paula. She despised a bully... of any age. Using sign language, she told them she would show them how to do it. The bullyboy was again rude and jeered at her too, really provoking her ire.

Without a moments notice or preparation, Paula took one step and did an aerial, into another aerial (making certain to land on her good foot first) on the second step after landing, she did a handspring into a back flip and after landing, (again on her good foot) did a handstand, first on two hands, then on one hand, back on two hands and a leg split, before returning to a perfect handstand and walking four steps on her hands before dropping into a dive roll to end up standing on her feet. The whole routine took less than a minute. She turned to the boys and bowed before walking away. She heard them running away and calling out to the adults and thought. What's the good of being a Safi-Mitiriki, if you can't put a bullyboy in his place?

The day was coming to a close; the cooking fires had been lit; dinner would soon be served. She would go back and study again the plant descriptions that Tamubu had written beside the drawings in her diary. Each pencil drawing was exquisite and the uses and formulations for each medicinal plant were complete. She missed Gomojo, with his kind bonhomie and insightful translations.

Wandering past the animal pens, she stopped to watch the goats being milked, and to pet the adorable newborn kids.

Arriving at her hut, Paula found a group of women and the two boys waiting for her. She smiled and thought. I'll bet the women think the boys are making up stories about me. The women all smiled back at her. One woman, different looking from the others, stepped forward and said, "I speak French. I am Rosata from Douala, married to Ovidio. These boys are saying you turn in the air and walk on your hands.

"Before they are thrashed or worse for lying, their mothers came to me and asked me to find out if what they say is true or not."

Paula went to the bully boy and said, "What's this boy's name?"

"He is called Sabuno. Why do you ask?"

"He is rude and a bully. What's this boy's name?" She laid her hand on the shy boy's shoulder.

"His name is Mbili. He is shy."

"Yes, and Sabuno was making fun of him... and me. I wanted to show Sabuno that he was not as good as he thinks he is. He should not laugh or make fun of Mbili or anyone else. Will you please tell the women what we have said so far?"

Rosata translated for the anxious mothers and fielded a flurry of questions before turning back to Paula saying, "The women all want to see what you did. They want to judge for themselves whether or not their sons told the truth. Lying is a serious offense and calls for serious punishment.

Paula was curious and said, "How serious is this punishment?"

The woman replied: "For a boy, only the tip of his tongue will be cut off. For a man, the whole tongue would be cut out."

Paula was aghast! She raised a hand to gain attention and taking a step went into the routine she had done for the boys. When finished, Paula turned back to her audience to see them on their knees, bowing to her. She thought. I hope my talents merit something more than tasteless stew for dinner.

She went to Rosata and raised her up saying, "Please tell them that I am a gymnast. I was taught to do these things as a child. There are many people who can do what I have done. It just takes a lot of training and practice."

The woman told the gathered group, which had been growing by the moment, what Paula had said in explanation. She turned back to Paula and said, "Our whole village is proud to have you as a guest. Is there anything we can do for you?"

Paula thought not a moment before saying. "I would love to have a bowl of oatmeal and some fresh fruit for dinner and hot water for tea."

When translated, the women looked perplexed, but one and all they left jabbering excitedly about something... hopefully the oatmeal recipe.

Paula retreated into her hut thinking, 'Fools rush in where angels fear to tread.' The awful repercussions that could have happened had not the mothers decided to confront her, were too horrible to think about. 'Go lightly, never show-off ... and you'll always be a winner.' Words her coach used to say when she pulled a stunt like she did today. She took off her soiled clothes and washed in tepid water, berating her self all the while for wanting to put a little boy, even if he was a bully, in his place. Who did she think she was anyway–a Safi-Mitiriki?

SHE HEARD A FAMILIAR voice say, “You will always be my Safi-Mitiriki.”

Paula spun around. There he stood, tall, handsome and sweaty with the impish smile she had come to love.

In a moment, she had flung herself into his arms. “Oh Tamubu, I am so glad you have come back–that we are together again!” He held her tightly, not trusting his voice. In a moment, she pushed back and said, “I think you would probably like to go and bathe. We can talk later.”

Tamubu put his head back and began to laugh.

Jon popped his head in the hut opening and said, “Did I miss a good joke?”

By now both Paula and Tamubu were convulsed with laughter. Tamubu turned, put his arm around Jon’s shoulder and said, “I’ll tell you the joke while we clean up.”

While they were gone, Paula’s oatmeal arrived–with coconut flakes and goat’s milk, hot water for tea and a platter of fresh fruit: a banana, an orange and some raspberries. She sprinkled the coconut on the gelatinous mass, eschewed the goat’s milk, instead thinning the oatmeal with a bit of hot water, and added the raspberries. A meal fit for a queen–or a Safi-Mitiriki–and she ate it all.

AFTER THE OATMEAL DINNER Paula added a colorful scarf to her shirt and put on her birthstone aquamarine ring and earrings and wore the scarab bracelets with her watch. She wanted Tamubu to know that she was glad to see him again, both as a friend, as well as a woman. She was barely ready when her hostess (as she thought of the woman who took care of her) arrived to escort her to an open pavilion, which had a brazier in the center and a low table (that looked like a bale of straw covered with a cloth) on which, was fresh fruit, a pitcher of lemon water, gourd-cups and the little cakes made of dates, coconut, honey and farina called tamutunda. These ‘sweet cakes' had been served after her dinner with the Elders. They were a special treat.

SHE HEARD THE DRUMS and arose just as Tamubu came into sight. He looked marvelous: clean, freshly shaven and showing his beautiful smile, with his kitu-kina draped over his shoulders like the cape of a Superhero. He was wearing safari khakis and knee socks with his sandals. His mop of honey-colored curls had been trimmed off his neck, but he still wore a brow band to keep his hair out of his eyes. Never have I seen such a gorgeous man. How had I not noticed his extreme good looks before?

Tamubu had watched Paula rise. She had such grace in her movements that she seemed to flow, not move. She sparkled: her eyes, her ears (that was new) and her bright silvery gold hair, which she wore with the sides pulled back and fastened at the back of her head. He slowed his steps, just so he could gaze at her a little longer.

All too soon he arrived at the open lanai. It was the courting lanai. Here, women received men who had made known their intentions of marriage. It was the only place the couple could meet until after the ceremony. Tamubu wondered why the Wahutu had chosen this place for him to meet Paula–had Gomojo suggested that Paula was to be his bride. While nothing would please him more, outwardly, their relationship had not yet passed beyond the friendship stage.

Paula took a step to meet him. Tamubu held up his hand to stop her; wearing his impish smile, he said, "Did you know this lanai is a special place?

Paula looked around and said, "No, why is it special?"

"It is the courtship lanai. It is the place where a man and a woman meet once a man has asked for the hand of a woman in marriage."

Paula blushed. Tamubu continued, "I wonder if Gomojo suggested that you were to be my bride to obtain the cooperation of the Wahutu to go and look for me? It would not be considered seemly for a woman to travel with a man, if she was not his wife."

Paula had given no thought to the mores of the natives. Now it was her turn to discomfit him. With her full smile, Paula said, “If you advance into the lanai, are you stating your position?”

Tamubu threw his head back and laughed. She has done it again! My, how I have missed the bantering we did on our travels. He turned to Jon, who stood just behind him, and said, “Jon, would you please act for Paula?” Looking at Paula he said, “A woman must have a man speak for her.”

Now Paula was abashed. What was he going to do? I’m not ready! I haven’t thought about this–oh, my gosh!

Jon entered the lanai and stood halfway between them. He smiled at Paula–he had been aware that she was in the courting lanai and had wondered if she knew it.

“Jon, I wish to speak to this woman. I would like her to consider me a suitor. Would you ask her to do so, please?”

Jon said, “Thomas is a good man; he has no vices that I know of; he promises not to beat you and he is quite wealthy. Will you consider him a suitor?”

Paula almost laughed–but caught herself. She knew this was serious, not a game in the eyes of the villagers, and so replied, “I am willing to consider Thomas a suitor, but I will need the permission of my father before I can make a decision. Will he accept this stipulation?”

Jon turned to Thomas and said, “You will be required to wait, possibly a long time, before you will know if this woman can accept you. Will you wait?”

Tamubu said simply, “Yes.” And strode towards the low courting table and sat down. He looked at Paula and said, “You may sit down now. We have satisfied the rules and customs of the Wahutu.”

Jon started to leave the lanai, when Paula said, “Jon, where are you going?”

“The chaperone usually sits outside–within calling distance,” he replied. “That too, is customary.”

“I would like you to sit here with us. Will that break any rules?”

“No, sometimes that is done too.”

"Well, Thomas and I want you here with us; come–sit next to Thomas so I can see both of you."

Paula was worried and asked, "Will I be allowed to leave with you if we are not married?"

Tamubu tilted his head to one side with a dimpled smile and saw the lines of anxiety around her eyes. He decided against stringing her along–she had had enough surprises. "Jon will be your chaperone until I speak to your father."

Paula was visibly relieved, but Tamubu saw the confusion in her eyes and to divert her attention, remarked. "You look lovely this evening–lovelier than I remembered. How is your ankle?"

"My ankle is a little sore from the walk here, but I bandaged it with some of your green powder and it feels much better. I have so much to tell you both; I don't know where to begin."

"Begin at the beginning," Thomas replied.

"Yes, of course, Douala. I left two messages for you at the hotel. One was misfiled under "F" for Paul Field; the other was still in your key box, Thomas, when I arrived. I had forgotten that this is a leap year, with an extra day in February, so March 5th was twelve days, not eleven."

"Why did Arthur say you had gone to the States?"

"BECAUSE THE OTHERS WENT to the States, and he did not know differently. I spent just the one afternoon on the *Just Cause*. Then I left with all my belongings and went aboard the *Wind Drift*. The next day we went upriver to Lambaréné to meet Dr. Albert Schweitzer and to visit his hospital at the leper colony. You remember... Captain Jones had been asked to ferry some missionaries to Lambaréné to study with Dr. Schweitzer... it was why we left the cove before Kasuku's foot was healed. When we returned to Port-Gentil, Captain Jones went to Omboué and I stayed at a Guest House until he returned. Arthur only thought I went home because Dr. Miles had been so unpleasant to me, and he knew I had resigned from the Expedition. It was the logical supposition, if he was not told otherwise."

"How did you find out where we had gone?"

"Mr. Pandi at the hotel said you had hired the landaulet each day and maybe the driver knew where you had gone."

"I see, but how did you persuade Gomojo to bring you here?"

"I did not persuade–he offered. Apparently you told him about my *5in1*. Ben saw it about my neck and asked me to demonstrate it for his son. Gomojo was quite thrilled and asked me if I was the Safi-Mitiriki?"

"Gomojo is a remarkable man, Thomas said. Living in a boy's body has made him very shy. You must have treated him like a man to make him want to help you."

"I was so desperate for help; I would have followed a newborn infant."

"Now that you have found us, what are your plans?"

Jon had been sitting quietly, just listening; but now was a crucial moment. He dreaded Paula's desire to go with them, for that would change everything. It would no longer be a one-on-one relationship; brother to brother, man to man.

Paula was stunned. "Why, I want to go with you and Jon and Kybo on your trek to Kenya."

Now, it was Tamubu who was perturbed. "The trip will take many months. There will be hardships... and possibly danger. It is not a trip for someone with a sore ankle." Tamubu watched the disappointment turn her features flaccid and thought: Why did I say that? It was my most heartfelt wish to travel to Kenya with her... but that was before I knew Jon was my brother... before Kybo had dedicated his life to me... when it would only have been the two of us... and before she injured her ankle. If I did not want her to go with us, why was I so unhappy when I thought she had gone back to the States?

UNBIDDEN, THE TEARS ROSE in her eyes. A lump formed in her throat. He does not want me to go with him anymore! What a fool I am! How many times did he have to save me in just the two weeks we were together? I would just be a huge burden to him.

Paula raised her head, squared her shoulders and said, "I

understand. So far I have been a great burden to you and was just too fatuous not to realize it."

"What is fatuous?" Thomas asked.

Paula looked at his impish smile and felt the rejection diminish, as she remembered all the times he had asked her to explain words to him in the same way. Her smile became a chuckle and the chuckle became a laugh and soon they were both laughing, and laughed until their sides ached. Jon did not understand the joke, but the humor was too contagious not to join it.

"Fatuous is foolish, silly and stupid." She replied, and the laughter became uncontrolled.

Jon was the first to recover from the tension-relieving humor. "Thomas is right, you know. Why just the night before last we had to sleep on the ground, out in the open (conveniently omitting that he had been in the radio tent)–and last night we had to sleep in the trees–with no fire and no protection from the elements and it was bloody uncomfortable!"

Thomas looked at Jon in surprise. He is jealous of Paula, yet there is a sincere concern for her too, so he said, "We all need to think about what is involved, and what allowances can be made so Paula can join us. Paula, you need to think long and hard about such a lengthy trip. Jon was not exaggerating the hardships–and three months is six times longer than our trek to the beach. Would you want to do that all over again–six times?"

Paula felt poleaxed: indeed, she had not thought of the trip to Kenya in those terms–yet that is exactly what she would be doing. It was a mountainous trek, especially through the Congo. With a heavy heart she said, "Maybe it would be best to sleep on it, before we make a decision."

Jon said, "You are the bravest woman I have ever known; but this is not a situation forced upon you, from which you must escape. You will be choosing extreme difficulties, and possibly a great deal of pain with your sore ankle from which, there will be no escape."

Tamubu said, "May we have a moment, Jon?" Jon smiled,

nodded his head to Paula and then left. He had had his say. It was not his decision to make.

Tamubu reached across the table and took Paula's hands in his own, stroking them softly with his thumbs. "I cannot find the words to tell you how glad I am to see my Safi-Mitiriki again. I would like to spend all my days seeing you. Nothing would please me more. But first, I must go to Kenya. Jon will help me to remember my youth and our family from his memories. But Jon failed to mention one important point: There is great danger from marauders along the rivers. A white woman would be a great prize. I don't want to expose you to these dangers. When I started out, I was alone. Alone, I could go anywhere safely. When it was just the two of us, I knew you could elude enemies through the trees, if needed. Now Jon and Kybo are with me–and I must look out for them–even though both are used to traveling in the deep forests. We now travel differently–more exposed–for none of us can travel through the trees as you can. You must see how different it would be, and what I'm saying is reasonable."

Paula did see that he was being reasonable. Her throbbing ankle made his point for him... but the reasons did not lessen the severe disappointment.

"Will it be acceptable for us to talk again in the morning?"

"Yes, as long as Jon is nearby."

"Would it be acceptable for us to share a meal?"

"I am thinking you might like some oatmeal."

"Yes, she smiled, I would, but only if you make it."

The Plan

PAULA THOUGHT ABOUT HER innermost desire, which was to trek to Kenya with Tamubu Jon and Kybo, but the weakness of her ankle worried her. After a few more days of trekking, I could be completely lame again–then what? I'd just be a problem for everyone. No, there has to be some other way ...

JON AND TAMUBU SHARED a hut for visiting bachelors. It was a small hut, with two low benches covered with greenery and pelts. There was a small firepot and a smoke vent in the roof.

Jon asked, "Did you talk to Paula?"

"Yes, I tried to talk her out of joining us, but it has to be her decision. We're going to talk again, in the morning."

Tamubu lay awake, thinking. With Jon as my teacher, do I really need three months to prepare myself to meet my parents again? I feel almost ready now. When I started out, time and exposure to others, was my only way to learn. This last month has put me far ahead of where I would have been in three months or even six months of traveling alone. I wanted to follow in Manutu's footsteps and cross Africa as he did, but then I was alone.

The whole journey has changed. I can no longer use my abilities to protect myself, or others. I must decide what is most important to me: the traveling... or the destination. I left the Zuri Watu to find my birth family. Meeting Jon has satisfied the need; yet has somehow made it greater. The traveling has changed. It is no longer the carefree trip that it was when I began; nor is it the same as it was traveling with Paula. Jon likes his creature comforts and is traveling cross-country only to please me. Kybo is an excellent traveling companion, and is accustomed to living rough; he has made a life commitment to me. I accepted it and now I must honor it, by seeing to his welfare.

But, most of all, I want to be with Paula now–not three or four months from now. She too, has made a commitment to me. If we are to have a successful future together, I cannot begin by neglecting her or hurting her feelings...especially when she went to so much effort to find us again.

I should ask Jon. He is well traveled; he might have some ideas–although he might just want to fly back to Kenya and be done with it. I may have to give up the idea of crossing Africa on foot as Manutu did, but I still want to experience some of the vastness of the continent. There has to be a middle road... somewhere.

When the birds began their morning-song, Tamubu awoke Jon. "We need to talk. I'll get us some coffee while you get dressed."

In a few minutes Tamubu was back. They took their coffee to the open-air privacy of a small grove of lemon trees, where Tamubu stated his dilemma and asked Jon for suggestions.

To his surprise, Jon said nothing about flying directly home; instead he asked, "What is it you really want to do?"

"I want to go home with you. I want to take Paula and Kybo with me. I do not want to subject her to danger, or further pain with her ankle. I want to see some of the vast beauty of Africa."

Jon mulled over Thomas' wishes, while Thomas went for more coffee and breakfast. When he returned, Jon said, "We have to go back for Kybo. From there, we could head for Yaoundé. It would be a week's travel–if we take Paula with us, maybe ten days. We could hire some canny Wahutu scouts..."

"What is canny?"

"Shrewd, well-informed... who would find good campsites, or even better, maybe visit overnight with other tribes–using your abilities as Manutu's protégé ..."

"What is protégé?"

"It means 'student of Manutu'... as entrée... means 'permission to enter'..." Jon glanced at Tamubu and they both began to laugh.

Tamubu said, "I will wait until you are finished before I ask again, but those words sounded so different to me."

"They are French words, but commonly used in English."

"As I was saying, the Wahutu scouts would also add to the safety of our group. We might visit the Gielli Pygmies south of Yaoundé. That would be a nice treat for me–put my education in African languages and the Paleolithic Pygmies to work."

"Paleolithic?"

"It is a period of time from the long past, commonly called the Stone Age, which refers to the era of the people living at that time.

"From Yaoundé, we could fly to Kisangani and make a day trip on the Congo River, before going east to The Ruwenzori Mountains and Lake Albert up to Murchison Falls National Park. You would also see Kampala and Lake Victoria before going on to Nairobi.

"Thomas, you would still see a great deal of the splendors of Africa and not take three months, or more, to do it. But best of all, we could all be together."

"Have you already seen these places, Jon?"

"Not all, but I have been to Lake Victoria and north to the Murchison Falls National Park and the Rift Valley to Lake Rudolph. I have not yet gone south to Lake Tanganyika or to Kasumo, the source of the Nile. I wanted to spend a summer visiting the Pygmy tribes there; but when I was home from school, the tea plantation and its business always seemed to need my attention."

"You have been fortunate to have traveled so much. Do you think we should take Paula overland with us to Yaoundé?"

"Why don't we let Paula decide what she wants to do; after all, it's her ankle and only she knows how it feels."

WHILE THOMAS WENT TO make oatmeal for Paula, Jon thought about his aborted grand tour graduation present. It had not been the tea plantation that kept me from my tour; it had been meeting Max Mason while on a visit to the Bambuti Pygmies. There, I decided to change my plans and go with him on his next trading tour; for Max had said he would go deeper in the rainforest, to tribes he had not traded with before, so I could look for my lost brother. I will never regret that decision–I found Thomas–even if it wasn't in a remote village. Someday I will finish that grand tour and see Kasumo and visit the Mosso, Hutu and Tutsi Pygmies.

PLEASED WITH THE NEW plans, Tamubu went to Mme. Ovidio's fire. He had already asked her if he could make some oatmeal for Paula.

"I never knew anyone who liked oatmeal so much that they would eat it for dinner and breakfast!" Rosata said.

Tamubu chuckled to himself. He knew the gelatinous mass that the Wahutu called oatmeal was much different from his gently cooked ground oats, farina and coconut slivers.

With the bowl of oatmeal in one hand and a banana and orange in the other, Tamubu joined Paula and Jon in the courting lanai. Jon had fetched hot water so Paula could make tea. While she ate, Jon outlined the ideas of their discussion for her. Paula had already decided she would only be a liability if she went with them now. Her ankle needed rest and mild exercise to heal properly.

"Oh Jon, what a wonderful itinerary; I would love to see the Congo and the Nile Rivers and Lake Victoria. Do you like this plan, Thomas?"

"Yes, I do, except for the flying."

Jon smiled at Thomas while he explained: "Planes have changed a great deal in fourteen years, Thomas, even here in Africa. There are now large passenger jet planes that fly from one continent to the other. Even the smaller commuter planes have full instrumentation and radio contact with the airports. There are still the small single engine planes and biplanes, but we will not be using them for our travels across the continent."

While Jon talked about the planes, Tamubu thought about

Paula calling him Thomas. She had done so before in jest, but this time he sensed it was a permanent change. For some reason it saddened him... it marked the passing of a time that had been one of the happiest in his life.

Paula said, "I have decided to return to Douala, get my luggage, and then take the train to Yaoundé and meet you there." This will give me time to write my parents and wire Uncle David to inquire about the progression of other business. "I will just wait for you at the Grande Hotel, until you arrive. But, before you go, I have something for you." Paula pulled out two paper-wrapped parcels and gave one to Thomas, and the other to Jon.

Opening his package, Thomas looked at Paula and smiled, "Did you make these?"

"No, I had a cobbler in Port-Gentil make them. I think he did a nice job. Try them on and see if they fit."

Jon was mystified. "What are they?"

"They are half-chaps. They will protect your lower legs from thorns and saw-toothed grasses. They are often worn in place of riding boots."

"Neato!" Jon said as he watched Thomas put his chaps on.

"Thank you," Thomas said, "I am very pleased!"

"You're welcome–they have your names stamped inside."

Jon opened out his remaining half-chap and saw his name tooled in the leather and was impressed. "I say, that's smashing!"

Wearing the new half-chaps, Thomas and Jon and the Wahutu scouts left a short while later to fetch Kybo on their way to Yaoundé. Paula arranged through Mme. Ovidio to hire a scout to take her back to the junction tomorrow morning, while the Wahutu drums sent a message, asking Ben to meet her at the trailhead at noon tomorrow.

Paula spent the morning writing in her diary. Mme. Ovidio hosted a lunch for her after which, she had a stringing glass beads lesson and sewing party, with Paula providing good fun and humor. She enjoyed learning to make the beadwork patterns. The application to the kitambas was truly an art, which Paula didn't even try to do.

For dinner, Paula was the guest of Chief Kusik and his wife. Present too, were their sons and their wives. The atmosphere was very different from the formal meal Paula had on her arrival, for the meal was served family style. There was animated talk and much laughter, since Paula's Bantu pronunciation often turned words around. The Wahutu were good hosts. She was not left to languish alone.

It was fortuitous that Paula had allowed extra time for the walk to the junction the next day. Her ankle was again swelling and painful when she and her guide, Pimio, met Gomojo, who had walked a ways down the trail to meet them. I am so glad Tamubu liked Jon's compromise to the overland trek to Kenya, she thought. In just a few miles, my ankle is so sore, I can barely walk.

Tirini had sent a delicious lunch of cold roast chicken, sweet potato salad with raisins and nuts and freshly baked corn bread for them. While she ate, Paula chatted about her stay with the Wahutu; and the decision to meet Tamubu, Jon and Kybo in Yaoundé, where they would all fly to Kisangani, to tour the Nile River.

During the drive back to the Douala Hotel, Ben thought about her story, which Gomojo had told them. So much has happened to this woman–so many perils from which she has managed to escape. I think the Wahutu Elders are right, 'she is protected by the gods...' and it is our good fortune to know her and her friends.

Paula felt replete, basking in the warm sun, while listening to the steady clip-clop of Sunny's hooves blending with the whirring sound of the carriage wheels. Paula had asked, "I expected to see Goldy today. Is he okay?"

"Yes, he is fine; but yesterday I used both horses to haul a big load for a builder. So Goldy had two days on and now Sunny has two days on. Tomorrow you will see Goldy again."

Ben thought about the bond she had developed with Goldy. It was unusual. Sunny was more tolerant of strangers than Goldy, who usually stomped a foot or swished his tail at a stranger's touch. The Countess did not believe in docking the tails of her driving horses. Instead, she wrapped the tail in a net and tied the net to the crupper. She said the weight of the tail kept the crupper from irritating the underside of the tail, which was true. But Ben let the tails flow freely so the horses would have them to shoo flies.

While listening to the relaxing sounds of hoof beats and carriage wheels, Paula thought about the new travel plans. A week or two of mild exercise and my ankle should be completely mended. Tomorrow, it will be four weeks since I injured it. Another two weeks should see me healed... if I am careful.

Ben and Gomojo waved as they drove away from the hotel. They would return tomorrow morning at 8:00 a. m. to take her to the train station.

Inside the hotel, Mr. Pandi joined her at the reservation desk. "Captain Jones has left a message for you. Were you able to find your friends?"

"Yes, we are going to meet in Yaoundé. I am taking the train tomorrow morning."

"I am so pleased. If I can be of any help... anything at all... just call me."

"Thank you. Do I need a reservation for the train?"

"I will be glad to arrange a first class ticket for you; anything else?"

"I think that does it for the moment. Thank you."

"My pleasure."

Paula left the desk for the Café and a cup of Earl Grey tea. She read her note from Captain Jones, which asked her to join him for dinner, as he planned to be in port for repairs for a week or so. Paula then went to her room, took a bath, washed her hair and gave herself a manicure. In her best traveling clothes, she hired a small jog cart for the ride to the pier.

Paula's heels clicked as she walked down the pier to the

Wind Drift. Captain Jones heard her coming and went to the gangplank to meet her.

"Permission to come aboard, Captain."

"Permission granted. I was just settling in to a dull evening with a good book. I hope you haven't had dinner. Jonas is making fish and chips, our usual, but delicious meal when tied up to the pier. He patted his slightly rounded belly–now you know why I try to keep on the move!"

This man was good for her. He was a witty raconteur, who was able to make inane topics interesting and enjoyable. No life or death topics for him. He will wheedle out of me everything that has happened, since I last saw him, in such a way that I will feel it was he who was telling the tales. I wonder why there isn't a Mrs. Jones–he's so charming. I think Anna Chumley would love the job, if she didn't have to live on the motor yacht.

Laughing together, they settled themselves comfortably in the canvas deck chairs. Jonas poked his head out on the afterdeck saying, "Why is it I'm always the last one to know when we have guests for dinner? Hello, Miss. It's good to see you again. It's fish and chips tonight, but I guess you know that."

Jonas disappeared as quickly as he had arrived, with Captain Jones saying, "Well, that's a first! I don't remember Jonas ever greeting a guest before. Have you enchanted him or something?"

Paula laughed. "I helped him fill out a job application on our way to Port-Gentil."

Captain Jones went serious. "That's not funny. Jonas is a superb cook. I could never replace him–unless Motozo needed a job."

Paula smiled, "In a way, it is funny. He was applying for the position of head Chef at the Ritz Carlton Hotel in Philadelphia. Did you know his mother lives there in the Rittenhouse Square apartments?"

"No, I didn't even know his mother was alive!"

"At some point Jonas had heard that I lived near Philadelphia and asked me to help him with the application.

You know, he may not have sent it. He didn't want to leave you. He just felt he should be nearer to his mother in her twilight years."

Captain Hannibal Jones was momentarily lost in thought. He had sought the sea after his young and lovely wife, and his unborn son, had died in childbirth. He had been inconsolable for years. My crew hands have come and gone, but Jonas came to me when I first came to Africa, fourteen years ago. He is not at all social, preferring to spend his time doing word puzzles; he was a cryptographer in World War II. He never seeks casual company, nor have we ever exchanged personal stories. So, Jonas has a mother living in Philadelphia–well, well.

Smiling at Paula, he said, "Forgive me. It was a surprise to find out about Jonas' mother. It made me wonder if he has other family too."

"I hope I didn't let the cat out of the bag. Please don't tell Jonas I told you. He is so close with himself; he might resent me for telling you."

With his jocular brogue he said, "Da na fash yoursel' lassie, me lips're sealed."

The pleasant evening flew by, and all too soon it was time to go. Captain Jones drove her back to the hotel and said, "I have your parents address. If I ever get to Philadelphia, I intend to look them up. If you ever feel the need to write a letter, I'd be happy to hear from you. Just send it care of the Douala Harbormaster ~ Cameroon, West Africa."

Hannibal Jones pushed his hands deep in his walking shorts pockets as he crossed the square to the Jeep. It had started to rain again. The only thing that made the climate bearable was the frequency of the cooling showers at night. Oddly enough, the humidity was not so intolerable on the open sea.

Paula fascinated him. He found himself wishing he was twenty years younger ... a first for him since Beth died.

In the morning, Paula was ready to go when Ben and Gomojo arrived. She was looking forward to the railroad trip, which was unique to the west coast of Cameroon. The narrow gauge railroad line had been built by the Germans, before the outbreak of war in 1914, when joint French and British forces invaded and conquered the Cameroons. The country was divided in 1919, under a mandate from the League of Nations and in 1944 the mandates were made trust territories of the United Nations.

Paula was aware of this from reading the newspapers. A new government had been formed on January 1, 1960, and rioting had ensued. The papers were full of background stories as well as the current news of French troops assisting President Ahidjo to restore order. The newspapers also said that the railroad was well protected, as it was the main transport from the banana fields in Bonaberi to Douala and Yaoundé. Mr. Pandi had mentioned that the line was antiquated and delays should be expected.

The passenger cars, Paula found, were truly antiques. The dark burgundy red velour-like upholstery was worn almost to the backing and the windows were held open by a stick in the corner. Her luggage was put in the mail car as the overhead racks had long ago been torn from their supports and were either missing or hanging precariously from a stubborn screw. The linoleum over the plank flooring was worn away in the pathways and only remnants clung tenaciously to the areas under the seats.

Ben had suggested she sit at the very front, in the seat facing to the rear to escape the dirty smoke spewed from the wood-burning engine. The seat facing her provided a convenient place to put her backpack and the basket lunch Tirini had made for her trip. The hand woven basket had a lovely diamond motif in colors of red, yellow and green in the spaces of open work. "It is a gift from Tirini. She made it herself," Ben told her. "She hopes you will remember us for as long as we are going to remember you."

Paula waved a sad goodbye to Ben and Gomojo as the train chugged from the platform; she hoped she would see these good people again one day.

THE FORWARD COACH WAS first class and the 'No Smoking' car.

It was about three-quarters full when the train departed. The next car was the 'Smoking' car or second-class seating, referred to as coach. It was packed–with sometimes three or four people sitting on the seats designed for two. The third car was the luggage and mail car. The rest of the train was racked flatbed cars designed for transporting the banana crops.

Looking at the scenery through the window after it passed by, gave Paula the feeling she would miss something if she looked away. Eventually the train left the pockets of villages and open areas and was enclosed by dense forest on both sides. Here, Paula noticed that she was the only woman on the train who was traveling alone. It seemed to her that everyone was watching her. It was a ghastly feeling.

She took out the book she had purchased in Douala–The History of Douala–about the narrow gauge train, the large and busy wharf and the various sights in the town. It also had a chapter about the Gielli Pygmies, who held a fascination for Paula from the stories Jon had told her. She had read a book on Africa, wherein the Pygmies were described as: '...the world's lowest technological primitives... a people who were more religiously moral and socially civilized than the Greeks, Romans or other nations of antiquity.' She hoped one day to meet a Pygmy tribe, so she could judge for herself if the statement was true.

The Douala travel book also included many interesting but odd facts: the rainfall in the area of Mount Cameroon reached 400 inches a year; the heavy rainfall was the reason the grass roofed huts of the region wore coolie hats: a second conical roof atop the first roof; while the Fon of Bikom, a local dignitary, was reputed to have more wives than any human being in the world! (Paula seemed to remember coming across this odd bit of information before and seemed to remember the number of wives was in the six hundreds.) Mount Cameroon is an active volcano, and covers seven hundred square miles at the base. The red-purple orchid (lissochilus), which Paula had already seen in her travels, but had not known the genus, grows to a height of fifteen feet in the rainforest. She had also heard the drums of the Wahutu village, which were claimed to have more advanced tonal communication than anywhere in Africa–except for the Congo.

Her travel book included a few facts about Yaoundé, the capital of Cameroon. She found it very distressing to read that it was sprayed by helicopter every night with DDT, in an effort to keep disease under control. Her studies of the flora and fauna had shown the devastating effects of DDT on wildlife, especially birds–making the eggshells so thin and brittle, they often broke during gestation. Some birds, especially birds of prey, were more susceptible to the cumulative effects of the spraying.

Other than having a European community of about 2500 people, and the many Greek businessmen to serve their interests; and lights for the tennis courts so people can play in the evening when it is cooler; Yaoundé seemed far less interesting than Douala, which was reported to receive, '20,000 tons of wine from France every year, for local consumption and distribution inland.' This little fact in her travel book caused her to chortle and then with paper and pencil, to figure the annual per capita consumption, which was a startling 3000 pounds, per year, per white resident, man, woman and child of Cameroon. Obviously, it was a misprint: the 20,000 tons should probably have been 2,000 tons.

In the heat of the day, in the shady alley formed by dense vegetation, the train stopped and people got off to relieve themselves in the bushes. Fortunately, the first class car had a rest room, which was not to be used when the train was stopped. When the passengers returned to the train, box lunches were opened and the contents eaten. Then everyone: conductor, engineer, stokers, and passengers took a nap–as best they could–sitting upright.

Before the train was once more underway, Paula moved her things to the backward facing seat and sat in the forward facing seat. The scrutiny of the sea of eyes had been a severe trial for her nerves. She did not blame the people for staring at her, for there had been little else to occupy their attention. But she felt immensely relieved to be able to look up and see the stained and peeling paint of the passenger car wall, instead of a sea of curious eyes.

SOMETIME AFTER THE NOON rest, the train stopped again to take on fuel and water. She had noticed the many tiny huts along the way, each manned by two men with rifles. It seemed Mr. Pandi had been right about the railway being well guarded. At the fuel and water stop, there was a large building, like a barracks, and the evidence of many armed men.

The train arrived in Yaoundé at 5:15 p.m. A carriage was found to take her luggage, as the hotel jitney was already full of passengers. Paula decided to ride with her luggage to the hotel. The driver was gregarious and asked her how long she had been in Africa. When Paula told him she had arrived on the 11th of January, he immediately asked her point of arrival. When she said Lagos, he was quite interested to hear from her first hand about the tsunami and how she had survived it. It was not long before he asked if she knew the lady who was lost on the yacht during the tsunami. Paula thought long and hard before she answered, “I am the lady who was lost on the yacht.”

The man’s eyes widened, then he smiled with pleasure. He was clearly pleased he had such an important fare, for her disappearance had been a leading story in all the newspapers at the time.

When they arrived at the hotel, the driver jumped down to assist her and unload her luggage saying, “My name is Gangis. If you need transportation while you are here, Missy, I would be honored to drive you. Just ask the concierge, he will contact me.”

Paula smiled at his sincerity and said, “I will remember your name. How much notice do you need?”

“I am usually not far away, near the park, but I should be able to be here in half an hour, unless I am at the train station.”

“Thank you Gangis. Will you see to the luggage while I register?”

“Yes Missy, thank you.”

Mr. Pandi had made it a point to contact the Grande Hotel to make the reservation for Paula. The desk was quite crowded so Paula sought the Tea Room for a cup of tea. A while later, the desk was unoccupied except for one man, who Paula thought, paid far too much attention to her business.

As she turned to leave, the man stepped forward and said, "My name is Cyril Latham," and handed her his card. Paula glanced at it briefly. "I have been waiting for you. Mr. Pandi said you would be arriving this afternoon. I was beginning to think I had missed you."

"The man looked elegant and charming, the perfect picture of the urbane attorney. I'm sorry, Mr. Latham. Why would an attorney from Nairobi be waiting for me?"

"I'm here in response to your letter to your uncle, asking for a recommendation of an attorney to handle your pharmaceutical acquisitions."

"My goodness, Uncle David contacted someone in Africa?"

"Yes, he seems to think you will be the next E. I. Lily. According to David, it seems that you have managed to corner the market in African herbal remedies."

"You seem to be on a first name basis with my uncle. How is that?"

"David and I went to college together. We were in the same Fraternity and then we both ended up staying in Philadelphia, and going to law school at Penn. I came to Africa to settle my aunt's estate for my mother. Her sister had lived in Africa all her married life. The estate was sizable; the records were poor; and it required a long time to get her affairs in order. In the meantime, I fell in love with Africa, and when the opportunity presented itself to stay–I stayed."

They had gravitated away from the front desk to a sofa and chairs grouping in the lobby where Paula ordered another cup of tea. Cyril ordered wine. When Paula chuckled at his order, his eyebrow went up and he said, "Are you a teetotaler?"

"No, I'm not, but I was reading a travel book on the train about Yaoundé and Douala. It mentioned that the European community used 20,000 tons of wine, imported from France, each year.

The irony was not lost on Cyril, and he threw his head back and laughed. “I wonder how many bottles of wine are in 20,000 tons.” They laughed together and Paula said, “I figured about twenty million–and how many glasses are in a bottle?”

Cyril liked this woman. She had a marvelous sense of humor ... and she was so free and unfettered: no wiles, no shy or retiring manners. He found most women too cluttered and for this reason, he had never married.

“Paula said, “How long do you expect to be in Yaoundé?”

“I have partners; so I am here for the duration.”

“Are you registered?”

“Tentatively, yes; I told them I would register after you had arrived. They may have taken care of it already. They are very efficient at this hotel.”

“Well, Mr. Latham, would you find it convenient to meet me for dinner... say at 8 p.m.? I am desperate for a bath.”

The more she talked, the more he liked her. “8 p.m. it is. I’ll take care of the arrangements. Would you like for me to call for you at your room?”

Paula cocked her head, began to smile and said, “If your male ego will not be bruised, I think I can find the dining room by myself.”

Cyril thought: Where has this woman been all my life? But, said aloud, “In the dining room at 8 p.m. it is!”

Paula arose; Cyril also stood up and bowed slightly as she left. He watched as she walked across the lobby and turned the corner. No make up, naturally blonde hair, no girdle and no artfully coy airs. She handles life honestly... more like a man than a woman. But, what an intriguing woman that makes her!

5

Cyril Latham

After the luxury of a hot shower, Paula sat on the edge of the tub soaking her ankle in cold water while she fluffed her hair dry. She was excited by Cyril Latham's visit. For him to come all this way from Nairobi, it must be very good news. She rummaged in her cases to find her best outfit. The simple sundresses she had packed for dinners on the *Just Cause* were just that–simple. One dress had a pretty dark green, black and white jungle print with a soft full skirt, with a white bolero jacket and narrow white belt; with her white sandals, it was the best she could do.

At 8 p.m. she presented herself to the Maitre D', who promptly escorted her to a table on the far side of the dining room. Cyril stood when he saw her approaching, and watched her progress in admiration. She had a big friendly smile and a charming eagerness in her demeanor. Her dress was simple, yet fetching; her hair hung loose about her face, curling under her chin ever so slightly, with the top pulled back and held, at the crown, by a large white barrette. He didn't think he had ever seen a woman look so lovely. Watch it, old boy. She's young enough to be your daughter! Cyril sighed. And, she might be a client too. If old Dave was right, she could be the client of the century.

Disregarding his inner voice, he said, "You look lovely this evening."

Paula said, "Thank you Mr. Latham."

"Please, call me Cyril."

"If it would please you, but I must warn you, I'll probably

forget. I'm not accustomed to calling my elders by their first names."

Ouch and double ouch. "Would you mind if I call you, Paula?"

"Please do. What did Uncle David tell you?"

"He said you had discovered all the ancient herbal remedies of the Medicine Men of the Zuri Watu."

"Well, I discovered a Medicine Man who drew some of the healing plants in my diary for me, along with descriptions of their preparations and uses. Here, this is my diary with his drawings. Are you familiar with healing plants, or herbal remedies?"

"Somewhat"... Cyril took the diary and opened it.

"Go to the back of the diary, the front is just personal."

He flipped the book to the back and found himself looking at a pencil drawing that had as much detail as a professional photograph. Next to the drawing was a description written in flowing script. Thumbing the pages, Cyril saw page after page of the same quality drawings and descriptions. He thought to himself, if these plants–most of which were unnamed–did what the descriptions said they did... this book was more valuable than King Solomon's Mines.

Cyril closed the diary and returned it to her. "You must know that your diary, if it is accurate and can do what it says, is extremely valuable and should be kept in a bank vault."

Paula looked at him and smiled. "Only four people know I have this diary: you, Uncle David, Professor Miles and me ... and of course, the artist. Professor Miles is a weak link, but he has gone to the States ... and he knows he would be suspect if anything happened to the diary."

"Have you any proof that these remedies actually work?"

"Some. The Ndezi gave me the kimmea while we were traveling in the rainforest. It put me to sleep gently and I awoke feeling rested and refreshed. It had no side effects: I did not feel groggy when I awoke; I did not experience appetite changes; I did not feel irritable or irrationally carefree, although in retrospect I was not nearly as apprehensive as I should have been. I had no bad dreams or lethargy. In fact, without any side effects, it was almost a week before I realized I was being drugged."

"What made you suspect you were being drugged?"

"I fell asleep minutes after I had eaten a meal, except for breakfast. This was unusual considering my dire circumstances, and not my normal habit. I often lay thinking and planning before I fall asleep– since I was being abducted–I certainly had a lot to think about."

"Did you have any experiences with the other plants?

"Yes. We used the natural antibiotics on a native boy who had a badly infected foot. It rid him of the wound infection and promoted deep healing."

"Does the artist know that you are seeking the advice of counsel?"

"No, but I have not yet asked him if he would share his remedies with the world. I just wanted to know what the procedures would be if we decided to do so; get off on the right foot, so to speak."

"If you are sure of the viability of these remedies; the best thing to do would be to set up a limited corporation with copyrights to protect your interests in this diary now and then patents for the specific remedies later on. Once secure, you would be able to sell your information to the highest bidder, or go into the herbal business yourself. There are no governing agencies here in Africa, but you would have to pass all the FDA regulations before marketing your products in the States.

"Since these are African plants, and your source is Africa; to mass produce the plants, they will probably have to be grown here. It is possible the growing conditions could be simulated elsewhere, but the earth and climate of Africa is unique and not so easily duplicated."

"I do not think we will want to go into business. If we do sell, it will be to the highest bidder with royalties. Whatever documents you need to draft should be based on that premise. It is possible that we could go into the growing business; supplying the plants in a dried form; but that would be a future consideration. Right now, I just want to protect the written knowledge in my diary."

Cyril asked, "Would you care for an after dinner liqueur?"

"Yes, an Amaretto would be nice."

They went to the Lounge, where it was secluded and quiet, with a piano player playing light classical music. Cyril wanted to hear about Paula's abduction and subsequent escape from the Ndezi. He listened intently; the story, from beginning to end, boggled his mind. He knew Africa was still savage and primitive, but abducting white women was just not done! He had never heard a story of personal danger told in such a rational and unemotional style. She was the first woman he had ever admired; where were women like her when he was younger? Long ago, Cyril had decided he was a man's man and avoided women, most of whom irritated him to distraction.

What he did not know was that Paula had never had a close interpersonal relationship with a member of the opposite sex. She had been kissed, but only casually, not intimately. There was some deep-rooted reason why she kept all men at a distance. Her friendly manner never invited intimacy. In fact, she could be quite condescending if casual liberties were taken. She had wondered if something was wrong with her, until she rode piggyback with Tamubu; for up to then her libido had been non-existent. She dated, but in groups and usually around an activity, like sailing, tennis, riding or hiking. In college, she hung out with the nerds, when she had time to hang out at all. There had been only one young man that had interested her. He was the Program Instructor for the Civil Air Patrol, but he was married. For some reason, she was perfectly happy that her brothers and her father and uncle were the men in her life. Them, she could trust... and now, she felt she could trust Thomas and Jon. In fact, for the first time in her life, she wanted a man's attention and company. She was so happy she had found Thomas again. She had to be honest with herself... she had deep feelings for him.

When they finally said good night, it was quite late. Cyril walked Paula to her room; his room was a bit further down the same hall. Paula was having mixed emotions. She was thrilled with the good the plants could do; but sorry to have this ancient knowledge be the pawn in a power game. Before they parted, Cyril told Paula he was going to return to Nairobi in the morning. Paula had already told him about her travel plans with Thomas, Jon and Kybo, and he had decided there was nothing more he could do here.

It would be better to have the necessary documents ready for them, when they arrived in Nairobi. Nothing else needed to be done until then. Paula had insisted on giving him a retainer fee and reluctantly, she had allowed him to take the diary with him for safe keeping. It was her personal piece of Tamubu–paging through the drawings always brought him close to her–giving her comfort. But, Mr. Latham was right. Her diary was valuable and needed to be kept in a vault.

CYRIL HAD MANAGED TO get a seat on an early flight that eventually arrived in Nairobi. He had finished the work he had brought with him and was rearranging his brief case, when he picked up Paula's diary to again look at the masterful drawings. The diary opened to a page that said in big block letters:

'I'm free! I've escaped!' and continued in normal print, 'I'm hiding inside a huge laprodis plant, called a devil plant by the natives. I hope and pray its evil reputation will keep me safe from the Ndezi, who are certain to come looking for me.'

Cyril closed the book, leaned back and closed his eyes. The pictures the words conjured-up were chilling. Now comes the test he thought: to read on or to put it away. He took the diary and put it back in his brief case thinking. It's going to tempt me, I know, until I have sinned.

He fought with his conscience for over an hour and finally rationalized: no one is going to know I have read it. No one told me not to read it.

The devil was working hard to undermine his principles. Finally, Cyril thought, just one more random page, just one!

He took out the diary and opened it to a page near the front of the book. His jaw went slack as he became riveted by the words on the page.

'I watched, as the traders were marched out of the village under escort. What did that mean? I was soon to find out!

A woman came to me and took off all my clothes, leaving me only my panties. She then braided my hair and greased my whole body. I was sick with worry as she led me to the edge of my aerie. I saw the villagers gathered below, circled around two women, who were greased and naked. One had a yellow stripe down her back–the other had a white stripe. Their right ankles had been tied together with a leather thong, with about fourteen inches between them. Their left arms were bound to their sides, above the elbow.'

THE PAGE ENDED. CYRIL closed his eyes and thought, I am damned, but I cannot stop. He turned the page and read on.

'THE INSTANT THE DRUMS began to pound, the women began tugging each other by the ankle, while striking out with fist and nails. Each was taking a severe beating when yellow was struck a blow to the stomach and doubled over. White was getting ready to drop a severe blow to her exposed neck, when yellow butted white in the solar plexus with her head and yellow's hand slid ineffectively off white's back, for she had lost her balance from a mighty tug on her ankle and fell backwards.

'A man came over with a wickedly curved hunting knife. He cut the rope that bound them and held the knife poised over the woman on the ground. I was horrified, I could hardly breathe; my heart was pounding in terror. Was this going to be my fate? Then, in a blur, the knife plunged down, and I turned away. The woman beside me poked me hard, and turned me back to look at the scene below. I saw the man with the knife help the woman to get up off the ground. She was holding her hand to her ear and blood oozed through her fingers. The woman beside me mimed cutting off the top of my ear. I felt dizzy and sick at the thought of such mutilation.'

CYRIL CLOSED THE DIARY and his eyes. He tried to put the blithe woman he had met yesterday into such a dire situation. She had weathered severe trials and still met life head-on. Maybe severe trials did that for you. He himself had never been threatened with physical menace. He had been too young for World War I, and a desk jockey in World War II. He had no affinity for danger, so he just couldn't fathom her feelings.

'Only a few minutes later, the old woman led me to the circle below. I too, was tied to my opponent. My left arm was fastened tightly to my chest, just above my elbow. Kira looked at me with hate and malice. She waved her long pointed fingernails and I knew she meant to scar me if she could. I drew on my years of gymnastic competition to close out the crowd and to focus on the challenge. At the first beat of the drum, I stepped into an aerial. I knew it couldn't be completed, but if we both fell, maybe we could avoid the penalty. With the centrifugal force of my right foot swinging up into the air, Kira had her right foot pulled so far up, she fell backwards and as she fell, I was able to raise my right foot even higher, which allowed me to fall on my hands and flex my elbows, for a springback onto my left foot. In less than five seconds, Kira was on the ground with me standing over her.

'The crowd stood mute in astonishment. I saw Bolbonga heading towards me with a huge smile, holding another nasty looking hunting knife. He handed it to me, hilt first. I bowed my head and prayed for strength. Was the penalty for falling, death? I wasn't going to kill anyone for these ghouls. Taking a deep breath, I knelt down and looked at Kira, who seemed unconcerned by her fate. What stoic strength she had. I raised the knife and plunged it down towards her enlarged and distorted ear, slicing part of it off.

'I heard the mass uptake of breath; the sound of astonishment and surprise from the crowd. I stood up and walked back to my prison aerie, where I stopped when Bolbonga spoke out.

'"The Bahariki does not know our customs. She did what she thought was required of her. I forgive her and ask you to applaud her stunning defeat of Kira."

'The men cheered, the women rattled bracelets and made a high warbling sound. I turned and went up the steps to my bower. Bolbonga ordered out the palm wine to celebrate my victory.

'I went quickly to my privy and wiped the blood off the knife, which I hid in the pile of furs. I lay down and pretended to cry when the old woman came up with hot water and soap. She guided me to a stool where she took the braids out of my hair. She washed the grease off my body, called for more hot water and left me to wash my hair alone.'

Cyril closed the diary and put it back in his briefcase. He was stunned. He now knew that, eventually, he would read the whole diary, and the knowledge made him happy, in a curious–I know something you don't know–sort of way.

Paula repacked her cases again. The Expedition related gear had already been sent home. She now packed a case of her best things to send on to Kenya. Her safari clothes had come back from the laundry, and her backpack was reorganized for day trips.

Paula put the grass gathering-bag Tamubu had made for her inside the turtle shell, which she put it in her bag for Kenya. She remembered how humble his gift had made her feel, and also, how inept. What if he had not waited and followed me that day, after he saw me coming through the trees? I owe my life to his curiosity... to a whim... or was it really destiny?

It was teatime when Paula heard a knock on the door. "Yes, who is it?"

"Tea, madam, compliments of the hotel manager." The kitchen steward had a full tray: teapot, cups & saucers, silverware, sugar, cream, scones, butter and jam, which he set up on the small table for two beside the window.

Paula was surprised but said, "thank you" and tipped the steward as he left. She never turned down a cup of Earl Grey tea... especially not at teatime.

Taking a cup of tea and a scone to the writing desk, Paula continued her diary entries. She was almost finished, having written her letters first. She had another cup of tea and finished the scone, while rereading her diary entries for omissions. Her eyes closed, her head nodded and then she was asleep.

When Paula awoke, it was dark and she felt chilled. Standing up to go and turn on the lights, she tripped over something on the floor. Feeling around on her hands and knees, she felt clothes, papers and possibly her suitcase on the floor. Crawling carefully to the bed, she reached for the bed lamp to find it gone. Feeling the way before her, Paula crawled to the door of her room, rose and rocked the switches back and forth–still nothing. Frustrated, Paula opened the door to the hallway. The hall lights were working, so it wasn't a power problem. She looked back into her room, now dimly lit by the hall light, and gasped. Her room had been ransacked! Staring, unable to comprehend what she saw, a passing bellboy greeted her.

"Good evening, Madam. Is there anything I can do for you?"

Turning to him, she motioned him over and pointed to her room–what they could see of it by the hall light. He passed her and went into the room to turn on the lights, but they didn't work for him either.

"Madam, I will be right back. Stay here in the hall." Good to his word, the bellboy was back in a few minutes with the hotel manager and two security guards.

While the security guards searched the room, the manager asked her, "What happened?"

"I don't know. I had been writing letters when your complimentary tea tray came, thank you, and then I fell asleep. When I awoke a few minutes ago, I went to turn on a light and fell over something on the floor. The lights wouldn't go on, so I opened the door to the hall for light just as the bellboy passed by. He saw this disaster and went to fetch you."

"We have the lights on sir. This room has been ransacked. You will have to move this lady to another room. Miss, come in please, and see if you notice anything missing." The security guard hovered over Paula as she looked around the room.

Paula could not believe that she had slept through such destruction. She had a terrible headache; maybe I was drugged, but by whom–and how?

The manager went to one of the security guards and told him to gather up the tea things as best he could. "I suspect our guest was drugged."

"Miss, would you please look to see if anything is missing."

Paula began to pick up her things and put them in order. The security guard put the lamps and drawers back in place and righted the furniture. She did not have that much with her, so it wasn't long before she noted that her new diary was gone and so were the letters she had written that day.

Immediately, she thought, thank you Cyril Latham! They were after my diary with the drawings and descriptions of the plants. If they had found what they wanted, would I still be alive? Her earrings and ring and bracelets were still in the secret compartment of her backpack, but everything else was scattered

"Mr. Shoby, only my papers are missing–my diary and letters."

"Were they valuable Miss?"

"Not to others, only to me. The diary was new today and the letters were just to family and friends."

"Did you have an old diary?"

"Yes, but I sent it to Nairobi."

"Would it have had any value?"

"Yes, I believe it would... but only to certain people."

"Do you know these certain people?"

"Yes, but he went to America two weeks ago."

"Are you certain?"

"No, it is just what I was told. I will make a few phone calls. Then I will have more information for you."

"The most important thing, Miss, is that you are unharmed. Gretchen here will show you to your new room and the bellboy will bring your things. I am most sorry that you have had this trouble under my roof."

"Before you go Mr. Shoby, may I ask: did you send me a complimentary tea tray?"

"No Miss, I did not. I'm truly sorry that this happened because of your trust in our staff."

"Will you call the police?"

"Since you are well, and nothing of monetary value

is missing, I can spare you the inquisition of the local constabulary. They are truly unpleasant. I will just file a break-in and damage report. Of course, you may replace any damaged goods at our expense."

"Thank you, Mr. Shoby. May I ask that you change my name in your guest register to Mrs. Maximillian Mason of Cape Town, South Africa?

"Of course, dear lady, anything for your safety; do you think they will be back?"

"I don't know–this was all so unexpected!"

Kybo Missing

JON HIRED FOUR WAHUTU scouts, including Bonomo, to guide them to Yaoundé. The warriors were honored to escort the Medicine Man of the Great Zuri Watu. Bonomo kept up a steady pace back to the camp where they had left Kybo, arriving as the dusk melted into night.

There was no sign of Kybo, but Bonomo, coming down from the tree, said their gear was still hidden high above. Tamubu immediately told them to find another place in the big trees where they could spend the night. No fire, travel rations only. Jon was going to spend his first night in a tree. Blast! And this is only the second day on the trail! But he was so tired from the fast trip back to Kybo's camp, that all he wanted was rest–anywhere!

When everyone was settled for the night, Tamubu left to *roam*. There was a full moon with only a scudding cloud cover. He made his way quickly to the river. There he found what he had hoped not to find... the deep V grooves of boats moored in the silt along the riverbank. It was no accident that they had stopped here–Kybo had lit a fire.

Tamubu knew that the river raiders would return down river, if they had a captive, or at least one boat would go back–for these sadists liked the safety of numbers, being basically bullies and cowards. He continued to *roam* down river and was rewarded when he found two boats pulled up on a silted-in snag below a high bank. There was a sentry sitting atop the bank under a tree swigging rum from a jug. Tamubu wished he had his pouches with him. Then the man would be asleep in minutes.

Looking for a way to scuttle the boats, Tamubu found Kybo lying on the bottom of the larger riverboat, gagged and bound in a net with his hands and feet tied. The other boat was empty. *Roaming* ashore, Tamubu found the motley group of misfits taking turns at another jug of rum. He listened to the conversation for a short time, none of which related to Kybo, but concerned: "...getting back down river before the hippos returned."

Tamubu saw that this had not been a meal stop. Once the rum jug was empty, they would return to the boats. Do I have time to free Kybo before the rum runs out? I need a knife to cut his bonds. As he watched, a ruffian arose and went into the bushes where he took off his thick heavy belt and laid it on the ground beside him, so he could pull his drawers down. Tamubu materialized behind him, picked up a rock and hit him on the head. The man went down without a sound.

Tamubu removed the knife from his scabbard and made his way back to the river, upstream of the boats, where he slipped into the water taking a small leafy-branched limb with him for cover. Drifting down the river, the limb came to rest beside the silted-in bank with jumbled debris. With cat-like stealth, Tamubu climbed into the riverboat under cover of the overhead branches and in moments, had Kybo free. Tamubu shook his head and put his index finger to his lips to indicate silence and signaled that a sentry was above them. He then gathered the ropes and net that had bound Kybo and took them with him as they slowly and quietly slipped into the water. Tamubu then let the current take the net and cut ropes away, knowing that they would sink once they were waterlogged. He gave Kybo the knife to put in his empty scabbard before they submerged to swim upriver.

Kybo had been hit on the head and trussed-up while he slept beside his little fire. The whole time, after he had awakened as a prisoner, he berated himself for not paying attention to the Kigozi and keeping a cold camp. To see the Kigozi in the boat, naked, with a knife in his hand cutting his bonds seemed to him to be the delusion of a man suffering from a head injury. Only when the water flowed over him did Kybo appreciate that the Kigozi was truly here; that somehow he had found him and saved him. Kybo had suspected that the Medicine Man of the Great Ziri Watu was allied with the spirits; now, he was convinced that Tamubu was Dogo Mungu (little god), as Motozo had said, and he would never again disregard his instructions.

The water held no safety for them. It was the home of crocodiles, poisonous water snakes, leeches and the unpredictable hippo. Only their slow and cautious movements kept them from attack. As soon as Tamubu passed the fallen tree, with its branches mired in silt, he left the water for the dark forest. Kybo followed close behind. The full moon shed intermittent light on the murky forest trail where the growth thinned along the river, but the night was dense in the thick woods, where Tamubu said in a whisper, "Climb this tree, to the top. Hide yourself there; cut little branches to cover yourself until I return for you."

"When will you be back, Kigozi?"

"By noon tomorrow; you will just have to suffer there until I come back for you."

"Yes, Kigozi, I will do as you say. May I offer you my clothes since you are naked?'

"No, my clothes are not far from here. I took them off before I went into the water. Also, you will never tell anyone that I was here. If asked, you will tell them that you found a knife in the bottom of the boat, and you rolled over on it until it was safe to use it to escape."

Kybo, who never lied, questioned Tamubu's reasons not at all.

After a short distance, Tamubu *roamed* back to camp where Jon and the Wahutu scouts were still sleeping–unaware of the deadly menace.

In the morning, the group returned to Kybo's hilltop camp and there read the story of his abduction. They followed the trail to the water and there Tamubu said, "They would go down river. They have a prize and would want to be off the river before the hippos return from the night's feeding ashore."

The Wahutu led the way for a bit, until Tamubu took the

lead and picked up the pace. At a rest stop he told them, "Be watchful and ready for the river raiders. They go ashore during the day, and wait to ambush hapless travelers."

The Wahutu knew of these foul men, for the Nyong River ran near their village. Sentries with drums were placed along the river to warn the village of their passing, but they could sneak by in the dark of the night.

It was nearing the apex of the sun when a forward Wahutu scout reported *sign* of an encampment ahead. Tamubu said, "There are *sign* of passage here too, one person, maybe two. We will follow the trail and see. Of course, Tamubu knew it was the twig he had broken to mark the way they had gone last night.

They moved inland seeing an occasional broken leaf until Tamubu stopped. He looked around, then looked up, and said, "Do I see Kybo high in a tree?"

Kybo moved the greenery and smiled. "Yes, Kigozi, you see Kybo."

There were huzzahs from the Wahutu as Kybo clambered down from the tree. Jon was suspicious. I have seen no trail to this tree. Granted, my woodsmanship does not compare to that of the Wahutu, but I sensed their reluctance too. They had decided to follow Thomas rather than question the omniscient Medicine Man of the Great Zuri Watu. No matter, Kybo was found, alive and well.

Tamubu cautioned them to travel quietly. He led them through the deep forest until they crossed a trail. Bonomo whispered, "Kigozi, these tracks go toward our village." Tamubu thought: I was afraid of that. But said, "Jon, what do you think about a change in our plans?"

"Such as..."

"Why don't we go back to Douala and take the train to Yaoundé? We have been going back towards the Wahutu village the whole time we've been looking for Kybo."

Jon sensed a purpose and said, "Yes, that is a good idea. We brought all the gear with us, so there is no reason to go back that way. I agree. A train trip to Yaoundé makes a lot of sense." What didn't make any sense was the rush. Jon now carried his own pack and the extra fifty pounds used up a lot of his energy.

He was about to speak up when Tamubu halted the group and said, "We must cache our belongings high in this tree, and take only our weapons with us."

Bonomo spoke up. "What is wrong, Kigozi?"

"I think the raiders have cut through the forest towards your village."

Bonomo smiled and said, "That would be foolish. We have hundreds of warriors. There can be no more than twenty raiders."

Tamubu turned to him, "Bonomo, they are already beyond your sentries. The raiders will not announce their presence. Only women and young children working near the forest will be taken. The raiders will be gone long before the women and children are missed."

The Wahutu men moved quickly and cached their belongings high in the trees. In a matter of minutes, Bonomo led the group at a double time pace, with Tamubu, Jon and Kybo bringing up the rear with the rifles and bandoliers of cartridges. A mile from the village, the group split up.

The Wahutu scouts returned home and alerted the chief; whereupon the warriors left the village to infiltrate the forest and surround these villainous scoundrels. Tamubu led Jon and Kybo towards the river, hoping to get behind the raiders, and so block them from returning to their boats if they already had captives.

When Jon and Kybo were safely ensconced in thickets beside the trail to the river, Tamubu left on reconnaissance. In a little bit, he stashed his things to *roam* to the river; where he found the river raider's boats, manned by armed guards, still waiting. Returning to the forest, Tamubu crossed an old trail that was no longer used because the wait-a-bit had grown so thick. Nearby, he found a trail freshly hacked through the leafy overgrowth. Scouting the newly hacked-out path, Tamubu realized that Jon and Kybo were too far to the east to intercept the raiders returning to the river; and hearing noises in the brush, feared there was no time to reposition them.

Tamubu moved toward the noises. He saw Jon and Kybo scouting for another path from the village to the river. Good, he thought: the main path to the river is already guarded by the Wahutu–now they will find the newly made path and be able to prevent the raiders from returning to their boats that way.

Tamubu moved past Jon and Kybo up the freshly cut trail. All seemed quiet and normal at the village, until he saw the glint in the brush, just before he saw the movement. He knew he had to intervene. Going to a comely young woman with a child weeding the beds near the forest edge, he whispered in her ear, "Take your child and go home–now! Vipers are lurking in the forest."

The woman looked around, her eyes wide with terror. She picked up her toddler and loudly cried out, "Snakes! Snakes! Run!" In moments the vegetable fields were clear. Tamubu *roamed* back to his belongings, passing the Wahutu warriors who were filtering into the forest, like fingers on a hand. These men were adept hunters and stalkers, who had special ways of dealing with the kind of snake they would find hiding in the bushes.

When the skirmish was over and the raiders were captured, Tamubu went to Jon and Kybo, who, hearing nothing, were still secreted beside the newly cut trail. "It is over. The raiders have been captured. We can go back for our things now."

"What about the sentries with the boats?" Jon asked.

"The Wahutu will get them too, unless they panic and sail away. I, for one, don't want to be here tonight. It will be a gruesome evening."

Jon knew the natives took revenge on these river marauders when they were caught. That was as it should be, but his curiosity was piqued. "What exactly will they do to them? Do you know? They seemed to be so civilized to us."

"Yes, I do know. And, yes, they are civilized until they are threatened. They have the right to protect their families, and their particular kind of punishment for the raiders will insure their safety for a long time to come."

"Are you going to tell me what they are going to do or not?"

"Use your imagination, Jon, and whatever you come up with will be a blessing compared to what is going to happen to them tonight."

Jon looked at Kybo, who shook his head and shrugged his shoulders, as if to say he didn't know either.

It was not long until they came to their cached possessions and Tamubu said, "This trail will take us back to the junction, do you remember it Jon?"

"Yes. The Wahutu have several rest stops hacked out of the forest, which is good, because we do not have time to reach the junction before dark. The drums had begun while they were recovering their gear. When the last bag was handed down and Kybo was almost to the ground, Bonomo and Gubu appeared to retrieve the traveling packs that had been stashed in the tree.

Bonomo said, "You are leaving, yes?"

Tamubu replied, "Yes Bonomo, we are leaving. This evening is not for guests."

"Do you require a guide?'

"No, I remember the way. But, if the drums could ask Ben and Gomojo to come for us at the junction tomorrow, we would be pleased."

"The drums will speak for you. Chief Kuteka has asked me to give you a message."

"What is the message?"

"The Wahutu are grateful to the Medicine Man of the Great Zuri Watu for his help in averting a tragedy in our village today. The Wahutu thank his associates too. We will always be ready to return the favor, if ever you need us."

"Please tell Chief Kuteka and the Elders that we are honored to have the Wahutu as our friends."

Bonomo and Gubu gathered the traveling packs, which Kybo had gone aloft to retrieve for them, and in the blink of an eye, they were gone.

Jon, never one to let a situation go without a comment,

said, "If Ben and Gomojo show up tomorrow at the junction I, for one, will feel we are even-steven."

Kybo, who was usually taciturn during the exchanges, said. "Kisha, Ben will be waiting for us when we arrive at the junction tomorrow."

Jon turned a swift eye to Kybo, who flinched not, but stood like an Archangel who had just announced the Immaculate Conception. Kybo had made up his mind that Jon was the assistant (kisha) and Thomas was the leader (kigozi) and his leader's word was gospel.

Tamubu chuckled to himself as he started down the trail. This change of plans, for some reason, made him happy. He had never been on a train, and looked forward to the experience. Soon, he would be with Paula again. He thought of seeing Ben and Gomojo too; he could inquire about Maybella. Maybe they would have time to visit her again.

They did not travel long before they came to a clearing surrounded by a thorn boma. "What do you think Thomas? Have we come far enough for today?" Jon asked.

"No, we will go on to the next clearing. There is a nice rock overhang there to keep us out of the rain tonight." Thomas replied.

"Well then, let's get cracking, I'm hungry!" Jon said as if he was whipping up the troops. Kybo, in the rear, smiled. He had become very fond of Jon and his gung-ho attitude ever since he had joined the trading safari. His whimsical good humor was contagious.

After a night spent snug and dry, Jon minded not at all the misty morning, for he had slept well. Thomas made oatmeal for breakfast and Kybo made delicious coffee. All was right with the world for Jon.

It was late morning when Thomas saw Gomojo coming down the trail to meet them. After greetings, Thomas said, "I hope we have not kept you waiting long?"

"Not at all, I just wanted to walk in the forest to meet you. Baba is reading the newspaper and my uniform is in the coach. We saw Miss Thornton to the train early yesterday morning. She would have waited for you, had she known you were coming today."

"We did not know we were coming today, until mid-day yesterday." Thomas replied. "How is your grandmother?"

"She is much better now. Will you have time to visit her?"

"I would like that, but first we must bathe."

Ben heard the voices and arose from the little stool where he had been reading his newspaper, close to the horse's heads. Today, both Belgians were harnessed. The drums had said three men and packs. Ben was meeting Kybo for the first time. He was glad he had hitched both horses. Kybo was a huge Nigerian, probably six foot, six and three hundred pounds.

Tirini had packed a picnic lunch. She sent homemade sausages wrapped in fresh bread, with pepper relish and mustard if desired. With such short notice, she had not had time to make bread pudding, but sent fried sweet potato chips and fresh fruit salad. They sat together in the shade of the sepele tree while they ate, with Jon waxing grateful for the delicious meal.

Gomojo said, "We would be able to eat like this every day, if you stayed longer." Everyone laughed. Especially his father who was still amazed at the change wrought in his son since meeting Tamubu, Jon and Missy Paula.

During the meal, Jon regaled them with the happenings of the past few days. His ability as a storyteller enthralled his listeners; even Tamubu and Kybo enjoyed his version of the recent events.

"There will be no train tomorrow." Ben said. "Rioters blew up a section of the track last night, and the repairs have only just begun. If you have no other plans, I am making my weekly visit tomorrow; Mother would be happy to see you."

Ben continued, "Kybo, we would be happy to have you as our guest until the train is running again–or do you have other plans?"

Kybo looked at Tamubu, who shook his head approvingly, before he replied, "I have no other plans and thank you for your offer."

"Good, then we will drop you off on our way into town.

Tirini has been after me to turn the soil in her flowerbeds, but I have not had the time. Possibly, you would do that small favor for me?"

"It is as good as done. I always turned the beds for my mother when I was at home."

Jon reflected on the exchange. If an Englishman asked a guest to do manual labor for him–it would be an insult–but for Ben to ask Kybo to turn the flowerbeds was to let him pay his way and not accept charity. It was a way of saving face for Kybo.

When they reached the hotel, Mr. Pandi said their former suite was occupied, but the owner's suite was available–but it had no balcony. Thomas smiled when Jon said, "My dear fellow, we don't need a balcony. We just need a hot bath and clean sheets!" Tamubu took a step back and looked at Mr. Pandi and shook his head slightly. Mr. Pandi immediately got the message. Mr. Jonathan did not know that Mr. Thomas had slept on the balcony during his previous visit.

Tamubu thought: One night in a smelly bedroom won't kill me. But he was pleasantly surprised, because the owner's suite was a 'no-smoking' suite and did not smell of cigars at all. And later, he was even more pleased to find the bed firm, like a pallet with many fur rugs on it. Maybe I was too hasty in forming a poor opinion of sleeping in a hotel.

Tamubu and Jon dressed in clean Safari togs after bathing. Jon wanted to walk about the town a bit and buy a camera. Tamubu wanted to walk to the café for dinner and have some bread pudding for dessert. So, with destinations in mind, they stepped out into the roadside bustle on a pleasant evening.

Plans Change

"THOMAS! THERE'S AN IMPORT Shop. Let's see if they have cameras, if you're not too hungry."

"I can wait." The shop had a good selection, and one camera, in particular, fascinated Jon. It had a zoom lens and automatic flash and was small enough to fit in his chest pocket. Tamubu browsed while Jon was occupied with the salesman. The shop was a Smorgasbord for him–the selections were endless–many of which puzzled him as to their use.

During dinner, Jon said, "I like the idea of a train trip to Yaoundé. I hope the track repairs will be finished in two days, as expected. I sent a telegram to Paula telling her of our delay. Is there anything you wish to do while we are here, besides visiting Ben's mother?"

"I think it is a mistake to plan each day so closely. I think it is best to see what will present itself and make decisions from there."

"That is fine when you are wandering through the forest, but train and plane trips require reservations, for which it is necessary to plan ahead."

"Yes, that is true; but who knows what is going to happen to change the need for those reservations?"

"I think what you are saying is: you want to *play it by ear*."

Tamubu smiled at his little riddle, but did not rise to the bait. Instead he said, "Yes, when the tracks are repaired, we will go to Yaoundé. Tomorrow I want to visit Ben's mother. Do you wish to go along?"

"But of course–you will need a translator." Tamubu smiled

to himself as he thought: I wonder why it has not yet occurred to Jon that Ben's mother speaks Bantu as well as French.

"Tamubu said, "We must take some gifts with us. We will go shopping again after dinner."

"I think I have turned you into a shopping monster."

"It is wonderful to go into the shops and choose anything you want. It pleases me."

"Once my traveler's checks run out, your pleasure will be over."

"What are traveler's checks?"

"Have you not seen me giving the shopkeepers pieces of paper on which I signed my name?"

"Yes, but I thought you were just giving them your name, so they would know you."

"Hardly, dear boy; I was giving them traveling money; money that only I can spend."

Thomas thought about this for a few moments before he asked, "Do you have a great deal of this traveling money; enough to pay for travel all the way to Kenya?"

"I believe so–but I also have a letter of credit."

"What is a letter of credit?"

"It is a letter that tells a banker that my drafts are good, so I can buy more traveling money."

"What is a banker? What is a draft?"

Jon threw back his head and laughed. "I think it will bc better to wait until the time comes when I need to use a banker and make a draft to explain the process to you. Suffice it to say, we have enough money to get home to Kenya... and to go shopping too."

Thomas smiled with pleasure, "Good, but I will be cautious in my choices."

Jon hated the thought of Thomas having to be cautious–he had fourteen years of shopping to make up for, so he said, "You choose the things you would like to purchase. I will tell you if they are too expensive, and you need to choose something else."

Thomas raised his eyes to this dearly beloved brother and replied, "You will not have to tell me–I will know."

And Jon thought, yes, you always did know... you always did the right thing... and I always wanted to be just like you.

Gazing deeply into Jon's eyes, Thomas said, "The world would have been a sadder place if there had been two of me and none of you. You have special qualities that no one else possesses. You are a gifted person." So saying, he arose and strolled towards the men's room.

Jon sat perfectly still, stunned, thinking–I used to wonder if he knew what I was thinking... now it seems he does know... but does he know all the time, or just at certain times? The enormity of this revelation was beginning to unnerve him when the waiter arrived with the check.

Out on the street, Jon asked, "Do you know all the time?"

Thomas thought for a bit; then said, "I know when you think with your heart."

They walked in thoughtful silence until Thomas saw a shop that had safari clothes and supplies in the window.

"Here is the shop I wanted." Thomas knew he would find the warm woolen knee socks he desired. He also found *3in1* whistles: compass, whistle and match holder, and bought four of them. Jon found a small air mattress that was pumped up with a foot pedal, which deflated to a small package. He was thrilled with his find, and while they didn't contemplate sleeping on the ground in the near future, he felt he had to have it. As an afterthought, he bought four of them. He also found camping hammocks, which had telescoping spreaders and tiny air pillows. He bought four of them too. He bought four waterproof ground cloths, because they were as light as air... with the comment, "You never know!" Jon asked that their purchases to be sent to the hotel.

They left the shop, letting their curiosity take them down different streets or through narrow alleys; it made the stroll interesting. In one such narrow alley, Thomas saw a beggar who had lost his legs from the knees down. He had beside him a small short hair dog that lifted a bowl in his mouth as they approached–and then sat up and begged, still holding the bowl. Jon and Thomas were touched. Jon put a liberal donation in the dog's bowl. The crippled man saw the generosity, and eyed

Thomas keenly. 'Your good hearts and generous alms deserve a good deed in return. Do not take the train to Yaoundé.'

Thomas met the focus of the almsman, and held his gaze so he could not look away. In a moment, the street and everyone in it faded away, until all that was left were the black eyes of the mendicant. Thomas was drawn into his gaze, beyond the obsidian orbs, to a place where he saw the wreckage of two passenger cars of a train. Closing his eyes, he broke the contact with the beggar.

Thomas reached into his medicine pack and took out a rolled leaf, which contained a salve. He leaned down to the beggar. 'This salve will help the pain of your legs and stop the festering. Wash only with boiled cloths and clean boiled water before using the salve. Asante.'

Turning to Jon, who was still amused by the little dog, which was now standing on his hind legs and turning circles to say thank you for the alms, he said, "Come, it is almost dark. I do not want to get lost on these back streets." Jon hastened along as Thomas strode away.

"I say, what's your hurry? The hotel is in the next square; look, you can see the widow's walk from here."

Thomas glanced up and then headed for the hotel at the next corner. Once in their suite, Thomas excused himself, leaving Jon slightly baffled, for he had not heard the warning of the beggar–for neither Thomas, nor the beggar, had spoken aloud.

In his room Tamubu prepared to *roam*, leaving through the window. He went to the train depot and listened to the talk of the station-master and would-be passengers:

"It is expected that repairs to the tracks will take another two days... possibly longer."

"Should we purchase our tickets now?"

"You could, but seating is still on a first-come basis, even in first class."

Tamubu breathed into the stationmaster's ear, whereupon he said to the couple facing him, "Why don't you wait until the tracks are repaired. If you have connections to make, you could take the daily commuter plane to Yaoundé, which leaves at eleven each morning. With all the unrest, it is the safest way to travel right now."

Tamubu left the depot and went to the local police station. Here too, he whispered into the constable's ear. The lieutenant stood up, straightened his tunic and bellowed for his sergeant. A head popped into sight and he began to issue rapid orders. Tamubu listened to the orders being given, before he felt satisfied enough to return to the hotel. He had done what he could to save lives, for he could not prevent the tragedy. The stationmaster would be reluctant to sell tickets for the next departure; and the police would alert the soldiers guarding the tracks.

Ready for bed, he rejoined Jon in the sitting room. "What did you say to Paula in your telegram?"

"I just said, 'we are delayed; the railroad tracks need repairs; will wire our ETA.'"

"What is an ETA?"

"Estimated time of arrival."

"Oh. I saw you talking to the Concierge, did you ask him about the train?"

"Yes, he thinks the repairs will take at least five days, maybe longer."

"Why did you not say that to me?"

"Shall we say? I felt the need for a little civilized living?"

"So, before we are even gone, you have had enough of trekking in the wilderness."

"Nothing of the kind, but I do enjoy my creature comforts."

"Well then, you will be pleased to know there is a plane to Yaoundé every day, except Sunday. How would you like to reserve three seats for the day after tomorrow?"

"That would be smashing! You sure you don't mind? I mean–small planes and all."

"No, I feel I have a destiny to fulfill, which does not include dying in a plane crash."

"Good show; how did you know about the plane?"

"Two men were talking in the men's room of the café. They called it a milk flight."

Jon laughed, “That means it stops at every little town with an airport.”

Jon picked up the phone. Concierge, please... Thank you. I want to book three first class tickets to Yaoundé for Friday... Jonathan Caulfield, Thomas Caulfield and Kybo bin Kimbo. Yes... I see. Well, have a go at it then, and leave the notice with my key.”

“Problem?”

“No, I suppose not. The concierge said seats were on a first come, first served basis, but he would see what he could do.”

“Ben will be here early tomorrow. Would breakfast at six be too early for you?” Thomas asked, as he walked to his bedroom door.

“Not at all; I suppose I should be delighted that the breakfast café doesn’t open at five.”

At six, just before first light, Jon and Thomas were seated in the hotel’s café, ordering melon, sausages, scrambled eggs, croissants and coffee–except for the coffee–foods that were not available on the trail and therefore a treat. The service was good and they found themselves able to return to their suite for their packages, and the necessary, and still be on time to meet Ben at seven.

HE ARRIVED WITH MUCH ado, for both Belgians were hitched to the flat bed wagon. Behind the driver’s seat, Tirini sat on a bench facing backwards with a large hamper under the bench. Up on the driver’s seat, Gomojo was sandwiched between Kybo and Ben, who looked odd without his coachman’s livery. Thomas and Jon stepped on the rear wheel hubs to gain the wagon bed and sat on either side of Tirini with their feet propped up on building supplies and tools. They greeted each other and indulged in some good-natured bantering with Kybo.

“I hope you are not up there to learn a new trade.” Thomas said.

“No, Kigozi, it is the only place I would fit. Ben needs my help to repair the cottage.”

“Well then, it is good we are doing it today–for we plan to fly to Yaoundé tomorrow.” Kybo’s mouth gaped in amazement. Thomas added, "The train will not be running for a few days."

The two Belgian horses worked well together. They were able to maintain their speed on the gentle grades built for fine carriage horses. Conversation was limited due to the noise of jingling harness, clopping hooves and metal-rimmed wheels, along with the roar of the ocean surf pounding the cliffs at high tide. But the vistas were so entrancing that no one really found the need to do much more than point and speak in monosyllables.

Gomojo stayed to water and pull grass for the horses at the wide turn-around under the sepele tree. Kybo carried the roofing slates, for the cottage was built in the Cotswold fashion of England, while Ben carried the tools. Jon and Thomas carried supplies and flowers, while Tirini carried the huge hamper on her head. Thomas felt more at-home at that moment than he had since leaving the Zuri Watu, and Jon had the easy feeling that he was back on the trading trail with Max.

The needed repairs were accomplished with much laughing and a workman's song, for Jon and Thomas would not be left out of the deeds of the day, and carried and fetched with alacrity. Tirini set out the luncheon feast on the sideboard. Ben's Mother, Maybella, set out the lovely china plates and fine silverware with linen napkins and cut glass crystal glasses on the dining room table. The Countess DuVries had given the contents of the cottage to Maybella, asking that they be kept in the cottage and used for special occasions.

Ben gave the Blessing, after which, Jon regaled them with their feats in capturing the river raiders. Over bread pudding and coffee, Thomas gave out his presents. He gave Maybella the woolen knee socks, and a *3in1* to Jon, Kybo and Ben. He gave a small nut chopper with attached bowl to catch the chopped nuts to Tirini, who was delighted with the gadget.

Jon was not to be outdone. He had boxes of confections for Maybella and Tirini and cigars for Kybo and Ben. While the women cleaned up, Ben returned to the wagon with his tools. Gomojo was then able to go and eat at the cottage and visit with his grandmother in the kitchen.

Soon, Gomojo, Tirini and Maybella joined Thomas, Jon and Kybo, who were sitting on the porch in the wooden rocking chairs. Kybo gave up his seat to Maybella. Tirini took the fourth rocker, and Gomojo sat with Kybo on the steps. Thomas presented Gomojo with a *3in1*, and Jon gave Gomojo a hunting knife in a tooled leather sheath with matching belt, which he had sized to fit him. It was a happy group that later strolled back to the waiting horses to go home.

The late afternoon sun was hot on the return, but the sea breeze kept them comfortable. They reached the hotel in time to have soup and a sandwich in the café before it closed at eight p.m.

Back in their rooms, Thomas said, "It is sad that Paula was not with us today. She would have been so pleased to see Ben, Gomojo and Tirini again, and to meet Maybella and to see the cottage. It was much bigger inside than it looked outside. It reminded me greatly of home, bringing back all sorts of memories that I had forgotten.

"You seemed as though you had never been away and were comfortable with your surroundings. I was quite surprised when you took your napkin and placed it in your lap before anyone else did so–you are not as far away from your upbringing as you think."

"I don't remember doing it. I was anxious to get to the special treats Tirini had brought for us. Nanoka used to make Kowanya, those fried liver and bacon wraps with the nut inside for my family day. I haven't had them in a long time."

"What's a family day?"

"Since Nanoka and Sashono did not know the day of my birth, they celebrated the day I arrived in the village, calling it my family day."

"The kowanya were delicious. I had not had them before. The whole meal was superb. It was a wonderful and happy day. It would have been super if Paula had been there, but I took a great many pictures with my new camera to show to her."

"Did you see the message from Captain Jones?" Thomas asked.

"Yes. It will be good to see him again. I am looking forward to American style pancakes and sausage à la Jonas." Jon replied, "And I'm looking forward to a nice hot bath too."

It was a hazy morning. The thick wispy fog would evaporate once the sun rose above the foliage; but the walk to the pier was eerie. People and horses would instantly emerge from the veil, and the piers themselves were gangplanks into an unknown abyss–only the high yellow light above the motor yacht gave them any assurance.

"Permission to come aboard" Jon called loudly.

"Permission granted" came the reply close at hand.

"It is a real pea-souper down here. Can you see us?"

"I'm standing next to you." Captain Jones replied as he stretched out his hand in greeting.

"Good of you to come along and show us below."

"There are three steps after the gunnel to the deck–here take my hand." Jon and Thomas negotiated the steps and hand on shoulder followed Captain Jones below. In the subdued lighting of the saloon, there was a strong delicious smell of freshly brewed coffee.

Jon spoke first, "Do you get many of these pea-soupers here? The closer we came to the wharf, the thicker the fog became; it was like walking with your eyes closed."

"We get a few, but they don't last once the sun comes up... unless there is rain too. I'm glad you made it okay. I hope your flight isn't delayed because of the fog. While it will probably be clear at eleven, take-off might have been delayed at Pointe-Noire or Port-Gentil."

"It will be as it will be." Thomas said. "We are in no hurry. The change from train to plane puts us in Yaoundé sooner than expected."

"What a lucky stroke it was that I offered to take the passengers from the *Dark Gypsy* to the hotel yesterday. Mr. Pandi saw me and mentioned that you were back in town. You must tell me why."

Over coffee Jon began to tell of the events that led to their return to Douala. He had just finished, after the fluffy pancakes and sausage patties were consumed, telling of their new plans to sightsee instead of overland trekking on their return to Kenya.

"I almost envy you such a spectacular trip–but in a week's time, I'd be longing for the sea." Over pipes, Captain Jones and Jon exchanged sea stories while Thomas went below to ask Jonas for his pancake recipe. Ten o'clock arrived all too quickly. Going topside, they found the day had cleared off nicely. Jon took pictures of the motor yacht, her sailors and themselves for Paula. In twenty minutes, they were at the airport, and true to his word, Mr. Pandi had seen to it that their luggage was waiting for them on the jitney.

After heartfelt goodbyes, Captain Jones left, waving a cheery hand.

Jon watched him go, feeling pensive, and thought: Will we ever see him again? He is such a bon vivant–I would like to have a life like his some day. I want to take Thomas home, but there are some people who make it very hard to say goodbye.

Thomas knew what Jon was feeling, for he felt the same way too.

Telegrams

PAULA RECEIVED THE TELEGRAM from Jon on Saturday. She was surprised that they had returned to Douala; but pleased that they would reach Yaoundé sooner–once the tracks were repaired. When she received the second telegram this morning, telling her they were flying to Yaoundé today and would arrive this afternoon, she was delighted and decided to hire Gangis to go to the airport to meet them.

Calling the front desk, she found the plane would arrive around one o'clock if it left Douala on time. The concierge said he would make sure Gangis was available to drive her to the airport after lunch.

Paula had spent yesterday evening rewriting her stolen letters, so after breakfast this morning, she mailed them, and obtained another diary from the gift shop in the hotel, courtesy of Mr. Shoby. She prefaced her new diary with a message to the thieves: 'Please do not steal this diary. It contains nothing but the daily events of the owner. The diary you seek has been sent to my attorney for safekeeping. P.M.T.'

Paula then brought the diary up-to-date. Rereading the preface, she decided to dash-off a note to Cyril Latham, saying he had been right to want to place her diary in a bank vault, and told him of the break-in yesterday. When she finished, she freshened up and went down to mail the letter and have a bite of lunch before going to the airport.

It was a lovely day. It had started out rainy, but now, the white fluffy clouds were high in the sky. The town looked fresh and clean, the daily coating of dust had been washed away. Gangis clucked to Molly who seemed a bit reluctant. "I don't usually go to the airport," he said. "The officials don't like having horses and mules near the terminal, as they can be quite difficult about the noise. It isn't the noise that bothers Molly, it's those enormous diving metal flies that terrify her." Paula laughed at his humor. "I will drop you at the terminal and then wait for the plane to arrive about a mile down the road. After I see the plane land, I will return for you."

Paula had not checked with the airport to see if the commuter plane was on schedule, she had expected the concierge to do so, and was therefore dismayed to find the flight was delayed two hours due to heavy morning fog.

Paula had never been good about waiting; she refused to stand in line for restaurants, movies, or shops. In college, when she saw a long line, she skipped the event or registered by mail. On occasion, she had even resorted to asking her father, a Professor, to get her in first.

She knew her impatience with lines, queues, or waiting rooms was a flaw, but the only line worth waiting in for her was the line made when her row was next at graduation to get their diplomas.

Paula decided to explore the little thatched buildings beside the runway and look at the planes parked down the field up against the thick undergrowth.

The mechanics were gruff and one said, "You shouldn't be out here, miss!"

She replied, "Are any of those planes for sale?" With that question, the mechanic's attitude changed to interest.

"Yes, two of them are for sale."

"Who do I see to inspect them?"

The mechanic said, "I can show them to you. How many hours of flight time do you have?"

"Several hundred, but none here in Africa; but I have twin engine certification in America."

"Well then, you don't need me. Here are the keys for the Cessna Twin and the puddle jumper at the far end of the field."

Paula took the keys and walked down the ballasted runway. She had no interest in buying a plane now, but she loved to look at them. Someday, she had vowed to herself, she would again take to the skies as she had in College with the Aviator's Club and Civil Air Patrol. Thinking about those stolen hours away from the books, she realized they had really been some of the best days of her school years. She had gained something valuable and had enjoyed every moment of the intensive flight school program. Paula had been one of two girls, and the only one not an ROTC candidate in the course. After a short time, the boys let up on joshing her–since she was tops in the class. Flying had been as natural for her as riding horses or gymnastics. In the air, she had a second sense as to what was around her all the time. She imagined herself an eagle and soared with absolute delight.

Paula had only cursorily looked at the single place BeechCraft. It was old and tired and had been used as a crop duster. But the Cessna Twin was a beauty. She climbed aboard and saw that it had less than two hundred hours flight time. She sat in the pilot's seat and imagined herself going through a pre-flight roster, checking gauges and flipping switches. Finally, she sighed, and alit from the plane, where she stood to lock the door.

She saw a man by the tail and thought it was probably the mechanic having second thoughts about giving her the keys... when she was grabbed, from behind by strong arms. A rough hand covered her mouth and pinched her nose before she could even react. She had never felt so completely immobilized. She could move nothing but her feet, and then her ankles were tied. She knew that she was being assaulted by two strong natives, from the slightly sour smell of their sweat and the many hands working in unison to overpower her. The keys were wrenched from her hand and she heard the distinct sound of a key being inserted in a lock.

Were they going to steal the plane? She would be blamed... but only if they took her with them: oh no, not again!

With her hands and feet tied, a gag in her mouth and a hood over her head, Paula was carried, even as she struggled, at a jog for a short distance. She was put down and rolled up in a musty old carpet. Again she was hoisted up onto broad shoulders and carried away. She began to feel dizzy and became nauseous, not only from the lack of air, but also from the unsynchronized jog of her abductors. She wondered what would happen if she had to vomit with a gag in her mouth... when she became aware of the idling rotors of a helicopter. She then heard a door latch, just before she was put down on a hard surface and pushed hard. She did not feel her abductors board the helicopter; she only heard the door close and then a voice spoke in French requesting clearance to take off.

Not only was it hard to breathe, it was also very hot inside the rug. She told herself to relax, for she was using up too much oxygen, but her nervous system was filled with adrenaline and paid her no mind keeping her reflexes functioning at top speed... and then she remembered nothing more.

GANGIS FELL ASLEEP EASILY–AND did so, as he waited for the plane to arrive. He slept lightly however, and knew he would awake when he heard the noisy Douglas DC-3 arrive. He did not like going to the airport, nor did Molly. The huge buzzing flies coming towards her made her want to buck and run off. It only took Molly five minutes, with an empty cart, to trot the mile back to the terminal. It would take longer than that for the passengers to deplane and gather their luggage.

Waiting almost in the same spot, where he had dropped Missy off, Gangis watched the passengers gather their belongings and head toward the Range Rovers. It cost ten times as much as he charged to ride in a Range Rover ... but, of course, it was ten times faster. It was much further to the airport than to the railway station. It would take him an hour with five and luggage to get back to the hotel. Molly was a huge, almost seventeen hands high, white mule and pound for pound she was stronger than a draft horse. But when Gangis had a big load he let Molly set the pace. At times, he had asked big heavy men to get out and walk up the steep hills–another reason he did not like going to the airport–too many hills.

All the passengers had gone to the Range Rovers and Gangis still did not see Missy Paula and her friends. He was not allowed to leave Molly tied–nor did he want to do so–to go in search of her. The last Range Rover to leave had a huge Nigerian hanging on to the back. As the vehicle neared his wagon, it slowed and the Nigerian asked, "Do you want a fare?"

"I have a fare. I brought Missy Paula to the airport to meet her friends. Did you see a pretty blonde woman?"

At his words, the doors opened and out stepped two men, one of whom commanded his attention, for he had a kitukina draped over his shoulders with an ancient ivory and gold talisman for a clasp.

He spoke in Bantu. "You say you brought a blonde-haired woman to the airport to meet her friends, and her name was Paula?"

"Yes, bwana, I did. But I have not seen her since the plane arrived."

"When did you last see her?"

"It was just after one this afternoon. I was told to take the mule and wagon down the road until the plane landed. I did not see her when I returned."

"Kybo, put our packs in the wagon and wait here with the driver. We will go inside and see what has happened to Paula," Jon said, before he traipsed after Thomas."

Jon jogged until he caught up with Thomas. "Wherever could she be?" He said, "There is no place else to go but down the road from the terminal."

With his jaw set, Thomas said, "We will find out."

The attendant manning the desk remembered Paula quite well. "She was too early since the flight was delayed and she left the terminal. Outside, Thomas saw the thatched huts along the runway and headed for them. The mechanic saw him coming and said to his co-worker, "It seems today is a day for tourists–here come some more."

When Thomas reached the man, he greeted him saying, "Have you seen a young woman with silvery blonde hair today?"

The mechanic was surprised, but answered, "Yes, she is down looking at the Cessna Twin. I thought she would have been back by now–there's not that much to look at when you buy a plane–until you take her up."

"What do you mean?"

"I mean that she wanted to know what planes were for sale and went off to look at them."

Amazed, Thomas glanced at Jon who stood with his mouth open. "What planes did she go to look at?"

"The two on the end–down near the undergrowth."

Thomas thanked the man who then called after him. "Remind her to return the keys when you see her!"

The mechanic turned to his friend and said, "What did you make of that lot?"

"Different... very different; the man who questioned you reminded me of the witch doctor in my village; he was very intense."

"Yah, that's what I thought too."

Thomas walked quickly to the planes at the end of the field. When he reached the Cessna Twin, he said, "Stay back Jon, there are a lot of scuffled prints here that I want to read."

Jon did as he was told, but ran his eyes over the plane where he saw the keys in the door lock. "Thomas, the keys are still in the pilot's door."

Thomas glanced up and saw the dangling keys and his heart plummeted. "Stay there Jon, I'll be back in a minute–don't come any closer to the plane."

To the plane, Paula's prints were quite clear for she was wearing shoes with small square heels. At the pilot's door, her prints were overlaid with the sandal marks of two large men, probably natives. These marks were scuffled and then two men with a heavy load walked towards the woods. In a moment, he found a wide flattened area and then the marks of the men, again carrying a heavy load, strode off. He followed them to a place where the helicopters landed. The ground was too hard for clear impressions, but it seemed the men's footprints went to the landing pad. There was a little building nearby, but it was empty. Thomas returned to Jon and said, "I greatly fear Paula has been abducted again."

Jon just looked at him speechless.

"We must go back to the terminal. I need to talk to the attendant there."

On their way back, the mechanic called out, "Did you find her? Did you remind her to return the keys?"

Thomas turned and said, "The keys are in the pilot's door of the plane with two engines. Do not remove them! Do not go down there! The spoor indications are that Miss Thornton has been abducted. The police will want to see this for themselves."

The mechanics just stood there looking at him, as if he had said, 'She flew to Mars'.

Thomas strode into the terminal and walked over to the attendant who was reading a tattered copy of Air and Space magazine. Young man, you must call the police. Miss Thornton, the blond-haired lady you saw earlier, has been abducted. Were there any other planes in or out of here today?"

The attendant stood transfixed by Thomas' words. Then realizing he had been asked a question, said, "No, no other planes today."

"Not even a helicopter?"

The attendant's mouth dropped open and his eyes widened. "Why, yes, there was a helicopter in today, but just to refuel. He was only here for half-an-hour or so."

"Do you have an identification number? Has the helicopter refueled here before?" Jon asked.

"Not that I know of... looking down at his log, he gave his number as 1-163 Nigeria. He said it was an emergency stop. The fuel mechanic said he only took half a tank, apparently he needs a new fuel gauge."

Jon spoke again. "Do you have a book that lists all registered fuselage numbers?"

"Yes, we do." The young man pulled out the book and gave it to Jon while he called the police.

"It is as I suspected. That number is not registered. It is not even the proper sequence for a helicopter." Jon told Thomas. "I wonder that the attendant did not notice it–unless he thought Nigerian numbers were different."

"Jon, stay here and wait for the police. I will go and tell the wagon driver he can go."

On his way back to the wagon, Thomas' mind filled with questions. Who had known Paula was going to the airport today? Why would anyone want to abduct Paula from Yaoundé? I wonder if anyone saw two strangers hanging about today. But why would they hang about–unless they knew she was coming here?

Thomas saw Gangis sitting in the driver's seat with his mule in the shade. He turned when he heard Thomas approach. "Did you find her?"

"No, the *sign* point to an abduction."

Gangis was shocked, thinking: Who would want to abduct the lady and why?

"You are free to leave now. Please take our luggage to the Grande Hotel. We have reservations there: Thomas and Jonathan Caulfield. Leave your bill at the desk. If you think of anything that was unusual, please, even if it seems silly to you, let us know."

Gangis drove off taking Kybo with him. Kybo had asked for a good place to stay in Yaoundé and Gangis had said his brother would put him up. He had a nice place with two bedrooms and would enjoy the company. Gangis was not only unhappy–he was very annoyed. He liked the blonde lady. He would talk to his cabbie friends when he got back. No one was going to abduct his fare and get away with it!

Jon and Thomas were tired and hungry when they finally arrived at the hotel, but the dining room was closed, as was the coffee shop.

Jon signed the register, and saw, several names above his, in room 210, a name he knew quite well. When the clerk turned back with his room key, Jon saw it was room 212 and said, "Do you know the lady in 210?"

The desk clerk looked at Jon and said, "No sir, I did not register the lady."

Shrugging his shoulders Jon went to find Thomas who was

wandering around the lobby, as usual. "Thomas, you'll never guess who is registered in the room next to us."

"I'm sure I won't...who?"

"A Mrs. Maximillian Mason, what do you think of that?"

"Isn't that the name of your trader partner?"

"Yes, but his wife has been dead for a long time. Odd, don't you think?"

"Yes, quite curious."

When Jon and Thomas left the lobby, the desk clerk went to the house phone and called Mr. Shoby. "Sir, two men, who had reservations, just came in and asked if I knew Mrs. Mason. I had given them the room next to her before he asked if I knew her. I denied knowing the lady, saying I had not registered her."

"You did the right thing in calling me. Are they in 208 or 212?"

"They are in 212."

Mr. Shoby took off his smoking jacket and put on his suit jacket. He sat to take off his slippers and put on his business shoes when the phone rang again. He reached over and said, "Shoby here."

"Mr. Shoby, we have had a room service order from room 212. The gentleman asked if I had delivered any trays to room 210 today. I told him I did not have that information as it had gone to the accounting department. We are preparing the tray now, what would you have us do?"

"So far you have done quite well. I will meet the steward in the hall. He is not to deliver the tray without me."

"Yes, sir," the steward replied.

Mr. Shoby pressed the receiver and rang security. "Shoby here, meet me in corridor 200 in ten minutes."

Jon was surprised when he opened the door to find two men in suits, with the room steward and tray in the rear. Before he had a chance to say anything, Mr. Shoby said, "I am the hotel manager. Might I have a moment of your time?"

Jon opened the door all the way and stepped back. Mr. Shoby directed the steward to set up the meal while he and the security manager stepped inside and closed the door.

"We are sorry for this inconvenience, but you asked the room service operator if there had been any trays delivered to room 210 today–why?"

Jon was wondering if the police had asked the hotel to question any inquiries about Miss Thornton, so he said, "I have a partner, Maximillian Mason from Cape Town, but his wife has been dead a long time. It was such a coincidence, that my curiosity was aroused."

"You also asked the desk clerk if he knew of Mrs. Mason."

"Why, yes I did!"

Mr. Shoby opened the door for the room service steward to leave before he replied. "Will you please tell us why you are here in Yaoundé?"

Thomas spoke up saying, "We are here to meet Miss Thornton."

Mr. Shoby felt the full force of Thomas' personality, so he directed his reply to him. Before we needlessly involve our guests with the police, who can be difficult, we wanted to examine the situation ourselves."

"We know that Ms. Thornton was abducted; I called the police from the airport." Thomas replied.

"What is your connection to Ms. Thornton?"

Thomas said, "She is my fiancée."

Jon smiled, "And I'm her duénna."

The humor passed over Mr. Shoby. He was much too concerned about his guest disappearing, especially since he had not reported the break-in of her room to the police.

"Please, gentlemen–sit and eat your dinner. I have a story to tell you. Yesterday afternoon, Ms Thornton's room was ransacked. Someone, acting as a room steward, brought her a complimentary tea tray. The tea was drugged and she fell asleep. When she awoke, the room was demolished, but she was unharmed. The only things missing were the letters she had written that day and a diary, a new one that she had purchased only that morning. She said they were of no value or importance, so we did not notify the police. I just placed a break-in and damage claim. We moved her to another room; and she asked that we place her on the register as Mrs.

Maximillian Mason of Cape Town. I now think she used that name to alert you when you checked in, since Mr. Mason is your partner.

We have been keeping a close watch on anything to do with room 210. We have been monitoring her calls and telegrams, so we knew you had wired her of your arrival today. The staff had been alerted to call me when you arrived. Then the police called from the airport to tell me that Ms. Thornton had been abducted and to monitor all calls and correspondence of any kind, which I had already been doing, for we take the security of our guests, especially the unescorted females, quite seriously."

Thomas said, "Thank you for sharing these past events with us. It has put an entirely different light on Paula's abduction today. Did she happen to say what she had done with her old diary?"

"Yes, she said she had sent it to Nairobi for safe keeping. She had also mentioned that only one person she could think of would have tried to get it from her... but she said he had gone to America. Ms. Thornton then said she would try and find out if he was in America or not. I can check the switchboard to see if she placed any overseas calls. Will that be of any help to you?"

"Yes, any information about her activities would be useful."

Before he left, Mr. Shoby said, "Feel free to call me at any time if I can be of further service to you or Ms. Thornton."

JON LOOKED AT THOMAS and said, "What would make her diary so important?"

"I used it to draw the healing plants and wrote a description of the uses and the preparation of the plants in the back of her diary. Paula said she had shown it to Dr. Miles when she resigned from the Expedition."

"Ah, yes! Now I remember, she said, '...the pompous egoist was blown away when he saw your drawings...' I had forgotten that comment. I hated to admit that I wasn't quite sure of her meaning."

"I wonder if he is the one responsible for having her room ransacked; and not finding the diary–had her abducted."

"I remember seeing your drawings when Paula was asleep on the beach with the pages fluttering in the breeze. Would they really be that important?"

"It is hard to believe, but it would seem so... for Dr. Miles, and possibly the drug company that sponsored the Expedition, are the only ones that know about the diary."

Jon thought aloud: "We only sent the telegram this morning from the hotel. Paula would not have had it long before she hired Gangis and his cart to go to the airport. Who would have known what she planned to do?"

They looked at each other and together said, "The concierge!"

Jon picked up the phone and said, "Mr. Shoby, please." The phone rang only once before it was answered, "Shoby, here."

"Mr. Shoby, Jonathan Caulfield. Thomas and I can think of only one person that would have access to the information about her activities, which would be necessary to coordinate her abduction... that being the concierge."

"I also came to the same conclusion; but the lad on duty in the morning went home sick and has not been heard of, or seen since. You have no idea how upset I am by these events. First, an unknown kitchen steward delivers a drugged tea tray; then a guest's room is torn apart; and now the concierge has passed on private information that might have facilitated the abduction; and now he has disappeared.

"After I spoke to you, I passed on these happenings to the Police. They were very annoyed with me, saying I withheld information–and they are right, it was a bad decision not to call them after the break-in."

Knowing the local Police could be extremely obnoxious to tourists, finding them to be all sorts of problems, Jon could understand why Mr. Shoby had not summoned them after the break-in. Now, not having done so put him in a negligent position with the authorities.

Gangis was more disturbed than he appeared when he heard of Paula's abduction. He felt responsible for her; she was his fare. He dropped the bags off at the hotel and then went home early. He saw to Molly, giving her a nice rubdown and fresh water and hay before he went in and told his wife of his day.

She suggested, "Why don't you go out and spend some time with the other cabbies. You might hear something."

"Yes, I'll do that." Gangis took two empty beer bottles and filled them with lemon water. He was not a drinker, but did not want to seem a prude to his fellow cabbies.

Each evening, the drivers gathered at a little café for beer and conversation. There were always different cabbies there at any given time, but all felt the need to talk... after listening most of the day. Gangis was pleased to see his good friend, Bube there. They had gone to Christian School together, and had both married girls they had met at the school. "Jambo, Bube!"

"Jambo, Gangis. Come sit with me. What is the news?"

"Gangis brought Bube up current on his personal news before asking, "What is going on with you? Why are you sitting by yourself?"

"I have had a bad day," Bube replied.

"I am sorry to hear that. Can I help you?"

"I wish you could... but the deed is done and cannot be undone."

"What deed is that?" Gangis' curiosity was now aroused.

"I do not want to speak of it. It is too upsetting for me."

"Well then, we will talk of other matters."

Gangis had the feeling that Bube was referring to Ms. Thornton's abduction. But he could not imagine that he had any part in such nefarious matters. He decided to prime the pump saying, "I had a fare stolen from me today. It has been a bad day for me too. We will just sit here and complain about our wives!"

Bube laughed. "Troli is such a good wife; I would have to make up lies." At this they both laughed, for this was a favorite pastime.

"What lie would you tell today?"

"Troli made a stew for dinner, but she forgot to put in meat or vegetables."

"Did you beat her for this?"

"No, because I forgot to give her the meat and vegetables; they were still in my cab!" They laughed, as friends do, before Bube said, "It is your turn."

"Noruda gave the baby a bath in a bucket. When she went to take him out, he was stuck fast; she had to call a neighbor for help!" They enjoyed making up these outrageous stories about their wives, and the laughter they evoked.

"But," Gangis continued, "It is hard for me to laugh. My fare was not only stolen, she was abducted; and the worst part is I have no idea how it happened."

"You too, Bube said, "I heard others talking about a fare that disappeared from the airport this afternoon."

"Yes," Gangis said, "That was my fare."

"I am so sorry to hear that. That is why I am so upset."

"Explain, please."

"I took two men to the airport today. I told them they were going much too early, as the flight was delayed several hours. They insisted I take them anyway. Before the flight even arrived they were back, and wanted to return to town. When Robergo, the policeman, heard this, he came to me and asked me for descriptions of these men. I did not know them. I had not seen them before. Wc did not talk much. They sat in the far back seat of the Range Rover. Robergo said two men overcame a woman at the airport and put her in a helicopter, which flew her away. I feel responsible."

"Do not be so harsh on yourself. You are a taxi driver. You drive those who want to go somewhere. You do not decide whether they should go or not! But I did not see you at the airport today."

"That is why I feel so guilty. The men asked me to take the service road that goes to the fuel depot. Halfway there, they told me to stop and got out. I saw them go into the forest, thinking they wanted to relieve themselves... but they were gone a half-hour. When they came back, they wanted to go back to town. I feel I should have suspected something. They were definitely not locals, I think they were Nigerians."

"The police will do what they can to find those scoundrels."

"I feel so bad Gangis, that if I didn't have payments to make on the Range Rover, I would get out of this business."

"You feel that way today, but tomorrow you will have the Prime Minister as a fare or someone else important, and then you will feel better."

"I hope so."

Gangis chatted for a while telling Bube about the adventures of Ms. Thornton being lost out to sea. "She is a survivor. She told me about Jon and Thomas. They are brothers. Thomas was lost in the rainforest when he was ten and only just found when Jon went searching for Ms. Thornton. Thomas, called Tamubu by his tribe, is a Medicine Man from the Great Zuri Watu and knows much. We will go and see them in the morning."

At 7:00 a.m. when Thomas and Jon came down for breakfast, Gangis and Bube were waiting for them. It took not long for them to tell their tale. Thomas was now positive that it had been the young man who had substituted for the sick concierge, who had given the information to the abductors. But this was now a police matter and meddling would be dealt with harshly.

SINCE THE MAU-MAU REBELLION in the fall of 1952, any European or American being abducted was under the sole purview of the Superintendent of the Police. At this point in time, Gangis and Bube were blameless, but could be harassed if they messed in affairs considered *not to be their business*. While the problem erupted in Kenya, Europeans (or whites) in the entire country had suffered a loss of confidence, for it had been the natives that were most trusted and who were allowed to move freely about their homes, that had murdered under the guise of loyalty.

It had shattered the ability of the whites to ever again completely trust the blacks working for them.

Black policemen were an entirely different species of native. They felt so superior to the rest of the black population that they dealt with their fellow man in a much harsher manner than the whites would have done, often beating them senseless for minor infractions. Interference would not be tolerated.

The Mercenary

Paula breathed in the dusty smell of the old carpeting and wondered about the sour smell when, through the miasma of drugs, she remembered being abducted from the airport. Whatever was the reason this time? She thought. Why does this keep happening to me? It was hard to breathe inside the rolled up rug and she was unable to move anything but her toes.

Panic crept over her with a hammering heart. Only by sheer will did she force herself to relax to use less oxygen. Then she heard the click of a door latch. Her cocoon was pulled along the floor before strong arms grabbed it, and toted her away. The bouncing ride ended a few minutes later when she was put down, and unceremoniously unrolled from the rug. Hands fumbled with her bonds and removed the hood and gag. She was told to keep her eyes closed as strong arms lifted her under the arms and dropped her in a wicker chair, where she was tethered. She heard footsteps and than a door closed.

After a few minutes of total silence, Paula tossed her hair from her eyes and peeked around the small shack. It was not a native hut, more like a large storage locker of some kind, and she was alone. There were three other chairs in the room, all pushed up against a small dining table. There were some boxes in a corner, and an unlit naked light bulb hanging from the ceiling. Daylight filtered in through two very dirty windows near the roof, which were opened out, awning style, to admit some fresh air. Her hands had been retied in front of her, but her ankles were still bound together. She had a rope around her neck that she thought might be attached to the wall, for she could not move her head forward at all. Being restrained in this unusual fashion terrified her and brought back the panic, making her heart thump and her breath labored.

Breathing deeply to slow her racing pulse, she forced her mind to examine the situation. Her eyes wandered around the shack and landed once again on the hanging light bulb. We must be close to civilization to have electricity... or possibly there is a generator nearby. The building looks like an airport storage facility–similar to the ones used by the Civil Air Patrol for emergency gear. I haven't heard any telltale noises of other aircraft. It was a short trip from the airport to this shack... for the sun is still high, but that doesn't mean much; I could just be in any field–anywhere. The room does smell musty and unused.

She hoped someone would come soon... she needed to relieve herself. No sooner was it thought, than the door was pulled open and a big Nigerian filled the doorway making her wonder if all Nigerians were so huge.

In Swahili, he said, "Do you need a pot?" Paula nodded a yes. He sat the pot inside the door before walking over to untie her bonds, which released her from the chair. Once done, he turned and went out the door shutting it behind him. Paula stretched and walked to the pot, which had several cornhusks at the bottom. Paula laid the husks on the ground, used the pot and returned to her chair. The Nigerian must have been waiting outside, listening, because, almost immediately, he opened the door, hung a canteen on a nail, and took the pot away.

After a few moments, Paula went to the canteen and smelled it. It smelled like water; she took a sip and it tasted like water so she slaked her thirst.

Moving around felt good–limbering exercises felt even better–until she heard someone outside the door. Quickly, she sat down in her chair. The door opened upon a tall man dressed in khakis, wearing a broad-brimmed hat pulled down low to touch large shiny reflective sunglasses–with a bandanna covering his nose and mouth western style; the man looked ridiculous. Paula didn't know whether to worry or to laugh. He pulled a chair from the table and sat down. He looked at her for a long time.

She has nerves of steel, he thought. I know men who would be sweating buckets in this situation. Yet, she is cool and calm. I don't think she will frighten easily. She must be alarmed, but her control is amazing. Why must I meet the first woman I have ever admired under these circumstances?

Paula sat thinking: Is this a war of nerves... or what? But suddenly, she felt empowered. If he intended to kill me, he wouldn't care whether I could identify him or not. He is doing this to intimidate me... and it is working... but he'll never know that!

The man spoke: his voice was fluid, soft but commanding. "It is not my wish to harm you–but I have been hired to obtain your diary, the one with the plant drawings in it... at **any** cost! It will be much better for you if you tell me directly where it is, and spare yourself the grief of interrogation."

Paula heard the tones of threat in his voice and knew that he was deadly serious. She thought for a few moments before she replied. "If I tell you 'directly where it is', what assurance do I have that you will let me go unharmed?"

"I am a man of my word; I have to be in my business; it is all I have for references."

"How will you go about setting me free?"

"I will return you to Yaoundé airport the same way you were taken from it."

"Then I have your word–all I have to do is tell you where the diary is, nothing more."

The man hesitated a few moments, sensing a trap of some kind, but he could think of none, so he replied, "Nothing more."

"The diary, with the plant drawings in it, is in my attorney's vault in Nairobi, Kenya."

Paula could not see the shock and surprise on the face of her captor, but it showed plainly in his body language; so she continued. "I do not know if it was you who ransacked my hotel room, but surely, if you did, you found only the new diary I had purchased, because the old one was no longer in my possession. I cannot give you what I do not have. Now, I have told you honestly where the diary is... will you keep to your word?"

The man said nothing. He sat for a long time looking at Paula. He was obviously considering his options. Finally he spoke. "What made you send your diary to Nairobi?"

"I had written to my Uncle, who is an attorney in the States, asking him for advice. He, in turn, contacted a friend from law school who has a practice in Nairobi. The friend was waiting for me upon my arrival at the Grande hotel. He later insisted on taking the diary back to Nairobi with him–for safekeeping. So, you see, it is not in my power to give you the diary."

PAULA'S INQUISITOR THEN AROSE and left, saying nothing more. Hours passed and no one came. The daylight faded and Paula dozed from the boredom and monotony of the jail-like shack. It was almost dark when the door opened and a plate of food was set inside the door. She saw no one. Soon the aroma of cooked food lured her to the wooden plate. She pulled the *5in1* from her chest pocket and ate the usual stew of vegetables, the biscuit and an orange. There was still plenty of water in the canteen to wash the meal down. Predictably, the food was drugged and she was soon asleep.

THE FIRST THING SHE heard was hollering voices in the distance, then nearby, "The lady is found. She is asleep in the crop duster. Come quick!" It occurred to Paula that the voices were referring to her and she opened her eyes to see the bare-bones interior of the old plane. A tremendous feeling of relief surged over her. The man had believed her, and was true to his word.

Opening the pilot's door, for there was no copilot seat, she made her way to the ground just as several people descended upon her, all jabbering questions. Paula raised her hand for silence, and in a calm manner thanked everyone for their concern, telling them she was all right. The group walked with her to the terminal building, where the clerk immediately called the police. Someone came with fresh water and asked if she was hungry. "No, I am fine. What day is this?"

"It is Thursday afternoon. You were taken yesterday afternoon. Where did you go?" asked the mechanic.

"I do not know. I was drugged and wrapped in a rug. I know only that I was questioned and then drugged again and returned here. Are the police coming to the airport? Could I not go to the hotel and talk to them there?"

The clerk picked up the phone and called the police station. When he hung up, he said, "The police are already on their way, so you must wait here."

"I need to wash up a bit." Paula told the group and headed for the restroom, where she locked the door and used her bandana with the cold rusty water, washing as best she could. Even so, cleaning up was refreshing, for the rug had been very dirty. The police arrived shortly after her ablutions, and questioned her only briefly, because she could tell them nothing. They put her in the Police Land Rover and took her to the hotel.

When she arrived, there was a group waiting for her: Tamubu, Jon, Mr. Shoby and Gangis, who was so overjoyed that he could hardly stand still. She went to him first, for he must have been extremely upset by her disappearance while in his care. "I am just fine Gangis, do not be upset."

"Missy, I thank the good Lord that you have come back to us safely."

Paula turned to Thomas and Jon and gave each of them a hug. Thomas held her close to him for a lingering moment.

Paula stepped away and said, "I'm so glad to be back... the more I'm abducted... the less I like it!" Her humor dispelled some of the tension. She looked directly at Mr. Shoby, smiled and said, "I hope there is plenty of hot water for a bath and I would love a pot of Earl Grey tea."

"Your wishes are our commands." Mr. Shoby replied. "You must stop giving us such frights. We will behave properly without them!" There was a titter of laughter, for Mr. Shoby was rarely jocular.

In the corridor, Jon left Paula with Thomas saying, "I'll meet you both later for Tea."

Tamubu took her hands and held them close to his chest, looking deeply into her eyes, and said, "I was beside myself while you were gone, for there was nothing I could do to help you. It made me aware of how deep my feelings are for you. We have much to talk about... after you have rested."

Paula was thrilled by his words. "Yes, we must talk. I was only gone a short while, but during that time I was desolate, because I knew you wouldn't be coming to save me. It made me realize how much it means to me, that I can count on you being there for me... as you promised."

Tamubu folded her into his arms, held her close and whispered, "Later."

Paula replied, "Yes, later." He released her; she smiled at him and went into her hotel room.

Jon was waiting for Thomas when he came in and said, "Well, that was a rum show... gone a day, and no valuable information at all. Thank goodness... at least she's back and safe, and no less for the wear. I say, do you really think this has all been over the drawings you did in her diary?"

"It would appear so."

"Then I must send a wire to that attorney in Nairobi, and tell him to ship the diary to his firm in London, or have them ship it to the States or something. He could be in great danger too. I say, this is pretty frightful stuff!"

"Yes... and I've thought of another problem too..."

"What's that?"

"If they feel the diary with the drawings is completely out of their reach... might they not go for the artist?"

Jon's mouth fell open–his eyes widened–and horror masked his face. It took a moment before Jon was coherent. "You! Do you think they'll come after you?"

"They seem pretty determined, so I'd say there is a good possibility."

"What should we do?"

"I don't have plans yet, but I feel it is necessary for us to leave this hotel and begin our trek at once. We must make no plans through the hotel or tell anyone what we are going to do."

Jon jumped up, "Kybo! What about Kybo? He is staying with Gangis' bachelor brother. We could go get him and leave from there." Jon picked up the phone, "Mr. Shoby, please."

"Shoby here."

"Jon Caulfield, Mr. Shoby. Would you be kind enough to come to our room? There is a problem I cannot explain over the phone."

In less than ten minutes, Mr. Shoby knocked gently on the door. Jon admitted the dapper hôtelier, closed the door and offered him a seat. "Mr. Shoby, we are sorry to have to summon you like this. It is most important that no one knows what we are doing. We perceive a threat to our lives, and want to disappear into the night. Can you tell us how to contact Gangis? Our man, Kybo, is staying with his brother and we need to alert him to our departure."

Mr. Shoby smiled. "Gangis is, at this moment, running an errand for me, a personal errand, so he should report to me directly when he returns... in about an hour."

"That is perfect. If you will personally prepare a bill for us, Miss Thornton too, and bring it to us when Gangis returns, we can pay you and you can square the hotel accounts tomorrow or the next day. It is vital that we have at least that much time before anyone knows that we have gone. We do not mean to insinuate that your staff is corrupt, but the men who mean us harm would not be averse to using force on your minions to obtain information."

There was a soft knock on the door. Tamubu went to open it. Paula stood there looking sparkling clean, but damp. She said smiling, "Jon promised me a proper English tea, and I am here to collect it!"

Mr. Shoby prepared to leave the room before the door was closed, pausing only long enough to say: "English tea for three coming right up."

Jon immediately explained the problem to Paula; she nodded her head in agreement.

"That's why I came over so quickly. It occurred to me that

they might try for the artist too... since the diary is beyond their reach. I am packed to go; I just have my backpack, and one bag that I can leave here to be forwarded to me later."

"How is your ankle doing?" Thomas asked.

"The rest this past week has made a big difference, but rough trekking might make it sore again. Maybe I should stay here and meet you somewhere later."

"No, we must stay together. Apart we are vulnerable." Thomas insisted.

The details were no sooner settled, than there was a soft knock on the door followed by "Room Service". Paula rushed to the door. She was famished for something besides the tasteless vegetable stew she had been given.

The tea was delicious. Scones, fruited cake, crusty fresh bread with butter and jam, and a shepherd's pie of chicken, potatoes, carrots, peas and mushrooms; and, of course, tea with clotted cream or lemon.

They were hardly finished with the afternoon feast when Mr. Soby tapped on the door. He had Gangis with him and the bill in hand. "If I can do anything else for you, please, just ask."

Paula spoke up. Would it be possible for me to leave a bag here until I have a forwarding address?"

"Of course, dear lady, do you gentlemen have bags to leave too?"

"No, we have no extra luggage, but thank you for the offer."

"Just leave your bag in the room, under the bed, Miss. Your rooms will not be let out for two days and I will see to your bag at that time. I wish you all a safe journey and Godspeed."

Jon paid Mr. Soby for their bills and, without checking, Mr. Soby placed the bills and payment in his breast pocket, saying. "For two days." He gave them a Cheshire grin as he left the room.

"Tamubu turned to Gangis and said, "We need to meet up with Kybo. No one can know that we are leaving Yaoundé this evening. We will be waiting for him at the native village on the eastern outskirts of town. What is it called?"

"Do you mean the Umpiti village, the one that has the big old ironwood tree where the old men sit?"

"Yes, that is the one."

"They do not like strangers there."

"I am not a stranger; I am Tamubu, a Medicine Man of the Great Zuri Watu; acolyte to Manutu, Medicine Chief of the Great Zuri Watu. I am welcome in all the villages of Africa!"

It only took a moment for the information to sink into Gangis mind. He had suspected there was something special about this man, but he never expected him to be a native dignitary. "Forgive me bwana, I did not know. When do you want me to have Kybo at the village?"

"We want you to take our things with you when you leave, Gangis. Later, the three of us can go for a stroll, before going to the Umpiti village. Go home, as usual, and tell Kybo to meet us at the Umpiti village later this evening. It would be best to let Kybo carry our gear and not take your cart to the village. Maybe, you and some of your friends could go with him just to be sure he gets there safely."

"It will be as you wish, Dawamtu."

"Yes, I am a medicine man, but I prefer that you call me Kigozi, the leader. I do not wish to make my identity known as general knowledge."

"Before I go to carry out your wishes, I want to tell you that it has been a great honor for me to know you Kigozi, bwana Jon and bibi Paula. Jambo na taz." (Goodbye and Godspeed.)

TAMUBU MOVED HIS GIRDLE of pouches to the rear, under his kitu kina, along with his knife, walinka and sling shot. Kybo had kept with him Thomas' bow, quiver and spear, as well as the rifles, bandoliers, radio and trekking supplies.

Jon put his pistol in his belt at his back and wore his safari jacket to cover it. Paula took the usual things in her pockets and wore her jacket. She felt naked without her backpack.

They strolled down the town streets, shopping here and there for a few supplies, laughing and talking as if they had no cares. At dusk, they stopped in the uptown café for dinner, so Thomas could have more bread pudding.

When it was totally dark outside, they left the café by the back door. Walking quickly, they moved into the shrubbery at the end of the street where the son of the owner of the café was waiting for them. He led them to a path in the woods that went to the Umpiti village. Within the hour, they were safely within the village being greeted by the village Elders.

Gangis had sent a young boy to the Umpiti village to make sure that the Medicine Man of the Great Zuri Watu and his friends received the welcome to which they were entitled. Consequently, the Elders had a council area set up to receive them when they arrived. After the formal introductions and amenities, Tamubu requested a sidebar meeting with the Chief and Elders wherein he told them of their travel needs: a short rest, an early start, four scouts and a week's supply of traveling food, for which they would gladly pay. The Umpiti told Tamubu that it would be their honor to supply his group while he conferred with the village Medicine Man about his patients.

Tamubu smiled inwardly. At least the Umpiti are willing to put a value on my services. Most of the villagers think I'm there just to do favors for them.

While Tamubu conferred with the Umpiti Medicine Man about his difficult cases, Jon regaled the Elders and villagers with stories of their trek. Paula added her story of being marooned and of her capture and escape, as the Umpiti also understood French. The Umpiti Village had not had such important visitors with such exciting stories for a very long time–so Jon and Paula knew their secret escape would remain just that–a secret.

As they walked to the visitor's huts, Paula said to Jon, "I could get used to being a legend."

Jon replied, "Yes, it is pretty heady stuff."

It was late when Tamubu joined Jon for the night. He had been gathering information about the trails, the people of the villages, and who could be trusted and who could not from the Umpiti Medicine Man. Jon spoke as Tamubu lay down on his pallet, "What did you find out?"

"We have had great good fortune: Long ago, Tundee, the

Umpiti Medicine Man, traveled to the lands of the Zuri Watu to visit Manutu. He studied with him for three rainy seasons. We will be able to travel a long way with his influence."

"Where are we going?"

"If I tell you, will you promise me that you will go to sleep?"

Jon thought, there is a hitch here, but said, "Yes, I promise."

"We go to Kenya!"

Jon spluttered, "But I knew that!" as Thomas laughed at his wit.

10

The Rainforest

THEY WAITED UNTIL FIRST light to leave the Umpiti village, so Paula could see the footing. The early path was wide and well used and easy to travel. When the trail narrowed, the two scouts in the lead hacked away the overgrowth. It slowed them imperceptibly as the men were adept at trimming back the encroaching greenery on the move. While there are main tracks that crisscross Africa, the little known hunting trails from village to village afforded them the greatest safety.

The group stopped for the mid-day break at a tributary to the Nyong River. They had covered almost fifteen miles. Here, hidden in the lush green tropical forest, the natives had felled a tall ebony tree, which grows like a lodge pole pine, for a bridge across the crocodile, snake and leech infested waters of the small tributary. Ahead were the lower reaches, the foothills, which rose to 2500 feet. The guides led them through creases formed by the downward rush of rainwater over the millennia. Above the often deep and rubble strewn watercourse, a shelf had formed from the roots of the tall trees, which kept the soil from eroding; this provided a habitat for soft springy mosses and lichen; so while they were climbing more, the footing was better.

Tamubu produced a lunch of grains, nuts, seeds and fruit mashed together and rolled up in mbogo, the large spinach-like leaves, with hot broth. After the quick, but satisfying meal, they separated into two groups for naps, with one group keeping watch for an hour while the others slept and vice-versa.

A group of eight adults is large enough to deter even the

boldest of predators; snakes and biting insects, however, were not the least bit intimidated. The noise of their passage and the rhythmic hacking thunks scattered the wildlife. They only glimpsed birds, monkeys and other tree dwellers. But the forest was full of animal and bird sounds, and once again, the jungle music from the Bridge on the River Kwai ran through Paula's mind as she walked beside Thomas.

About five miles from their destination, when the day had lengthened into the long African dusk, an escort of Machozi warriors met them on the trail, for the drums had told of the impending visit of important travelers. Once their charges were in capable hands, the Umpiti scouts turned for home.

Following the ritual greetings at the Machozi Village, the guests were shown to huts to freshen up for the dinner meal. The chief, the medicine man and two elders, along with their wives, which was a concession to Paula's presence, dined together in the open square around the central fire. The food was first served to the village leaders, then the guests, men and boys, (who had completed their manhood trials). When they were finished eating, the women and children ate what was left. The dinner was served in wooden bowls, and eaten while sitting cross-legged on animal skins. Fire hardened gourds of unusual shapes served as cups for the Palm wine or minted lemon water. Dinner was the usual vegetable stew, but the chief's cook had worked wonders with spices.

The evening followed the same pattern as previous evenings, as the rituals for important guests varied little from tribe to tribe. Tamubu soon went off with the medicine man while Jon regaled his listeners with excerpts of stories from their experiences; Paula enjoyed that which she understood, for her Bantu was still limited; her problem was the dialects, as each one added subtle meanings within the group of languages, which compromised Bantu. Paula almost blushed at the curious glances when Jon told the listeners, who were quite impressed, about a beautiful young white woman: how she had been a castaway by the tsunami; was captured and escaped; and was in the jungle, alone and unarmed, until she met Tamubu.

After the story, Jon and Paula were presented with feathered jangles, which were tied on just below their elbows and above their calves. The drums and pipes began. One male warrior, adorned with feathered jangles, began to dance and stomp around the fire, using a bejangled spear to mime hunting in his graceful and inventive dancing. He was soon joined by another bejangled warrior, and then another and another until twenty or so men were dancing in unison around the fire in front of them. The first dancer came and took Jon into the dance with them, where Jon gave a very creditable, if laughable, version of the ritual dance. The drums and pipes ended suddenly with a great coordinated stomp. The watchers warbled and cheered.

Soon the drums and pipes began again. A stunning young woman dressed in a short grass-like skirt with feathered jangles in her hair and on her elbows and calves began to dance. She mesmerized the crowd with her fluid movements, interspersed with intricate stomping. Soon, one by one, other unmarried women joined the chorus line, and lastly, Paula was drawn into the dance with them.

Jon had told of her ankle injury, so no insult was inferred by her lack of stomping. In deference, the young women dropped into a circle, leaving Paula to improvise alone. Paula enjoyed the limelight and gave the watchers a good show: first she pirouetted and then stepped into an aerial, into another aerial, a pirouette into a cartwheel, and slowly into a handstand split on one hand, back to a perfect handstand where she dropped into a dive-roll into a pirouette into two illusions and a backspring into a floor split into the Valdez lift into a final pirouette. The watchers roared their approval. When she sat down, Jon said. "That was a smashing show; these villagers will talk about your version of dancing forever!"

"I told you, I enjoy being a legend. I also like bringing new things into their lives–opening doors and minds–so to speak."

"Well, you certainly did that! I don't know where you found the energy. I, for one, am dead tired and ready for bed. How about you? How is your ankle?"

"It is aching, but it is better than I expected after twenty five miles. I think the washing up before dinner refreshed me, but I'm sleepy now.

Paula found the leather basin, suspended on a tripod, once again filled with hot water. She had the luxury of a hot sink bath before donning her nightshirt. She sat on the raised pallet covered with soft pelts, brushing her hair when she heard Tamubu say: "Knock, knock. Paula, would you like me to wrap your ankle for you?"

"Yes, please come in... if that is allowed."

"As a medicine man, it is allowed." He prepared the herbal anti-inflammatory salve, saying, "Jon told me about your gymnastics this evening during the dance. You will be the talk of the village for a long time. I always used to be the center of attention when I arrived at a village; but between you with your gymnastics and Jon with his stories, I'm hardly noticed anymore." Tamubu looked up with his whimsical smile of mischievous humor. "But, your talents will pave the way for us."

"What do you mean?"

"The drums will talk, and they will talk of you and Jon."

"Oh, do you mind?"

"Not at all, it might lessen the number of unusual cases waiting for me in each village."

"Is that what you have been doing each evening–tending the sick?"

"Yes, I'm glad I had the time to prepare my medicines while we were on the beach. I've gathered a few more plants to prepare, but some plants are found only in the bush."

"Yes, I noticed you cutting plants with your knife and hanging them on your medicine pouch to dry. Are any of these plants in the diary?"

"No, these plants are used mostly for infections, heart problems and bowel problems. How are you doing? Your ankle seems well. Are you in pain at all?"

"Just an ache now and then; with you walking in front of me, clearing the path of loose debris, I have had good footing."

"And the mud huts?"

"So far, all the huts have had smoke holes and mud plastered walls, which seems to preclude the dank and smelly problem."

"What is preclude?" They both chuckled at his unexpected return to their old ways on the trail.

"It means to prevent something from happening–to stop it."

"There, your ankle is all ready for our hike tomorrow. You did well today. Did we go too fast for you?"

"I felt the need to put as much distance between us and Yaoundé as possible today, but if we could slow down a bit tomorrow, it would be best. My ankle is not yet sore, but it is throbbing a bit."

"We will walk a bit slower for the rest of the trip. We now have a good distance between us, and that evil man. The tribes will see to it that we are not followed."

"How long will the Machozi scouts stay with us?"

"Two or three days; we will be in the foothills of the mountains where there are not many villages; so we may have to sleep out. The forest trails close in when they are not used, so our progress will be slower, which will be good for your ankle. I talked to Rubio, the lead scout; he feels that the only people we might encounter are Pygmies. He knows of no villages until we reach the Duibo. Jon had his maps out and says it is a hundred and fifty miles to thc Duibo, at Lomie.

"Without villages, there are no drums to tell of our arrival. In this wilderness, not many know of Manutu, so a visiting medicine man could be looked upon with suspicion... but a story teller and a woman who can dance on her hands will always be welcome!"

Paula laughed. "Are you serious or just joshing me?"

"I am serious. You will guarantee our safe passage through uncharted territory."

They chatted a while longer, and as they parted Tamubu asked, "Would you like me to make some oatmeal for breakfast?"

"Silly boy, why ask a question to which you already know the answer?"

Smiling, Tamubu thought: this woman makes me glad; and went off to bed down with Jon, who, when Tamubu arrived, was already asleep.

THE MACHOZI SCOUTS LED the way at a moderate walk. Paula loved the equatorial forest: the delightful and varied calls of hundreds of birds; the chatter of the monkeys as they passed; the occasional throaty sounds of the carnivores in the distance and the noises of the cicadas and tree frogs close by; all accompanied by the jungle travel music from the Bridge on the River Kwai, which played continuously in her mind.

The need to watch where she put her feet left scant opportunity to gaze at the profusion of flowering vines with their extravagant bright red, yellow or pink flowers hanging like tinsel on a Christmas tree; or to enjoy the lavish display of velvety burgundy and cream orchids that rooted in the mosses growing along the decaying lower limbs of massive trees; or glimpse the rare black, white and purple-tongued orchid that grew in stunning clumps in the deep mossy crotches of rough-barked trees. But those she did see in their resplendent profusion reminded her of strolling through the tropical plants exhibition in the conservatory at Longwood Gardens–with the dull shade of the canopy, the misting showers and the myriad ferns.

The Machozi did not talk on the trail, but moved silently through the rainforest, with only the occasional "siasa" (watch it) to alert the following person to a hole, a tangle of vines or thorny creepers. The lunch stop was the time for talk and discussion. Even the short water stops were mostly silent, while she sat, for precious moments, on a fallen log gazing up at the vast floral cathedral built by the most discerning architect of all: primitive nature.

On the rolling trails, which skirted the slopes, they saw the effects of altitude on the vegetation in the rainforest. Some of the changes occurred– almost one step to the next–from ferns and broad evergreen leafy undergrowth to tall, almost leafless trunks of what would have been, at home, garden flowers, but here under ideal conditions year-round, grew into small trees.

The constantly hilly terrain also accounted for the sparse population–an average of three people to a hundred square miles.

Everyone watched for a good campsite as the day lengthened into the long twilight. When a small level spot was found, the Machozi built lean-tos around the cooking fire from saplings, which they covered with large green leaves; the proximity of the fire gave a bit of security from curious nocturnal animals. The scouts took turns keeping watch and replenishing the fire. Jon was vindicated as he passed out the rubberized canvas air mattresses to Paula, Thomas and Kybo, thereby eschewing the usual, and often buggy, camp bed of fronds and leaves.

Tamubu did the cooking. He liked doing it, and since he was so good at it, no one tried to dissuade him from his chore. Tonight, it would be the usual stew. Tamubu used strips of dried turtle meat, which he simmered with wild onions, garlic, wild barley and spices, before adding the root vegetables and spices. Lastly, he would add the chopped-up stems from the mbogo leaves and cassava powder to thicken the stew. While the stew cooked, he lightly steamed the leaves of the mbogo; made biscuits for dinner and the flat pancakes for tomorrow's lunch. Later, he would take the residue of the stew, if any, and mix it with finely chopped nuts, grains and dates for a paste for the lunch roll-ups.

Kybo gathered wood for the fire; Paula wrote entries in her diary; Jon made coffee and heated water for tea and broth. In general, Jon helped where he was needed, and tonight he decided to make a rain lean-to for the cooking fire. As he drove the thick sticks into the ground, Tamubu asked, "What are you doing, Jon?"

"I am making a rain lean-to for the fire. It is going to rain tonight and it could be a swamper. This way you will still have a nice fire to make breakfast."

Tamubu smiled inwardly at his younger brother, who was always concerned with the next meal. "What makes you think that it is going to rain heavily? It has been getting cooler."

"Aha! That's just it! The tropical rainforest can vary from mile to mile, as you've seen. In some areas, it rains hundreds of inches, much more than the eighty or so inches a year required to maintain a tropical rainforest. I'm sure you've noticed the changes in the vegetation as the ground has risen; well, in the tropical rainforest the air is warmed by the ground at sea level, for little sunshine actually penetrates the canopy. As the land rises, the heat from the ground decreases; the vegetation changes with the cooler ground and allows an increase of sunlight through the canopy, which causes the cooler moist air to rise during the day, and to precipitate at night. We have been feeling cooler air, the vegetation has changed: viola–heavier rain at night!"

"Did you learn all that in school?"

"Yes, in college, but it was my personal choice to learn about the different areas of the west coast of Africa, the inland terrain, the various tribes and the languages. In my studies, I became fascinated by the Pygmies."

"Why?"

"Because their line is so ancient–old–and too, there is a hypothesis–theory–that they were the first men on earth, and that the area of the Mbuti Pygmies in the Congo was possibly the site of the Garden of Eden, where God created the first man and woman."

"I thought I was learning much, but I see I still have a great deal to learn. Do most people know of this Garden of Eden? The Zuri Watu have legends about the first man, but I thought them to be just Zuri Watu stories, not general knowledge. Well, dinner is ready, gather everyone, will you?"

That evening Jon told the bible story of Genesis and of Adam and Eve in Bantu as he remembered it. The Machozi listened in rapt wonder as... 'On the first day God created the Earth–and found it good...'

The second day with the Machozi scouts mirrored the first day. They were good scouts and seemed to magically know where there was the least undergrowth to make a path. They seemed to be able to find many paths that nature or animals had made, which required only light trimming. The only sound they added to the cacophony of the forest sounds was a steady beat of solid thunks as the machetes sliced through offending branches.

Late in the day, they came to the headwaters of the Dja River. From here, the Dja went west and then south and then southeast to Lomie. Here, the river was little more than a raging creek. The Machozi scouts suggested they climb nearer the top of the slope to find a level place for their camp. Tamubu agreed with them. They had the three hours of lengthening dusk to find a suitable camping spot. In not much more than an hour they came upon an unusual rock formation. It was a wide, long and level plateau of stone surrounded by trees. Here, they could hang the hammocks and use the ground covers for rain covers by suspending them on a line above the hammocks; for the igneous rock would not support the stakes needed for lean tos.

Jon was again in his glory, and soon had the string hammocks strung in the trees. He had bought four, although Thomas had said he didn't like hammocks, and preferred the trees. They had left Yaoundé so impetuously that Jon had not left the excess behind. Kybo told Jon he would prefer to sleep on the ground, on an air mattress under his hammock. Paula was soon quite comfortable resting in a hammock, for it was the perfect relief for her throbbing ankle. It put her feet higher than her heart.

She was luxuriating in the comfort, planning her diary entries–for writing in a hammock was frustrating–when she dozed off She awoke to hear Jon speaking a peculiar language. When she opened her eyes, she saw a troop of little people, Pygmies.

When Jon finished talking to them, he turned to Tamubu, who stood nearby, saying, "These people are a whole family clan of the Gielli Pygmies. They say the Goliath beetles, huge six- inch long fruit eating insects are swarming in the treetops of their old campsite, and the children are frightened of them. I'm not so sure that I, myself, wouldn't be a bit put out by flying beetles as big as rats!

"When I told them we were going to Lomie, two of the young men volunteered to guide us to the Duibo hunting lands, in exchange for the staples we carry, which, of course, we can replace in Lomie. The clan leader will leave *sign* to guide the young men to the new camp, for the clan will continue to travel until they find a place that suits them. The Gielli say it is two, maybe three days of travel to the Duibo Village. Their drums, which are any hollow logs, will tell the Duibo we are coming."

The Machozi scouts were not displeased with the change in plans. It cut the trip in half for them; and they knew that the Pygmies were excellent guides.

After dinner, Jon and Tamubu went to the Pygmy camp, which was a few hundred yards away, near the spring where Kybo had filled their water containers, earlier. Tamubu had seen several children with infected sores on their legs and arms and he wanted to administer to them. Jon was able to explain that his brother was a medicine man, who could make the sores go away. The mothers exhibited worry about his skills; so Tamubu went up to a boy who clearly had a displaced arm at the shoulder. Tamubu had Jon tell them that the boy had hurt himself when he fell out of a tree.

"Yes, yes, that is true."

"I will fix his arm; after I touch him he will be well."

Tamubu took the boys arm above the elbow, which easily fit in his right hand and felt his shoulder and arm gently with his left hand. Smiling at the boy, Tamubu raised the boy's arm with one hand while he braced the boy's shoulder with his other hand. Tamubu gave a tug and a twist and the arm bone popped back into the socket.

The boy looked at Tamubu in amazement and then shouted. "I am well! The pain is gone! I can move my arm again!"

The mothers lined up with their children and in a short time, the wounds had been cleaned with an antibiotic paste and bandages applied. One wound was deep and needed stitching. He gave the little girl some kimmea in broth and told Jon to tell her mother that she would be last. He then had Jon tell the mothers; "Always boil the water to clean wounds; never allow children or anyone with open cuts to go into the river water. Devils, in the form of germs, would enter through the wounds and make them very sick." While the little girl slept, Tamubu cleaned the deep gash thoroughly, stitched it closed and applied his antibiotic paste and a bandage from Paula's first aid kit. He then made three more bandages with antibiotic paste already applied and had Jon tell the child's mother to change the bandage every other day and not to let the wound get wet in any way until it was healed. Then, the child's father should cut the knots in the stitches and pull them out with his teeth. The Pygmies showed their appreciation for Tamubu's attentions to their children by inviting Tamubu, Jon and their friends to come and sit with them for stories.

While Tamubu went to get the others, Jon worked out a system whereby he would translate the stories. Once introductions were made, everyone settled around the campfire in order of status. The clan leader stood and gave a greeting to their guests. He thanked God for bringing such special visitors to the Gielli, His children. He then asked if the guests would tell them why they were traveling to the Duibo village through the forest and not on the road?

This question made the Pygmies laugh and Jon immediately saw the humor of the question. Why were these people wandering in the forest? Without translating, Jon gave them a synopsis of events, which lead up to their *wandering in the forest*. The Pygmies often oohed and aahed and sometimes laughed. It was a tale of strange and unusual happenings and thrilled them all.

The clan leader arose again and said, "I ask Muklu to come forward. Muklu is the Keeper of Legends for our clan. She will tell our esteemed guests the Legend of Fire".

Jon was quite excited as he translated this statement for them. Having the Keeper of Legends tell a story first hand was akin to hearing Moses recite the Ten Commandments. With great anticipation, the guests waited for Muklu to settle herself and compose her thoughts. Then she began, her voice was strong, yet pleasing and mellow:

"In the beginning, God gave man everything but fire.

"Life was wonderfully pleasant in the blessed land of

Paradise. In the chilly evenings, however, the people had to cover themselves with leaves and fronds to keep warm.

"Then one day a man wandering in the forest came upon a bright, leaping light that did not come from the sky. Beside the leaping light was a woman, who seemed to care for the leaping light. As the man approached the woman he said to her, 'What is that brightness called?'

"And she replied, 'It is called fire.'

"As he neared her, he felt the warmth of the fire and asked, 'How do you get fire?'

"After a while she said, 'Only God gives fire.'

"'Would He give me fire?'

"'I do not know, you must ask Him yourself.'

"'How do I do that?'

"'You must pray.'

"'What is pray? How do I do it?'

"'To pray, is to talk to God; to thank Him for all the wonderful things He has given you.'

"'Oh! I talk to God all the time, but I have never thanked Him for the Paradise He has given me.'

"'If you are not grateful for the bounty you have already received, why should God give you more?'

"The man thanked the woman for her advice. He went back to his sleeping place where he told his brother what had happened to him while he walked in the forest.

"'I am going to go to the great water and talk to God; do you want to come with me?'

"'Why do you have to go to the great water to talk to God? Can you not talk to Him here?'

"'Yes, I could, but I think better at the great water.'

"It was a long way to the great water and the man was thinking as he walked: I know I told the woman that I talk to God all the time, but, in truth, I do not–at least not with my voice. All I have ever said is, 'I like these oranges that God has put here...' or... 'It was good of God to give us the flowers which are so pretty.' I can't remember ever thanking Him by saying the words, 'Thank You.' I wonder if that will make any difference to Him.

"All the way to the great water, the man thought and wondered.

"When he reached the great water, he sat on a boulder and looked at the vista before him. It was so beautiful, so immense, and so splendid that he blurted out, 'Dear God, where did You get all your ideas for the beauty of earth?'

"Immediately, he was embarrassed. Who was he to question God? To make up for this mistake, he said, 'I came here to this beautiful place, which makes me glad, to thank You for giving us so much beauty to enjoy. Each flower, each tree, each hill, and each stream–they are all so wonderful. I came to thank You for giving us all these marvelous creations to enjoy.'

"The man arose to begin his journey back to his sleeping place when the clouds roiled and a great shaft of light blazed through a rift and streamed down to the water where it shimmered. He stood gazing at the beam of golden, pink and dazzling white light, when he heard a voice say, 'It was my pleasure.'

"The man was overjoyed. He had talked to God and God and had talked back to him. On his long walk home he pondered the phenomenon. Why had he never actually talked to God before? It was wonderful!

"His brother listened eagerly to his story and then asked, 'What did God say when you asked Him for fire?'

"The man stared at his brother in amazement before he answered, 'I forgot to ask God for fire.'

"'You walked all the way to the great water and back, and you forgot the reason you went?'

"'Yes, I realized that I had never talked to God before, and I felt ungrateful, as the woman had suggested. I was nervous about talking to God at all... I mean who am I anyway? The woman had said to thank God, so that is what I did... and I am glad that is all I did. We have gone this long without fire, we can go on longer.'

"That night the winds blew and the rain came in torrents. Looking out the opening to the cave, the man said, 'Thank

you God for this cave to keep us dry. We are pleased with it.'

"He no sooner said the words, than a flash of lightning came and lit up the night, then another and another, coming closer all the time. Everyone hid their eyes from the great flashes of intense light, so no one actually saw the last flash, which struck a bush just outside the cave. But soon, they felt the heat from the wildly burning bush and looked up to see the fire.

"Everyone laughed happily and cheered for God had given them fire. The man sent them out to gather wood, for he remembered seeing the woman placing little sticks in the fire, and each time she did, the fire had flared and burned brighter.

"The rain stopped. Soon there was a pile of sticks and dead brush inside the cave to keep God's gift of fire burning. So ends the story of how man was blessed with fire."

THE LISTENERS CLAPPED WHEN Muklu finished telling the legend. The guests then stood and thanked their hosts. The hour had grown late. They would start for Lomie at first light.

The Machozi scouts spent the night with them; they too had listened to the Pygmy 'Legend of Fire', which would cause considerable excitement in their village, when the story was retold word-for-word as they heard it. All the tribes knew of the Pygmy legends, but none had ever heard one told by the 'Keeper of Legends'. In a land of peoples who had mostly no writing or record-keeping skills, all was memory. Children learned to carry messages word-for-word. To mis-speak a message was to bring shame or ridicule on oneself. The Machozi scouts were gone, but the Pygmy lads had taken their places before dawn, when Tamubu arose to make breakfast.

Traveling with the Pygmy scouts was a revelation to all of them. The young men were about four feet six inches tall and seemed to flow through the rainforest like air, barely moving the vegetation at all. Kybo followed closely behind Asu and Ocha using his machete to enlarge the path for Tamubu, Paula and Jon, who followed him.

The Pygmies, they found, do not sleep during the noon stop. It is customary for the women to make a light meal and feed the children. While the smaller children nap, the women and older children gather plants, fruits and roots for the dinner and breakfast meals. The elderly women watch the babies, while the elderly men protect the campsite. The rest of the men take their bows and arrows, with which they are very proficient, and hunt small prey: rabbits, snakes, birds, bush babies, squirrels and the like. Sometimes they even kill a dik-dik, a small antelope, no taller than sixteen inches at the shoulder, which is found in the deep rainforest.

Since Jon was the only one who could speak with the Pygmies, he became a font of information, which he eagerly imparted to them over meals. A great source of interest was the paucity of their belongings. Each Pygmy over the age of four carried his own water bag, bowl and kijiko, which is a small wooden stick with a depression like a spoon at one end, and a sharp point at the other end. It was usually made out of teak and was used to spear food from the eating bowl.

Some adult Pygmies carried or wore a sleeping blanket or kitamba if they had one. They obtained these old kitambas by trading nuts, fruits, snake skins, small pelts and carved wooden beads in the native villages. Most did not have a kitamba, so made nests of dried leaves and soft fronds and covered themselves with elephant ears, the same large waxy leaves that were used to make lean-tos.

The men wore uumenea (penis covers) while the women wore shuka (loin cloths). The children went naked: until the boys reached the age of twelve and until the girls began menses. The older children amused themselves by painting intricate designs on one another–with pointed sticks and vegetable dyes–all over their heads, faces, chests and backs and legs. The small children played games with a variety of nut husks, sticks and pebbles.

In the rainy season, they used the same water impervious elephant leaves for umbrellas that they used for huts or lean-tos: or for nurseries, for ponchos, for ground-cloths, for pallet covers, for food storage, for just about everything. If nature didn't provide it, they didn't need it. Even the kitambas were considered unnecessary. They were merely a status symbol for the elderly men.

Each Pygmy had a distinctive woven pouch for their belongings, carried by a woven strap across the shoulders and chest. Small babies were carried in woven net sacks across the mother's chest; older babies were carried on their backs. It was not unusual to find that the father carried his wife's personal belongings while she carried a child or two.

Jon finished by saying that the Pygmies are truly nomadic. They stay in one place as long as the food supply lasts; then they move on, making new shelters wherever they decide to stay, usually near a source of spring water and far away from rivers.

While the Pygmy scouts were with them during the day, they went off on their own for the night; but returned before daybreak.

Late in the afternoon of the fifth day of travel, the second day with the Pygmies, four Duibo scouts met them on the trail. The Duibo had gifts for the Pygmy lads: a small pouch of salt, a small pouch of brown sugar, and two bags of cornmeal. Jon had already given the Pygmy clan their staple supplies, as agreed, but Tamubu insisted on giving the lads the rest of his prepared antibiotic paste, for he had gathered enough plants to make more. They watched as the Pygmy lads melted into the forest. Traveling alone, they would be back tomorrow in time to have lunch with their family clan.

JON WAS SORRY TO see Asu and Ocha leave. It had been a wonderful experience for him, even better than he had anticipated, for the lads were quite open and honest with him. He had almost despaired of ever using the knowledge he had worked so hard to obtain in school–for all his teachers had to be special tutors in African languages, which he studied in addition to his other classes.

It was a long day to the Duibo village. The four Duibo scouts retraced their path back to the village. It was a hilly trail, but one that was never used by anyone but the Duibo.

It went through their ceremonial burial grounds, which was a lethal trap for those who did not intimately know the area. It was a quagmire of sucking bogs that looked no different to the inexperienced eye than did the level ground.

No one said a word in the waning daylight, as each lived with the dire stress that a misstep–could be the last step. It was a great relief to pass the quagmire minefield without mishap. The guests were taken to their huts where they were able to wash up in hot water and don clean clothes before being escorted to the chief and elders for introductions and the ritual greetings.

A small wild pig had been roasted with sweet potatoes and squash for the arriving guests. When they finished the sumptuous repast, the chief and elders sat with them to talk. Paula excused herself for she had never felt so tired. Tamubu took her back to her hut and rewrapped her ankle for her. He had added kimmea to her broth to relieve the stress and to help her sleep.

Jon was in full form when Tamubu returned to the elders and the gathered villagers who listened to him as he related their adventures. Jon had an amusing way of telling a story that kept his audience hanging on every word. The medicine chief sat listening too, while he waited for Tamubu to return to the fire. When Jon finished the story, he left to confer with Tamubu about their craft. At the moment, no one in the village was sick.

Just past noon of the sixth day of travel they arrived at the small town of Lomie. They would replenish their traveling supplies here, and rest a day. Paula's ankle throbbed a bit at nights, but gave her no problems during the day. Tamubu insisted that she keep it bandaged for support in case of rough or slippery terrain, for it rained steadily every night now, and sometimes, there were heavy showers during the day too.

They looked forward to the respite from traveling, and to the simple amenities of the rustic lodge: beds, sheets, showers and real towels–what luxuries.

11

Lomie

LOMIE'S MODEST GUEST LODGE was a popular stop for birding safaris and was usually fully booked; but as the rainy season drew near, rooms were available. Each room had a sink but water was brought as needed. The showers were canvas affairs in the back yard with a wood-fired hot water heater and the necessary was also a canvas affair with a seat over a hole–after which you pushed a bit of dirt into the hole from the surrounding mound with a stick shovel. There were also night pots in the rooms. It was only a few steps up from the village huts–but the windows in the walls made the rooms positively delightful. The lodge had a small dining room and the fare was stew, fresh bread and salad for dinner; or eggs, sausages, oatmeal, fruit and toast for breakfast– a giant step up from the villages. Lunch, if desired, was peanut butter and jelly sandwiches, and fresh fruit. Coffee, tea, and lemon water were available all day long. Palm wine was available at dinner for a small charge.

At breakfast, Paula asked, "What are your plans for today?"

Tamubu replied, "Jon and I are going to attend to our provisions. The village elders have been generous in return for my help with the sick, but we are going into the sparsely populated areas again. It is as far to Gamboula as it was from Yaoundé to Lomie. Jon, have you asked about guides?"

"I talked to the desk clerk. He has given me some good suggestions for guides." Jon replied, "We can check them out when we go shopping. What are your plans for the day, Paula?"

"Me, I'm going to shower and wash my hair and then catch up on the entries in my new diary... and maybe, nap a bit."

"Shall we meet here... let's say at 1 p.m. for lunch, or shall we just do dinner together today?" Jon asked, arranging meals as usual.

Simultaneously, Tamubu and Paula said, "Let's just do dinner;" laughing at the coincidence.

"It seems I'm the only one up for a spot of peanut butter." Jon said with his *poor boy, woe-is-me* demeanor, causing them to laugh again.

Back in her room and freshly showered, Paula moved the small desk over beneath the window and sat to bring her diary up to date. The scene outside the window caught her attention. Not a hundred feet away, three young boys–maybe seven to nine in age–were stuffing things from the lodge trashcans into burlap sacks. The sight distressed Paula, as she continued to gaze out the window after the boys were gone, thinking about the children of Africa.

It was while she mused that she saw Tamubu stop to speak to a beggar sitting beside the walkway to the road. She saw him give the beggar a coin and one of his little leaf pouches of his herbal medicines. She smiled as she thought. He has such a good heart and cares so much for the souls with the least. Will he remain unchanged when he is with his family again? To her surprise, a few minutes after Tamubu left, the beggar arose and went away. It is early in the day to give up such a good spot. Maybe Tamubu was quite generous to the mendicant and he felt his day's work was done.

Returning to her diary, Paula scribbled for hours until she had a call of nature. On her return to her room, she stopped for a cup of tea and a slice of fresh bread with peanut butter. She wrote for a while longer then took a nap. The bed had a real mattress, though thin, and many quilts, blankets and feather pillows... such luxury!

Thomas went to hire scouts for the next leg of the trek, while Jon purchased supplies. He found the man the desk clerk had recommended and coincidentally, found Kybo. "I thought you were going to stay in the Duibo village," Thomas said.

"Yes." Kybo replied. "But Ruffo, he bring me to work with him this morning; he want to know about our trek to Lomie."

"Well, I'll leave it to you, then Kybo. Arrange what we need with Ruffo. It would be best to have three scouts to the next village."

"Ruffo, him say next village kali-taz."

"Unfriendly warriors, huh, well what do you recommend, Ruffo?"

"Go north and east into the Kaaka lands away from the Dzem to the east."

"Will we be able to find a friendly village in a day's walk going north and then east?"

"Yes, small camp Pygmies, friendly, live in open, no huts just leaf roof, leaf bed and small fire."

"We have small tents. What do they need?"

"Foodstuffs: cornmeal, flour, powdered milk, sugar, salt."

"Is this what you usually take to them?"

"Yes, small bags. Too much, it rots."

"Will they supply scouts for us?"

"No, Duibo stay with you three days to Kaaka village."

"Will you have your own supplies with you?"

"Yes, each man takes his own food."

"Good, well, carry on Kybo." Thomas went off to browse in the shops with Jon and to buy the needed foodstuffs, for eating and barter. Jon was pleased with the change in plans, and the opportunity to visit yet another Pygmy clan of the Gielli tribe.

A SOFT KNOCK ON the door roused Paula from her slumber. Looking at her watch, she was startled to see it was so late. "Just a moment, please."

"Hot water, missy."

Paula opened the door. "Come in... thank you." Paula closed and locked the door after the hall porter left and washed her hands and face enjoying the mint scented water. She brushed her teeth and combed her hair and put on her bright scarf for dinner. She was rereading her diary entries for omissions, when there was another knock on the door. She thought it was Thomas and rushed to the door...but something, an odd feeling, made her stop and say, "Who is it, please?"

"It is the steward. There is a message for you." The voice sounded familiar, but it was not the steward and a prickle ran up her spine. Going on intuition, Paula decided to be cautious.

"Just slide the message under the door, please." There was silence and Paula saw the handle of the door turn slightly. She had the deadbolt fastened but she grabbed the desk chair and jammed it up under the doorknob.

"Did you hear me? Please slide the message under the door."

There was no reply... and no message. Paula felt weak. The mercenary couldn't have found us... not after the long trek through the rainforest. What to do? I dare not leave the room, but I must warn Thomas and Jon... my whistle! Paula pulled her red *5in1* whistle from her shirt pocket and leaned out the window and started to blow and blow and blow. She made an awful racket before she heard someone knocking on her door. "Missy Paula, what is wrong? Can you open the door, please?"

"Who is there?"

"It is me, Umpopo, your porter."

"Umpopo, go and get Mr. Thomas and Mr. Jonathan right away."

"Yes, miss... are you alright?"

"Yes, bring Mr. Thomas and Mr. Jonathan here at once." It was only a few minutes before Jon and Tamubu arrived. Both had heard the whistle and both had realized it might be Paula calling for help. They converged at the stairway and met the steward rushing down for help.

"Paula, it is Tamubu." Paula opened the door, apologized to Umpopo and thanked him for his help as she pulled Thomas and Jon into the room. "They are here," she said. "Someone came to my door saying they had a message for me. I don't know why, but I told them to slip it under the door. Then I saw the doorknob turn and jammed a chair under the knob. Who else would try to fool me into opening the door?"

Jon looked at Thomas and said, "These men are very determined. They have gone to a lot of trouble to post lookouts in the towns surrounding Yaoundé, hoping we would show up somewhere sooner or later. I'm afraid our rush to Paula's aide may have tipped our hand to them. They did not know what you or I looked like until now. Did you see the tall man with the scarred face at the end of the hall? He may have been waiting to see who came to the rescue or for Paula to leave the room. He had the nefarious look of a mercenary to me."

"I remember him. He did look out of place, but tourists come in all shapes and sizes." Thomas replied.

"Jon," Paula said, "did he wear a western style bandana around his neck?"

"I thought it was an ascot, not properly tied... but yes, he did! It was a red print thing, quite gauche."

Paula slumped down on the bed. "It was him, the man who questioned me when I was abducted. How did he ever get here? I was feeling so safe."

Tamubu went to her side and sat beside her. "We will figure out a way of eluding him. It may be that he is here alone, and if so, he will have to sleep. If he has help, we will get help. One thing is certain. We must stay together at all times."

Jon spoke up with a bit of cheer. "I have my pistol. Thomas has his knife and you have your whistle. How can he get past those defenses? But let's go down to dinner–before the food is all gone–I'm starved!"

During dinner the problem was dissected and it was decided to leave as soon as it was dark. This might be a problem for the mercenary unless he had native help to guide him. They would go to the Duibo village for Kybo and the scouts, stay in the village until morning and then be off.

"Do you think we are putting the villagers in danger?" Paula asked.

"We will alert them to the problems," Jon said. "They will be well prepared to deal with a few mercenaries, if there is more than the one you saw."

"I will talk with the medicine man too," Tamubu said. "He is in a position of power over evil spirits in the form of mercenaries."

"Will we ever be able to stop in another town?" Paula asked.

Tamubu smiled at her saying, "This is not like you, to worry so. What is bothering you?"

"It was just such an awful shock–so unexpected. I thought we were well away from him and then he pops up here in the wilderness. Why? Will he keep popping up wherever we go? Will we always have to creep about? I don't know that my nerves can take it. It took me weeks to get over the Ndezi chasing after me–even after I was safe with you. I tried not to show the angst I felt, but that doesn't mean I didn't feel it."

"What is angst?"

Paula looked at Tamubu and smiled. "You have a way of bringing me out of myself when I get frazzled." And she smiled back at him.

"What is frazzled?" The question was so ordinary in the face of such distress that the simplicity made her laugh.

"Angst is a feeling of anxiety or dread. Frazzled is stressed out or drained."

The waiter came to the table and said, "The dining room is now closed."

"Let's go get your things and take them to our room. We can leave from there later," Tamubu said.

Jon added, "I settled with the innkeeper earlier today and meals are included, so we can be off whenever."

ONCE ENSCONCED IN THE larger double room, Tamubu said to Paula, "You have had a bad time, but you must look at the problem like you would a hungry lion, a black mamba or a rogue elephant. You must know what they are capable of doing, where they will do it and why... to keep yourself out of harm's way. We are going into the deep rainforest. The mercenary cannot follow us there. He does not have the skills and the natives will be against him. So, his only choice is to wait for us at another town as he did here in Lomie."

"That is our strength," Jon added. "We know what he must do, because we know what he cannot do. So, we plan accordingly. We traveled southeast from Yaoundé on a path to Nairobi. He probably only had one other man at Ebolowa in case we went south. East was Lomie and north was the mountain, which he ruled out because of your ankle. To continue on our present course would put us at Guinguo in a week, but we would have to pass through the Dzem who Kybo has found out are hostile warriors. If the mercenary also has this information, he will know that our next stop must be northeast to Gamboula.

"But," Jon continued, "I suggest we go southwest to Meuban, which is in the opposite direction, about 80 miles. Fifteen or twenty miles due south of Meuban is the Kom river which flows due west to the ocean along the southern border of Cameroon. It should be navigable. This will keep us out of Gabon, which is a quagmire since the deforestation in 1952."

"Why are we going west to the ocean?" Paula asked and Tamubu added, "Yes, why are we going west, Jon?"

"For several reasons: One, the mercenaries might not suspect that we will go that way... since we just spent a week going southeast in the rainforest to get here. Two, I think our friend Captain Jones will be glad to take us to Port-Gentil where we can get a plane to Mbandaka to Kisangani, then to Kampala on Lake Victoria. At any of these stops, we can tour the area before traveling on.

"What, you mean go back to Campo?" Paula asked.

"Yes, do you know it?

"I don't know it, but Captain Jones stopped there for fuel and told me it was on the border of Equatorial Guinea and Cameroon."

"Right, I don't think our pursuer will ever think of it. We have told no one and the Duibo are loyal to us. It is so implausible–not believable–that we should be quite safe. From Port-Gentil, or even Libreville, we can fly to many places. We can change our itinerary–list of expected places of travel–at any time. What do you think Thomas?"

Tamubu snorted, "I think that if I need to know the meaning

of a word, I will ask." The ensuing laughter at Tamubu's umbrage relaxed them a bit.

"I think that is a very good plan, Jon, Tamubu said. You are right. Why would he even consider that we might go west; we were just there; why would we go back? Yes, I like this plan. How about you Paula, what do you think?

"I'm still too frazzled to think right now. I'm going to have to rely on the two of you to do it for me."

Jon continued. "Paula, think of what could happen if we had this man following us, for whatever reason, and we were not aware of it. It is much better that we know he is there so we can take evasive measures. Our advantage is that he does not know what we want, what we plan to do, or what we are capable of doing. Who do you think has the upper hand?"

"I understand your logic," she replied. "I see that we have some control; but he is still out there somewhere... lurking, and having met the man up close, he terrifies me. He could strike at any moment."

"Before he can strike, he must find us again... and we are going to make that very difficult for him to do." Jon said in an assured tone.

Tamubu said, "We are going to travel deep in the rainforest. Without the cooperation of the native tribes, this would be impossible. They do not allow strangers on their lands without permission. The mercenary cannot follow us in the rainforest. If he is foolish enough to try, he will die. So, you can put him out of your mind. He will not be following us where we are going."

Paula sighed, "I do not understand the trepidation I feel. It is a new and unpleasant experience for me. I appreciate your concern... give me a day or so to get over the panic his sudden appearance caused. Once I'm in the rainforest, I will feel better. Have you thought of how you will contact Captain Jones to let him know of our plans?"

Jon replied, "All we need is a village with a short wave... Kybo! I forgot! Kybo is carrying my short wave radio." I was going to leave it in Yaoundé, but he offered to carry it saying, 'If we need it–we will have it'. He took it with him when he went to stay with Gangis' brother. I haven't thought of it since. I wonder if the batteries are rum. But we can get batteries in most towns. Everyone uses them these days."

Thomas asked, "What if Captain Jones is not available to help us get further down the coast? What then?"

Jon replied, "We will just have to hire another boat to take us where we want to go. Campo is a major refueling stop."

Thomas smiled at Paula, who said, "I feel much better now. I feel we are back in control. We have a plan and a good one. I feel we can elude this mercenary long enough that his bosses will let him give up on us."

Thomas spoke softly, "I don't want to upset anyone, but I think we should change our final destination. I do not think we should go to Kenya." Jon and Paula just stared at him... before Paula finally said, "But you want to go home, don't you?"

"Yes, I do. But it might not take long for this mercenary to find out why we are going to Kenya... other than the attorney in Nairobi who has the diary...and that could put the rest of the family at risk. I had a thought Jon. What do you think of writing a letter to Mom and Dad asking them to meet you at Murchison Falls or Lake Victoria? You could tell them that you have found me, and that I want to get together before we go to the farm in Kenya."

Jon thought a while before he replied. "I have to admit you are right, we could be putting the family at risk. At this time, it is probably still believed that you are a Medicine Man of the Zuri Watu. If they delve further into our affairs, they will see that you have registered in the same name as me–but they might think that was a ruse to get you into the hotels as a white man. You certainly don't look like a white man, with your darkened skin, long hair held back by a headband and that cape your always wear and those native sandals... and all the pouches and weapons you carry."

Laughing Jon said, "Now that I think of it, it is a good thing you never went to the front desk, we might have had a problem if you did!" Tamubu and Paula smiled at the irony of the thought.

An introspective silence followed. Then Jon said, "Yes, that's what I'll do. I'll write a letter to Mom and Dad. Thomas, you too must write a letter too. We'll mail them home from Campo."

12

The Wilderness

It was the dark of the night–the moon and the stars were hidden behind dense cloud cover–the rain would come later. Jon passed all their gear out the window to Thomas waiting below. Then, with his revolver in his deep safari jacket pocket, Jon and Paula left by the front door and strolled to the end of the walkway where the beggar had been sitting that morning. They heard, "pssst, pssst", and turned to see a man in the shadows who resembled the beggar, but who stood up straight and tall, wearing decent clothes.

The man beckoned to them saying, "Come with me. The medicine man is waiting for you in the park. It is not far, come!"

Jon and Paula were surprised, the beggar, no longer hunched over in his rags, was also well spoken.

"Who are you?" Jon asked.

"I am a friend of the Medicine Man of the Great Zuri Watu."

"Lead on," Jon whispered. The trio zigzagged through streets and alleys to end up at the wooden archway to a little park. A short way up the path, they found Tamubu sitting on a park bench with their gear.

"Well done, Hemeti. Thank You. Hemeti knows a secret path to the Duibo village."

"Yes, Bwana, the path is good, but it is a long walk."

"You were not followed?"

"No, Bwana. I had friends watching. We were not followed."

The night was so dark that Paula, literally, could not see

her hand in front of her face. She walked with her right arm around Tamubu's arm and held on to Jon with her left hand. She was beginning to get disoriented and dizzy, for she had never experienced walking over uneven ground in the absolute dark.

Hemeti took out a flashlight and lit the trail in front of them. The light was channeled downward and did not cast much light into the thick brush. Hemeti kept the light focused just a few feet in front of them to pick out the obstacles on the trail. It felt like wandering into an unknown abyss, for the path seemed to curve and turn endlessly. Fatigue from disorientation and the winding dark paths began to overcome her when she smelled the smoke of campfires and saw a dim light beyond the trees. Paula heard a soft jangle and turned to see the dark outlines of armed warriors following them.

A few minutes later they arrived at the village of the Duibo. People came out of their huts to stare at them as they passed. Like everyone else, Kybo turned to stare at the unannounced visitors and was astonished to see Thomas, Jon and Paula being led into the village by the man he had thought was a crippled beggar. "Ruffo! Ruffo! Come quick. It is the kigozi, the kisha and Missy Paula!"

Tamubu went up to the chief, who had heard the sea of murmurs and had come out of his abode. After the formal greetings, Tamubu said, "We come unannounced Chief Agnozo, and seek your indulgence, for there is a mercenary in Lomie who would do us harm. He has, in the past, kidnapped my betrothed and now seeks to harm me. Will you give us succor for the night?"

The chief raised his arm in royal greeting and said, "It is our great good fortune to have you as guests in our village for the night or for as long as you need our protection." He waved his hand and the women came and took Paula away to the visitors hut. She hated to go but understood that for tonight, she was just a betrothed woman in a man's world.

"Have you had your late meal?"

"Yes, we have eaten, but a cup of water would be appreciated, shukrani."

"Come; sit with me and the Elders of the village. We would hear more of your reasons for returning to the lands of the Duibo."

They talked far into the night. But long before he retired to his bed, Tamubu had obtained scouts who would guide them to the Dja River where dugout canoes were kept high on the land. If the river had risen from the rains, they could do forty miles in one day, before heading south to Meuban, which was only about ten miles from the Kom River, which flowed to the ocean.

Chief Agnozo continued, "If the river is too low, we will take you overland to the Meuban village. My oldest daughter is married to Chief Chabo's oldest son. The drums will not announce your coming, just in case the mercenary has someone who understands drum talk. They will tell only of my visit to see my daughter and her newborn son."

While Jon held the Duibo Elders in his storyteller's spell, Tamubu attended to Paula's ankle and gave her the good news. The Duibo medicine man had asked Tamubu if he would look at a seven year old boy who was wasting away but had no fever or pains. Tamubu examined the boy closely using Hemeti's flashlight. He saw a small puncture wound under his little toe in a small space that had not calloused over. There he found and removed a small thorn. Tamubu suspected it was an unusual case of jaw cramp. He gave the medicine man some of his oral antibiotics and suggested that all the boy's meals be liquefied (boiled to pulp and mashed) and taken through a reed for the next ten days. The Duibo medicine man was impressed by his skill and discussed the use of other plants and their preparations. So, it was early morning before Tamubu finally fell asleep on a pallet next to Jon.

They left at first light with four scouts, who not only led the way, but also helped to carry supplies. This, in itself, helped Paula on the trail, for she carried nothing that was not in her pockets. Kybo still carried the two-way radio, because he thought of it as the magic box. Tamubu carried his usual gear as did Jon, but the camping gear and the gift and bartering supplies and Paula's backpack were carried by the scouts.

The Duibo scouts set out at a fast walk where the way was open; later, they slowed a bit, which was better for Paula.

KYBO HAD NOT YET heard about the mercenary at the hotel and was wondering about the complete change of direction. When he could stand it no longer, he said. "Kisha, why are we going west?" Jon, annoyed as ever by the demotion, said, "We have been followed and found by the mercenary who abducted Paula. We are hoping a total change of plans will lose him for good."

"Where are we going now?"

Jon moved close to Kybo, stood on his toes and whispered in his ear. "We are going to Campo, on the coast. It is a secret."

CHIEF AGNOZO HAD TOLD them that the Pygmy village they would pass was the only semi-permanent village in the vast Gielli territory. The Pygmies stayed there because they were able to trade with the Duibo who were close enough to Lomie to replace the bartered staples. The Pygmies did not travel into towns.

They came to the Pygmy village late in the day, where leaf-covered domes–similar to a one-man tent–had already been erected for the guests. A hot meal of stew, which had been salted for their enjoyment, awaited them. The customs of the Pygmies were different in that they talked to their guests and one another all through the meal. The guests were given honored places closest to the cooking pot. Everyone helped themselves from the communal pot, with parents serving the younger children. The Duibo made their own camp not far away, and ate their own food, as was their custom. The Pygmies had so little extra food that sharing with the honored guests was enough good will in return for the gifts they had been given. Jon requested permission to cross the vast Gielli territory. Permission was given, but he was warned that the hairy ones to the southwest were cannibals.

The dignity of the Pygmies, the little people, enchanted Paula, especially the adolescent children. The Gielli clan here had more contact with outsiders, so the children were not as shy as the Gielli youngsters they had met six days ago. Two little girls, maybe six and eight, had elaborate designs painted on their faces and shaved heads. The children looked healthy and were very pleased with the cookies Paula gave them. A year old baby boy had blonde wooly curls and huge blue eyes and was carried in a sari-like cloth on his mother's back. The men were about four feet nine inches with big broad feet and nicely proportioned bodies. They looked to weigh about ninety pounds. The women were three or four inches shorter with skin colors from light brown to a dark cream. An old man had a wiry mustache peppered with erratic curly white hairs, which also grew below his lower lip and chin. His face was unlined and serene–the pepper and salt hair and gnarled hands were the only signs of his advanced age.

Before they went off to their beds, Jon said, "I asked the Gielli not to send a message with the drums alerting the rest of the clans to our passage; and they agreed." Tamubu nodded his head in reply.

TOWARDS THE END OF the second day, in the long lingering twilight dusk –for they were about a hundred and sixty miles north of the Equator–they met the Djoumani warriors. Greetings were exchanged and Dodi, the Duibo lead scout, explained the situation to the wary, if not overtly belligerent warriors.

Jon, never one to be put off by tribal differences, soon had the Djoumani eating out of his hand. He knew the dialects and subtle differences of the Bantu language and quickly had their attention. Jon apologized for not sending a drum message of their coming, but told them that professional killers were following them to abduct Tamubu, the Medicine Man of the Great Zuri Watu, who was an acolyte of Manutu.

The Djoumani knew of Manutu, the Medicine Man who walks with the spirits, for Manutu had traveled the Dja River on his voyage to the Congo River. They immediately closed ranks, giving the Duibo scouts leave to spend the night on their land, before returning home in the morning.

With six Djoumani warriors in front and six in the rear,

they traveled at a fast pace until they arrived at a much-used camp. There was a large, roofed shelter; maybe twenty feet square, with an unusual number of pole supports, which turned out to be posts for hammocks. The roof had a smoke hole with a second thatched cover above it. All of which, was surrounded by a high thorn boma.

Kutoto, the leader of the Djoumani warriors, told Jon, "This is a good game area. We come here to hunt several times a year." He also warned, "It will be a long day tomorrow. To travel to the Djoumani village near the Kom River, we will leave before first light."

Permanent tripods with leather basins were filled with warm water for washing up. A few kitambas were draped over poles to give Paula a bit of privacy in her ablutions and while asleep in her hammock. After the usual meal of vegetable stew, Jon regaled the warriors with Paula's escape from the Ndezi and Tamubu's timely arrival.

The dialect was different enough that Paula did not understand most of the story, but saw the approving and admiring glances of the warriors. A brave woman was unusual. A brave white woman was extraordinary.

The next day they arrived at the Djoumani village in the waning twilight. All was in readiness for them as two men from the group of warriors were sent ahead to tell of the coming of important visitors. Most of the African villages took great pride in welcoming special travelers from distant places. They liked to be tidy, swept up and have a nice meal (fresh stew) prepared for them. So advance notice was necessary if people were to go and listen to the stories told by the visitors; chores must be done, animals must be penned and small children must be put to bed.

The village ceremonies for important guests were a ritual that varied little: the Elders and Chief greet the visitors; guests go and clean up and rest until dinner; the meal is served, and then an area is arranged for story telling. The tribal leaders question the visitors and then invite stories based on the answers to their questions. Since Jon was fluent in their dialect, he answered most of the questions and retold Paula's story, for it was a favorite theme among the natives: a stranger lost and alone in Africa. Jon ended the story with Paula doing dancing handstands with the Machozi dancers.

There was an immediate request for a demonstration. Jon tied the feathered jangles, which the Machozi had given them as gifts, to their legs and arms asking the group to sing a chanting song. Jon danced first as he had in the Machozi village. Then he drew Paula up and she walked around the circle shaking the jangles on her calves and elbows before suddenly going into the same routine she had done for the Machozi. The watchers were amazed, and warbled and cheered loudly in praise. Again, Paula was a hit.

Tamubu missed the demonstration for the second time as he had started a conversation with the medicine man at dinner, and it wasn't long before they left to look at some puzzling cases. It was an honor for Tamubu to consult with the local medicine men about unusual problems and a tribute to Manutu when he was able to help.

In the morning, Chief Chabo sent four scouts and four warriors, (warriors do not portage) with them, for the river might not be navigable all the way to the ocean. He said, "It is a long way to the ocean." (Jon figured about 225 miles via the Kom River) "There are some rebel clans that might attack a small group of strangers if there are no warriors with them. Our hunting rights go all the way to the big water. No one will challenge my Djoumani warriors. You will be safe." Chief Chabo assured them.

Paula enjoyed traveling with the Djoumani. They liked to sing marching songs as Motozo, Kimbo and Kybo, Ubendi and Obi had done on the trek back to the beach, after her escape from the Ndezi. It made the time pass in a happy frame of mind. Sometimes, Jon and Tamubu laughed heartily at the risqué suggestions in the lyrics.

Paula delighted in the cadence of the words, but didn't understand the double meanings. There were times of extreme quiet too when she listened to the symphony of bird calls or happened to glimpse the ruffed faces of the Black and

White Abyssinian Colobus monkeys as they screeched and scampered away through the trees.

Most calls were just heard for the wildlife was naturally shy. Always, there was the vast panoply of flowering vines, the parasitic air plants, the gracefully draped tree ferns and the shy clumps of orchids hiding in the deep moss of tree crotches–dwarfed by the giant, flowering red-purple lissochilus that grew to an incredible height of fifteen feet; all were stunning in their profusion.

At the lunch stop and in the evenings, the Djoumani kept to themselves. Mostly they played a game of stones and laughed often. It was very pleasant to have their company close by. Kybo made the fire and prepared the areas for the tents. Tamubu did the cooking. Jon and Paula did small chores and clean up.

TAMUBU HAD BEEN QUIET these past two days so Paula asked. "Is everything all right with you? You have been so quiet. Jon and I have been doing all the talking."

Tamubu looked at Paula. She was so lovely, so sincere that it made his heart thump a bit. "I have been thinking about all the unexpected changes in our plans of late. I am more than a little bit worried about seeing my parents again; I have no idea what to say to them in the letter Jon wants me to write."

Paula, who could write anything at anytime, started to make light of his worries; but then she thought, what if I was going to meet my parents again, after fourteen years, and I hardly remembered them... yes, it would be hard to know the right things to say.

"You must say what was and what is. You must say you were sick with malaria for a long time after you were rescued. You must say that by the time you were well, you were an important member of the tribe that had adopted you. You were the son of the Chief. You must say that Nanoka loved you deeply and cared for you day and night through your long illness. You must say that you were happy in your life with Manutu as your teacher... that each day of learning was a joy; and that you could hardly wait for each new day and the discoveries you might find. You must say that it was only when Nanoka was sick unto death that she told you about the missionary doctor, who had brought the quinine, and who had told her about a missing white boy. It was only then that you knew you had another family, and it was then that you went looking for them.

"You must say that you found me lost and in peril and in helping me, Jon was able to find you. You must say that you have grown to be a different man than you would have been if they had raised you and you hope with all your heart that you don't disappoint them when you meet again. You must sign it with Love."

Paula looked up from her peeling chores and thought she saw a tear run down Tamubu's cheek. She got up and went behind him and put her arms around his shoulders and laid her head on his neck. "They are your parents," she said softly. "Their love for you is boundless. Just be open with them so they know where they stand. I've told you this before, but I'll say it again. You must be you, for you can be no one else." She gave him a squeeze and got up and walked over to Jon who was fiddling with the radio. He looked up at her approach and said. "I don't think I can get this thing working without new batteries, which means waiting until we get to Campo. I was hoping we could give Captain Jones a heads-up and have him there when we arrived."

"If he is in Douala, he can be there in a day; it's about a hundred and twenty miles. If he is off somewhere, it will be what it will be."

"You are very philosophical today."

"It is a good day for philosophy. Where's Kybo?"

"Off playing that game of stones; one of the Djoumani scouts challenged him to a game and it has turned into a tournament."

"Is Kybo good at it?"

"It would seem so. He has beaten all challengers so far."

"Traveling with the Djoumani has been very relaxing. They are a happy lot, don't you think?"

"Jolly good men, none better."

"I wonder what makes them so happy."

"Kings of all they survey, most likely. Not too many worries, not too many cares and almost no enemies, for they are a warrior nation and can be deadly when opposed."

"How do you know that?"

"I studied most of the African nations when I was in school and the tribes that make up each nation are quite diverse: like the Ndezi that abducted you. It is a dictatorship as you no doubt found out. No council, no elders, just a few lieutenants and the Medicine Man. It has always been so, but Bolbonga is a good leader, if a bit arbitrary when he wants something. But you found that out too."

"Was there any particular reason you chose to study the African tribes?"

"Yes. I knew that someday I was going to go looking for my brother and I wanted to be able to communicate with the natives."

"Well, you should go and communicate with your brother now. He needs you and he needs your assurance that your parents will accept him and love him." Jon turned sharply to Paula. "Is something wrong?"

"Not really, he's just scared to death he will disappoint your parents."

"Balderdash!"

"I agree, but you must find a way to make it easier for him. Put yourself in his place. You'll see what I mean."

Jon started to stuff the radio back in the carry pouch when Kybo appeared with a big smile. He saw Jon with the radio and said, "Kisha, does the radio work?"

"No, we need new batteries."

"Wait, I get them for you." Opening his personal pouch, he pulled out two packages of new batteries and handed them to Jon, beaming."

"Did you get these in Lomie?"

"Yes, Ruffo he take me to town. I see radio in shop, buy batteries for you."

"Kybo, you are a jolly good fellow!"

It was just a few minutes before Jon had the batteries

installed. He said, "I will wait until we climb higher tomorrow to see if anyone can pick up my signal." Jon put the radio in the case, patted Kybo on the back, and strode off, with his lips pressed into a grimace. He headed toward Thomas–but slowed as he approached.

"Do you know what a plum Kybo is for us? He remembered to get batteries for the short wave radio in Lomie. I can try for Captain Jones once we get a bit higher tomorrow. I say old chap, I wanted to ask you what I should say in my letter to our parents. Maybe it would be best if you wrote your letter first, then I could fill in the gaps in my letter."

"Has Paula been talking to you?"

"Goodness, yes. She talks to me all the time."

"You are being evasive. She told me what I must say in my letter and I agree with her. It's the doing it that is hard. I don't want to hurt their feelings by telling them I forgot all about them."

"Well, don't then; be positive. Say how it was. Tell them that you were happy, boy and man. It will please them to know you were loved and an important member of your tribe. It will make them happy to know that you are a respected Medicine Man and an herbalist with great knowledge. All they have ever wanted for their children is that they were reasonably happy, well cared for and grew up to be productive and responsible adults. In my opinion, you qualify on all counts."

"We will make the time for letters when we get to Campo. With you and Paula to help me, I don't know why I worry. Dinner is almost ready, round up the troops."

After dinner, Dodi, the lead scout spoke. "Tomorrow, we will be passing the lands of the Chukikibeti and then we will be at the river."

Jon said, "What do you mean, nasty Pygmies?"

"The Chukikibeti are small of stature like the Pygmies, but their nature is very different; and so are their looks for they have heavy brows recessed eyes and are hairy. They live in an area of dense vegetation where the trees grow so closely together they almost form palisades along the path. The Chukikibeti are tree dwellers and have come to like the taste of man. There is true danger for they use blowpipes and poisoned darts. It is impossible to see them coming or to give chase for reprisal. They are not on our lands or the lands of the Gielli, but adjacent to them in Gabon. Normally, I would not go this way, but this is the trail to the river. We have canoes stored after the double bend of the rapids."

"How long will we be in danger?" Jon asked.

"It usually takes about half a day to travel past the Chukikibeti."

"How soon will we come to this trail tomorrow?" asked Tamubu

"We are just an hour from the trail now."

"Could we travel it at night? You say the trail is closed in, so animals should not be a problem," Tamubu asked.

Dodi thought for a few moments. It was a new idea to him and he wanted to go over the possibilities in his mind before replying. "If we are very quiet and walk with our shields above our heads and hand to shoulder, I think it could be done. There is no moon tonight, it is overcast and will soon rain."

Tamubu turned to Paula. "What do you think? Are you game for a night stroll? You will not be able to use your flashlight."

Paula disliked walking in dense darkness; but sandwiched between Tamubu and Jon, she should be okay. "I think it is a better choice than being targets for poisoned darts."

"Jon?"

"Suits me if it suits you; but I think we should douse the fire and start to get our vision acclimated for the dark night."

Dodi returned from talking to the other Djoumani. "We are for it, one and all. We will sleep now and start out after the midnight hour."

Paula curled up in her tent and thought about her escape from the Ndezi. There was a full moon that night with wispy high scudding clouds. She remembered how, as the moon traversed the night sky, it waned, but she could still see well in the trees. Jon was right; her night vision had improved without the light. Feeling confident that she was not going to embarrass herself, she soon fell asleep.

13

The Trap

TAMUBU PUT A HAND on Paula's foot as he softly called her name. "Time to get up–we must leave in a few minutes." Paula clambered out of her little shelter to see large shapes gathered and ready to go. The long days of continuous exercise made her sleep deeply. It took her only a few minutes to do the necessary, wash her face, brush her teeth and comb her hair. Tamubu handed her a roll-up with cold oatmeal mixed with crushed berries and coconut, and her metal water bottle filled with tea. I might be in the wilderness, but Tamubu and Jon take such good care of me, I could be in a resort hotel. Paula reveled in the long trek, although the reasons for it still rankled. It had been six weeks since she wrenched her ankle, which now gave her little trouble mostly due to Tamubu's nightly ministrations.

The first hour on the trail was difficult. The total darkness of the rainforest was like walking with your eyes closed. Her right hand was tucked under the woven belt Tamubu wore with his safari shorts, so she could feel his steps–if he was going up or down or moved sideways–it alerted her to what to expect. Jon was right behind her off her left elbow should she need extra support.

They stopped. The word was whispered down the line: no talking–no noise. The tension of the stealthy progress had Paula breathing in shallow breaths. She soon felt the fatigue from a lack of oxygenation in her muscles. Breathing deeply, she concentrated on breathing in through her nose and out through pursed lips. The heavy rain came suddenly. Paula was glad she had suited-up before she left, as she watched Jon scramble to put his poncho on before he was soaked. Tamubu wore his kitu kina, which he simply raised up over his head and the Djoumani either did not mind getting wet or were satisfied with the protection of their hardened leather shields overhead.

The rain made a racket on the foliage and on the leather shields, so they picked up the pace a bit under the cover of the noise–mistake! They heard a shrill desperate cry and then nothing. Everyone stopped and crouched low, to make themselves smaller targets for poisoned arrows. Nothing else happened. They remained crouched for long minutes, until the awful word was passed back to them.

Kutoto, the leader of the warriors, had fallen into a pit dug in the middle of the trail. There were sharpened stakes at the bottom and Kutoto was dead. The Djoumani had no intention of leaving his body for the Nyelamosi [ni-el-a-mo'-see] (hairy ones). Paula offered her cliff-climbing ropes to pull him out of the pit. They made loops for his legs and arms and pulled them snug. Then with two men on each rope, they lifted him to the trail, where they wrapped him snugly in his kitamba, before tying him to his shield. Two of the warriors hefted Kutoto to their shoulders so they could be on their way. The Djoumani left a bloody arrow in the hole with a long black feather attached to it–the native declaration of reprisal or war.

THIS TRAIL WAS ON Djoumani hunting lands and the Nyelamosi had provoked extreme vengeance by digging the pit. A month later, the Djoumani would send all their troops into Gabon in a raiding foray. The warriors would spread out and form a huge circle around the Nyelamosi home territory. Slowly, they would tighten the noose, driving the Nyelamosi into the densest part of the forest. Here they set a ring of fires, which burned for days on end, until all the forest was destroyed and hopefully, the Nyelamosi with it.]

BUT TONIGHT, THEY MOVED with care. Tamubu offered to go ahead on the trail to make sure there were no more pits. Paula cried, "You can't do that! What if there is another pit?"

He smiled at the concern in her voice, as he said, "I will walk with Manutu, and he will find the way for me." Unseen in the dark, Tamubu gave his things to Bahati, who was Kutoto's lieutenant, to carry for him while he *roamed* the trail to the river. He should have done this before, but it had not occurred to him that the hairy ones would place death traps on a trail in the Djoumani hunting lands. In a short while he returned to retrieve his things from Bahati. They had not traveled far, as the three remaining warriors were walking abreast down the trail, poking their spears in the ground before them as they walked. Now, four scouts carried Kutoto between them.

Tamubu knew the closed-in trail opened up ahead and led them to the place. Here they sat to rest for a bit. Hoping to relieve the tension, he said, "There are no more pits on the trail. I believe the Nyelamosi are sleeping in the caves made by the huge roots of the Mora trees–and are not out in the rain. In another hour, we will come to an old clearing. I think we should rest there until daylight and then move on."

Bahati, known for his perception, observed Tamubu and wondered how he had obtained so much information in such a short time. He pondered the reasons why Tamubu had given him all his things, including his kitu-kina, which he wore always. Bahati asked, "Is the river flowing enough for the canoes?"

Tamubu almost fell into the trap, for the river was indeed flowing smartly enough for the canoes, and they could use some good news about now. "I would expect so; we will see when we arrive at the river." He replied.

The rain stopped before they left the forest-walled trail. It was a relief to leave the narrow confines of the enclosed path and once more climb the less densely treed hillsides, where a bit of starlight penetrated. Here, they came to an old camping site.

Tamubu suggested rest and a meal, and began gathering pieces of an old thorn boma for a fire. He made broth for everyone and added a bit of kimmea to relax them, which he served with cookies from Paula's pack. She smiled at him when, with pantomime, he asked if she would share the cookies with everyone. Even under extreme stress, he never seemed to lose his good humor.

When everyone was gathered around the fire, sipping broth, Tamubu asked, "What do you plan to do with Kutoto's body?"

A group of blank stares greeted him like he had grown horns. "I mean, you cannot carry him for the rest of the trip. What funeral arrangements do you prefer?"

The Djoumani had not thought that far. They were still in shock from the sudden loss of their leader and friend.

Tamubu prodded them a bit, saying: "The trail climbs a bit higher from here to the summit of a hill. It is very stony ground up there. I'm sure we could find a depression and then cover it with many stones." He had found just a spot when he *roamed* earlier. Now, he wanted to give the Djoumani time to adjust to the thought of leaving their friend behind in a strange place.

Tamubu pulled his kitu-kina around him and stretched out for a nap. Paula too, was soon asleep and Jon was not far behind her. Kybo was playing a game of stones with the sentry, while the other Djoumani took turns napping

The sun streamed through the breaks in the canopy and after another cup of broth with a leaf roll-up of grains, coconut slivers and mashed figs, they were on their way again.

It was a long hour before they topped the hill, for carrying a big man, who probably weighed over two hundred pounds, uphill was difficult work. The plan was to spread out and look for suitable burial sites.

After a few minutes, Tamubu *joined* with Paula and sent her in the right direction. In a bit, she called out, "I think I have found a suitable place, come and see."

They agreed that it was a good place, and gathered elephant leaves to line the depression. Kutoto was untied from his shield and gently arranged in place. It was a good fit; he lay perfectly flat a few inches below the soil line. They now covered him with elephant leaves, and then his shield and spear, more elephant leaves and then small rocks were placed over the elephant leaves, fitting them together as best they could. Then larger rocks were laid upon the small ones and finally really big rocks that took two men to carry were placed all over and around the low mound.

Paula had wandered into the forest to find a small sapling that could be placed as a marker, but instead, near a watercourse she found a small bamboo plant growing out of a root well away from the parent plant. She dug it out with the machete and took it back to the grave. A small hole was dug and filled with water, and the little plant, only two feet tall, was placed in the hole. Small pebbles were gathered to stabilize the base and to allow rainwater to penetrate to the fragile roots. Bamboo is a hardy plant, once it takes root, and has been known to grow up through macadam.

Jon was asked to say the customary funeral prayers and eulogy: "Dear Lord" he began "God of our ancestors, we pray that you will take Kutoto and give him a home in your abode of many rooms. You will find him strong and dependable, as he was in life. He will serve you well."

The Djoumani each added some sort of praise for the man they knew and loved... "He was a good father and husband"... "He never beat his wife or his children"... "He was honest and never told a lie"... "He was always faithful to his friends"... "He never shared a secret"... "He was always ready to help those in need"... "He was kind, never mean or boastful". Jon finished up with the "The Lord's Prayer" or "Our Father", the prayer most well known among Christians.

Paula walked away thinking: I hope I have a funeral like that– where the people who knew me stand around my grave and say nice things about me. It was lovely.

The night and the day so far had been very difficult for everyone, physically and emotionally, so Tamubu said, "Why don't we camp here on the high ground for the rest of the day and tonight? It will give us time to hunt fresh meat and dry some jerky for future meals." The suggestion was greeted with relief. No one wanted to be the first to say they didn't feel like going any further today.

The three warriors and the lead scout went off to hunt. The three remaining scouts and Kybo went looking for building materials. Tamubu went off looking for edible plants... and medicinal plants if he happened to find them. Jon stayed with Paula and prepared the campsite and built a fire pit with a rain cover. At least he had the sticks in the ground–all he needed was the roof.

Looking at the nice fire in the fire pit, Paula thought about lunch and wandered over to Tamubu's gathering pouch. He had some stubby carrots and some vegetables that looked like rutabagas and wild onions. There was a bird that Tamubu had snared that morning while we napped, and some of the cut-up big chard-like leaves that tasted something like spinach. She remembered a stew her Hungarian grandmother used to make... for most of the ingredients were here if Tamubu had some rice. She almost missed it, for it was a larger sack, like the ones they had taken for the Pygmies.

With that, she took his big turtle shell pot and suspended it over the fire, on the sticks Jon had already put in the ground. She tossed in the fatty neck and skin of the bird and sautéed them until they were crisp. By then she had the onions cut up. She removed the neck and skin and added the onions. She smelled Tamubu's little cooking pouches until she found one that smelled like sage and one that smelled like thyme. She put the sage in with the onions and proceeded to hack up the bird with the hunting knife she had taken with her when she fled the Ndezi. Tamubu had already eviscerated the bird, burying the entrails with the head and feet, as he was wont to do. She put the cut up bird in the pot and seared it to seal in the juices before covering it with water, adding the thyme, salt and pepper corns. She covered the pot to let it simmer. While the bird cooked, she wrote in her diary.

Jon had taken the radio to the top of the hill to contact Captain Jones and he was still gone. She wondered why? Walking to the top of the hill, she saw him sitting there with his head down. Had he fallen asleep? She crept up and saw that he was writing on a pad, and surmised it was probably a letter to his parents. She turned and crept away.

When the meat was tender, Paula fished it out of the pot, added more water to bring it to a boil then added salt and the cut up vegetables, and some of the wild barley. The rice was brown rice, so she saved it for when she returned the cut up fowl to the pot. She banked the fire, so the pot wouldn't boil over, but would simmer gently. I wonder if Tamubu has any of his biscuit mix already made up. Then, I will only have to water down the coconut milk.

She was again looking through his sacks, when she heard, "I'm not gone an hour and come back to find you rooting in my packs!"

Paula laughed as she turned to see him loaded down with plants, another bird and another turtle. "I was looking for your biscuit mix... to see if you had any already prepared."

"Now, why would you want to do that?"

"I was going to make biscuits to go with the Hungarian stew I made."

"You made stew?" Tamubu dropped his gleanings and went over to the fire; lifting the leaf lid, he sniffed. "It smells really good. What's in it?"

"Your bird, onions, carrots, that big round rutabaga thing, rice, barley, spices and water, but it really needs biscuits."

"May I taste it?"

"Of course, let me know if you think it needs anything."

Tamubu drew out a small cup shaped ladle on a long stick and put it in the pot, stirred and took out a bit. He saw the rice and barley were not yet cooked, so he put the sample back and took just a bit of the broth. He sipped, then sipped again and finally finished the sample. "Delicious, absolutely wonderful, where did you get the recipe?"

"From my grandmother; she never measured anything when she made stew, so I figured I could do it too. I knew the ingredients from helping her make it."

"Well, it is nice to know I don't have to do all the cooking anymore!" I'll make the biscuits while you bank the fire around those rocks. Did you make the fire pit too?"

"No, Jon did; that's what started me thinking... that and my stomach... about making lunch. So, I looked through your stuff to see what I could find and found the makings for Hungarian Chicken and Rice."

"Well, I must go off gathering and let you look more often."

At this point Jon appeared and asked, "What do you mean 'you must go off and let her look more often'?" For some reason this struck Paula and Tamubu as extremely funny, while Jon just stood there and gazed at them saying, "I'm always glad to bring a spot of cheer into the conversation."

As if everyone could smell the stew, the men all returned in the next five minutes with their missions accomplished. Paula's stew was a big success. Hardly a word was spoken, for no one wanted to stop eating long enough to say more than a few complimentary words.

Jon spoke up first. "I was able to contact the *Wind Drift* on the radio today. Captain Jones was in town, but I spoke to Jonas. I told him we needed help to get to an airport further down the coast. That we were on our way to Campo, and would get in touch with him when we had an estimated time of arrival; right now we're about two hundred and forty miles away." Jonas said he would relay the message.

"I wondered why you were gone so long. Were you waiting for Captain Jones to radio back?" Paula asked.

"Yes, for awhile. I wanted to ask him if the Kom River was navigable for his cruiser."

Bahati spoke up. "We have been to the big water on the Kom River. It is a good wide river until you get to the rapids, about sixty miles from the big water. The big rapids go for twenty miles, maybe more, and then you have the little rapids for another ten miles or so. It is only about twenty miles from the big water to the little rapids."

"Did you go down the rapids in a canoe?" Jon asked, incredulous.

"Not the big rapids, they also have waterfalls. We portaged

past the bad places. In between the rapids, we stayed close to the banks where the current is not so fast."

"How long did it take you to make the trip?"

"We were three days on the river and three days of portage."

"Why... that's sixty miles a day on the river, if you can portage twenty miles a day. That's very fast."

"Yes, the river runs very fast to the big water. If you could stay on the water the whole way, you could do it in three days."

"Do you think we will be able to use the Kom River to the big rapids now?"

"Yes, the water never gets too low for a canoe, but when the water is low, the hippos can be a big problem."

"Ah, yes... the hippos, of course!"

"They get cantankerous and territorial when the water is low and challenge anything new or different. They can easily capsize a canoe and will then savage the occupants trying to swim away. Then the crocs get excited and the snakes and usually no one survives.... if it is breeding season, the water height doesn't make any difference, then the bulls are always looking for a fight and chase everything away, even the crocodiles."

No one said much; they were thinking about the hippos. Paula spoke up first, "Is there a good trail beside the river?"

"Where it is necessary to portage, yes, otherwise, no; even with the hippos it is so much faster on the water that no one goes by land near the river." Bahati read the consternation in Paula's face and added, "We will take rolls of sudd with us in the canoes. If the hippos seem unduly interested in us, we will use our tupa shindo [sling-shots] to shoot wads of this favorite food out into the water. The hippos will, almost certainly, go for the food."

Tamubu listened to the exchange. Paula was the bravest woman he had ever known; but the hippos were a concern, even for him. He was constantly amazed, as he traveled, at the unique ways in which the different tribes managed to co-exist with the wildlife around them. He caught Paula's gaze and held it as he moved into her thoughts, '*you must not be worried; the scouts have done this before, and are still here to tell you about it.*' He looked away and saw Jon watching him, and smiled, for with the eye contact, Tamubu read Jon's thoughts. '*Why's he looking at her like that? Oops, I'd better be careful.*' And Jon smiled back, feeling foolish.

DURING THE CONVERSATION, TAMUBU had built a low three-sided shelter on the hillside in which to dry his plants. He bedded coals over the floor, with a low wall of rocks at the rear; there he hung the turtle strips over a smoky fire. In front of the meat, he hung his plants to dry, for the draft moved through and over the hanging plants first.

Tamubu then began to make a stew from the parts of the turtle meat not suitable for drying. He'd found several manioc plants, sweet potato tubers, and the young shoots of wild celery on his afternoon foray; as well as limes and figs, and a sweet fruit with a tough fuzzy skin, which would not draw insects. He'd replenished his supply of root vegetables, which kept well and had gathered more of the chard-like leaves he used for the lunch roll-ups, which did not keep well and had to be gathered daily. The Djoumani too, had gone out gathering in the late afternoon, returning with coconuts, bananas, tinder for the fire and fresh bedding.

This was the first evening that there was time to sit around the fire after dinner, before going to bed. Jon looked at each face, smiled and said, "Well, whose turn is it to tell a story?"

The Djoumani all shook their heads, except for Bahati. Jon jumped on this lack of denial and said, "Well, Bahati, it seems you have been chosen to tell a story."

"I would like to tell a story about Kutoto: He was my mother's sister's son and two years older than me. As small children, we played together often, but as we grew, the two years separated us in our duties and learning. He was always kind to me and often asked me to go with him when he went hunting or fishing. He particularly liked to go fishing. A mile or so from our village, there was a big pond. It had the usual crocodiles, snakes and leeches, but it also had good fish. The men had built a pier over the pond, so people could be safe above the water to fish. It was a good place for boys to go to talk about anything and everything."

"Kutoto had asked me to go fishing with him early the next morning, saying we would be back in time for chores. I agreed and I met him before first light. It was a big adventure for a ten-year-old boy. I was proud that my mother had agreed to let me go with Kutoto. She even made a small breakfast pouch for us to take with us, for the cooking fires had not yet been lit.

"The trail was open to the pond, as it was well used. The sun was just peeking over the horizon when we arrived at the pier. We went to the end and sat to bait our hooks. I had a rough branch from a willow for a rod, but Kutoto had a tamarind branch, which tapered nicely to the end. We tossed our worm baited hooks into the pond and waited quietly. It was a good morning to fish. The haze stayed over the pond until the sun rose. We soon had eight nice fishes in a pail of water. It was time to go home and do our chores.

"I got up and as I bent over to pick up my gear, I stepped on a wasp's nest that was in the crevices between the logs of the pier. The angry bees came at us, so we grabbed our stuff and ran. I took only two steps before I dropped my net and tripped over it and fell tumbling into the water.

"The splash aroused the crocodiles. They immediately moved into the water and sped to the site. Kutoto did not think at all... he just dropped his things, except for his walinka, which was in his waistband, and jumped into the water to help me. I was on the ladder to the pier, which had been built for such emergencies, when a huge crocodile surfaced with gaping jaws going directly for Kutoto. I was frozen with fear. I could not even make myself climb higher in my terror. I did not know what to do. I was going to see my best friend grabbed by a vicious crocodile and taken down to drown. As I watched in horror, Kutoto took his walinka from his waist, and with it pointed up and down in his fist, he shoved it into the crocodile's mouth, where upon the crocodile

immediately closed upon the object. I scampered to the top of the ladder, and belly down on the pier and put my hand out to help Kutoto who was rapidly climbing up the ladder. We sat there to catch our breath and let our hearts return to normal as we watched the nasty beast as he thrashed about in the water; for until he closed his jaw further, he could not reopen it either. If he did not dislodge the walinka, the crocodile would die of starvation or drown.

"The bees had gone back to their nest. We gathered our things and filled the pail with more water for the fish and headed home. Nothing was said for a while, but when I calmed down, I sincerely thanked him for saving my life. Kutoto said, "It was nothing. You would have done the same for me." As I walked home, I wondered if I would ever be as brave as Kutoto was that day. I asked him if he was going to tell the story at home. He said to me, "If you ever want to go fishing at the pond again, you will tell no one what has happened this morning."

"And this story has never been told before... for we have always kept it our secret. I will sorely miss Kutoto, for he has been my best friend all of my life." The End.

IT WAS CUSTOMARY TO warble and whistle at the end of a story, but instead, there were repeated praises and short tales of other of Kutoto's accomplishments. Paula was impressed; the dead man had been well liked, well admired and well loved by all who knew him. She wished she had had the time to get to know him better.

As she rested in her little shelter, she thought again of the story Bahati had told, and wondered if she would have had the courage to go to Bahati's aid when she was only ten years old? She had almost decided probably not, when she remembered an incident that had happened when she and her twin brother were thirteen.

They had gone sailing with friends off the New Jersey shore in their friend's catamaran. It was a blustery day

and they ran aground on a sandbar. Eric jumped overboard to lighten the load; as he regained the deck he was knocked overboard by a wild swing of the boom. Paula tied a line around her waist and jumped in after him. All their weight was on the one side as she helped him back aboard, when another strong gust came along and lifted the catamaran off the sandbar. It flew away over the sea, keel hauling her as it went. Her friends finally managed to lower the sail and pull her in, but there had been some dicey moments. Still, when she jumped in to look for Eric, there hadn't been any sharks... or at least none that she was aware of... so it wasn't really the same was it? She concluded just before she fell asleep: you will never know what you will do in an emergency until the time comes... and that's the way of it.

14

The River Kom

THE START WAS A bit later the next morning. Tamubu needed time after first light to organize and pack the medicinal plants he had been drying all night in the leaf shelter. The others had a general repacking to do to make places to carry the sudd they would gather on the way to the river. It was not a long journey, just twelve miles. Even with the late start, they should be there well before noon. Paula missed the singing and marching songs today. The Djoumani were silent and in mourning for Kutoto, their lost leader and friend.

THE TRAIL PARALLELED THE run-off water from the mountains to the river. It was an animal track that wandered up and down, but the footing was good. The dim gloom of the rainforest was dispelled by the sunlight that streamed through the wide gap in the trees over the watercourse. The variety of birds here was delightful. Paula saw a flight of Grey Parrots with their conspicuous red tails, and a Green-Breasted Touraco, which was a huge teal blue bird with yellow breast and a loud strident cry in flight, when the crimson wings were visible. It had a tall black crest atop its head and hopped in a strange progression from branch to branch after it landed on a perch.

On the dry rocks in the watercourse, she saw a number of the Lemon-Rumped Tinker birds getting a drink of fresh water; they were a common little glossy black bird of West Africa, with a bright yellow patch above a short tail, their 'touk...touk...touk' calls could be heard all day and for long distances.

As they approached the river and the open grassy areas

where the hippos fed at night, she saw the White-Crested Touraco: a bird only a bit smaller than the seventeen inch adult Green-Breasted Touraco, but entirely different in coloring. The bird attracted Paula's attention with his deep guttural 'karoo', which he repeated many times, before she saw the distinct white head with purple and red eye patch. When the bird moved, Paula saw the emerald green breast and the vibrant purple wings and tail. This morning, she was walking in a birder's paradise.

Just before noon they reached the Kom River where the natives had suspended the canoes from the trees. Tamubu made a fire while the Djoumani brought the canoes down to the ground. He heated water for tea and broth and made the roll-ups for lunch.

Over lunch they discussed canoe etiquette, the dos and don'ts that were vital for their safety. The canoes were large with high prows, which was an advantage where the river had white water. They were made from a light but durable wood that had been covered with pitch and fired to harden it.

Each had a wide keel shaped bottom on the outside with adzed log benches (thwarts) crosswise for seats and strength on the inside. Each canoe had four seats: two in the front and two in the rear and each bench seated two. The center of the canoe was an open flat bottom to accommodate gear and supplies. Overall the canoes were about twenty feet long. Each canoe could hold eight adults and personal gear.

Since there were only eleven of them, it was decided to have two warriors manning paddles in the rear of the one boat with Kybo and Bahati manning paddles in the rear of the other boat. The scouts would be in the front of each boat manning the paddles, for they had the experience, having made the trip before. Paula and Tamubu would be in the first canoe with Kybo and Bahati. Jon would be in the second canoe with the short wave radio and his camping gear.

Jon who was familiar with canoes asked, "These are very nice canoes. Who made them?"

Bahati answered, "Years ago, the Djoumani found three men who were suffering from illness on the banks of the river. They were almost dead from hunger and thirst. They were taken back to our village where, in time, they recovered. When they were well, they went back to the river and built these boats. They had much money and gave generously to our chief for their care, and to purchase the tools needed for building the canoes. They had worked building ships in England and had a very strong reason for going back down the river to the big water. We brought them supplies while they worked on the canoes and some Djoumani stayed to help, as they were also generous to the helpers.

I think they were going to go to sea in the canoes, for I once heard them talking about making holes in the rails to fasten the canoes together when they reached the sea. Also, they had purchased canvas and ropes with the building tools.

One day when the Djoumani brought supplies for them, they found them all dead, killed by guns. Our friends, who were helping them were dead too. We buried them all in the clearing over there. One of the canoes was gone. They had built three. The one that was different, wider, deeper with a top in the middle was gone. We took one of the canoes down river to the rapids, but never saw anyone with guns.

Twice since then, we have ferried travelers to the big water. Once we took our chief, for he wanted to see the river meet the big water. When we returned, the water was too shallow to continue back to the camp where they were made. We left them here. The canoes have been in the trees for four rainy seasons now."

"Did these men tell you their names?"

"Yes, they were Smitty, Jonesy and Peters."

"Good English names," Jon said. "But, of course, they tell us nothing. What happened to the canvas you mentioned?"

"We used the canvas to wrap the bodies before we buried them."

"And the ropes?"

"We used them to make the nets to raise the canoes to the trees and which you are using to hold your goods in place in the canoes."

"And the tools?"

"They were gone, as was all the personal property of the white men. Only the canvas and ropes were still here. Even the cooking pots were gone."

"What an unusual and sad story!" Jon remarked, "But there is always the unexpected, isn't there?" "Well, let's get cracking–I wonder if you could lend a hand here, Bahati?"

The group was ready to embark shortly after lunch, without the noontime rest. The canoes had been packed with care; the goods covered with nets, which were secured through holes in the coping rail. The bank here was high enough to keep crocodiles away, but too high to easily enter the canoes. With ropes attached fore and aft, they walked the canoes down the stream to a hippo groove near the lea.

River progress was slow in the beginning. Only the scouts and Bahati were familiar with the canoes... and Jon had some experience too, but in smaller craft. As they became familiar with the changes in the handling of the craft, caused by the movement of body weight and current, they experimented with the paddles in the rear for guiding and stabilizing the direction of the craft. They practiced moving closer to the bank and moving away from the bank; and maintaining direction. The current was swift and they felt the strength of it when they moved away from the banks.

It was not long before they came to the first snag, where a tree had fallen into the river and other debris had collected in the branches. A line was tossed from the first canoe to the second and the second canoe tied the line to a stout branch above the water line of the snag, playing out the line as the first canoe ventured into the stronger current. Once around the snag, the paddlers worked mightily to escape the strong pull of the current into the slower waters near the banks. The second canoe made it around the snag in the same way, without incident, but now everyone understood the immense and possibly deadly pull of the fast river current.

They had seen only the one hippo groove on this side of the river–where they boarded the canoes. The rest of the afternoon passed uneventfully, with the paddlers gaining skill and confidence. Paula and Jon were gauging the speed of travel. Even near the banks, they were doing eight miles an hour, more than three times faster than on land.

Dusk had already begun its long approach when Bahati called out. "There, see that snag, we can beach the canoes on it. There is a clearing not far from the water." He beached the canoe in the silt surrounding the snag. The two paddlers jumped out of the canoe onto the wide silt island and tugged the canoe higher before fastening it to a stout branch in the snag. The second canoe did the same. Everyone was relieved to be on terra firma again, without incident; and all clambered onto the fallen tree trunk to gain the bank, where they made a beeline to the brush.

Everyone had a job to do to set up the camp for the night. It was a ritual of efficiency and dinner was soon on the hob. Once the lean-to shelters had been built, a party went out to get fresh spring water, returning with sweet potatoes, the chard-like leaves called gojani, wild onions and muhogo, the large turnip that looked like a rutabaga. It stayed firm in the stew and had a pleasant sweetness to it. They also had coconuts, bananas and wild lemons. Bananas are rarely ripe when found, except in villages where the monkeys fear the presence of man.

Jon looked at the cornucopia, for the sight of food always pleased him, and said, "I do believe we have enough food to swamp the canoes!" Paula and Tamubu laughed, but the Djoumani looked worried and Jon took pity on them saying, "I was just kidding... but we do have to be careful of the load."

After a fine dinner of turtle stew with biscuits, and lemon water sweetened with coconut, Bahati said, "Does anyone have questions?"

Kybo said, "We were watching the paddles of the first canoe, why did you turn them on edge, so the paddles did not work?"

Bahati smiled and said, "If you turn a paddle edge first into the water, you transfer the power to the other paddle, and by turning it under the water, you add to the power of the other paddle. I will get the paddles and show you."

While Jon, Tamubu and Paula were not paddling, they found the explanation quite interesting with Jon saying, “Tell us all you know about using the paddles, Bahati, we’ll never know when the information might be useful.” Bahati told them all he knew, which was considerable, about the steering and handling of the big canoes. Bahati ended the evening, saying, “There are several hippo grooves on our side of the river tomorrow. I think we will pass two of them early enough in the morning so that the hippos should be resting and ignore us; but the last one is in the late afternoon and hippos get restless late in the day, for they are hungry.

The tension and apprehension of the day just gone made everyone tired and wanting to sleep. Tamubu took the first watch so he could prepare his plants. Jon kept him company for a while and told him that he had written a letter to their parents and if Thomas wanted, he could read it, so he could get a feel for what to say and how to say it in his own letter.

“I have not had much time to think about my letter. Reading your letter would be a big help to me, as I really do not know how to start. It will be the first letter I have ever written.”

Jon thought, the things that Paula and I take for granted, because we have done them so often before, must seem like giant obstacles to Thomas. I’m glad I thought to let him read my letter; I think it will help him.

He said, “It is quite easy... you just pretend you are talking to the person with a pencil. Let’s say I wanted to thank you for our nice dinner but you were out gathering and I was going to go to sleep. I would write: ‘Dear Thomas, Thank you for the delicious dinner you made for us. My stomach is quite happy that you are such a good cook. I can’t imagine what we would be eating if I had to do the cooking! Love, Jon.’

“In a letter or note, you can say things that might make you feel a little embarrassed if you said them to the person out loud. I think that is why people like to say difficult things with letters. Other good things about letters are: you can stop and think about how you want to say something... or change the way you did say it, or add to it something you might have left out... or take something out that you did write, but when you reread your letter, you found you didn't want to say that at all."

Tamubu smiled at Jon, "You make it sound easy."

"It is easy. In a long letter, it is helpful to make a list of the things you want to say and the order in which you want to say them, like the order in which things happened to you: lost, found, cared for, healed, important member of the Zuri Watu, happy as a boy, educated to manhood by Manutu, and finally learning of your natural family from Nanoka before she died; your travels to home, meeting Paula, then me and that we will soon be together again.

"I do not want to say anything that will hurt them."

"Then only say what was or what is, and that you have always been happy in the life you have lived. It will please our parents to know that."

"Have you have been talking to Paula? Those were almost her exact words."

"Paula and I have not discussed what you should say in your letter, only that you should write a letter. If I have given you the same advice, it is because we are both experienced letter writers. Well, I'm about to nod off as I sit here. Do you have much more to do with the plants?"

"I should be finished when Dodi and Efo come to relieve me."

In the light of the campfire, sitting all alone, Tamubu reached for his pack and drew out the diary Paula had given him for drawing plants. So far, he had only a few plant entries, for his time always seemed to be occupied with chores or gathering. He turned to a blank page, wrote the outline as Jon had suggested. Then he began:

Dear Mother and Father,

I am so happy that I will soon see you again, but I think I should tell you a bit of what has happened to me in the years that I have been lost to you...

The next day the start was delayed until it was full light.

By then, the hippos should be back in the river. The canoes would stay in the shallow water of the banks, while the hippos would be further out in the stream, standing where they would be submerged and have only their eyes, ears above water. During the rainy season, when the water level rose, the hippos stood closer to the banks, where they could maintain their submerged but watchful stance.

The preferred method for a hippo to travel in the water is to submerge and walk, or trot, along the bottom of the stream or river, which they can do easily as their specific gravity is higher than that of water. This presents a clear danger to canoe travelers; as a hippo walking on the bottom of the river could surface to breathe at any time underneath a canoe and in so doing tip it over. The average weight of a hippopotamus is 2500 to 3000 pounds with some bulls getting as large as 5800 pounds. A full canoe with its occupants weighs less than 2000 pounds and the balance of a canoe is, of course, critical.

They slowly passed the hippos grouped near mid-stream about mid-morning. The hippos seemed to give them no notice at all, which greatly pleased everyone. At the lunch stop, well away from the gregarious pachyderms, that preferred to stay close together, Bahati gave the passengers instructions in loading the tupashindo [sling-shots] with the sudd and how to fire balls of sudd into the area around the school... should the hippos seem too interested in the canoes. They practiced for a half an hour after lunch before regaining the river. The hippos would leave the river after dusk to forage on land. They wanted to be well past the hippo grooves in the bank before then.

The afternoon was idyllic. Birds of all kinds flew across the river from the trees and vegetation on one side to the other. The most startling was a spectacular demonstration by a Giant Kingfisher who swooped down from the trees just above their heads and snagged a large fish that was probably trying to escape the passage of the canoes. He was a huge bird, eighteen inches in length with a massive black bill, a slate gray body speckled with white, a white throat, rufous breast and a black and white barred belly. Needless to say, we ducked. Bahati said, "Tomorrow night we will have fish for dinner too." His humor relaxed the nascent canoeists.

Rounding a bend in the river, Tamubu and Paula saw a very large school of hippos, possibly thirty animals. They stopped the canoes near some overhanging foliage and watched the school for a while. The cows and calves were grouped closer to the opposite bank and seemed quiet enough. A few bulls were yawning at each other showing their tushes [long canines], but it seemed more a display than a serious threat. The canoes continued along the riverbank. The occupants maintained absolute silence. They did not make eye contact with the animals gathered away from the bank of the river.

As the first canoe passed the groove leading from the river to the grassy fields a loud creaking groan was heard, then another and another. Survival instinct dictated that they look at the hippos to see what was happening, and saw the bulls, with mouths agape, coming towards the canoes.

Bahati said, "Time for the sudd. Send it all out. We don't want them to submerge!" Paula, Tamubu and Jon fired ball after ball of the sudd at the advancing bulls. On they came; Paula took a ball and aimed directly for the gaping maw of the leading bull. It was a direct hit and the bull closed his mouth. Finding a favorite food he chomped and seeing more in the water stopped to feed. The other bulls also stopped, and then began to challenge one another for the food.

This was just as dangerous as an attack, for the bow waves caused by the hippos plunging about would hit them broadside, and could capsize the canoes. The men paddled as fast and as hard as they could to put some distance between themselves and the huge hippo bulls, who when they finally stopped to feed had only been fifteen or twenty feet away; much too close–for just the movement of the bulls vying for the food had rocked the canoes, tipping them sideways. Only the forward speed and the reflexive movement of the passengers to the high side had saved the canoes from overturning.

They paddled furiously for a mile and then fatigue forced them slow a bit. It was such a close encounter that Paula could still see in her mind the jagged, broken tushes of the bull hippo closest to her. She saw the damage those teeth could inflict in the deep pink gashes on the scarred hides of the other bulls.

According to Bahati, that was the last channel until tomorrow. The river went very deep here and the drop-off from the bank was straight down as the river narrowed in this stretch and the current strength increased. It was a very fast run for the next two hours. Rounding a bend, the river widened and the current slowed. There were sand banks in the lees with crocodiles lazing in the last oblique shafts of sunlight for the day. Two miles further on, they came to a silted-in snag where they could beach the canoes and reach the overgrown river bank.

"This is a new place, Kigozi. Bahati said. "I do not know it. But we shall soon see if it is suitable." He called the other scouts and off they went. Paula, Jon and Tamubu sought the privacy of the bushes; and it seemed no time at all before they heard the scouts returning. Bahati said, "There is an old encampment just beyond those trees, with an old thorn boma around a clearing. The antelopes and deer have kept the grass down, so it is a good place to camp. Each person grabbed a pack once the canoes were secured to the bole of the fallen tree. The clearing was delightful. The thorn boma, while old, was still a deterrent even if many plants and vines had grown around and though it. It seemed no time at all before they were settled in nicely, and the men had gone off to find fresh water. Jon was busy putting up sleeping shelters and Tamubu was making dinner. Kybo had gone off with the warriors to hunt and forage. Paula decided to catch up on the entries to her diary.

When the scouts returned with water, Bahati was holding a long club with what looked like the remnants of a metal pail attached. He came to the fire and handed it to Jon. "Look what we have found."

Jon was perplexed, "What is it?"

"It is a metal adze. We found it near the spring. We found cooking pots and other gear there too. We think the people who shot the canoe builders were camped here, and left the things they no longer wanted to carry. I find it curious, for

I know the tree snag where we tied up was not here before. It makes me wonder if they had an unpleasant encounter with the hippos and lost their canoe. We said in our drum messages that the killers were in a canoe. We wondered why the drums never told of their passing. If they were trekking, they might have reached the sea unnoticed. It would explain why we never heard of them again."

Bahati now had Jon's complete attention. "Show me the place where you found this thing." And off they went. They were back in a short time with Jon saying, "There is not enough light to see the details. I will go back in the morning. Thomas, will you go with me?"

"What can you expect to find after so many years?"

"I am looking for something that will identify the murderers."

"Why would you want to do that?"

"Because, if we don't care about what happens to our fellow man, and try to right the wrongs, our civilized society will deteriorate into chaos."

"What is deteriorate?"

"To worsen–or become worse; fall apart; crumble; decline."

"I will go with you in the morning. Sit with me; I have something for you to read." Thomas reached in his pack and pulled out the plant diary and showed his letter to Jon. Jon read the letter and then read it again. It was succinct. A lifetime in two pages; if he has never written a letter before, he is a natural for it. And his handwriting, it's practically copperplate. Why does this not surprise me? I loved Thomas as a boy, but it was puppy love compared to what I feel now. Mom and Dad are going to be so proud of him!

Jon handed the diary back to Thomas. "It is a very good letter. You have a gift for many things and letter writing should be included."

"I have you to thank for that. You made it sound so easy; I decided to give it a try... just as you suggested."

"May I show it to Paula?"

"Yes, she was worried for me. Seeing it finished will please her."

Jon went to Paula's little lean-to, expecting to find her scribbling away, but she was sound asleep. Well, those hippos were awfully close today. She is such a good sport. Never a word of complaint; I can see why Thomas loves her. I love her myself. He went and sat by Thomas. "Paula is asleep."

"Well, dinner is ready. Get the others, but tell them to be quiet. If Paula is asleep, she needs the rest. I will put a bowl of stew aside for her."

Tamubu again took the first watch. Everyone else went to bed; but he still had work to do. He was preparing some of the antibiotic paste, pressing a white sticky liquid from the tough stems of a plant into a shallow bowl and then mixing in the powdered plants. It would gel and he would roll it into an arnica leaf to keep in his pouch. He was almost finished, when he felt a presence behind him and then heard Paula say, "Why did you let me sleep so long? I'm starved."

"If you were asleep, you needed it. Your dinner is here, keeping warm." He handed her the coconut bowl of stew and a biscuit he had rolled in a wet leaf before sitting it on top of a warm rock, so it was still soft and fluffy. He made a cup of broth and added a bit of kimmea and a curl of cinnamon.

"Ummm, that smells so good; tastes good too. After I left you in the cove, the thing I missed most was your broth. Nothing comes close the hearty flavor and the delicious smell of your broth..."

"Did you miss only my broth; nothing else?"

She smiled, with a flirting look and said, "I missed you too. Did you miss me?"

He returned her look with a sensual smile, raised his eyebrow and with a smile in his eyes, he said, "More than I expected. I was heartsick when Arthur said you had gone home."

Paula's heart fluttered–she felt ecstatic, but said simply, "Me too, I was crestfallen when I found that you were gone."

"What is crestfallen?"

"Sad in spirit, disappointed."

Into the long silence, she said softly. "We have been making very good progress. I figure about one hundred and twelve miles, maybe more. Did Jon happen to say how far he thought we had traveled on the river so far?"

"No, Jon was tired and went to bed early too... everyone did, even Kybo. It must be hard work to paddle those big canoes."

"I'm sure it is... but do you think it is harder than hiking with all the gear and supplies they carry? I think it is because we have had no afternoon naps."

"You're right! It is probably a combination of both." They heard a rustling sound and Dodi and Efo came to the fire. Tamubu fixed them a cup of broth and they sat and thanked him while Paula asked them which they preferred: hiking through the forest or canoeing down the river?

They thought for a moment and then Dodi replied, "The River is faster and mostly easier, but we like walking in the forest too."

With that, Paula arose and said, "Believe it or not, I'm ready to go back to bed again."

"Would you like me to rebandage your ankle tonight?"

"Will the morning be okay? I want to wash it first, it itches."

Paula no sooner put her head down on the air mattress pillow, than she was once again asleep. Tamubu went to his lean-to and rolled himself in his kitu-kina, thinking about the verbal exchange of deep feelings, and he too fell asleep. Dodi and Efo were already playing a game of stones in the firelight.

15

The Pymtu

THE HEAVY RAIN HAD come and gone in the night. Dodi and Efo had extended the leaf roof over the fire to keep dry, while they played their game of stones during their watch. Tamubu appreciated the enlarged shelter as he prepared breakfast, for it was still drizzling. Jon made the coffee and then went to pack up.

The cooking bags were the last to be packed and the first out each night, and sometimes they were even needed for the mid-day break. Feeding so many at each meal, Tamubu was running short of staples. Seeing Bahati with a parcel headed for the canoes, Tamubu asked him, "Bahati, are there any villages in the next two days?"

"Yes, tomorrow before we portage around the rapids, there is the village of the Pymtu."

"Will we be able to barter for supplies? I am running low on some staples."

"I do not know these people well. They are a poor village of fishermen. I think they will share, but who knows if they will have it to share?"

Tamubu considered this and said to himself: I must finish preparing my medicines tonight, for they may be worth more than barter to the villagers.

Jon chatted with Paula while Tamubu put a clean wrap on her ankle. "I say, this river travel must be a good rest for your ankle."

"Yes, I suppose it is. It hasn't been throbbing at all during the night, but it has been getting a little stiff from all the sitting."

Tamubu said, “You must walk a bit more when we are stopped, and elevate it at night. There is a bit of heat; you don’t want it to swell again.”

When Tamubu was finished, he and Jon went to look at the campsite that Bahati had found last evening. It was overgrown and Jon remarked, “Why would anyone camp over here, when there was a perfectly good thorn boma over there?” Jon took a thick brown stick and started to push the brush around.

“Jon! What do you have there?”

“What do I have where?”

“In your hand–let me see that.”

“It’s just a stick.”

Tamubu took the “just a stick” and looked at it carefully before he took his knife and pried the dirt out of the end. “It is not a stick, it is a leg bone.”

“Really? Blast, here are more.” Jon was using his long knife to cut away the vegetation. “I wondered why the grass was eaten inside the thorn boma and it was so overgrown nearby. Now I know. The animals knew something had died here.” Together, they cut away the brush and found, almost completely covered with debris, the remains of several men. Some of the bones were missing. All the arm bones were gone, but when the Djoumani came to help, they found enough of the remains to determine that there had been six men. Once the site was cleared, Tamubu powdered a bit of rib bone and added the juice of some berries. When the watered-down berries fizzed in the piece of coconut husk, he said, “These men were poisoned; there is a plant that looks much like gojani, but has pointed leaves, they are deadly. They cause a person to crave water, so the men gathered here beneath the spring to drink. The water hastens the spread of the poison and death occurs in a few hours. That is why the cooking pots were here with them, to gather water... and the adze, to cut away the vegetation to get closer to the water.”

“What shall we do with them, I mean the bones?”

“For myself, I would just leave them.” Looking at the Djoumani, they nodded their heads in agreement.

“It doesn’t feel right to me,” Jon said, “but I suppose it is fitting. I wonder what happened to their guns and the other things."

Bahati spoke up. "If they lost their canoe to the hippos, the heavy rifles would have sunk quickly. Light packages would have floated away. The adze with the wooden handle might have floated a bit and the pots might have been in a crate. The canoe builders had built crates for their campsite, to sit on and to store things, and they too were gone. It might have been all they could rescue from the swift current. It would also explain why they were eating leaves, not meat."

"I haven't seen a crate, have you Bahati?"

"No, but the crate could have been used for firewood."

"You should be a detective Bahati; you're no end of valuable information and quite good at figuring out what might have happened." Jon said.

"It is necessary to learn from what you see to survive in the wilderness."

THE MORNING ON THE river was idyllic. A cloudy mist floated a few feet above the water until the sun rose over the trees; then as the direct rays made the mist gleam and shimmer, the layer thinned to wisps and then was gone. In the background, like a concert on the radio, the morning birdsong filled the air, interspersed with cries from the forest denizens. They floated silently with the current–only the soft splashing sound of the paddles announced their presence.

A LITTLE AFTER NOON, Bahati cried, "The Pymtu village is just ahead." They all watched as the village appeared when the thick bank foliage thinned. There were several large boulders in a semi circle along the bank behind which, the women were washing clothes on smaller rocks in the shallows. The women called out to the villagers when they saw the canoes. "Mjeni, (visitors) Djoumani mjeni na msafiri." (And travelers.) The men and children came to the water's edge and helped beach the canoes. Bahati talked to the men, who laughed at some arcane joke.

As they assembled on the beach, the introductions were

casual. The guests were led to a thatched pavilion where the Chief, the Medicine Man and their sons awaited the guests. Bahati began the introductions with: "This is Tamubu; he is a Medicine Man of the Great Zuri Watu, an acolyte of Manutu. This is kisha Jon; he is the brother of the Medicine Man. He also speaks our language and others well. This is Missy Paula. She was marooned alone in a cove beyond the great mountain by a tsunami. She is the intended of Tamubu. Jon is her chaperone. Kybo, who has gone with your lieutenant, is a Nigerian who has dedicated his life, as afisa, to the Medicine Man of the Great Zuri Watu.

When the formal introductions were completed, the chief asked Tamubu, Jon, Paula and Bahati to join him for the noon meal. His lieutenant had already taken the rest of the visitors with him to share his noon meal. Actually, it was the village stockpot–a huge pot that simmered all the time, with bits of meat, fish and vegetables added as they became available. This way, they always had a broth to start other pots of stew.

While the lieutenant entertained the visitors, his wife took broth from the stockpot, added fresh water and bits of dried meat, which she placed over a hot fire; when the broth boiled, fresh vegetables, barley and spices were added. While the stew simmered, his wife made kiazi taz (potato pancakes) which she served with honey. There was also freshly made lemon water.

While the mid-day meal was being prepared, the chief satisfied his curiosity about these important visitors. He spoke to Bahati, "It is pleasant to see you again. Why do you journey to the big water?"

"We are taking the Medicine Man of the Great Zuri Watu and his companions there to meet a friend. The party of four were traveling overland to Kenya, but they encountered a mercenary in Lomie who would do them harm. The Duibo helped them to escape into the forest. They are now returning to the big water to avoid the dangers of traveling overland to Kenya with enemies following them."

"The Pymtu are glad to be of assistance to you and your friends. We will watch the water for you."

Bahati continued, "We are hoping the enemies do not know that we are taking the river to the big water. We are hoping they are still waiting in towns east or north of Lomie for the Medicine Man and his friends to arrive. We will have failed to keep their passage secret, should there be followers."

"We will be alert. We will keep your secret." Chief Mzutu turned his attention to Tamubu and said, "If you would be so kind, my daughter is sick. Oduri will welcome your opinion on her illness."

With that, Tamubu followed Oduri to a large thatched hut with mud walls and several rooms, with the center room having small stools and a tiny fire. Two women arose when they entered, bowed and then left. The little girl was in a small adjacent room on a raised pallet. She smiled to see Oduri and then fear came into her eyes when she saw the stranger. Tamubu smiled at her and her fear fled, for she could see the kindness in this man.

Tamubu gently examined the girl, who was eight years old. She had been languishing with a fever, no appetite and nightmares. She had been sick for two weeks. She had a roseola rash on her face and neck. Tamubu asked if the girl could be carried outside so he could examine her in the daylight. Quickly, an enclosure was made of kitambas, while skins were placed on a shelf supported by two tree stumps. Tamubu then examined the little girl, especially her legs and asked. "What caused all these long thin red lines on your legs?"

The little girl said, "I was running and tripped and fell into some briars."

"Would you show me these briars? I will carry you." Tamubu picked up the child and walked as she directed.

"Over there, see the briars by that log."

Tamubu did indeed see the briars by the log. They had an elongated heart-shaped leaf, which tapered to a point. The tiny thorns along the stem of the vine were often toxic to women and children. He had never seen such a bad case of blood poisoning from them. He put antibiotic salve on the still red scratches and gave the child some kimmea with powdered herbs to cleanse the blood. In a few days, the child would be well. Tomorrow she would begin to eat again. Today, she would drink broth all day with the powdered herbs.

Tamubu said, "Chandi, you have been such a good patient that I am going to send Missy Paula to see you. She will show you a whistle that can tell you which way to go in the forest; can light a fire for your dinner and then helps you eat it." Chandi laughed happily at such nonsense. She was already feeling better.

Tamubu left with Oduri, and the women went back inside to be with the sick child. He said to Oduri, "Those briars over by the log have caused blood poisoning in the child. See that they are removed, roots and all and burned. This is a man's job; tell them to use tools, not their hands to dig out the briars and then burn them. Men are not so susceptible to the poison of the thorns, but if they are scratched deeply, they too could get blood poisoning."

Paula went to entertain the patient with her *5in1* whistle. Oduri told the chief that Chandi would soon be well. Tamubu had found the cause of her illness. It was a very pleasant noon meal. Chief Mzutu was extremely grateful as Chandi was his only child; he said he would gladly part with the staples they needed for their trip. He was also going to send bearers with them to carry the canoes past the rapids, as the Djoumani scouts had gear to carry.

Chandi was thrilled when she saw Paula. She looked like a goddess with her silvery gold hair and creamy skin, her sparkling blue eyes and the pale red lips of her smile. Paula demonstrated the *5in1* as she had for Gomojo. Chandi laughed and laughed until tears ran down her cheeks. The women attending her had watched from the doorway and they too giggled with delight.

As they sailed away, for it was still eight or ten miles to the rapids, Jon, who was now in the canoe with Paula and Thomas said, "Well, that was certainly an expeditious encounter. I didn't even have the opportunity to tell a story!" They all smiled. Jon was getting used to being the center of attention with his stories, and today he had taken a back seat to Tamubu and Paula. His ego was a little bruised.

Thomas queried, "Expeditious?"

"Fast, efficient, quick."

IT WAS EARLY DUSK when they reached the bend before the rapids and a large sand bar, which was occupied by crocodiles. The Pymtu, who had the huge and dangerous reptiles as a constant presence in their lives, had an unusual way of dealing with them. Instead of confrontation, they fed them. The bones, tough skin and sinew scraps and unwanted fat not fit for the stockpot were rolled into bundles. When a croc was in the way, they tossed a bundle out into the water. This, in essence, trained the crocodiles to head into the water when they saw the Pymtu coming. For being on the beach meant other crocodiles would get the food... and it was a good way for the Pymtu to get rid of their garbage.

Chief Mzutu had sent five bearers with them, with Hamoso being the leader. They had brought their own traveling food for the return and once the canoes were unpacked, went fishing. Hamoso returned in a short time with a string of large catfish saying, "Good eating." Tamubu had prepared them before and asked Hamoso to cut the fish crosswise in thin slices, once the heads tails and internal parts were removed. He rolled the sliced fish, the size of long fat fingers, into cornmeal mixed with ground peppers and rolled them in a papyrus husk, which he buried in ashes at the side of the fire. With the catfish they had baked sweet potatoes and greens boiled with garlic. Chandi's mother had given Tamubu a papyrus bag of honeyed dates to thank him for helping her daughter. These he shared for dessert with spiced broth.

The campsite was tucked into a corner at the edge of a grassy savannah, which was a long narrow stretch of grass about a half a mile wide. The hillsides around the grassy lea were covered by forest. Along the river was the usual dense tropical growth. Tamubu asked, "Hamoso, what feeds on this grass. Do the hippos come here?"

"No, bwana, elephants feed here."

"How long is the savannah?"

"It stretches to the end of the fast water."

"Has it ever been a problem to camp here?"

"Only when the bulls are in *must*."

"Isn't that just before the rainy season?"

"Yes, bwana, the *must* season is over now."

"Does the elephant herd stay here all the time, or does it travel?"

"We get enough rain here all year for the grass to grow. The cows and the young elephants stay here for it is not a large herd. The bulls travel."

"When you camp here, do you usually sleep on the ground?"

Hamoso smiled, "No, bwana, we sleep in the trees." Tamubu looked around. All the lower limbs of the trees had died from the elephants eating the foliage; and the closest limbs were twenty-five feet off the ground.

"What trees do you sleep in–and how do you get up there?"

Again Hamoso smiled. "We go deeper into the woods. The elephants can go there too, but need a reason to do so. There, the limbs are closer to the ground."

"Would you suggest that we all sleep in the trees?"

"Yes, bwana, come, I will show you." They followed a worn path that led to into the foothills of the mountains. Hamoso turned down a narrow track and led Tamubu to a small clearing. "This is where we usually camp, but it is too small a place for so many people. But, you see, here it is easy to climb into the trees. The elephants do come here, but not often. Sometime lions come, but mostly just leopards and wart hogs." Tamubu liked the spot. "We will move the camp. This space will do."

They returned to the clearing, where the others waited for Tamubu and Hamoso to return. The other scouts had said that they did not usually sleep here, so it was not much of a surprise when Tamubu told them they were moving the camp into the woods. But it was a huge surprise when he told them they would be sleeping in the trees. Paula turned away when she saw the dumbfounded look on Jon's face, so he would not see her smile–no air mattresses or hammocks tonight!

The trees were spreading oaks with good crotches and wide limbs. They grew best in the woodlands near the savannah, where the giraffe and elephants ate the parasitic plants and vines off the trees, while the vines were still young, tender shoots, before they smothered the tree.

Paula found two nice forking branches and showed Jon how to make a comfortable pallet with the big waxy leaves and how to tie himself to the branches, so he would not fall in the night.

Paula put on her rain poncho, hung her backpack on a limb nearby and drank the rest of the hot broth she had put in her metal water bottle. She knew Tamubu had laced it with kimmea, and she would need it to sleep well in the trees. Today had been an easy day physically, but the crocodiles and hippos still made river travel stressful; and while she felt they had eluded the mercenary, the nagging and insecure feeling of being pursued never really went away.

DURING THE NIGHT, PAULA awakened to the sound of deep rumbling, a long and constant sooothing sound. Looking down, she saw the elephant herd cleaning up the leaves and fallen fruit and nuts from the forest floor. Now and then an inquisitive trunk moved along the trunks and lower branches of the trees looking for the tender shoots of the succulent parasitic vines. They moved like wraiths on a Scottish moor, now you see me, now you don't. The rumbling sounds were comforting–an elephant lullaby, and she fell back to sleep with a smile on her lips and contentment in her heart.

When she awoke, Tamubu was sitting and watching her. Paula smiled and asked, "What are you doing?"

"I was wondering where you learned to sleep in trees."

Paula chuckled, "You, better than anyone, should know that. How did you sleep last night?"

"I slept quite well. Did you hear the elephants?"

"Yes, it was lovely. The rumbling sound they make is so comforting, I fell back to sleep listening to it."

"It is not often that a person can be in the midst of an elephant herd and hear the soft assuring sounds the cows make for the youngsters. Elephants take very good care of the young. The bull calves stay with the herd until they are twelve or so. Then they leave and are solitary, or form small herds of two or three bulls together, especially if they were raised together in the same herd. The cows always stay with the herd they are born into and help care for the young calves until they themselves become mothers. Nowhere else in nature do you find this sense of lifetime belonging and caring that is found among elephants. Manutu and I used to climb trees near the herds hoping they would come during the night to forage beneath us, so we could hear them softly reassuring one other."

"Did you know they would come last night?"

"No, but elephants have been known to wander through native camps and villages at night, doing little harm, if they perceive no danger from the humans. Come, the oatmeal is ready."

The only good thing that could be said about the morning's portage was: the trail was easy. The insects were dreadful. Paula used her bug repellent, but was still bitten many times, especially under the loose part of her clothing.

"Hamoso, you did not tell us the bugs would be so bad."

"I did not know. These are nits, just hatched; they seek the water spray of the river for moisture, and for the air currents to buoy them. We are their first meal. They are annoying, but as yet, they have no diseases to transfer when they bite. We must find some mint leaves and rub ourselves with them. They do not like the odor."

Away from the river for the noon stop, the biting bugs were gone; but everyone went out looking for mint while Tamubu made the roll-ups and broth. Tamubu insisted that everyone wash in boiled water and then he put salve on any bites that had festered from being scratched. When that was done, all wiped one another down with the mint leaves and put the used sprigs in hair and browbands and sandals, for the bearers had many bites on their feet too.

Today, the afternoon rest was welcomed. Tamubu waited until everyone was asleep, except for the sentries, and went off gathering. As soon as he was well away from the campsite, he stashed his things to *roam*. He had found and prepared the herbs necessary for spirit travel when he was making his antibiotic paste. It felt wonderful to be free and he *roamed* all the way to the ocean. He found good campsites and many sources of food. He found fresh water and coconut trees and banana plants. When he strolled back into camp, he had gojani (the chard-like leaves), muhogo (the rutabaga-like tuber) and asparagus in his gathering sack. The men had everything packed and ready to go.

The afternoon was pleasant. The bugs had diminished and those that were still buzzing around did not bite them. It was a time of majesty. All the forest wildlife came to the water. Paula saw several different species of Kingfishers including the tiny five-inch Pygmy Kingfisher. A profusion of birds in all sizes and in varied brilliant colors abounded. There were no crocodiles or hippos in the rapids, so they often caught a glimpse of gazelles or antelopes watering by the small pools that formed close to the banks. Even the tiny dik-dik was glimpsed momentarily. Monkeys scolded them from the trees for intruding on their serenity, while baboons came in small troops and sat on the boulders edging the torrents and groomed each other in the water-misted shafts of sunlight. Occasionally, they heard a lion roar, or an elephant trumpet; but the birdsong and mating calls of the rainforest surround-sound orchestra never diminished, only segued.

They came to the portage campsite as the long dusk began. Even with the bugs, they had covered twenty miles. Tomorrow they would be able to use the canoes again. The water would still be swift, but there would be no white-water rapids or waterfalls in the next ten miles.

Hamoso said the men wanted to bake fish for them as they did at home. Tamubu said he would make the biscuits and vegetables while he made the flat pancakes for tomorrow's lunch roll-ups. The camping area already had the leaf-covered domes, made by the Pygmies when they came here to fish, which were surrounded by a thorn boma. So, there was little work to do to set up camp.

Paula found a nice place in the shade and began to bring her diary up to date.

Jon decided to take Kybo and the radio and go up the hill to see if he could contact the *Wind Drift* and Captain Jones. There was less than two days of travel to Campo.

"Jon Caulfield calling the *Wind Drift*; Captain Jones, do you have your ears on? Over."

He fiddled with the squelch and called again: "Jon Caulfield calling the *Wind Drift*. Over."

He sighed and said, "We might not be high enough Kybo... feel like climbing higher?"

Jon was getting ready to call once more when he heard, "This is the *Wind Drift*; Captain Jones calling Jon Caulfield. Where are you Jon? Over."

"We're about thirty eight miles up the Kom River. We expect to be in Campo in a day and a half to two days. Could you meet us there? Over."

"That's an ETA of Monday, the 30th, in Campo. Is that correct? Over."

"That's a ten-four. Over."

"See you then, Jon. Over and Out."

Without warning, Jon felt elated. He was so happy; he could have danced with Kybo. As the sudden euphoria dulled, Jon examined the reasons he felt such glee. He didn't like what he found. He was glad the trekking was coming to an end. What if they still had fifteen hundred miles to go? Well, they didn't and he didn't have to tell anybody how he felt.

Kybo said, "I suppose the kisha is happy that the traveling in the forest will soon come to an end. Will you not miss telling stories at night?"

Peeved at his perception, Jon thought. Don't tell me Kybo can read minds too. This is getting annoying. But he said, "I am just so happy that the days of danger to Thomas will soon be over."

"Yes, that has been a worry to all of us." Kybo now had

the radio packed up; he hoisted it over his shoulder, and they started down the hill to camp.

OVER DINNER, AND THE superb baked fish the Pymtu had cooked, Jon told everyone the good news. He had reached the *Wind Drift* and Captain Jones had agreed to meet them in Campo on the 30th.

Paula looked at Thomas, and smiled before saying, "Now, the fun part of the trip is yet to come. All that is required is that you write the letter to your parents."

"I have done so. Would you like to read it?"

Paula was astounded. "Yes, I would... if you don't mind."

Tamubu reached into his pack and drew out the diary. As he handed it to her, he said, "I wrote it the night you fell asleep before dinner. Jon took it to you to read, but didn't want to wake you. Later, I forgot to show it to you."

Paula took the diary, which Thomas had opened to the page and read the beautiful letter. She had tears in her eyes when she looked at him and said, "It is just wonderful. It is perfect."

"Jon was a big help. He gave me instructions in letter writing. After he went to bed I decided to give it a try. With his help, it was actually easy; because I did want to explain to our parents, before I saw them, why I didn't go home."

"Now, it's your turn Jon."

"I'm finished too. I had offered my letter to Thomas, so he could see what a letter looked like and what one said... but he did a smashing job on his own."

"He certainly did." Paula felt so pleased. The letters will give their parents time to adjust to seeing their ten-year-old boy as a grown man–an important man... a man with incredible talents.

THE HOUR HAD GROWN late, for the fish were baked whole, after they were cleaned, deboned and stuffed with a paste of ground nuts and figs. Tamubu had watched the process, asking questions, so he could make this fish dinner for his parents. It was the best fish he had ever eaten. He hoped they had carp in Kenya. The Pymtu said that the ten-mile stretch between the rapids was the only area they found carp in the River Kom. Now he knew what the water baskets were for: they were going to catch carp on their return and take them home.

EVERYONE WENT TO BED. The Pymtu offered to take the watches. As Jon watched them set up the game of stones, he thought. I wonder who made up that game. It is certainly a game of strategy. Much later, Jon would find out it was a game from ancient Greece, called Pente, brought to Africa centuries ago by the Arabs from the Mediterranean.

16

To The Ocean

THE RIVER WAS INDEED swift; Hamoso had not exaggerated. They put the canoes in the water below the last cataract where the banks had silted in amongst the rubble below the sheer rock walls of the mountains that lined both sides of the river canyon.

"Hamoso, how do you portage around these rock walls?" Paula asked.

"There is no portage around the rock walls on this side of the river, Missy. We must go on the river or not go at all."

"You have done this before, correct?"

"Yes, Missy, the water is fast, but not rough. This is just a crease where the mountains meet. For a bit, it will be exciting. Once we are through the passage, the water slows down for the river widens out again."

"How do you get back... if there is no portage?"

Jon said, "I'm glad you asked that question Paula. Yes, Hamoso, how **do** you get back?"

Hamoso replied, "A mile or so, after the last rapids, there is a silted-in area on the other side of the river. Behind it, there is a wide crevice in the rock, which goes all the way past the gorge, where it climbs to a high ledge, which is a dead end. We have to use lines to lower the canoes and ourselves to the water." He pointed to an undercut ledge, high on the sheer wall on the other side of the river. "There, that is the place where the crevice ends."

HAMOSO WAS RIGHT. THE trip through the gorge was exciting. They were amazed by the speed of the water. Jon guesstimated that they were doing twenty miles an hour through the gorge; it seemed that they were no sooner flying along at breakneck speed–totally controlled by the speeding flow of the water–than the canoes slowed, and the paddlers were able to move, once again, into the slower water along the banks. Jon looked at his watch and said, "That five miles took only fifteen minutes–we were going twenty miles an hour!"

Everyone laughed, both from relief as well as Jon's enthusiasm, which was contagious, for his sense of humor never seemed to fail him. He was the first one to make light of his sensibilities. His ability to enjoy the smallest thing and to accept all challenges made him a boon companion. Even his grumbling was a source of amusement.

Before the hour was gone, they were beaching the canoes for the last leg of the portage around the waterfalls and the white water, before the river widened and flowed to the sea.

As they walked the stony path, Paula once again had her hand tucked in Tamubu's belt, with Jon right behind her. She was now carrying her own pack. She was used to walking with it, and had developed a rhythm over the years for walking uphill and down with a full pack. She felt she actually carried herself better when she had the pack. With the pack, she was always aware of her footing; without it, her attention tended to wander to the magnificent flowers, the colorful birds and the marvelous vistas.

Along the river, the views were sometimes incredible, especially near the falls. The sun sparkling through the misty water spray turned all it touched into glittering diamond-studded fantasies: the long draping vines of velvety orchids in cream and dark burgundy were resplendent with diamond drops and contrasted by the dainty and graceful sprays of miniature white orchids with purple stamens. All seemed touched with pixie dust as they glistened and glittered. The stunning beauty made Paula want to stop and paint the scene; but alas, Sallee Anne her sister painted, she did not. Paula had used up all her film and Jon had taken so many pictures of the Pygmies, he too was out of film; so if they wanted pictures of these awesome sights, they would have to come back another time.

WHEN THE PATH WAS closed-in and the visual distractions diminished, Paula's thoughts wandered. I need to talk to Thomas. He has been quiet for days. He seems dispirited and distracted. I don't think he is worried about seeing his parents again; but something is bothering him. Maybe I'm wrong... just because I think his parents will be thrilled, beyond belief, to have their first born son home again–grown strong and healthy and so accomplished–does not mean that he feels the same way. Tonight, we must get off alone and have a talk–like we did the other morning in the tree–just the two of us–like it was on the trek back to the cove. I certainly miss the togetherness of our first trek. Even when it is just Jon and Kybo, it is not the same. I wonder if we will ever do anything as companionable as that again... just the two of us... and if we did, would it be the same as those first magical days together.

THE TEN-MILE PORTAGE WAS difficult. It was hilly and the footing was uneven with many loose stones. There was little shade for not much grew in the stony earth. It took them almost six hours to pass the last of the waterfalls. Then the rainforest reclaimed the earth and it became thick and luxurious again. The old campsite was completely overgrown and had to be cleared inside the thorn boma. The grasses were tall and dry and had to be cut down, but they would make good fodder for the fire.

The African landscape could change from one mile to the next, often so completely, that it was like stepping through a magic portal.

With the mountain to shield the foothills, they received much less rain, so a savannah covered the lower reaches, with rainforest along the river where the availability of water was constant. There was evidence of antelope, gazelles and elephants having fed here... and where there are game animals, lions and cheetahs abound.

Until the men cleared the thorn boma enclosure, there was a bit of time free before the fire would be ready. Paula approached Tamubu, who was rooting through his food bags, and said, "Do you have time to go for a walk with me?

Tamubu looked up and read the concern in her eyes. He immediately said, "Of course I have time to go for a walk with you. Any place in particular you want to go?"

"No, you pick the way. We can gather as we go."

"Excellent idea, I need root vegetables and greens. I see you brought your grass gathering bag."

"Yes, I had packed it with the turtle shell to send on to Kenya, but put it in my backpack in Yaoundé... just in case." She smiled at him.

"That quiet time seems so long ago."

"It does, yet it has only been twenty three days. So many unexpected things have happened to us that they would fill a lifetime elsewhere."

"Yes, our travels do not fit my thoughts of trekking across Africa. When I first started out, Manutu told me, 'It will be the story of your lifetime.' I was not sure what he meant, but I knew I would find out. I think even Manutu would be surprised at all that has happened."

"Are you sorry that you will not be crossing Africa as you planned?"

"Yes, it is hard to give up a desired plan, but I would not change what has happened, if I had the choice to go back and start again."

Paula smiled at the compliment. They had already gathered plants and some vegetables when she said, "You seem dispirited and worried these last few days. Is something bothering you?"

Tamubu thought: She sees into my soul. How am I ever going to tell her that I want to meet my parents alone, having only Jon with me? I don't know why I feel this way–I have been arguing with myself for days. What difference can it make? Be honest with yourself... you don't want her to see the disappointment in your parent's eyes when they see a native... not their son. She has always accepted you for the person you are and you don't want that to change...why? Because I want to spend the rest of my life with her and I don't want her good opinion of me diminished.

Paula kept her eyes fastened on the ground as she dug out some stumpy carrots. She could not believe the thoughts that came to her when she closed her eyes. Was Tamubu thinking these thoughts? Where were they coming from? How could he possibly think these things? My mother! My supercilious mother! She has always been condescending. It is her way. She doesn't mean to be that way; she just doesn't know that she does it. I'll have to make this easier for him...

Tamubu arose with a large muhogo just as Paula arose with the stubby carrots. They looked at each other's gleanings and paroxysms of laughter seized them. His was obscenely huge and hers was impossibly small.

When she could speak, Paula said, "I asked you to walk with me because I have something to say to you. I think you might be wrestling with the same problem that concerns me... the diary. I gave it to Cyril Latham for safe-keeping and I'm glad I did; but I never had the opportunity to discuss with you my thoughts on what to do with the knowledge contained in your drawings, if anything.

We are not committed to anything at this point. Do you want to share your knowledge with the rest of the world? Do you want to have the herbal remedies, like kimmea, available to all those who need it?"

"I have been thinking about that, but I have not yet made a decision. There are many things I need to know before I decide. We have been so occupied with escaping the mercenary that I have had little time for thinking about the plants in the diary."

"Yes, his coming into the picture has certainly made a difference in my attitude about using the plants for profit. I was wondering if you would mind if I traveled on to Nairobi to meet with Cyril Latham by myself; maybe, while you were meeting with your parents? That way, when we are together again, I might have the answers to our questions, for I have reservations too. Tamubu was stunned. She has been wrestling with problems of her own and has solved mine in doing so. I am so glad we took this walk and had a chance to talk. "I do not like the idea of you going to Nairobi alone."

"I was hoping to take Kybo with me. Would you mind?"

She always has the answers. How am I going to be parted from her again? I told myself when I found her again at the Wahutu Village, that we would be together in all things... and now I want to be alone for a bit, and she has given me the space I need. "No, certainly not; take Kybo, he will like that."

WITH BULGING GATHERING BAGS, they wandered back to the campsite. Paula could tell from his walk that his problems had been solved. I was the cause of his fretting. He needed time alone, and did not want to hurt my feelings. Now I know why I care for this man so–he considers me before he considers himself.

Jon approached them as they came out of the forest. "I was just getting ready to go looking for you. You have been gone a long time; but I can see that you were busy." Jon took Paula's gathering net and went to the fire to help Thomas prepare the dinner. Paula went off to bring her diary up to date.

The leaf shelters had been built and her backpack was in the one under the African tulip tree. For a few moments, while she gathered her thoughts, she watched Tamubu. He was so changed, back to his old self... still quiet, still composed, but taking an active part in the conversation around him, and he was laughing. I think that's what made me aware of his anxiety–he had not been laughing at all.

It was a short day, but a physically difficult one. After the meal was finished, Jon said, "It seems my days of telling stories over a campfire are almost at an end, so I have saved a special story for the last. Is anyone interested in hearing it?"

There were shrill whistles and many huzzahs, and then the "huh-huh-aah" started, until Jon raised a hand and began.

"Once, a long time ago there were two boys; they were

brothers. One was nine years old, the other seven. When the oldest boy reached the age of eight, he was assigned a wilderness tutor by his father. The duties of the tutor were to teach him the ways of the forest: about the different animals and the plants growing there. He was to teach him how to survive–if he ever found himself all alone in the deep woods.

"The younger boy wanted to tag along, but his father was strict about the rule: 'You must be eight years old; then, you too, will have a wilderness tutor.'

"The older brother was the younger brother's best friend. He looked out for him whenever they were out playing, and had often kept him from harm. It was difficult for the younger boy to enjoy himself without the companionship of his big brother. The long hours when he was away with his wilderness teacher were hours of tedium for the lonely boy.

"The big brother saw the sadness in his younger brother and began to share the happenings of his tutored day with him. The hours after tea, before dinner, became the happy hours for the younger brother. The two boys went out to their tree house fort, and there the older boy imparted all he had learned that day to his brother. It was a fascinating and wonderful time.

"There were two days a week when the men did not work for the farm. One day, Saturday, was for taking care of personal gardens and personal chores; the other day, Sunday, was for God, when everyone went to Church and then rested, or visited.

"One Saturday, the boys went out to the woods to put into practice what the older boy had learned that week from his tutor. They told no one what they intended to do, fearing that they would be forbidden to go. It was a perfect day: sunny, but not too warm.

"The older boy made peanut butter and jelly sandwiches. He added bananas to the sack and took a jug of lemon water. The older boy had a knife in a scabbard and an assagai, [spear] a gift from his tutor who had lived with the Zulus. The younger boy took his small bow and bullet-head arrows.

Both had walinkas in their belts, but neither had yet gained any proficiency with the throwing club.

"The older boy walked along in a wary way, looking for enemies in the bush. The younger boy imitated him. Several hours later, after chasing small animals out of the bush by throwing the walinkas at them, they stopped their hunt for lunch. As they ate a rustling sounded in the tree above them–a rustling not connected with the breeze. Looking up they saw a leopard poised above them. He had the remnants of an old kill stashed in the high crotch, but the leopard much preferred fresh meat. They were caught!

"Keeping eye contact, the older boy told his brother to move slowly, and hide in the hollow log on which they had been sitting to eat their lunch. Now, nothing is faster in the trees or more agile than a leopard. Even squirrels fear him and dash to smaller branches that will not support his weight.

The older brother knew this, and he also knew the leopard would not be able to resist a running prey. The older boy dashed off. In an instant, the leopard was on the ground and closed the distance with mighty leaps... with the last leap a killing strike–with claws extended and lethal canines bared. But the leopard closed on thin air.

"The older boy had grabbed a dangling vine as he ran. At the apex of the vine's arc, he swung out and up on the vine, using the momentum to raise his legs up over his head high on the vine. In a flash, he wrapped his legs around the vine and used his stomach muscles to sit-up, raising himself out of harms reach, as the vine swung back over the frustrated leopard. He shinnied higher and with strong pushes, kept himself swinging back and forth over the leopard's head. The older brother was now high above the ground, and too far from the tree supporting the vine for the leopard to reach him. He continued to sway back and forth, keeping the leopard intrigued.

"Meanwhile, the younger brother had crawled far enough out of the log to grab his bow and arrows. He took aim for the leopard's rump, and let fly one of his small, bullet-shaped

arrows, and quickly notched another. When the leopard turned to see its antagonist, he let fly the second arrow, which struck him on the upper part of his front leg. Neither arrow went deep, but the leopard had had enough from the unseen enemy, and, snarling viciously, took off through the forest.

"The boys waited a few minutes, then retrieved the abandoned assegai, before they scurried down the trail towards home. It had been much more of an adventure than they had bargained for and they swore one another to secrecy.

"The younger boy did not know it then, but in less than a year, his adventures with his older brother would be over. The memory of this day would stand out in his mind and make him lonely for the next fourteen years. The moral of the story is: live each day to the fullest–for one never knows what the future holds in store for us." The End.

THE HUZZAHS AND HIGH-PITCHED trilling were hearty, for the listeners soon intuited who the brothers of the story were in real life.

Tamubu had to gather all his inner reserves and stoicism to keep his emotions in check. Paula made no effort to do so, and the tears ran down her cheeks as she sniffled into a tissue.

Kybo wondered again about the great man to whom he had dedicated his life. He had once been an ordinary boy. When had he changed into a savant? When had he acquired his powers? Had he had them all along, but just didn't know it? The story made him glad he had decided to go with the Medicine Man of the Great Zuri Watu, called Tamubu. Life had been an adventure ever since.

WITH THE SUNRISE, THE rainforest came alive... as if someone had turned on a '*Sounds of the Jungle*' recording, with speakers everywhere. Hundreds, if not thousands, of birds chirped, hooted, called and made joyful noises. Other denizens, not to be left out, added their cymbal-like interjections.

Only a mile of portage remained to the embarkation site.

On the river, the clear and distinctive sounds of the forest became muted, as the banks with their overgrown foliage flowed by in a dense, impenetrable wall.

The river mist lifted and the river took a big bend around the base of a hill. The shouts from the first canoe, alerted everyone to the surprise. Several hundred yards past the curve, anchored in mid-stream, was the impressive motor yacht, the *Wind Drift*. Her Master tooted his foghorn in greeting when he saw them. Captain Jones descended from the flying bridge to drop the stern plank, so the canoes could disembark their passengers. His crew of three, waited to give a hand and to take the traveling packs, which couldn't really be called luggage to the staterooms.

Jon tried to talk the Djoumani into coming aboard, but he was unsuccessful.

Bahaiti said, "If we go back now, we will have time to portage around the lower falls and make camp before dusk–when it is a good time to fish for carp."

Tamubu replied, "I understand, Bahati. Thank you, one and all for your help and the safe passage you provided us. We will always consider the Djoumani kings among men–the noblest tribe of all. Please tell Chief Chabo we are grateful for his friendship. We hope one day to meet again."

Shouts of "Jambo" and "Kwaheri" rang out from the canoes, as they paddled upstream in the shallows.

When the Djoumani were out of sight, Tamubu turned his attention to Captain Jones and his crew saying, "I meant every word of that. Did you understand what I said?"

Captain Jones replied, "Jon was translating for us. You've been fortunate to make friends with the Djoumani. They are greatly feared by the other tribes. Come, Phil and Steve will show you to your cabins. When you're ready, I'd like you to join me here on the afterdeck. Jonas has been cooking for you all morning. I have no idea what he is making and I'm dying of curiosity."

Thomas said, "I hope he has made pancakes. I've not been able to duplicate his recipe over an open fire." Everyone laughed, ruefully, for they had had to eat the flat, hard attempts to duplicate Jonas's pancake recipe, which thudded when dropped.

Later, after Jonas had served his fluffy pancakes with maple syrup and link sausages with bacon scrambled eggs, he asked, "Did you use eggs?"

"Yes, I used two eggs, just as you said, and the francolin had just laid them, and didn't like parting with them either."

"Francolin? What is that? How big were the eggs?"

"The francolin is a bird about fourteen inches tall that nests on the ground. The eggs are about the size of a chicken egg and have very tough shells. I knew they were fresh, as I had found the nest the night before, and there was only one egg in it"

"Did you use milk or water?"

"I used coconut milk cut in half with water."

"How much baking powder did you use?"

"Baking powder? I didn't use baking powder! You didn't tell me to use baking powder!"

"You have to use baking powder if the flour is not finely ground. I don't have to use it myself, but over a campfire, I think it would be necessary."

This exchange had everyone in fits of laughter. They knew how serious Thomas was about his cooking, and how much the flops had annoyed him.

Kybo said to Jonas, "Let me help you with the clean up. I will go mafuu (crazy) without something to do."

Jonas eyed the big Nigerian and said, "If you fit in the galley, I will be surprised, but come along."

Over a second cup of coffee, after raising the anchor, Captain Jones said, "Now, tell me. What is going on?" Thomas looked at Jon and nodded for him to tell the tale. You could tell that the story had captured Captain Jones's attention by the number of times he raised his eyebrows and grimaced.

"Well, where to then..." he asked when Jon finished. "I don't think we should go to Campo. That's the reason why I left and came up river. Some strange toughs arrived yesterday by cigarette boat. They stayed, but the cigarette boat left and did not come back, which is quite unusual. Accommodations are scant in Campo. It is mostly a fuel and water stop. I headed north and then out to sea yesterday before I circled around to approach the Kom River from the south.

Paula said, "How would they know we were coming here to you?"

Captain Jones looked at her sadly and said, "I fear they were monitoring the radio channels when you did not show up further east as expected."

Jon's mouth fell open, and then his face crumpled. "Blast and double blast! Stupid me! I never gave that a thought! I must have mush for brains! I can't believe I was so dim-witted."

"Give over, lad. You had to contact me, or else I wouldn't be here to help. We're ahead of them now, but I need to know where we are going. The nearest commercial airport going south is Luanda in Angola. It is about 650 miles in a straight line. We will have to go about 700 miles to get there. I am fueled for 2,000 nautical miles, the most I've carried in a long time. We will cruise at 15 knots or 17.5 miles per hour, so it will take us about 40 hours, if the good weather holds. We can also go back to Douala or northwest to Lagos. Those are the major airports with Kenya as a destination."

"What about Libreville, Port-Gentil or Pointe-Noire?" Jon asked.

"I am sure they will have Libreville watched. Port-Gentil and Pointe-Noire are just local stops. You would still need to go to a major airport to fly to Kenya.

Jon said, "We are going to Kampala first.

Paula spoke up, "But I am going on to Nairobi before I return to Kampala."

Jon looked at Paula askance, "Why?"

"I am going to see my attorney, Cyril Latham. We need answers to our questions before we can make a decision about the information in the diary."

"We need a destination, folks. What's it to be: Luanda or Lagos?"

"Which do you think would be best?" Paula asked Captain Jones.

"My money's on Luanda. It is as far away as Lagos and further from Kenya too. If they know Kenya is your final destination, they might rule it out."

Everyone agreed on Luanda in Angola. Captain Jones went below to set a course on his charts. Steve was at the helm. After leaving the river, he had been heading due west out to sea.

Later, when Kybo did not return to the afterdeck, Jon's curiosity got the better of him and he went along to the galley. He heard shouts: "Hah!"... then, "Gotcha!" He peeked into the crew's mess, where he saw Kybo and Jonas playing a game of stones. Jon returned to the afterdeck and hollered up to Captain Jones, who now manned the wheel on the flying bridge, "I fear we have had our last meal."

"Wha' did 'ja say laddie?" Captain Jones called down in his brogue. "Did 'ja say no mor' meals?"

Not one to be outdone, Jon replied, "Aye, that I did... yer cook 'n' Kybo 'r' playin' a game a' stones an' I fear they're deep in it."

Captain Jones laughed. "Where did you pick up your brogue?"

"At school, we had lots of Scots and Irish who used it in jokes."

"Come on up, lad. The view is great."

Jon climbed the ladder to the bridge where Captain Jones said, "What's this about no more meals?"

"Kybo has a game that he is very good at playing. He is now playing it with Jonas. I fear the strategy consumes the players."

"I'm glad to hear it. I'm not one for games and Jonas is besotted with them and puzzles. The other lads won't play with him anymore. He beats them too badly."

"Well, he may have met his match. The Djoumani had a tournament with Kybo and he bested all comers."

"I hope so. Jonas needs a challenge now and again. We have good weather today, but rain is forecast for tomorrow.

We will travel south about fifty miles offshore to avoid the changing currents; should be smooth sailing."

"Thomas and Kybo are the only nascent sailors aboard. The rest of us are pretty well seasoned."

"Good, then we should have a good trip. Tell me more about this 'diary' that seems to be the crux of the situation." Jon told what he knew and was just about finished when Phil came to the bridge to relieve the Captain for lunch.

"Ha! You were wrong. We're still going to eat." Phil chuckled and smirked in an odd way when he heard Captain Jones's assertion.

Lunch was served on the afterdeck on nice days; when the ocean swell was low, and the yacht wasn't plowing though high seas. Today, each place was set with plate, flatware and mug. In the center of the table was a long flat serving dish. It was filled with roll-ups.

When Jon saw the table, laughter consumed him; he could hardly speak to say, "I told you so." Captain Jones, ever the good sport, stalked off to the galley where he found Jonas and Kybo still engrossed in a game of stones. He saw Thomas at the cutting board, making another batch of roll-ups.

In his best stentorian voice, Captain Jones said, "I am looking forward to the roll-ups Thomas, I understand they're delicious. Are you by any chance looking for a job? It seems my cook has found occupation elsewhere."

Thomas laughed. "I offered to make lunch. I needed something to do, but I am not looking for a job as a cook." He smiled and continued, "We have a tournament going on here. Jonas has bet Kybo that he can't win ten games in a row. They are now on game three–with the score three to nothing. I fear Jonas has met his match."

"Will you be cooking dinner too?"

"I am not prepared to do that. This kitchen is too fussy for me."

"Well, come along. Bring the soup pitcher. I'm hungry." Lunch was indeed delicious. Thomas had used fresh ingredients, with sliced ham, cheese and a paste of mustard-spiced figs with lettuce wrapped in the tortillas Jonas had in the refrigerator.

"Did you make these roll-ups on your travels on land?" Captain Jones asked.

"Yes, we had them for lunch each day, with different ingredients, of course. It was a quick and easy meal and a satisfying one too. I made broth instead of soup. That too, is easy to make."

"Well, they say an army travels on its stomach... no wonder you were able to travel so far, and come out looking like you'd just walked around the block."

Jon added, "Thomas is a superb cook over a campfire. All our meals were as good as you can get anywhere. Even Paula can whip up a delicious dish called Hungarian Chicken and Rice over a campfire. We traveled in the lap of luxury when it came to the food."

Paula and Thomas exchanged glances, smiling. "Jon has high standards, I'm glad we were able to please him." Thomas said mockingly.

Jon, not one to be outdone... ever, said, "There's always the unexpected, isn't there?" Captain Jones laughed heartily and his eyes twinkled, as he thought, this is going to be a fun trip.

17

Hannibal Jones

THE GAME OF STONES tournament was over before dinner. Jonas had lost to Kybo. He had to part with his egoistic supremacy. It was hard for him to do. He had been superior to all comers for so long, he felt invincible. He told Kybo, “You are just plain sneaky!” and Kybo agreed, “I am! We can play again after dinner.”

Jonas jumped at the offer. “You’re on!”

Meanwhile, Captain Jones spoke to Paula, Thomas and Jon, Phil and Steve. Our trip will be about 880 miles, which at 17.5 knots will take us about 51 hours. We need to man the watches if we are to run straight through. I’ve made a schedule, which I will post in the galley:

4 p.m. to 8 p.m. - Steve and Thomas
8 p.m. to midnight - Phil and Jon
Midnight to 4 a.m. - Capt. Jones and Paula
4 a.m. to 8 a.m. - Steve and Thomas
8 a.m. to noon- Phil and Jon
Noon to 4 p.m. - Capt. Jones and Paula
Kybo can relieve Jonas in the galley.

That gives everyone eight hours before taking the con again. We will follow the same schedule each day; any questions?

Thomas asked, “Why are two men scheduled at the same time?”

“Good question. I have to go to the head, who is going to take the helm? I could use a cup of coffee, or an aspirin, who is going to take the helm while I go and get it? It takes one at the helm and another to keep watch. We have an autopilot, but nighttime watches are difficult enough without short staffing them. We all have bio-rhythms, which regulate our sleeping and waking times. Midnight to 4 a.m., for the majority of people, is the time to sleep. Staring at a dark sea can make you very sleepy–even if you just woke up. With company, you have the ability for conversation to break the monotony. Very few people fall asleep while talking to someone else."

After lunch Paula unpacked, took a shower and washed her hair, before washing out a few personal items and hanging them in the shower to dry. She found a manicure set in her stateroom and when she was finished her toilette she felt like a new person. Weeks in the rainforest was an adventure, but a dirty one; she was surprised she came clean. Walking aft she saw Thomas, who had also bathed, shaved and changed his clothes. Jon had found a laundry room next to the galley. He was off doing their laundry.

"Well, this is a nice change, is it not?" Paula remarked.

"I have been so busy, for so long, I don't really know what to do with myself. There are no vegetables to gather, no meals to make, no herbs to dry and prepare, no sick people to treat–I am at a loss."

Paula chuckled, "You can draw plants in the new diary, if you aren't bothered by the motion of the motor yacht."

Thomas smiled. "I think I am finished drawing plants for awhile. I don't want anyone to get bashed over the head... or worse, for another diary."

"Have you given any more thought to the plants? I thought we might just market the kimmea. What do you think?" Paula asked.

"The kimmea is a very helpful plant. It is a common plant, found almost everywhere in woods and the savannah. I have even found it in the rainforest, but not where the vines blot out the sun."

"Do you think it would grow like squash if you had it in the garden?"

"Many people pull it out of their gardens as a weed. When the kimmea plant is mature, it gets a small red berry.

"Are the kimmea berries of any use?"

"Yes, they are the seedpods of the plant."

"So, they could be grown in a hot house environment?"

"What is a 'hot house environment'?"

"It is a building made of glass that is heated by the sun during the day and heated by wires running under the plant beds at night. A constant temperature between ten degrees difference is maintained. Water is sprayed from pipes above the flower beds to maintain the desired moisture."

"I should like to see a 'hot house'. What do they grow there?"

"Special flowers for florists: like gardenias, orchids, roses, carnations. Hot houses are used for starting nursery stock too for many garden plants."

"If they can grow orchids, they can grow the kimmea plant."

"Now all we need is a supply of the seed pods and we are in business."

"I have a supply of seed pods. When I find a spot where the kimmea plant would grow, I drop a few in a shallow depression. That way, I always have a supply of plants. Most of the medicine men that know about the kimmea plant, also plant the seeds. Once the plant is cut down; it does not grow again from the same roots."

"When I get to Nairobi, I will send the diary to my Uncle David in America. He will put it in a bank vault. Would it be all right to allow Mr. Latham to proceed with the kimmea plant? Is that okay with you?"

"Yes, just the one plant, that will be enough for a start. We can always add others later."

Paula sighed, "I'm glad I sent my suitcase to Cyril Latham from Yaoundé. I will have clean clothes, and dresses to wear when I am there. We can buy safari clothes for Kybo in Luanda. I might just buy a thing or two for myself." Paula felt euphoric. They would just deal with the one plant for now. It was a common plant, easily found by anyone. There was no reason for mercenaries to pursue them any longer.

A light dinner was served early: tomato soup, a tuna casserole with mixed vegetables and egg noodles in mushroom and sour cream stock, with grated Swiss cheese...and popovers, foods that were not available on their trek, which made the meal delectable.

Paula lay down to nap after dinner and it seemed only moments before a tap came on the door. “Eleven o’clock Missy,” Kybo called. “We have tea and scones in the galley.”

In fifteen minutes, Paula was sipping Earl Grey tea in the galley. When Captain Jones arrived, they took their hot drinks and scones to the dining room. Kybo had helped Jonas with the snack preparations, and was taking the galley watch to 4 a.m., so Jonas could get a full night’s sleep.

“Well, who won at that infernal game of stones?” Captain Jones asked.

Kybo smiled, “I won bwana; but soon Jonas will find the secret to winning. Then I will have my hands full with him. He is a master at puzzles.”

“Yes, he is a master at puzzles, especially word puzzles. He was a cryptographer during the big war. He said, “If a man made the code, another man could figure it out; for each code has a key.”

About ten minutes before the midnight hour, Captain Jones and Paula went up to the flying bridge. Unless the seas were tropical storm rough, it was the preferred helm as the visibility from the flying bridge was awesome.

The flying bridge had two roomy Naugahyde upholstered chairs on high posts with wide footrests and seat belts. It is permanently enclosed on three sides, with a squall cover that can be lowered to cover the open back. A Plexiglas cover protects the instrument panel. The windshield and swiveling side window panels are made of thick reinforced Plexiglas. The flying bridge canopy and the Plexiglas frames were made of aluminum reinforced fiberglass, as is the hull of the yacht over a steel bottom. The flying bridge windshield is higher than the bow spray in all but high seas, but all three sides have windshield wipers for rain. There is a bank of four large spotlights, controlled by folding handles on the ceiling between the pilot and co-pilot.

The swell was light tonight with small whitecaps. There was

no moon, for the cloud cover was heavy. It would rain before the night was out. Paula was cozy in the big upholstered, high captain's chair, which swiveled when you pressed the button on the arm.

"Do you stay up here even in the rain?"

"I only go below for high seas. It is not safe up here then."

"Are you often out in high seas?'

"No, I stay in port when storms are expected. I really don't have to go anywhere, except when I want to go somewhere." They laughed at the whimsy of the remark. You know I'm really very glad to see you again–I just wish the circumstances were different."

"Me too, it has been awful fleeing from men with nefarious intentions. The natives were wonderful to us. They have so much respect for Thomas. He is a healer, you know."

"Yes, Ben told me how Thomas had helped his poor crippled mother. He gave Ben some salve to relieve the pain in her knees. He also gave him some powder to put in her tea, which helps her sleep through the night."

"Yes, that was kimmea. We might just sell that formula to a drug company. That is why I need to go to Nairobi. I want to talk with our attorney about it. It is a helpful drug that has no side effects of which I am aware. I was given kimmea for the first time after the Ndezi abducted me from the cove. In such a frightful situation, I should have been constantly terrified, but I wasn't. I slept easily, awoke refreshed. It was a week before I realized that they must be drugging me, for there were no side effects at all."

"Did it take away your inhibitions?"

"No, I just didn't worry. Sometimes I was anxious, like when we ran for miles to escape the lions, but when I was safe, the fear quickly went away. It does make you mellow, non-confrontational. I was not afraid when I had to fight Kira, I just knew I had to win or die." I have been using the drug now for almost eighty days, for one reason or another. I still can't put my finger on a change and say: that is the kimmea. But, I think I can truthfully say that, without the kimmea I would be a nervous wreck with all that we have been through the last few weeks."

"I don't think a drug that takes away the strain of worry and helps you to cope and sleep well at night can be a bad thing. I could have used it many years ago."

Paula waited for further confidences, but none came. As generous as he was with his time and yacht, Captain Jones was still reserved about his personal life.

"I saw the Expedition yacht, the *Just Cause*, when I was in Port-Gentil to see Anna. It is for sale. I suppose that means that the Expedition fizzled out after you had your little talk with the good professor."

"It wasn't my talk as much as it was his unprincipled disregard for me. The other men refused to work for him. They fouled lines, ran aground, dropped gear overboard and generally made it impossible for him to continue his research. He lost his humanity when he thought he saw the Golden Fleece. No time to worry about a lost assistant–onward and upward–full steam ahead! It doesn't take a rocket scientist to figure out that if he'd abandon me, he would also abandon them, if necessary. No one likes to feel expendable."

"Who do you think has hired these mercenaries?"

"I don't know. I don't think the professor has the wherewithal to finance them. But I can't imagine that a respectable drug company like APCO would get involved with anything so sleazy. I have been thinking that the professor might have sold his information to someone who has no scruples; like an unprincipled private investor, who sees a chance for big profits with little risk. It would be the only way Dr. Miles could recoup his losses."

"What losses did he have?"

The professor had to resign from his position at Penn. It was either leave or be prosecuted for reckless endangerment and malicious misconduct. He had too many witnesses against him. He had little choice. My Uncle David told Cyril Latham that in his letter, when he asked him to represent me... us. Uncle David and Mr. Latham went to Penn together and Law School together. They are brothers of the tie, the fraternity tie." Paula chuckled. "They always know the scuttlebutt at Penn."

"Why are you going on to Nairobi alone?"

"I'm not going alone, Kybo is going with me."

"You know what I mean."

"Yes, well the plans may have changed again for Thomas and Jon were not able to mail their letters from Campo. Jon feels it is necessary to prepare their parents for Thomas's sudden reappearance, and I agree. Jon has not yet told his parents that he has found Thomas. The letters were to do that: one from Jon telling them how he found Thomas; and one from Thomas telling them why he never went home. They will need time to adjust to the idea that their son is coming home again–after fourteen years."

"I should say; both sides are going to have to adjust!"

"Yes, Thomas has memories of class distinction when he was young. He is worried that his parents will be rebuffed by his native appearance. He is Zuri Watu almost to the bone. He loves his native heritage, and I know he will not give it up. 'Love me, love my kitu-kina.'

"Thomas has very great powers. Did you know that?"

"No, I didn't; what kind of powers?"

"I do not feel it is my prerogative to tell you about them. Suffice it to say that he can do things that neither you nor I would even dream of doing. He is a medicine man who has the knowledge of the ages. I wish I could go and meet his parents first; get them ready for the changes and laud his attributes; but I cannot interfere. Jon will be with him. Jon loves Thomas so much, that I think he would leave his family and not look back if they were to make Thomas uncomfortable."

"All this tells me that you love Thomas deeply. Is that so?"

"Yes, we are soul mates. We belong together. I will go where he wants to go. I will be with him in all things... except the reunion with his parents."

"What about Jon? How does he feel?"

"Jon is Jon. He goes with the flow. He makes no waves. His ambition in life was to find his brother. He spent fourteen years preparing to do so–only to find him when he went to find me. He has said that he believes he was summoned to find me. He said he had no choice in the matter. He believes Thomas summoned him, by thinking of him, while he returned home. It is possible. Thomas has great gifts. I know Jon was unhappy that I was going on the trek with them; but it was what Thomas wanted, so Jon wanted it too. Jon is a bon vivant in all things."

"I could go for a cup of coffee; how about you, a cup of tea maybe?"

When Paula returned with the hot coffee, tea and a scone for Captain Jones, she said, "While we have this time alone, I want to tell you how much your friendship means to me. You have been unfaltering in your support of me and my family and friends. You are, without a doubt, the very best friend I have ever had, and I love you for your friendship. I just don't understand why you go to so much trouble and expense for other people, many of whom are total strangers."

It was quiet for a while. Paula sipped her tea and waited for Captain Jones to reply. She hoped he would eventually answer her. Her mind wandered to the sound of the cruiser plowing through the sea. Other than the passage of the motor yacht, it was quiet on the water... no birds, no jungle noises. The deep drone of the powerful diesel engines was muted by insulation and distance. It was a comforting sound; almost like the rumbling of the elephants when they passed under the tree where she was sleeping. She missed the surround-sound orchestra of the forest; but the diverse and incredible sounds came back to her whenever she thought of the traveling music in the movie, The Bridge on the River Kwai.

Captain Jones cleared his throat and said, "You will be the first person to whom I have ever said this. I hope you will keep my confidences secret to the grave."

"When I was a young man, newly married, I wanted to be successful. I wanted to be a partner in the law firm where I was employed. I wanted to hear my name spoken with the

reverent awe the secretaries used when they referred to the partners. Now you know, in a law firm, working sixty hours a week is normal, but I worked eighty hours a week or more. My wife, Beth asked me to go at a slower pace; to spend more time with her and our families. I was impervious to her pleas. We did not need the money; but I needed the glory. Beth and I both came from prosperous families. She had already inherited when her father died, which was before we met.

"Then, Beth became pregnant. Good, I thought, now she will have a child to care for and stop pestering me to be with her all the time."

Captain Jones stopped and sipped his coffee and nibbled on the scone. He heaved a deep sigh and continued.

"I tried to be home for breakfast and dinner each day, but I usually went into my home office after dinner and worked 'til the small hours of the morning.

"In the seventh month of her pregnancy, Beth's mother was killed in an automobile accident after leaving our house. She came over often to keep Beth company, and that day, she'd been helping her to get the nursery ready.

"The ensuing weeks were terrible for Beth. The funeral arrangements took a toll on her vitality. She was now the executrix of a large estate and the sole heir as an only child. Her parents had a May and December marriage, but they had loved one another deeply. I would help Beth a bit in the evenings with the legal issues, but other than that, she saw to everything else alone.

"In her eighth month of pregnancy, she came to my home office door saying she was in great pain. As I looked at her standing there, her water broke. I called the doctor and he said to bring her in to the Emergency right away. Those were the most awful hours of my life. Twelve hours later the doctor took me into his office. 'It is with great sorrow that I have to tell you, your wife died in childbirth, as did your son.' After he had given me a sedative, and a glass of brandy, he continued. 'It was a breech birth, with buttocks presentation. The baby was already in the birth canal when she arrived at the hospital, so a "C" section was impossible. We could

not turn the baby, so we performed a double episiotomy to allow more room for the birth. He was a big baby, almost eight pounds. He was blue when he was born. We could not revive him. Your wife began to hemorrhage, then went into shock and then stopped breathing, all within moments of each other.'

"The Obstetrician lived just a few blocks from us, so he took me home in my car, saying, 'My wife can drop me off at my office in the morning, it is on her way to work.'

"Once I was alone, I began to cry. I cried for two days. My parents came to be with me and took care of callers and the funeral arrangements. My older brother, a medical doctor, stopped by to see me each day; he gave me sedatives and mood elevators. Nothing helped. I was so deep in depression that I considered taking my own life. But, each time my Mother came with a meal or a cup of tea... or each time my Dad came and sat with me in the matching lounge chair, saying nothing, just being with me; I knew I could not condemn them to the same horrible feeling of unbearable loss. It was all that saved me.

"I resigned my job, but I was told when I was ready, there would be a place in the firm for me. My Mother hired a housekeeper for me. She and my Dad redecorated the nursery. My Dad, who was an Investments Advisor, managed all the paperwork and the finances for me. For months, I was just numb and cried all the time. I had such an awful burden of regret. I really hated myself, because I now saw myself for the terrible person I really was: selfish, arrogant; concerned for no one but myself, my happiness, my esteem. I had paid not a bit of attention to Beth's needs. I had ignored her almost entirely... and the saddest part of that is: I loved her more than life. Just let me achieve the status I want and then we can be happy together for the rest of our lives.

"It took me a year before I could get through a day without crying. I took to building the sailboat Beth and I had started when we were first married. It was my only therapy. When it was finished, I sold it and gave the money to the Nursing Mothers Association. I knew Beth would have liked that.

"While I was building the boat, I thought about what I would do with the rest of my life. I couldn't stand the thought of being a lawyer again. I talked to my Dad, my Mother, my brother, my friends. Everyone, in his or her own way, helped me to find myself again. We lived in Westchester, New York and my parents told me they wanted to sell out and move to Florida. They said, 'Come with us. Sell this place. Make a new home. Florida has lots of boats, which you love. It would be good for all of us.' My brother had already considered moving south. He'd had a great offer from a Practice in St. Augustine. He took his family with him for the job interview. They fell in love with St. Augustine. So, he took the job on the spot.

"We all moved to St. Augustine, Florida. A few months later, I was hanging around an upscale marina, looking at the fabulous yachts, when the marina owner realized I knew as much about yachts as he did. He offered me a job, and I took it. It was a place to start.

"It was a good life, but it wasn't enough for me. I needed to expiate my sins against life and nature. My job was to take people out on yachts for a demonstration, when they were considering a purchase. I'm afraid that I talked more people out of a purchase, than I talked into one. Don, the owner said honesty was great, but I was never to tell anyone that they didn't need a yacht, or one that big, or that buying one used to start would be a better idea. Then, Don took the **Wind Drift in** *trade. The man wanted something bigger with larger crew quarters and a fully enclosed and internally accessed high bridge. Don called the* **Wind Drift** *a white elephant: too big for a week-ender; too small to cross the ocean and not designed right for a luxury fishing boat. He was right on all counts. The boat just sat in the marina for the next two years. I took it out several times to show to customers, but it was never just what they wanted. I heard Don talking one day to a customer about the* **Wind Drift**. *He said, 'I can make you an offer you can't refuse...' He stated a price I'd be willing to pay for the yacht. The customer declined, figuring there was something terribly wrong with the yacht–to get so much*

boat at such a price. I had gone nowhere near the customer. He was Don's friend. When I asked him if he had sold the ***Wind Drift****, he said, no. 'I don't think I could give it away.'*

"I said, 'I'll buy the ***Wind Drift*** *for the price you stated to Mr. Hadley.' Don just stared at me. 'You'll never get financing,' he said, 'and you can't afford it anyway.' I told him I could get the money, so we signed an agreement of sale. Then, I told him it would be a cash deal and he nearly fell off his chair. I continued working at the marina, but I also worked on the* ***Wind Drift****.*

"One day when I was talking to my brother, he told me about a children's clinic that was looking for an outing for the children. He said, 'They've done pony rides and fairs to death and are looking for something unusual.' Later, when I was cleaning up the ***Wind Drift****, the idea came to me. What about a day at sea? I called Ed back. At first, he thought it was too different, but he said he would get back to me. The next day he called and said, 'Your idea went over really big with the staff. How many children can the boat handle?' I asked, 'How many children do you have?' He said, 'Twenty two.' I said, 'Bring them all, there's plenty of room.'*

"That was when I finally began to heal. After the day at sea with the children, I felt good for the first time in four years. I tried doing charters, but I hated it. I was beginning to think myself a real fool for buying the ***Wind Drift*** *when southern Florida was hit by a hurricane.*

"I took food, medical supplies and medical personnel to the disaster site. The emergency personnel used the boat as quarters but the injured were taken to the hospital. During the day, I ferried supplies to the emergency center, for most of the local yachts had storm damage of some kind. The days were a whirlwind. I hired a cook and another crewman. We had become vital to the rescue efforts; many roads were impassable and bridges were unsafe... and for a time, the power was out. When something was needed, I went and got it. Other yachts began to show up to help. The Mayor put me in charge of the ***Aid by Sea*** *efforts.*

"Now I had scheduling, fuel and personnel problems–but

I never felt more alive. Two months later, when things were getting back to normal, the local paper ran a headline story about me. It was picked up by the wire services. Overnight, I was a hero. I didn't feel worthy of the praise, until I looked into my parent's eyes and saw their admiration of me. That was when I knew what I had to do with my life.

"Two years later, I heard of a freighter leaving Baltimore empty, bound for West Africa. I had read a great deal about the problems of Africa, so I contacted the freighter's owner who agreed to pick up the **Wind Drift** *in Fort Lauderdale.*

"I went to Africa. I was thirty-six years old. That was twenty years ago. My parents came every other year until they died. My brother and I trade years for visiting. I go to the States every other year for a month, usually in the rainy season.

"This is **Wind Drift III***, but I don't use the numbers. I consider each one to be the only one. This pretty lady is fit to go to sea. She is ninety-five feet long and sleeps twelve, with crew quarters for six. The first* **Wind Drift** *was only sixty-two feet long, but she was a sailor's dream. She handled like the breeze. I gave up a bit of that for the length and a wider beam, but, now I'm sea worthy. So, helping you and your family is what I do. If it weren't for people needing help, I wouldn't have anything to do with my life. I wouldn't have any reason for living. So, I should thank you that you have asked me to help you, so I can go on doing what I need to do."*

PAULA WAS QUIET. WHAT could she say? She could say nothing. He had bared his soul to her and she had to keep his secret forever. "I'm glad you considered me worthy of your secret. I will treasure it, as I've treasured our friendship, forever."

The ship's bell sounded the hour as Steve and Jon appeared to take over the helm. "All's quiet." Captain Jones said. "She's running with the current now, but you'll have to head south by southwest in an hour. Hold that course for an hour and then head south by southeast. Keep your eye on the depth gauge, keep her at 500 feet."

18

Ocean Travel

THE RAIN CAME LATE in the night and lasted until dawn. The day was overcast and hazy. They had entered the doldrums, an area of almost no winds, so this haze might last all day.

Below decks, meals were served from the galley, buffet style. Jonas was in his glory. He liked cooking for a crowd. He had bacon, sausages and waffles, plus cold cereals with bananas and toast as breakfast selections and bacon, lettuce and tomato sandwiches and chicken noodle soup for lunch selections. For the hearty eaters, there were fresh scones and pan-fried potatoes too.

Without the sun to herald the day, Paula slept until noon. She arrived at the galley to find Thomas preparing a tray to take to the dining salon. "I was wondering if you were awake yet?" he said. "Jonas has set out a feast for us."

"So I see and I'm famished too." Thomas looked at her with his head cocked to the side with a quizzical smile that showed his dimpled cheeks but not his teeth. Paula chuckled and said, "Famished is very hungry." They smiled knowingly at each other, as they had when they first traveled together. It was a special connection, a unique feeling. It was a great way to start her day.

Paula led the way to the dining salon, where Captain Jones was finishing brunch. "One thing I like about having company on board is: Jonas goes all out. I can't tell you the last time I had his homemade chicken noodle soup." Paula had chosen the BLT with soup and pan-fried potatoes. Thomas had sausage, waffles with maple syrup and pan-fried potatoes.

Thomas said, "I wish I had known it was homemade, I

would have taken a cup." Paula took his spoon and dipped it into her cup and passed it to him saying, "Take a taste, you will definitely want this recipe."

Thomas tasted the soup. It was delicious. "That was so good; I'm going to get a cup. Anybody want anything else?"

Captain Jones said, "I could use another cup of coffee, cream and two sugars, please."

Paula asked, "How long do you expect this dreary haze to last?"

"The sun usually burns it off by now. But, I suspect the day is overcast. In the doldrums, there is very little wind and sometimes the cloud cover lingers."

"Does it affect navigation?"

"Yes, because you can't see much; but we have radar, so we won't run into anything."

"What are the doldrums? I've heard of them, but I'm not sure what that implies."

"The doldrums are an area in the ocean where there is almost no wind, because the cold water currents moving north from the Antarctic meet warm water currents moving south. The currents do no blend, which forces the two currents to turn and flow east towards land before turning south."

"Why do the currents flow towards land and turn south?"

"Both currents are below the bulge of West Africa when they meet. They have to turn east and then south, because of the land mass of the African Continent. It was a place to be avoided by sailing ships because of low winds, which is why the Slave Coast, the Gold Coast and the Ivory Coast are all in the southern portion of the bulge, before the currents meet and turn south."

"Thomas told me the story of the Zuri Watu nation. It was originally a coastal tribe, but because of the slave traders, they went far inland. I remember him saying that an archeological dig was set up in the place of the old coastal village. From other things he said, I thought the old village might have been near Douala, which is below the bulge."

"There is a time of year when the currents merge a bit and lessen the effects of the doldrums. It is when it is summer in

Antarctica. The cold water is not as cold as it travels north, and the waters from the north in winter are cooler. When the currents meet, they blend some and form a current that goes first toward the coast and then down the west coast of Africa from Douala in Cameroon to Namibe in southern Angola. It was a wise sailing master who might have known this and pillaged Douala, which is just north of the confluence of the currents."

"Well Lassie, it is time to take the watch."

Thomas came up with the coffee. "Sorry it took so long. We had to make a fresh pot."

"Just in time lad, we are headed for the bridge."

The haze cleared, but the day remained dull. The only breeze was the one made by the moving cruiser. In a moment, when there was no one on the afterdeck, Paula asked Captain Jones, "Why did you choose to come to Africa? There must have been places in the States that needed you."

"I felt I needed a complete change. Too many things kept reminding me of my loss. I needed to get away from the reminders. Africa was perfect for that. I had so much to learn: new customs, new language, different peoples and different sailing conditions. It was a panacea for me"

"I wanted to ask you. How is Anna doing?"

"She is just fine. She asked about you when I last saw her. She will be disappointed not to have seen you again, before you left for Kenya."

"This pursuit by the mercenary has changed everything for us. He is intent on kidnapping Thomas to extort information from him. It is vital that I go to Kenya and put an end to his pursuit by filing for patents or copyrights or whatever it is that makes the medicine off limits to others."

"Patents, for medicines, I wish you success. Tell me about your trip here from Yaoundé." So the afternoon passed in a pleasant way. As always with Captain Jones, Paula felt loquacious. He asked perceptive questions, probably a trait held over from his law career. It seemed no time at all before Steve and Thomas showed up for their watch. Paula left the bridge first and Steve ascended once she was down. Paula had a few moments to talk with Thomas before Captain Jones left the bridge. She asked him, "Have you eaten?"

"No, I was not yet hungry."

"I am going to take a nap now–could we meet for dinner when your watch is over?"

"I can think of nothing I would like better." Thomas said as he smiled at her and caressed her with his eyes.

Captain Jones came down to the afterdeck and said to Thomas, "Steve forgot his sunglasses, Thomas. Come with me. He told me where they are... Paula can sit second chair for a few more minutes."

Thomas followed Captain Jones to the crew's quarters and on a desk just inside the door were the sunglasses. As he handed them to Thomas, he put a hand on his arm and a finger to his lips and motioned Thomas to follow him. Captain Jones opened a door and stepped inside. It was the Captain's quarters. He shut the door saying; "I picked up the same ship twice today, following the same course, only twenty miles further out. She was a small ship like the *Wind Drift*. It may not be anything, but I am familiar with most of the craft in the area, and there are no others like the *Wind Drift* south of Lagos. I didn't want to say anything in front of Paula. She is showing the signs of stress already. As I said, it may be nothing, just a coincidence."

"Thank you. We will be alert."

"I made notes of the time and distance in the log; get Steve to do the same if he spots the ship too. You go now. I'll stay here for a bit."

Thomas thought as he went forward: I was hoping we had evaded them. It was too much to hope for after Jon's radio message was intercepted. These people are really determined. Maybe I should go and put an end to their pursuit. It is beginning to wear on my nerves too. Paula descended to the afterdeck and smiled at Thomas before heading off to her cabin.

Steve was glad for his sunglasses, saying, "I'm not up here much during the day so I forgot how bad the glare can be–worse than the sun."

"Captain Jones spotted a ship on the same course this afternoon. He wants us to keep a watch for it. He said to note it in the log."

"Okay. He told me to read the log, but I decided to wait and read it when you got back. Take the helm–maintain the heading. Do you know how to do that?"

"I've never done it before, but I've been watching you."

"Give it a try, I'll be right here. If you have a question, ask it!"

It didn't take Steve long to read the log. It did pose some questions for him though, the foremost being, 'Why would Captain Jones care if there was another ship on the same heading?' Thomas was doing well at the helm, so Steve decided to let him go on for a bit longer, and turned on the radar. There it was: a blip, eighteen knots out. Steve set his chronometer; he would take a reading every 30 minutes. He noted the time and distance in the log. He said to Thomas, "You are a natural helmsman. You kept a perfect course."

Thomas smiled. He was having a great time. Seems he had an affinity for the sea and seagoing ways.

When the watch changed, Thomas went to his quarters to change and wash up. The heavy sea air had made his shirt feel damp. He found Paula in the mess hall off the galley playing a game of stones with Kybo. He laughed, "Not you too! Are we going to have to throw this game overboard to get any work out of you Kybo?"

Kybo grinned. "Missy Paula beat me, second game. Jonas wants to play her next."

Thomas was impressed. Jon had said, "No one beats Kybo." He himself didn't play, as he had an unfair advantage–did Paula have one too... and didn't realize it?

"Just a minute Thomas, we are almost finished." Paula said.

"It looks to me like there are still a lot of stones to play." Thomas said.

"Yes, but this one will end the game." Paula put a stone down and shrieked, "Gotcha, gotcha, gotcha!"

Kybo surveyed the board and shook his head bewildered.

Jonas came, with cooking spoon in hand, to see the rout, and laughed and jumped up and down with glee. "She's gotcha! Ha, ha, she's gotcha for sure!"

Paula stood up, "Excuse me gentlemen, my date is here." She took Thomas' hand and went to the buffet Jonas had set up in the pantry. She took a plate and chose the fish filet, the macaroni and cheese and a dinner roll with a side dish of salad, iced tea, a napkin and flatware. Thomas watched and imitated her, and her choices. They went into the dining salon and chose two chairs by the window near the end of the table.

"I feel so good," she said. "I love being at sea in this marvelous ship. I loved our sailboat too, but being at sea in her was like living in a tent, compared to being aboard the *Wind Drift*. Do you like the yachting?"

"Yes, I do. I liked it from the first, when Captain Jones took us for a cruise out to sea. I had high spirits from it."

"Exhilaration, high spirits is called exhilaration, or you feel exhilarated."

"Yes, I was exhilarated!" and he laughed. "I like that word!"

"If all goes well, we will be in Luanda tomorrow afternoon. It is a shame we can't use the radio to make plane reservations. Let's hope there will be a plane with four empty seats."

Thomas replied, "Later, we need to get Jon and Kybo and sit down and talk about our plans once we reach Luanda."

"Yes, a plan of action is always good; but, it makes me wonder why you think we need to do this?'

"We don't know who might be watching for us. We don't know how far the tentacles of this mercenary will reach. Don't tell Jon I said that; he feels bad about giving us away."

"I wondered about him. He has been so quiet."

"Yes, he is quite upset."

"He shouldn't be. None of us thought to tell him not to use the radio. I didn't think of it, did you?"

"No, none of us thought of it until Captain Jones said it."

Thomas walked her to her cabin. She reached up and gave

him a little buss on the cheek, saying, "I saw the blips on the radar screen too. Good night."

Shaking his head, Thomas walked away with a smile on his face. She is the greatest! Knew all along why I was concerned. She doesn't want me to worry–I don't want her to worry. Somebody's got to worry. I guess it will have to be Jon."

Jon came in a little after twelve. Thomas turned on the light and said, "We have to talk."

"Oh no, what did I do now?"

"Jon, no one blames you for using the radio. None of us thought about the message being intercepted...

"Boy, that's a big one. When did you learn that?"

"Captain Jones used it, remember? Now, what we have to do is outwit these men and do it like we passed off the face of the earth. Leave them with no clues to follow."

"How do you plan to do that?" Thomas outlined the plan. Jon liked it, but added a few changes.

"I will go to the bank and use my letter of credit to get cash, so we don't leave a paper trail. The bank would never divulge my business to someone else. By one o'clock in the morning, they had a good plan and turned out the light.

In half an hour, Jon was asleep and snoring. Thomas took off his clothes, put them under his blankets, and left to *roam*.

The ship, twenty miles out to sea running on a parallel course, was a beauty. She was named the *Gallant Lady*. She must have had at least five levels with a fully enclosed bridge seating five at the helm high above the prow, with three areas of cushioned leather banquettes seating twelve around the sides and back of the bridge. Thomas saw at least four crewmembers moving about the ship. There were three uniformed officers on the bridge and two working on charts at one of the sofa and table seating areas.

A quick look through the ship told him that there was someone occupying the three main staterooms above the lounge and dining salon. Below, there were five men, in suits, playing cards. There was one man in the galley and eight men asleep in the crew's quarters. He decided to watch the card players for a while. They put colored discs in the center of the table, put cards with them and took more. Then, one man took all the discs and they started over again. They talked very little, except to say words like: "I'll call" "see ya" "raise ya" and other terms that had no meaning for Thomas.

He thought they were never going to talk and had decided to go back to the bridge, when a white-jacketed man from the galley came in and said, "The boss wants to talk to you, Max."

A big burley man got up and left the room. The man from the galley sat down in his chair. Thomas followed Max through the magnificent yacht to the stateroom nearest the bridge. Max knocked lightly on the door and heard the word, "Come" before he opened the door. Inside were four people. They too had been playing cards, but they had no little colored discs, they had numbers on a paper. The three people said, "Good night" and left the room. Max closed the door after them and said, "You wanted me, Mr. Hunter."

The man remaining in the room was tall and well muscled. He had the shiny-pebbled flesh of a burn scar on the left side of his face and neck. He said, "Max, sit with me a moment." He gestured to the club chair beside him. "I am fairly sure now that our prey is headed for Luanda. We are going to arrive there first so we can follow our man when he gets off the boat. In a suitable place, we will drug him, bring him back to our ship and leave again. He will not suspect us, for he thinks he has evaded us. It should not be hard to surprise him. We do not want the girl or any of the others, unless we have no choice. Should they bypass Luanda, they will have to go to Cape Town. I am sure they are trying to get to Nairobi and the attorney that has the diary. So, unless they are going to sail the whole way, and I doubt that, they need a commercial airport."

"Would it not be good to take the girl too and threaten her with harm to get him to talk?"

"I have thought about that, but I admire the girl. If I had my choice of women, I would pick her. There is something about her that pleases me deeply. I could never harm her, so the threat would be useless."

"What about the brother? We could take him."

"You know Max, there are so few truly good people in this world, that it pains me to reduce the number. Another possibility is that so much time has passed that a copyright has already been obtained, and the information in the diary is now useless to others. The only thing that keeps us going is the possibility that he knows more than is in the diary. So, it is either the medicine man or no one. I don't think our employer, who is letting us use his grand ship, wants to be involved in a capital crime. No, it has to be just the medicine man. We can make him talk with drugs. Once we have the information, we can leave him in an alley and go. He is the one with the knowledge. He is the source. The others know nothing."

When Max opened the door to leave, Tamubu left with him. He now had much to think about. Curling up under a nice warm blanket in his bed, for the air conditioning in the stateroom had chilled him, he thought about ways to avoid the mercenary's plans.

He was drifting off, with the only plan being always to travel in a large group, when another idea occurred to him. What if we offered to sell them the diary? What if we made them our partners? They could do all the work and have the profits. We would be free!

Tamubu looked at the clock. It was 3 a.m. He decided, now was the time, the only time that it would be safe to work his plan. He prepared for spirit travel and *roamed* back to the *Gallant Lady*. He went to an alcove that was lined with books, where there was paper and pen. He took a sheet of the paper with the words: *The Gallant Lady* embossed in gold at the top. On it he wrote:

'I am Tamubu, Medicine Man of the Great Zuri Watu. We are weary of your pursuit. We would consider a business association with you. Tomorrow, come to the *Wind Drift* one hour after we dock in Luanda. Mr. Hunter, do not bring anyone with you but Max. Do **not** bring weapons of any kind.'

Tamubu walked through the corridors hoping he would meet no one at this hour of the night and slipped the piece of paper under the door to Mr. Hunter's stateroom. He immediately *roamed* back to the *Wind Drift* with a smile in his heart. He would have liked to have seen Mr. Hunter's reaction when he read the note.

Mr. Hunter, as it happened, was not in bed. He was still sitting in the chair by the window alcove, and he saw the note slip under the door onto the carpet. Annoyed, he got up and went to pick it up. He opened the door to chastise the sender, but there was no one there.

He took the paper to his chair, and by the light of the dimmed lamp read the note. He read it again, and again, and again. The more he read the note, the more questions it raised in his mind. *Is someone on this ship working against me? Even I did not know the medicine man's name. How could Max and I be sent to a rendezvous in Luanda, if the medicine man didn't know about it?* He sat in his chair unable to fathom how the note was delivered? *He is on the **Wind Drift**... so how was the note written on ship's stationery? Who slipped it under my door? How did the sender know my name? How did he know about Max? How did he know about the **Gallant Lady**?* His whole body ran cold. For the first time in his life, he was truly intimidated, and the icy fingers of irrational fear ran up his spine.

THERE WAS NO SENSE in going back to bed. It was almost time for his watch. Thomas met Steve in the corridor and followed him to the bridge. Paula came down the ladder and Thomas took her hand and led her to the afterdeck. "We are going to meet the mercenary today after we dock and talk about a deal. Is that okay with you?"

"I guess so... how did you..."

"Not now, I will explain everything later. We will soon be free of this man with his evil intentions. Sleep well, my love."

Thomas met Captain Jones at the foot of the stairs and said. "Would it be possible for someone to relieve Jon at the start of the 8 a.m. to noon watch?"

Surprised by the request, Captain Jones said, "Yes, of course, may I ask why?"

“We need to have a talk: you, me, Paula, Jon and Kybo, when you arise from your rest. We are going to deal with the mercenary and put an end to his pursuit.”

Paula listened to Thomas speak to Captain Jones; then she wandered off to her cabin. The meeting was a mystery; but she only thought of his last words to her: ‘Sleep well, my love.’ Her heart hammered with joy. He did love her, as she loved him.

19

Luanda

THE *GALLANT LADY* WAS already berthed alongside the long land pier. It was the only mooring that could accommodate her 167-foot length. Captain Jones piloted the *Wind Drift* past the *Gallant Lady* to the fuel dock to refuel before docking at a pier near the *Gallant Lady.*

It was almost one in the afternoon. Captain Jones had taken the con after their morning meeting. He felt baffled by the things that had transpired at the meeting; but he remembered Paula's admonition: 'Thomas is capable of things, of which you and I would not even dream.'

THE HOUR OF THE meeting arrived. They watched Mr. Hunter and Max go down the gangway from the *Gallant Lady*, walk along the pier and hail Captain Jones with: "Permission to come aboard".

Thomas shook his head. It was the signal that the visitors were armed. Once they boarded the ship, Paula stepped to the side of Mr. Hunter and Jon stepped to the side of Max. They raised pistols and poked them in their backs. Thomas said, "In my note, I had said no weapons. Already, before we even begin, you have shown yourselves to be untrustworthy."

Mr. Hunter again felt the icy fingers of abject fear creep up his spine, which caused an eerie feeling of déjà vu that left him confused and helpless; his thoughts whirled: *You! You wrote that note to me. How did you get on our ship? How did you get back to yours? How did you know our ship was following you? How do you know my name and Max's name? Have you been listening to us? How could you possibly do that?*

In the next few milliseconds Mr. Hunter retreated... in reality, he gave up. He knew he was going to cooperate in every way, thinking: *I am being paid big money; but no amount of money is enough to deal with a person who can do such things. What if we had abducted him? His vengeance might have been horrible.* The very idea of such power terrified him, and he was not a superstitious man.

Thomas went to Mr. Hunter and reached into his chest pocket and took out a cigar case, which cleverly held small throwing knives, and tossed it overboard. He went to Max and took the snub nose pistol from his ankle holster and tossed it overboard. He found the knife in his jacket sleeve and, wagging a finger at him, tossed it overboard. Then he turned to Mr. Hunter and said, "Take off your shoes." Mr. Hunter complied, and Thomas held out a bag for them. Then he said, "Ah, the ring. That too must come off Mr. Hunter." The ring followed the shoes into the bag. "When you leave, you may have your things back. But, just a minute... Max, Mr. Hunter, remove your belts." They took off their belts and Thomas put them in the bag. "What is that in your ear, Max? I think that should go in the bag too." Thomas looked them over carefully and then patted Max down. There was a peculiar bulge low in his suit pocket. He reached in and found a syringe, loaded with who knew what and said, "That definitely goes overboard. Our guests are ready now, Captain Jones."

The new passengers seated themselves in the indicated chairs on the afterdeck. There were six of them sitting around the table: Mr. Hunter, Max, Captain Jones, Paula, Thomas and Jon, who placed a tape recorder in the center of the table. Kybo stood beside the ladder to the bridge. Steve was on the flying bridge while Phil was in the salon, behind the blinds at the opened window, with a blowpipe and tranquilizer darts. Jonas had gone ashore to run errands.

Captain Jones began the formalities by stating the date, Saturday, April 2nd, 1960 and the time, 1:15 p.m. and the place,

Luanda Harbor, Angola, Africa for the record. He then asked those at the table to state their names for the record.

Acting as attorney for the proceedings he said, "We have called this meeting to discuss an Agreement of Sale with the people who have hired you to abduct Thomas. It is not to your advantage to be dishonest with us in any way.

"At this time, we have enough proof of serious crime against you to call the authorities; to have you put in jail for kidnapping; and stalking with the intent of kidnapping, as well as breaking and entering and theft.

"Whether you talk or not, is of no moment, for your employers will also be prosecuted on the same charges. Allowing you to use the *Gallant Lady*, a multi-million dollar private motor yacht, to follow us with nefarious intent, was a big mistake because it obviously indicts the owner too.

"My clients have agreed to sell you certain information regarding homeopathic remedies for ten million dollars. If, at any time, they are molested or once again stalked–or even watched–the offer is gone. We will then bring criminal charges against all of you. For the record, please state that you understand these conditions." Mr. Hunter, Max Smith, Thomas and Paula all said, "I understand the conditions and agree to them."

"How do we know that these remedies are worth ten million dollars?"

"Your source, Dr. Miles, has told your employer of their worth. That is why you have pursued my clients over a good portion of Africa. The ten million dollars is only to bind the deal. It is not the final price."

"We do not have the authority to make such a deal."

"I fully expected that. Here is the offer. In sixteen days, on Monday, the 18th of April, a meeting will be held in Nairobi, to iron out the terms and conditions of this offer. We will expect your employer to have the ten million, as a binder, in a cashier's check at that time. It is to be drawn on a bank that is yet to be specified.

"If we cannot come to an agreement, you may leave and

take your cashier's check with you. We will then press charges for kidnapping, breaking and entering, theft, stalking and extortion, against you and your employer, whose name is a matter of record as owner of the *Gallant Lady*.

"In the meantime, we will need an address where we can send you a copy of the tape of these proceedings and preliminary copies of the agreement; and a phone number in case we have further questions."

Mr. Hunter took the paper and pen offered to him and wrote an address and telephone number. "Use my name. I have no authority to release the name of my employer."

"We expect you to leave Luanda after you refuel, if that is not already done. If you wish to contact my clients, you may do so per my associate, Cyril Latham, Esq. ~ Rue de la Maison ~ Nairobi, Africa."

No one shook hands. It was not that kind of meeting. It was more an armistice; the treaty would come later... or not. Mr. Hunter and Max Smith disembarked. Max picked up the paper sack while Mr. Hunter sat on a nearby bench to put on his shoes. They left without looking back.

Mr. Hunter went directly to the bridge of the *Gallant Lady*. "Are we refueled?"

"Yes, sir."

"Then get us out of here."

"Yes, sir! Where to sir?"

"Take us back to your dock."

"Yes, sir."

Mr. Hunter went to his stateroom and took off his clothes to take a shower. He had been sweating profusely. Under the water, he heard a voice say, "Don't be foolish and plan a reprisal. You will die a horrible lingering death, if you do." Hurriedly he opened the shower door, but he already knew there would be no one there. He had stepped into a terrifying nightmare and he didn't know the way out.

He had to call Mr. Athos and tell him about the meeting.

Aboard the *Wind Drift*, the conferees had gone to the galley, where Jonas had left a tray of wrapped tuna sandwiches and fruit salad for a quick lunch. Captain Jones waited until Thomas finally joined them at the table before discussing the meeting.

"I thought that went well, he said. They were certainly subdued. Tell me Thomas, why did you have Mr. Hunter take off his shoes and both of them take off their belts?"

"Thomas smiled. "Mr. Hunter had metal in the toes of his shoes. Both had metal in their belts. I thought it very unusual, so I had them remove them."

Paula said, "There was a spy story where a woman had knives in the toes of her shoes... could that have been it?"

Jon laughed, "That reminds me of a book I read: where villains had garrotes, thin wire ones, secreted in their belts that they could whip out instantly... I wonder how they got the garrotes back inside the belts."

Everyone laughed at Jon's whimsy, which relieved the tension. It did make them wonder, though... how **did** they put the garrotes back into the belts?

Paula said, "Maybe they just got new belts with garrotes already in them."

Jon chuckled, and in his best British Inspector's voice said, "I say, Mr. Hunter, why do you have ten belts, all exactly alike?"

The laughter continued. But no one asked how Thomas had known these things. No one asked how the meeting had been arranged either. It was a conundrum that had been exacerbated when Thomas had said, "I told you in my note, no weapons." Captain Jones again thought of Paula's statement about Thomas's abilities and decided to let his questions go unanswered.

"And the ring and the hearing aid? Why them?" Captain Jones asked.

"Is that what that was, a hearing aid? I had never seen one before. I was just being difficult with them;" which brought peals of laughter.

Paula said, "I suppose this is our last meal together. I have had such a wonderful time... that I wouldn't mind going all the way to Kenya on the *Wind Drift*".

"I, too, have greatly enjoyed myself. So far, it has been a grand voyage. I've never sailed around the Cape of Good Hope. It would be four thousand miles or more to Kenya. I would need a much larger crew to consider such a voyage." Captain Jones replied. "But, it would be the trip of a lifetime!"

JONAS CAME ABOARD THE *Wind Drift*. He had gone ashore to mail the fat express letter to Kenya for Jon and to do some shopping. He had also called the airport from a pay telephone.

He sat down at the table and said, "There is a flight tomorrow morning at 7:15 a.m. for Nairobi, via Kinshasa, Kisangani and Kampala. You will need to confirm the reservations–actually pay for the tickets–by 5:00 p.m. today."

Jon looked at his watch and said, "I'd better go to the bank. Want to come along Thomas? You will get to see me use my letter of credit."

"Yes, I'd like that. Shall we also get a hotel room while we are out?"

"Nonsense, lad, Captain Jones said. You'll stay with us on the *Wind Drift*. Jonas has planned a farewell dinner for you... and the others have shore leave for the rest of the day. Besides, I think Jonas and Kybo are headed for the mess, with the intention of playing that infernal game of stones one last time."

"Are you coming with us Paula? Jon asked.

"No, now that we are docked, I need to catch up on the entries in my diary."

AT THE BANK, JON asked to speak to the manager. A Mr. Jordan came and said, "How may I be of help to you?"

"I have a letter of credit. I would like to draw a sum of cash against it."

"Come with me please." Once seated in Mr. Jordan's office, he said, "May I see your letter, please?" He looked at it carefully and said to Jon, "Please sign your name here on this draft." Mr. Jordan compared the two signatures, rose and said, "I'll be back in a moment."

True to his word, he was not gone more than two minutes. When he returned, he asked for the sum required. Jon told him the amount and said, "I would like half of the amount in Travelers Checks; the rest in cash, large denominations, please."

"This will take a few minutes. May I offer you coffee or tea?"

"If you don't mind, I think we will go to the mercantile across the street. We will be back in half an hour or so. Is that convenient for you?"

"That will be just fine, Mr. Caulfield. We will be ready for you then."

Once outside, Thomas said, "A letter of credit must be very special. It was a great deal of money you requested."

"That bank happens to be an affiliate of our bank in Nairobi. Apparently, we are in their system. It usually takes much longer."

"What are you looking for in the mercantile?"

"A present for Captain Jones; do you have any ideas?"

"No, but that's a good thought. We'll find something nice."

The mercantile was a large store. Thomas thought it would have been fun to spend the rest of the day there. They had everything that anyone could ever want... and many things for which he knew not the purpose.

Jon and Thomas bought khaki safari clothes for Kybo and underwear and several pairs of thick knee socks; laughing at the reaction they knew the underwear would bring from Kybo. Jon bought him a neckerchief too, a paisley print of reds and blues, and a belt made of braided strips of tooled leather.

Past the clothing section, a perky young lady had a table set up displaying, so the sign said, Polaroid Cameras. Jon, who loved cameras, asked her what a Polaroid camera was–she lifted the camera, pointed it at Jon and Thomas, said, "Smile" and clicked the shutter. A flash went off. Then, in moments, the camera began to whirr and out came a piece of paper, mostly black. Smiling, the young lady placed the piece of paper on the edge of the table in front of them, saying, "Watch, but don't touch it yet." As they stared at the rectangular shape, images began to appear. In less than three minutes, there it was: a picture of them standing together. The young lady picked up the picture and took a roller and ran it across the picture, "This process seals the picture, so it doesn't fade or fingerprint."

Jon said, "This is it! This will be our gift to Captain Jones! What a great thing it is! We want a camera and lots of film–gift wrapped–please."

"The young lady said, "The film has a shelf life, so it is best to buy it fresh; unless you can keep it refrigerated."

"Refrigeration is not a problem. Six boxes of film, please."

Jon paid the young lady with Travelers Checks, and left her to wrap the gifts. They had gone not far, when Jon stopped, turned around, and went back to the table. Thomas watched him; in a few moments Jon returned. "What did you do?" Thomas asked.

"I bought another camera with film as a present for our parents. They will just love it! While she is wrapping, let's go back to the bank. Mr. Jordan should have the new Travelers Checks ready for me to sign."

"Why are you going to sign the Travelers Checks now?"

"When you buy them, you sign them at the top. When you use them, you sign them at the bottom. That way, unless someone is a good forger, no one else can use the Travelers Checks if you lose them."

Mr. Jordan was indeed ready for them. It took Jon not long to sign the twenty checks. Mr. Jordan than made them into a booklet for him and gave him the list of check numbers to keep separately. Jon tucked the list into Thomas's pocket. When they were on their way back to the mercantile, Thomas asked, "Why did you put that paper in my pocket?"

"It is a list of the numbers of the Travelers Checks. It needs to be kept in a different place from the checks themselves."

"Why?"

"Because, if I lose the checks, I can take the list to a bank and they will give me new checks to replace the ones I lost; except for the ones I may have already used. As I use the checks, I cross off the number on the list."

"This is very good money. I like it." With parcels in hand, they caught a cab to the airport. Jon asked Thomas to stay with the cab and parcels while he went into the airport building to pay for the tickets.

THOMAS SPOKE TO THE cab driver. "What tribe are you?" he asked.

The driver was surprised at the question, but replied, "I am Ibo, why?"

"My afisa (aide), Kybo, is also Ibo. You are a long way from home."

"Yes, I came here to escape being educated at Ibadan. I did not like the college in Nigeria. It was boring and restrictive. I came to Luanda on a summer job. I liked it here, so I stayed. What is your man's name?"

"Kybo bin Kimbo." (Kybo son of Kimbo.)

"What is your name?"

"My name is Rubio. I think I know of them. Were they employed by the Afrikaner trader?"

"Max Mason, yes."

"I met them when the trader came to our village to hire bearers. How is Kybo? Is he well? Is his father still with the trader?"

"Kybo is well. Yes, his father is still with the trader."

"Why are you here in Luanda?"

"We are getting ready to go to Nairobi tomorrow by plane. Ah, here is my brother, Jon." Jon got in the taxi and Thomas said, "Jon, I would like you to meet Rubio. He is Ibo. He knows Kybo and his father, Kimbo."

"Nice to meet you Rubio, would you take us to the docks please?"

"Yes, sir."

Jon nattered on, "It's almost five o'clock. I'm ready for tea!"

Thomas replied, "I look forward to English Tea, too. When we get to the docks, Rubio, I am sure Kybo would like to say hello to you. Will you have time to stop?"

"I will make the time, sir."

"I am called Tamubu. I am from the Nations of the Great Zuri Watu."

Jon thought: One day, I must meet these Zuri Watu of whom he is so proud. They must be a very special people.

Rubio was puzzled: He introduced the white man, Jon, as his brother, yet he says he is from the Zuri Watu. Maybe he meant brother as in brotherhood.

Kybo saw the taxi arrive. He hastened down the ramp to help with the packages. The taxi driver got out of the cab and gave Kybo an Ibo salute. I know this man. Kybo thought.

Tamubu took the initiative and said, "Kybo, this is Rubio. He says he remembers you and your father when Max went to his village to hire bearers."

Now I remember him. He wanted to go with us. Max had hired him until his father came and said he was going to college to be educated. His father was the first son of the Chief, who had not yet succeeded to being Chief himself.

"Rubio, what are you doing driving a cab? Do you work as well as go to college?"

"No, I did not like college. I stopped going. I will get my education here in Luanda. I go to the Library and the lady there helps me to choose books that will educate me without boring me to death." They laughed knowingly.

"When you go home; if you see my father, tell him I am well and happy."

"I will do that, Kybo. Have you been gone long?"

"No, not long; a moon has not yet passed."

"I wish you well on your journey to Nairobi. Kwaheri."

JON AND THOMAS HAD taken their purchases aboard the *Wind Drift*. Then Jon bolted for the galley. He gave a sigh of relief when he saw that there was still a pot of potato soup, freshly baked bread and scones.

Jonas left Kybo in the crew's mess and came to serve him. "What would you like, mate. I have grilled fish in the oven."

Jon said, "Oh, a fish sandwich would be super! I haven't had that since I left England."

Jonas took a thick slice of his homemade bread and asked, "Tartar sauce?"

"Yes, please."

Thomas watched as Jon passed him with a huge smile, on his way to the dining table on the afterdeck

"I think I will have the same as Jon. He looked positively delighted."

"Coming right up," Jonas said, "One fish sandwich with Tartar sauce and a cup of potato soup."

Captain Jones joined them with a cup of coffee and a warm scone. "I will be sorry to see you go, but my waistline will be happy. Jonas has had a grand time cooking for you. My simple tastes don't challenge his culinary abilities. Did you get all your errands accomplished?"

"Yes, we did," Jon smiled. Paula arrived; soon Steve and Phil joined them. Jonas came on deck bringing a tray with a pot of coffee, cream and sugar and mugs, with Kybo carrying a plate of fresh raspberry scones. Captain Jones wondered: What's going on?

Thomas, who had excused himself to go get seconds, arrived on the afterdeck loaded with wrapped packages.

Jon, Paula and the rest, shouted, "Surprise!" Thomas walked to Captain Jones and sat the wrapped gifts before him.

"What is this? You're not supposed to give me presents! There's no room on this ship for presents. What am I going to do with you?"

"You are going to open the presents," Jon said, "I can hardly wait." As Captain Jones reached for the smaller parcel, Jon said, "Open the bigger one first. It will make more sense to you that way."

Captain Jones opened the large flowery-papered gift. He

saw the box and said, “Polaroid Camera, what is that?” He continued to open the box and saw the clunky big camera. “Not exactly a pocket model, is it?” Everyone burst into laughter. But Captain Jones opened the instruction book and said, “Oh, my; it takes and prints the picture all at once.” In a few minutes more, he had the film package opened and had the film in the camera. The first picture he took was of Paula, sitting across the table from him, smiling. He sat it on the table and everyone gathered round to watch the picture develop itself. Jon took the little roller, and showed him how to apply the sealing coating when the picture was fully developed.

Captain Jones laughed and said, “What a marvelous gift. It is about the only thing that I don’t already have three or four of... thank you, I’m really pleased.” He continued to take pictures of everyone individually on the afterdeck. Even Jonas posed for a picture, and then asked him to take another so he could send one to his Mother. Lastly, he took group pictures of Thomas, Jon, Paula and Kybo; Phil, Steve and Jonas; then Jon took pictures of him: on the wharf beside his yacht. He also took some head shots of the Captain with his crew. In the end, they used three packages of film. But everyone had mementos to take with them. Jon told Jonas to put the other three packages of film in the refrigerator saying, “The saleslady said the film keeps better that way.”

Phil and Steve left for a night on the town. Jonas went to the galley to prepare dinner. He already had two stuffed chickens roasting in the oven. Paula went back to her diary.

Jon and Thomas took Kybo to their room and dressed him in his new togs. As expected, Kybo refused to put on the underwear. But Jon ignored him; when he was dressed, he said to Kybo, “Sit here... no, sit over there in that chair. No, that’s not right either. Sit over there on that bed. No, maybe you should sit on this bed.” Kybo was making a wry face. Jon smiled and said, “Would you like to try the underwear?” Once Kybo was fully dressed, they went to the afterdeck where Jon took two pictures of him. One for Captain Jones and one for his father with his kitamba draped across his chest and over his shoulders like a chief.

Now, to the packing–it would be a very early day tomorrow. Rubio had said he would be here at 6:00 a.m. to take them to the airport. He would certainly get an eyeful when he saw Kybo decked-out like a white hunter... except that Kybo wore woven leather sandals with his high socks instead of boots.

Farewell cocktails were served on the afterdeck at 8 p.m. and dinner was served, buffet style in the dining salon, at 9 p.m. The roast chicken was the best Thomas had ever eaten and the stuffing and gravy were seasoned perfectly. Jonas served fluffy white mashed potatoes (made from canned Idahoan potato flakes), glazed carrots and peas, Julienned cabbage slaw with celery seed and pecans, guava jelly relish and crescent rolls.

It was a meal fit for the Ritz-Carlton Hotel and Paula said so to Captain Jones.

"Please don't tell Jonas that. I am planning on taking him to see his mother in May. Her birthday is the 20th. It is a surprise for Jonas. But I don't want him to have time to place any applications for a job before we leave. I know that is selfish, but having you on board has made me realize that I could never replace him."

Thomas insisted on clearing the table and fetching coffee and tea. He had to get the recipe for the glazed carrots and peas. He had never eaten such tasty vegetables. Jonas and Kybo were playing a game of stones... what else? But Jonas jumped up and said, "I have a surprise for dessert."

"Dessert, I don't think anyone has room."

Well, we'll take it up with the coffee and tea and see."

Jonas had made a carrot cake. It was the most fantastic thing Thomas had ever seen. It had little carrots made of orange icing arranged around the edge on top with sprigs of fine green leaves, also made with icing. There was a decorative carrot for every slice. The bottom edge on the side near the plate was covered with walnuts in half circles to match each decorative carrot on the top.

"That cake is so beautiful; no one will want to cut it. I have never seen such artistic talent applied to food. You are a marvel!"

Thomas preceded Jonas with the coffee pot, teapot, cream, sugar, cups, saucers and spoons. He placed the tray on a side table and said, "May I now present Mkuu (chef) Jonas with his dessert masterpiece. Everyone turned to watch Jonas come in with the marvelous cake. He sat it down on the table in front of Paula amidst clapping and cheers. Kybo followed with plates, forks, napkins and the cake cutter.

Captain Jones was astounded. The cake was so professional, that he thought: maybe I am holding him back by keeping him here. Aloud he said, "This cake is fantastic."

But moments later, Jonas said, "I enjoyed doing the cake for you, but I'm glad I don't have to do it for a living. I'd rather cook than bake and decorate."

The cake was delicious. Thomas knew he could never duplicate it, so he didn't even ask for the recipe. Paula, though, wanted the recipe. Carrot cake was her favorite dessert. She had never had better–ever.

Jonas was glad to share the recipe with her. He said, "The secret is in the beating, a full five minutes on high to make the batter light, and to get the excess moisture out of the pineapple, because it is so heavy."

Jonas and Kybo cleaned up and in between returned to their game of stones. Jonas stacked the dishwasher several times while Kybo put the clean dishes away. Jonas had never liked having anyone in his galley; but Kybo was quiet and efficient. If he didn't know where something went, he either asked or left it for Jonas to put away. The work went quickly with four hands. Pots and pans disappeared and were replaced by dishes needing a final scrape. All the dishes were buttercup yellow Melamine with a wide purple border. The flatware was stainless steel. The glasses were plastic too, but looked like crystal. They were clear, lightly cut for grip with thick bases... they were made in Lund, Sweden.

"Life is going to seem so dull when you are gone. I am especially going to miss playing this game of stones with you." Jonas said to Kybo.

"I do not know what life will bring me. I have dedicated my life to the Medicine Man of the Great Zuri Watu. He walks with the spirits and talks with the spirits. He can heal almost anyone who is sick. I have never met such a great man who is so humble and likeable. It is my greatest good fortune that he has allowed me to go with him wherever he walks. I have been blessed." Kybo replied.

"Yes, I know what you mean. I, too, am blessed. For I have a life that is exactly what I want. It is quiet and restful and interesting. After the World War, I was so weary that I could not bear the thought of my life at home. We were in North Africa when the war ended. I went home to see my Mother; but I soon returned to Africa. I love this continent: the animals; the smell of the air; the forests and savannahs; the people and I love the sea. I settled in Douala and had a small boat; but I had no direction to pursue. Then I saw the ad for a cook aboard the *Wind Drift* and here I am–I want nothing else. It is a good life. Captain Jones is a good man."

"We, you and I, are fortunate. So many people live out lives of sadness and have no work to do that they enjoy. I went with Max Mason because he needed strong men. My father left Safari work and joined him too. I liked the trading, and the travel was interesting. We met many people and saw many places; but when the trading safaris stopped for the rainy seasons, I was lost. I had nothing worth doing. I disliked village life. I found it restrictive and boring. Then we met Tamubu and Missy Paula. In a few days I knew what I wanted to do with my life, if Tamubu would have me. My father was sad when I left him. He knew he might never see me again, but he wished me well. I have liked being on this ship. I am pleased to have you as a friend. I hope we will meet again.

Jonas took Kybo's hand in a strong clasp saying, "For some reason, I feel that we will meet again. I just sense that our fates are intertwined."

20

The DC3

THE LUANDA AIRPORT WAS a long open building that had the feeling of a converted airplane hangar. Multi-colored Formica airline counters were arranged along the runway side of the building in front of the waiting areas and doors to the tarmac. On the opposite side of the building were kiosk-like partitions for the car rental counters, the Western Union counter, two sets of entrance/exit doors, a snack bar, a news shop and a souvenir shop.

Jon led them to the Sabena–Belgian World Airlines counter to check-in for the flight to Nairobi, via Kinshasha, Kisangani and Kampala. Thomas' carry-on items were his medical and herb pouches. His clean clothing was in Jon's bag. The pretty Sabena check-in clerk looked at the pelt pouches and said to Thomas, "Would you like a zippered bag for your carry-on items, sir?"

"Yes, that would be nice. Where do I get one?"

She smiled at him; he was so good looking, so earthy and feral. She had never before seen such a magnetic man. "I have one here for you, sir."

Thomas accepted the nice heavy cloth bag of red and gold. It was zippered along the top and had SABENA–BWA printed on the sides in large gold letters. Pleased, he gave the clerk a full smile and said, "Thank you." She sighed and almost fainted on the spot.

Tamubu turned to Jon and said, "Our tickets go all the way to Nairobi. I thought we were going to Kisangani."

Jon said, "Let's go get a cup of coffee." When they were seated at a small table, Jon continued, "We've been so busy

I forgot to tell you about our marvelous itinerary. For just a few dollars more for each ticket through to Nairobi, we have the option of getting off at any stop, as long as we book the stop and the day we want to reboard the plane, when we buy the tickets. The tickets are good for seven days. Our itinerary is to fly to Kisangani for two nights and tour the Congo River. On the third day we will fly to Kampala on Lake Victoria. Paula and Kybo will be with us in Kampala for two nights and then, on the fifth day, Paula and Kybo will fly to Nairobi. Mr. Latham is expecting you. He is booking you and Kybo at the Mayflower Hotel. Thomas and I will remain in Kampala with our parents, while you do your business with Mr. Latham. On the seventh day, we will all fly to Nairobi to meet you. After a visit in Nairobi, we will go home to the tea farm together. Imagine it! All this traveling on just one ticket–and all for the one price! Isn't that wonderful?"

Paula and Thomas just looked at one another and smiled. Jon will always be Jon... impulsive, generous and delighted by himself. Paula had to admit it was a very good plan. But she hated to be parted from Tamubu, even for two or three days.

"How will our parents know to meet us in Kampala?" Thomas asked.

"I sent them a telegram... from that counter over there, yesterday."

"What did you say to them in the telegram?"

"I said: 'Letters will arrive soon. Will meet you in Kampala at the Victoria Hotel on April 7th at 2:30 p.m. Love, Jon.' Does that suit you?"

"Yes, you are very clever."

"I also have reservations for us at the Stanley House in Kisangani; and at the Victoria Hotel in Kampala."

"How did you manage all that? You were gone only a short time."

"It was a service included in the special promotion provided by Sabena for travelers going the full distance to Nairobi. Everything was included in the ticket surcharge–we still have to pay for the rooms, of course, but they took care of the reservations for us. I would have told you when I got back in the cab, but you were busy talking to Rubio. When we got back to the *Wind Drift*, I was intent on Tea and just forgot."

Paula looked at her watch. "It's 6:50 a.m. already, I think we should go to the gate and wait there."

The flight was boarding when they arrived, a Sabena employee led them out across the tarmac to the waiting plane. Thomas was stunned by the size of the plane: the huge wing span of almost a hundred feet, the sixty-five foot length and sixteen foot height, and thought: I don't have to worry about crashing in the forest; this plane will never get off the ground! Kybo, on the other hand, couldn't think at all. He was in a state of shock.

On board, the co-pilot checked their tickets before closing and locking the door. They were the last to board and the co-pilot directed them to the last two rows in the rear, which were marked 'Reserved'. Paula took the seat on the aisle, with Thomas at the window. Jon and Kybo sat in the row in front of them; with Kybo in the window seat, Jon sat on the aisle. The DC3 wings are quite broad where they attach to the fuselage under the cabin windows, and only the last seats have a downward view.

The co-pilot made sure all seat belts were fastened as he walked up the aisle, where he turned and said, "Ladies, gentlemen, thank you for flying Sabena-Belgian World Airlines today. We have a high ceiling today and will be flying below the clouds at about 7,000 feet. Our ETA for Kinshasha is O-ten-hundred. Please obey the seat belt sign at all times and keep your seat belt fastened when you are in your seat." He went into the flight deck and closed the door. Paula asked Jon, "Have you flown the Douglas DC-3 before?

"Yes, I have flown in the DC-3 before; but for Kybo, it is his first flight ever, how about you Paula?"

The plane began to taxi to the runway as Paula replied.

"It is my first flight in a DC-3. I flew to Europe last year in a Boeing 707. The bulk of my flying has been small aircraft with single or twin engines."

The pilot spoke through the intercom: "We are cleared for take off, all seat belts must be fastened, thank you."

They sat silently as the plane gathered speed down the runway and lifted off. The moment of flight, when the wheels left the ground, always gave Paula a thrill, no matter how many times it happened, as pilot or passenger.

She turned to Thomas who was looking out his window.

"Isn't taking-off a thrill?"

"Yes, it is. I didn't believe this big plane could do it."

"Believe it or not, there are much bigger planes than this one, but even so, it is still quite impressive when they leave the ground. The Wright brothers would be soooo amazed by today's aircraft!"

"Who are the Wright Brothers?"

"The men who built and flew the first plane off the ground... for fifteen seconds... and then crashed. But they didn't give up and we have their tenacity to thank for air flight today."

Paula leaned forward and said, "How are you doing Kybo? Did you watch the take-off from your window?

"Yes Missy, I did. When we went to the plane I looked down the runway. When I saw no plane bones, I had hope; when the plane was going so fast, I wondered if the forest just beyond was filled with plane bones, but then I thought: why would people get on planes if they crashed. So, I looked out my window and saw the miracle happen."

"Yes Kybo, this is an incredible experience." Thomas agreed.

"Bwana, everything that happens when I am with you is an incredible experience. I never knew life could be so different; I am trying to get used to it. Will we ever have an ordinary day again?"

Paula looked at Thomas who had a smile on his face. He was thinking what she was thinking. They had never heard Kybo speak so many words at one time–it was a window into his soul.

"Now that you mention it, our lives have been unusual. We will soon long for adventure again once we have arrived in Kenya."

"I will take you at your word, bwana. I will wait patiently and see."

Kybo looked out the window, thinking: Never, in all my days, would I have dreamed that I would fly across Africa in a plane; nor did I ever imagine running the gorge rapids of the Kom River in a canoe; nor did I ever think I would lose sight of land for days because I was on the sea in a ship; nor did I ever suppose that I would be the afisa (aide) to a medicine man who walked with the spirits.

I did not believe that I would ever like the dullness of the village. I always felt that there had to be something better in life than carving animals from ebony all day. I had no idea that going on a trading safari with Max Mason would change my life so completely.

I know I will never see Laalu again. She will be a good mother to someone else's children. She has been my good friend since I was twelve. I will have to write her a letter. Maybe Missy Paula will help me with it. She writes letters all the time. I don't regret leaving the village, but I do regret leaving Laalu. She would have enjoyed the adventures we have had, especially flying in this airplane.

PAULA THOUGHT ABOUT THE exchange and said to Thomas, "How are you doing? This is an act of courage for you, after your first experience."

"I, like Kybo, 'am just trying to get used to it'. It is so different from my first and only experience with flying. I don't really feel like I'm in an airplane. It is so much bigger, quieter and stronger... steady and very comfortable, with these big comfortable seats and curtains on the windows."

Paula smiled at his reply. She reached over and took his hand, then dropped her head to his shoulder and closed her eyes in tranquility.

It had been an early and busy morning, so Paula was soon napping. Not so Kybo and Thomas. The nascent passengers remained absorbed by the bird's-eye-view of the scenery below. Kybo felt the thrill of an eagle soaring, while Thomas was awed by the vast vista to the horizon and the incredible diversity of the land beneath them. He too, felt like the mighty eagle.

Jon sat and smiled smugly to himself. It had been worth the price to have the last seats reserved for them. On the DC3, the two rear seats are considered first class because they are the only ones where the view is not blocked by the wings.

About a half hour before the descent into Kinshasa, the co-pilot came on the intercom saying: "We will soon be on the approach to Kinshasa. For those traveling on to Kisangani with us, we are offering lunch. Today we will have ham and cheese sandwiches with mustard on dark bread, or peanut butter and grape jam on white bread. Both will be served with potato chips, cookies, lemonade or bottled water. Please indicate your choice on the paper you received with your ticket. I will pick them up after we have landed." Paula chose the ham and cheese, as did Jon. Kybo chose the peanut butter and jelly, as he had not tasted it before, and so did Tamubu, because he had not had peanut butter and jelly since he was ten years old.

It seemed no time at all before the "Fasten Seat Belts" sign started flashing. Thomas was a bit apprehensive about the landing of this big plane, and was therefore astounded, that he felt almost nothing when the wheels touched down. The passengers clapped and cheered. "Why are they doing that?" Thomas asked.

"It is a cheer for the pilot who did such a good job landing the plane so smoothly." Paula replied.

The plane taxied to the terminal, where the passengers were required to deplane during the refueling. The terminal was surprisingly modern and one and all they headed to the kiveo, (rest rooms–African style) after agreeing to meet at the coffee bar. Paula was the first to arrive and already had a cup of tea when Thomas and Kybo joined her. Jon had gone off to buy a book to read. It was a five-hour flight to Kisangani.

"The DC3 has seven rows of passenger seats–two seats on the right as you face forward–from the lavatory to the bulkhead–and a row of single seats on the left, from the door hatch to the bulkhead–and all were occupied. The four of them occupied the last two rows of double seats before the lavatory. Men in military uniforms occupied the single seats. Looking up from her puzzle, Paula watched a man in the first row get up to take something out of the overhead bin. Before he sat back down, he turned to face aft, speaking to the person in the seat behind him. Paula drew in a sharp breath and quickly lowered her head to look at her puzzle. Thomas sensed her tension and asked, "Is something wrong?"

"I thought I saw Mr. Hunter in the first row of the double seats. That couldn't be. It is an infringement on our agreement. Why would he be here?"

Thomas went up the aisle. Paula had not been mistaken. Not only was Mr. Hunter there, but Max was with him too. Thomas stopped and looked at Mr. Hunter saying, "Is this a big coincidence... or is your boss not interested in our offer? We didn't expect to see you–ever again. I'm sure you'll be glad to tell me where you are going and why."

"I don't have to tell you anything. We can go where we want, when we want. If you don't like it, get off the plane."

"My, my, how hostile; that's not a good sign. Let me say this, just once. If I see you again, for **any** reason, when we are off this plane, you will get what was promised you in the shower." Thomas returned to his seat and said to Paula. "You were right. It is Mr. Hunter and his boon companion, Max. I think it is just a coincidence. If they get off the plane in Kisangani, I will have to deal with them."

Paula asked, "What will you do?"

Thomas replied, "You do not want to know."

The DC-3 moved forward, the engines roared and the plane gathered speed. Before the "Fasten Seat Belts" sign turned off, Jon was opening his bag lunch, which was handed to him as he boarded the plane. Bottles of lemonade or water were sitting in cases inside the door and you were told to help yourself.

Jon said, "I don't know why I'm so hungry, it is only eleven in the morning."

Paula said, "We had breakfast at five in order to be at the airport by six-thirty. I'm hungry too."

Kybo, after a bite of his peanut butter and jelly sandwich

said, "It is so much taste! With the salty potatoes, it is a mouth treat."

Thomas smiled, remembering this favorite food of his childhood saying to Paula, "How do you like your sandwich?"

"It is potted ham and canned cheese... I don't know what I was thinking... but it is tasty. The bread, though, is freshly baked."

Thomas turned his attention to a National Geographic magazine, which had fascinating pictures of Kenya in the main article, which was about the Great Rift Valley. One of the pictures showed a tea farm and Thomas wondered if he could keep the magazine. It reminded him of his drawing that had won a prize so long ago. This was the first printed matter that he had seen in fourteen years. He was pleased with the magazine because of all the pictures, but he did not know some of the words. No one treks with books, so it was the area in which he was weakest. He thought: no one else will know that I did not understand all the words, only I know, but I must speak to Paula about this problem.

Paula awakened Thomas when they were on the descent into Kisangani. He had fallen soundly asleep after lunch. Paula had been napping off and on, as the complexity of the crossword puzzle made her sleepy. Jon and Kybo both had their eyes closed the entire time, so maybe they were sleeping too. This was the longest leg of the flight. They had passed through a time zone going east and lost an hour. It was after six p.m. in Kisangani when they deplaned.

The through passengers had to change planes for the leg to Kampala and Nairobi; and walked across the tarmac, with their luggage following on a cart. Thomas waited while the other passengers boarded the waiting plane, and then stepped in front of Mr. Hunter saying, "We have decided to take your advice and not reboard for Nairobi. Should we have contact with you again, in any way, before our scheduled meeting... the deal will be off!"

He could see the surprise in Mr. Hunter's eyes. Good, he thought, he needs to be shocked every now and again. At the foot of the stairway, he said, "Kybo, stay here until they close the door and the plane taxies to the runway. I will be in the terminal, with Jon and Paula, getting our luggage. When Kybo came into the terminal, he watched with Tamubu until the plane took off saying, "I wonder where they are going?"

"They are ticketed through to Nairobi. I asked the lady at the ticket counter saying, "I lent my reading glasses to Mr. Hunter and forgot to get them back. If he is going through to Nairobi, I can have someone pick them up there. Can you check his destination for me?"

She said, "Yes, he is ticketed through to Nairobi."

When they were in the air, Mr. Hunter said to Max. "I didn't expect that, did you?"

"No, but it was your suggestion. It might have given them the idea. Seems funny though, paying for four tickets to Nairobi and then getting off halfway."

"We couldn't get off either. He had that Nigerian waiting at the bottom of the steps. Mr. Athos said not to queer the deal, but to watch them. Once he pays me, I'm outta here; you going to stay or get out too?"

"I think I'll stay; I'd like to see what happens. You have a lot to lose; me, I'm just hired help. I didn't stalk or kidnap anyone, or break and enter either."

"You know Max, I like being a mercenary. I pick the jobs I want to do at a price that pays me well. I've never had to hurt someone physically; my facial scars usually scare people into giving in easily; only a few got hurt when they tried to bolt. I can get out now and still feel good about myself. If I were you, I'd get out too. There are things happening here that I cannot explain to you–you wouldn't believe me even if I tried. I think I will take the money, get out of the mercenary business, and open a bridge club in Florida."

Max thought: I feel a bit dubious too. Mr. Hunter had that note before we docked. It was written on Gallant Lady Stationery. Then, that man Thomas said, "I told you in my note...." How did he write a note on *Gallant Lady* stationery when he was aboard the *Wind Drift*? Now, he says, "If I see you again, you will get what I promised you in the shower." What shower? What promise? This is getting really weird... but

I have to find out what is going on here. Mr. Athos asked me to watch Mr. Hunter and I agreed. I think Mr. Hunter should get out. He's never been spooked before. It has affected his reasoning. He should never have suggested that they get off the plane. He gave them the out. Mr. Athos doesn't want to queer the deal before he has a chance to find out what exactly is involved. And... the money he has offered me is really good. I wonder if Manny still runs a day-trip boating business on the Congo River; I'll call him from Entebbe.

The Stanley Hotel was decorated in the late 1800's style. Paula looked at it with distaste. It was too fussy. There were huge ferns and uncomfortably low furniture everywhere. You'd think that by now, the stuff would have rotted or something. No one would purposely decorate in this overly ornate décor these days; but the guest rooms were a pleasant delight. They were richly utilitarian with a taste of Victorian that was livable. They had adjoining rooms with double doors opening from the bedrooms to the sitting room.

Entering the little parlor, Paula said, "This is a bit much for just two days. We will hardly ever be here. Where's Kybo?"

"He has a room on the other side of the hotel." Jon said. "He will meet us here for dinner at eight o'clock. I ordered for everyone. Is that agreeable?

"It's fine with me. I'd really like to go for a walk." Paula said, "Anyone interested in going with me?"

"I'll go with you... Jon?"

"You two go on, I'm going to take a soak before dinner."

"Okay." Paula said. "I have to change shoes, Thomas. Come over when you're ready to go."

"It will have to be a short walk Jon, it is almost seven now. Paula says we passed through a time zone and lost an hour."

Jon thought: I should have known that. I feel like a fifth wheel on this trip. I wonder how Kybo feels; but we can't do anything about the apartheid in hotel accommodations.

I'm now sure Thomas and Paula are in love–they just don't know it yet–or, if they do, they're keeping it low key. Where does that leave me? I've spent most of my life imagining what would happen when I found my brother. Now that I have, nothing is as I thought it would be... except between us–the harmony is still the same... that does make up for some of the differences.

I could never have known that Thomas would be a medicine man; never could have known that he would be enthralled with his new life; never imagined that he would only want to visit the life he had known as a boy; our parents will see that too. I don't know what I'm going to do if he chooses to return to the Zuri Watu... I will feel so lost.

Jon's naturally upbeat personality pulled him from his blue funk. No sense in giving him up before I have to though... I'll bathe later!

JON WENT TO GET Kybo while Paula and Thomas stopped by the concierge to get a walking map of Kisangani. "Are there any good places to see on a walking tour?"

The concierge was most helpful and recommended: "The Stanley Museum, which is now closed for the day. It has wonderful artifacts from Stanley's travels in a delightful diorama. The best shopping is on the street behind the hotel. There are many quaint shops there. European type stores are just down the street from the hotel."

"Are there day trips upriver to Boyoma Falls?"

"Yes, at the end of the street behind the hotel, there is a kiosk where the boat trips are booked." Paula and Thomas left the concierge just as Jon and Kybo arrived.

"We are all set. We have a good map. Let's go!" Paula said happily.

They walked to the street behind the hotel. Most of the quaint shops were closed for the day, but one or two were open and they browsed, making mental notes for tomorrow. Thomas was anxious to get to the kiosk where the tours on the Congo River to Boyoma Falls were booked. He took Kybo and left Jon and Paula browsing in a gift shop.

The man at the boat tours kiosk intrigued Tamubu. His face was dot-painted across his cheeks around his eyes and down his nose, in a design like bunting. He wore strings of beads criss-crossed on his chest and under his arms, with a large Ibis-feathered headdress. Tamubu could hear him singing a melodic chant softly to himself, as they approached. He stood immediately and said, "Good day to you sir. Can I interest you in a fascinating trip on the Congo River to the Boyoma Falls, which are also called the Stanley Falls? It is a trip to be remembered."

Tamubu replied. "How long is the trip?"

"We leave at nine in the morning and return to the pier at one in the afternoon. There is also a trip at two in the afternoon, which returns at six."

I would like to book four of your best seats. My brother will pay you in the morning. What tribe are you?"

The man was surprised, but he had already sensed a man of power and importance, and so replied. "I am Luba."

"I am Tamubu, Medicine Man from the Great Nations of the Zuri Watu. Kybo here is Ibo. He is my afisa (aide) in all things. We are pleased to meet you. How are you called?"

"My given name is Manchester. My father was piataz (top caretaker) for the Earl and named me in his honor. I am called Manny." Manny looked at his schedule and said, "I only have three first class seats left on the morning trip. I do have four seats available for the afternoon trip."

Kybo took Tamubu's arm. "Kigozi, I would be happy with second class seating, if you want to go in the morning."

Tamubu looked him in the eye. He was being honest. He smiled to himself. I think Kybo has had enough first class experiences to last him his lifetime; but he is just going to have to get used to it. He said to Kybo, "Nonsense, we will go together in the afternoon."

He said to Manny, "Book four first class seats for the afternoon tour. What services do you provide?"

"We provide coffee, tea and lemon water, crackers and cookies for everyone and tea sandwiches for first class. Bring sun lotion with you, mostly for the wind. There is a canopy over the first class seats. Bugs are not a problem."

Jon and Paula were no longer in the little shop; it had closed for the day. So Thomas and Kybo returned to the hotel.

Thomas saw them sitting near the entrance to the Lounge. "We are booked for the trip to Boyoma Falls, for two o'clock tomorrow afternoon. Does that suit you?" Jon and Paula said that was fine. "How did you pay the fares?" Jon asked.

"I told him you would pay him tomorrow, so don't forget your Travelers Checks." Jon had ordered lemon water for all of them and a tray of cheese and crackers and fruit. Thomas saw the packages on the floor, next to Paula and asked, "What did you buy?"

"We're not going to tell you. It's a secret." Paula replied.

Tamubu laughed, "I can see that I am going to have to be careful and not leave you two alone together too often. Jon loved to hatch plots when he was a boy. I'm sure he is at it again, using you to help him now."

Paula chuckled saying, "Jon, he has your number... but he doesn't know what we've done... yet."

THE NEXT MORNING THEY left early for the Stanley Museum. It was not only interesting, but fun too. The *talking buttons* for the miniature picture stories at each diorama thrilled Thomas and Kybo. Their delight enhanced Jon and Paula's pleasure in the pictorial display.

The shopping was a collector's dream. The quaint shops offered an assortment of African art that was simply exquisite. There was everything from intricate filigree necklaces, carved from tiny tubes of ivory and spaced with polished semi-precious stones; to large animal sculptures done in ebony, podocarpus, teak, mahogany and oak, using the natural colors of the woods in an intricate manner to simulate the coloring of the animals. The workmanship of the carvings was extraordinary. The designs and presentation of the works were original and creative. It was much better than going to an art gallery, for you could buy the things that pleased you at reasonable prices. Jon and Paula bought many things, which the shops were equipped to wrap, either for shipping, or to take with you as carry-on luggage.

All too soon, it was time to return to the hotel for lunch,

stash their parcels, and leave for the boat tour to the Boyoma Falls on the Congo River.

21

Letters

Lady Mary and Sir Peter ate breakfast together every morning in the sunny breakfast room on the east side of the house–just as the sun peeked over the sepele trees that edged the east lawn. Here, they discussed their plans for the day, for they usually did not see one another again until cocktails at seven in the evening, before dinner at eight.

After breakfast, over a second cup of tea, Lady Mary conferred with the household staff: the housekeeper and cook about the needs of the day. The cook received her weekly menus each Monday, but checked each morning for unexpected changes.

On the verandah, over coffee with his farm manager, Sir Peter discussed the schedules of the tea business: new bushes to be planted; cultivation and fertilization of the plants and vines; the harvesting of the tea leaves or grapes; and the progress of current rotation projects.

Sir Peter liked to oversee the plantation from horseback and did so each day after the meeting with his manager. He noted anything that he thought needed attention in a small spiral book and these notations were the basis of the morning discussions each day. The farm manager dealt with the overseer who was in charge of the workers. Sir Peter's system worked well. On his rides, he made notes, which kept the workers on their toes. He never failed to notice the extra effort of any one of his employees. His observations were communicated by the manager to the overseer, who used the praise to obtain a cooperative spirit of effort among the men and women.

Sir Peter was mounted and long gone before Lady Mary

made it down to the barn each morning to work with her horses. She loved the training more than the competition, but still competed locally in several disciplines. She had a marvelous Dutch Warmblood stallion to cover her Andalusian, Lusitano and Arabian mares. His size [17.2hh] and his superior conformation were passed to his offspring. The mares imparted the flash, agility and speed of their breeds to produce spectacular sport horses with super abilities. The horses that did not have the required mental set for dressage were used for other disciplines. All excelled at whatever task they were trained to do. As a result, she had more buyers for her horses, than she had horses to sell.

Pompito helped her work the horses each day. The other lads, Suffo and Abumi, cleaned stalls, groomed horses and cared for equipment. Pompito helped Lady Mary longe-line the horses. He also rode the green horses with Lady Mary on the lunge line until they knew the leg and seat aids that went with each movements. Reining was taught on the longe-lines as the proper head carriage and collected body movements were better learned without a rider.

Each day of training was different. New things were repeated and done at least three times correctly before moving on to something fun, like cavalletti. Work in hand was done each day before and after any learning session.

Doing first, the easy work they knew well gave them the confidence to try new work... and if the new work was less than perfect, going over easy, or already learned work, afterwards ended the session on a positive note. Some days, there were cones or parallel rails; some days, horizontal rails were laid at varied distances, which required the horse to lengthen or shorten their stride to develop agility and finesse. Young horses were worked on the round-pen rail, running free, at the beginning of a training session to rid them of too much exuberance, and to bring their minds to the task at hand. As the horses progressed in training, new, and sometimes unusual, obstacles were added to encourage their acceptance of new things. This trained the young horses to be inquisitive, not fearful, when something different was added to the regular routine.

It was a delicate line: to keep all the learning available; adding enough new work to keep the horse mentally involved; keeping the horses interested in what they were asked to do by rewarding them immediately (with the spoken words "good boy/girl") and with change, when they did it correctly two or three times.

Lady Mary used voice commands as well as the usual aids. She believed that "...your voice is the one aid that is always instantly available..."

Each day, there were three horses to work at a given stage in their training. Horses were not worked every day, but every third day. No training was done on Sunday. This meant that only nine horses could be in training. The longest days were the days 'up'. Riding three horses usually took an hour each. A session that was too short made young horses impatient with the successive sessions. Sessions that were too long made them fretful and difficult. By working every third day or twice a week, Lady Mary found the horses eager and willing in their training. Horses that were doing particularly well in training, were often the ones chosen for the Sunday afternoon pleasure ride. These gatherings of friends and family for a slow pleasure ride though the forest trails and along the edges of the hay fields often put a contented and cooperative attitude on a young horse's psyche that lasted their whole life.

Lady Mary usually returned to the house for lunch around one. Sir Peter took a packed lunch and thermos each day, saying, "It takes too much of my time to take the horse to the stable and then clean up–just for a sandwich." Rather than eat alone in the breakfast room, Lady Mary had a tray in her study where she kept track of the horses: their pedigrees; their training; their feed and vaccinations: their likes and dislikes; good days and problem days. It was where she kept track of the household accounts and wrote her correspondence. The mail, that arrived while she was down in the barn, was placed in a box on a table inside her study door. (The local farmers each took a day of the week, Monday through Friday, when they sent a driver to Nairobi for supplies, and also picked up the mail.) Lady Mary showered and put on a clean shirt and breeches, her preferred daytime attire, before she went to her study for lunch where she usually spent the entire afternoon.

Once in a while, she fell asleep while reading. The house was so quiet. The open windows, during the day, allowed a breeze to flow through the rooms. The windows were closed at night on the ground floors, even though they still retained the decorative, but functional wrought iron bars that had been installed during the Mau-Mau uprising.

Today, her mailbox was almost full. Lady Mary quickly scanned each envelope until she reached the telegram, which she set aside and then a large envelope from Jon, also set aside. There were two other letters, both from England, a note from a local resident, possibly an invitation. The rest were bills or horse related correspondence.

Turning back to the telegram, she opened it. It was from Jon, and the message was cryptic. She then opened the express envelope from Jon. Inside were two envelopes. One said, "Open this envelope first."

Dear Mom and Dad,

I have had the most extraordinary experiences since I left you to go with Max Mason on his trading safari.

In one village we encountered an American girl who had been abducted from the beach where she was marooned alone on a yacht after the tsunami that hit Lagos. You might have read about the missing scientist in the newspapers. The Chief would not consider letting her go. After desultory trading, we were marched from the village back to our camp by fifty warriors. The next day Max set up a military rescue effort, which failed because the American girl had escaped during the night. Most of the men in the village were out looking for her. Can you believe it? The natives came back without a clue as to her whereabouts!

Max and I, of course, could do nothing more and headed out to our next village to trade. I could not sleep. It bothered me that the American girl had gone off in the rainforest; this unfortunate woman was alone, unarmed and uninformed. When asked, Max let me take four men, his cook and a radio to go and look for her.

It was quite something, but I actually found her. She was resting in the lee of a native traveling hut. She had been making her way back to her yacht in the cove. She had injured her ankle in an encounter with a rampaging bull ape.

Even more unusual, the American girl had found a traveling companion, who was well acquainted with wilderness travel. The man was walking across Africa from Cameroon to Kenya. We joined forces and traveled to the beach together. It was where the yacht was marooned, but when we arrived, the yacht was gone.

A few days later, I had the very best day of my life! I became certain that Tamubu, who was the man traveling with Paula, was your son and my brother, Thomas.

Lady Mary could read no more. The tears flowed liberally down her cheeks. She sniffled and blew her nose. A big lump had blocked off her breath and made her heart pound. She closed her eyes and thought: Can it really be? Has he truly found Thomas? How can he be sure? Oh, dear God, please let it be true. She picked up the letter and continued reading through her tears.

Thomas was on his way home to us. He had only a few months before, found out that he had another family in Kenya. It was when his adopted mother was sick unto death that she told him how he came to be with them. Thomas was sick for two years with Malaria after he was found wandering in the rainforest by Zuri Watu scouts. By the time he was well, he remembered us only as dreams he had had while he was sick.

Mom and Dad, you are going to love him so much. He is so wonderful. He is so talented. He is so kind and helpful. He is the son you would have made of him if you had done the job. He is different, to be sure, but I wouldn't change a hair on his head nor an idea in his mind.

The other envelope is a letter from Thomas for you. I love you. We will see you soon. Love Always, Jon

With shaking hands, she opened the other envelope. She was instantly startled when she saw once again his beautiful handwriting, and read through her tears:

Dear Mother and Father,

I am so happy that I will soon see you again, but I think I should tell you a bit of what has happened to me in the years that I have been lost to you.

The plane had engine trouble and landed in the river. It hit a tree that had fallen across the river and killed the pilot and my teacher. I was uninjured and was able to climb out of the plane to the tree trunk and then to land. I was alone for two days until I saw some natives, and followed them to make sure they were not cannibals before I approached them. They gave me food and water and told me there were no tribes in the area; that I would have to go home with them. I agreed, but on the way to the village, I became very sick, and they had to carry me for the rest of the way.

I was very sick for a long time, longer than four rainy seasons. Nanoka took care of me night and day during all that time and I came to love her because she loved and cherished me.

A Missionary Doctor gave Nanoka medicine (quinine) that healed me. After such a long time being sick, I remembered you only as dreams I had while I was sick. Nanoka and Sashono, who is the Chief of the Zuri Watu, had adopted me, for they had no children of their own. My tribal name 'Tamubu' means 'Sweet Gift.' I was happy, man and boy. I was taken by Manutu as a protégé, which is a great honor, as Manutu is the Medicine Man of the Great Zuri Watu and his skill is known and respected in much of Africa.

From the time I was twelve, for ten years, I learned how to care for, and heal the sick. Manutu taught me all the ways of nature and the gifts God has given man in the plants, animals, water and stars. I loved the learning.

When Nanoka was near death, she told me the story that the Missionary Doctor had told her of a lost boy from Kenya. She told me to go and find you, and to tell you that she was sorry that she loved me too much to give me back to you, once I was well. She hopes you will forgive her for being so selfish.

On my trek to Kenya, I saw a woman traveling in the trees. She was as agile as a monkey and seemed so at home in the trees that I watched and followed her for days. One day she strolled into an area of lion dens, and after I chased the lions away, we talked high up in an old oak tree. She was lost and needed my help to get back to her yacht in the cove, where the Ndezi had abducted her. I agreed to help her.

We were almost to the cove, when Jon showed up at our camp. He had met Paula when she was a captive of the Ndezi; but his partner had not been able to persuade the chief to let her go. When Jon heard that she had escaped into the jungle alone, he went looking for her and found us both.

We were going to travel overland to Kenya, but our plans changed when Paula injured her ankle.

This is just a short story. It is so you will know that I was well cared for and an important member of the tribe that adopted me. I was happy all the time–once I was over the Malaria–and wished for no other life than the one I had.

Since I met Paula, so many forgotten memories have returned to me; and once I knew Jon was my brother, a floodgate of buried memories came back to me in our conversations about our childhood.

We have much to tell each other... I never forgot my father reading bedtime stories to me. I never forgot watching a smiling woman riding a dancing horse. I just thought they were recurring dreams–and I treasured those dreams.

Your Son, Thomas

Lady Mary read and reread the letters. She heard the Grandfather clock chime the hour in the hall. It is only two o'clock. I must let Peter know right away. She stuffed the letters and telegram in her shirt at the waist, while she ran to the pantry and washed her face. She called Pompito on the intercom, saying, "Saddle *The Wizard* for me. I'll be down in two minutes. Do you know where Sir Peter is? ... Find out please; send Suffo or Abumi to find out now and hurry!"

"Helen? Are you there?"

"Yes, Lady Mary. What can I do for you?"

"I have to go and find Sir Peter. Please answer the phone... or get George to do it." She ran out the door.

Helen just stared out the door, amazed. She didn't know Lady Mary could run that fast.

Pompito had the horse saddled for her as she ran up. *The Wizard* caught her sense of urgency and pranced around. She took a moment to calm him and then took a leg-up from Pompito as Suffo came running across the yard. She walked *The Wizard* to him and said, "Did you find out where Sir Peter is?"

"Yes, maam; he's in da so'th field where dey's plantin' new bushes t'day."

She had a rule: 'walk the first mile out and the last mile back' but today, she let *The Wizard* into an easy trot once they were out of the yard. It was two miles to the south field, but her anxiety made it seem like fifty. It only took ten minutes until she was at the edge of the south field. She saw *Midnight Rider* tied in the shade of a tree and stood in her stirrups to look over the field. There he was, directing the planting himself. She trotted *The Wizard* around the edge of the field to the row where Peter was supervising the work. "Peter!" she called and had to press her lips together to keep from crying again. Peter looked up, astonished to see her, and hurried to the end of the row.

"What's wrong? Mary. You look like you've been crying." The tears flowed again. Peter took hold of *The Wizard's* reins and Mary slid off and rushed to him. He put his arms around her and thought: What is going on? Mary never comes out to the fields. She usually sends someone to find me. He said,

"Let's take *The Wizard* over to the shade with *Midnight Rider*. Then we can talk."

Before Mary took *The Wizard's* reins back, she took the letters out of her shirt. "I think you will want to sit down before you read these letters." In a few minutes, they had the horse tied to the tree next to his barn buddy. They sat down in the shade and Mary handed Peter the telegram. He read it quickly and held out his hand for the letter.

She saw his jaw muscles working and then he closed his eyes. Mary said, "I know... I know, but it is true. Thomas is alive."

Peter opened his eyes and finished the letter from Jon. His eyes sparkled with unshed tears as he held out his hand for the letter from Thomas. As Mary had done, he startled at the remembered graceful handwriting, and then reread the letter several times. There was a pressure in his chest–a joy so great that he felt as if he would burst.

Peter held Mary tightly. "Our boy... he is alive... he is well; he is coming home." They just sat holding each other for a long time. Each lost in thought. Mary thought her agonizing wound had healed in the past fourteen years. The first four years were dreadful. Peter went off to look at dead boys for two years and then had to stop going. His nightmares had been terrible. The screaming in his sleep had forced Mary to sleep on the third floor in Thomas's old room.

After Thomas was lost, Jon came down to the guest room on the second floor that was next to his nanny's room. Peter gave Jon a native teacher to interest his mind and to assuage his grief. The nanny then left to work for a neighbor with small children. It was a good change for all of them.

That was when she had purchased *Diablo*, the Dutch Warmblood stallion as a yearling colt. She needed to be busy and work to exhaustion during the day to be able to sleep at night.

Peter reread Thomas's letter again. He knew he was going to like his son. The letter told him of his strength of character. It told him the boy, now man, was straightforward and uncomplicated. He was kind and considerate. He said, "I think he is a bit afraid we will not like him."

"How could he ever think such a thing?"

"It was the way he praised Manutu and his work. Natives raised Thomas, so his ways will be like those of a native. He might remember how much the natives aggravated me when he was young; how I railed against their laziness and inability to take pride in their work. I know all those things have changed now. We have good men here. They now realize that men of worth do an honest day's work and support their families. It was not always so."

Mary said, "He had a native teacher here too. He will remember Kaizii. Jon will tell him things have changed. Jon–he must be the happiest man in the world–all he ever wanted was to go and find Thomas. He dedicated his life to learning what he needed to know so he could look for him. I think he learned to speak every language in Africa."

"Well, if we are to catch a plane from Nairobi for Kampala on Tuesday, I'd better get back to work. I'll have to do a week's planning with Simmons. I wonder how long we will be gone."

"I am going to plan on being gone to the end of next week. Nothing in my life is more important than being with our firstborn son again."

"Of course, you're right! It will be what it will be. Simmons can handle things until we get back."

22

Kisangani

IT WAS A LOVELY afternoon for the tour to Stanley Falls, for the morning haze had given way to sunshine. A small ferry had been converted for the express pleasure and comfort of the sightseers, with small tables between padded swivel chairs, which were fastened to the upper deck over the wheelhouse and facilities. The seats were arranged in groups of two around the canopied deck and provided a panoramic view. Kybo was seated with a lone missionary. Jon was seated next to Mr. Harold Holmesby. His daughter, the lovely Miss Anna Louise Holmesby was seated in front of him beside her mother, Julia Holmesby. The family was on Anna's college graduation tour. Anna Holmesby mentioned that they were from Wiltshire at Swindon. Jon was delighted. He told Anna that their ancestral home was in Berkshire near Lyford in the Cotswold Hills. We are almost neighbors.

THE FALLS WERE SIMPLY spectacular. The awesome abundance of water cascading from such a great height made a deafening noise, which eliminated all conversation. The dense spray from the falling water created an ideal habitat for a spectacular profusion of flowers. The constant mist encouraged moss to grow on the trees, and dotting the moss like sequins were tufts of brilliant parti-colored orchids, dripping long stems of exquisite flowers in a lavish display. The movement of the boat changed the scenery like a kaleidoscope, with shafts of light filtering here and there to make glistening rainbows, which shimmered in the mist for a few moments until others took their place. The opulence of the grandeur was overwhelming... in variety, scope and magnitude.

To and from the falls, there was the lush scenery on the uninhabited islands, which dotted the Congo River. Each island teemed with a plethora of diverse and exotic birds, the sounds of their calls and their stunning mating displays. It was almost a sensory overload. Among the species she saw, Paula recognized the African Sand Martin, a brown and gray bird the size of a robin, gathering mud from the banks for a nest. In a boggy lea amidst the undergrowth, she saw a number of Finfoot: large birds similar to the Cormorant or Grebe that are shaped like mammoth ducks. Some were swimming through the reedy growth with only their heads above water–possibly walking on the bottom with their oversized and long toed web feet, to churn up the thick silt for edible tidbits. She saw the flashy kingfishers, the dull brown and gray grosbeaks, striking weavers with their bright yellow breasts, and vividly colored doves and pigeons with parrots in sparkling colors of iridescent green, red and gold, and black wing stilts with long flamingo-like legs and long tapering bills, like thin straws.

Yet, it was only one lone dove that enchanted Jon–the demure Miss Anna Louise Holmesby.

"We are staying at an English Guest House." Julia Holmesby said, "We like to meet fellow travelers wherever we go. We enjoy the casual acquaintances as much as the traveling." Before they disembarked, Paula said to Julia, "We would be delighted if you would join us for dinner at the Stanley Hotel this evening–cocktails at seven. We'll meet you in the lobby." Julia was pleased and accepted the invitation, which overjoyed Jon.

On the walk back to the hotel, Jon was once again his bombastic self. He insisted on stopping at the florist's shop to have small orchid corsages and a carnation boutonniere sent to the Holmesby's Guest House. Paula and Thomas walked about the shop, intrigued by the variety of hothouse flowers.

Listening to Paula's voluble delight over the exquisite blooms, Jon decided to send a corsage to Paula and boutonnieres for themselves. Kybo would be non-plused, a thought which made Jon chuckle to himself

THE EVENING BECAME A not-to-be-forgotten memory. Harold and Julia were good conversationalists, and purred their pleasure over the flowers. Jon and Anna Louise often talked softly together in their own little world. Anna Louise told Jon about the delightful jitney tour of Kisangani saying: "It is an attractive town with all the charming red-roofed houses, and many of them have such lovely gardens. You get to see so much more on a motor tour, rather than a walking tour. We took the tour from the airport when we arrived. Maybe, you could take the tour on the way to the airport, tomorrow morning."

Kybo had dined with them for dinner. Thomas and Jon were quite pleased that the Holmesbys had not made Kybo feel out of place, but had shown a keen interest in his position with Thomas. Kybo's grasp of English often left him unsure when the conversation went back and forth so fast; so he was relieved to be able to excuse himself when the meal was finished.

On the way to the lounge for coffee and dessert, Jon asked Anna to join him while he made reservations for the same tour in the morning. It was then convenient for them to sit at a nearby table alone. Anna laughed often for Jon was being effervescent and irresistible.

THOMAS AND HAROLD DISCUSSED butterflies. The variety in Africa was stupendous. Harold showed him his log where he had sketched several species that were new to him. Thomas told him their names, larval and pupa stages and genus. Harold was delighted and scribbled in the notations.

Julia talked to Paula about horses, which were her passion, saying, "I'm a member of a Hunt Club in England, and try to make the Saturday hunts. I have a passion for riding. I did a fifty mile Quiltie in Australia on a borrowed mount last summer... what with it being winter down under when it is summer in England. I would like to do more Endurance riding, but my time to condition a horse properly is limited by my job as a school principal. Right now I'm on sabbatical year. That is one of the reasons we chose Africa. None of the teachers at school have ever had any first-hand experience in Africa. And, I must say, there are quite a few things that we have experienced so far that would be hard to put in a text."

"Where is your next stop from Kisangani?" Paula asked.

"We are headed to Kampala and then to Nairobi."

Paula smiled, "That is our itinerary too. Do you know where you will be staying?"

"Yes, the Lake Guest House in Kampala and the Mayflower Hotel in Nairobi."

Paula replied, "We are staying at the Mayflower Hotel too! What is your itinerary?"

"Let me see; ah, here it is: we leave Kisangani on Wednesday morning, the 6th of April, and arrive in Kampala at noon; we are there Wednesday, Thursday and leave at noon on Friday, the 8th for Nairobi, arriving Nairobi late afternoon. We are in Nairobi until Tuesday, the 12th, leaving on an early flight for Moçambique in Mozambique and a boat tour to Madagascar; a flight to Goborone in Botswana and the Kalahari; then Cairo, Tripoli, Algiers, Rabat and then home."

"Sounds wonderful; call me Thursday morning, after you arrive at the Mayflower. Jon and Thomas might be there by then."

"You're going on alone, then?

"Kybo is going with me to Nairobi. I have business there. Thomas and Jon will join us when they are finished here."

"Will you be going to England in May when Jon's sisters, Hanna and Sara, graduate from college?"

"Julia, I have no idea what I'll be doing two weeks from now... let alone two months. We have so many irons in the fire. But I want to be there... so if I can, I will."

"We would love for you to visit us, if you do come to England. Let me give you our number and address."

THE REST OF THE evening hurried away. All too soon Julia said,

"My, what a delightful evening this has been. We thank you so much for inviting us to dinner, but the hour has grown late. We must be off. Harold, Anna, it is time to say adieu. These lovely people have an early day tomorrow."

Paula said, "Thank you for coming on such short notice."

Julia replied, "That is one of the pluses about travel. You have the flexibility of doing what pleases you most, with little notice."

Jon walked the guests to the lobby door and saw them into a cab. Paula and Thomas sat chatting about the pleasant evening, while they waited for Jon to come back. Paula asked, "Did you really enjoy all that talk about butterflies?"

"I did. I have a huge butterfly collection back in the village. Manutu helped me collect them. He likes butterflies too. I listened to you talking with Julia with one ear. I did not know that you also competed on horses. Is there anything that you haven't done?"

"Yes, but I hope to remedy that soon." She gave Thomas an alluring smile.

He liked the twinkle in her eyes and replied, "Soon, will not be soon enough."

Jon returned saying, "I thought you two would have gone up by now. I would have missed you sitting in here except that I left my mechanical pencil on the table. Wasn't that a fine evening?"

"Yes, we were just saying what a nice time we had." Paula said as she rose to go to her room; adding, "But Julia was right. We have an early day tomorrow."

Jon had arranged that Kybo meet them for breakfast at eight in the morning.

THE JITNEY TOUR WAS all that Anna Louise had promised. The tour guide was an expert at making facts and figures interesting. He started out with the comment: "No African is happy under foreign domain in his country. Once he is educated, he will want to rule himself."

Jon said, "We are leaving Zaire, and going to Uganda.

Do you know anything about Uganda?" The tour driver, a transplanted Ugandan, smiled and replied:

"Uganda is 99% African of Bantu, Nilotic and Hamitic origins. Uganda is Swahili for Buganda.

"Originally Uganda was thought to be unfit for European habitation due to the tsetse fly, so it was avoided by whites. The potentates of the four major provinces of Uganda devised a policy that excluded whites from ownership of land. The policy exists to this day. Uganda has almost 6 million natives, 50,000 Indians, who are mostly tradesmen, and 8,000 British. Neither the Indians nor the British are land owners except in minor instances.

"Uganda is a Socialist country, on a par with England. In 1953 the King of Buganda, which is one of the four major provinces of Uganda, was dethroned and exiled by the acting British Governor. This caused a major political crisis in a once very peaceful country. Sadly, the political unrest and turmoil exists to this very day in one form or another.

"In 1908 Winston Churchill advocated harnessing the power of the Nile River. Forty years later, his advice was finally acted upon. The Source of the Nile is Ripon Falls at Jinja, the northernmost point of Lake Victoria. The Ripon Falls were flooded out of existence by the Owen Falls Hydroelectric project, which Her Majesty Queen Elizabeth formally opened on April 30, 1954. Because of the strong feelings against the British for exiling the King of Buganda, the people of Uganda refused to show up to honor her during her visit.

"The western side of Uganda is bordered by the Ruwenzori Mountains, known as Monts Mitumba or Mountains of the Moon. Ptolemy had been told of these mountains by travelers, in the 2nd century A.D. He thought they were the source of the Nile River. While run-off from the mountains does contribute to the flow of the Albert Nile, it is not the source. The Monts Mitumba remained mostly unknown until modern times, when Stanley explored them in 1875. To the north of Uganda is the Sudan and vast swamps. Along the entire western border are the mountains. Beyond them are the dark forests of Zaire, formerly the Congo. On the east is Kenya. On the south is Lake Victoria, which is the second largest lake in the world, after Lake Superior, which is exceeded in size only by the Caspian Sea. On the south, too, is Rwanda, from Lake Victoria to the Monts Mitumba."

Jon said, "I say, you are an encyclopedia of knowledge. What do you know about Kampala?"

Pleased by the compliment, the tour guide said, "I began by giving tours in Kampala, so I can highlight Kampala for you, if you like."

"Yes, please do. We are leaving for Kampala today and might not have the time to do a Kampala tour." Paula replied.

"Lake Victoria covers an area the size of Ireland, 26,000 square miles and lies at an elevation of 4,000 feet. It is dotted with islands, which are dense with the tsetse fly and uninhabitable.

"The water of the lake is infested with bilharzia, which is a deadly microbe that enters the human body through cuts and bodily orifices. The lake is also teeming with hippopotami and crocodiles. On sailing the waters, one is exposed to mbwa flies that carry onchoceriasis, which causes blindness. The flies are scent seekers, so they can be avoided by taking large doses of chlorophyll.

"Entebbe is an island in Lake Victoria, off the shore of the mainland at Kampala. Kampala is the Ugandan seat of government. Entebbe is the British counterpart and the location of all the official British buildings, including Government House, as well as the residences for the British elite and the celebrated botanical gardens. Entebbe has one of the most modern airports in Africa although the airport is remote and surrounded by thick jungle.

"Kampala, like Rome, has seven hills. Three of the hills feature churches: Catholic, Anglican and an Islamic Mosque. Another hill is occupied by the University College of east Africa, Makerere College. It was the only school with University rank between Khartoum and Johannesburg until the building of a University at Salisbury in Southern Rhodesia... hence, Rhodes Scholars. Near Kampala, at Budo, is a preparatory school for boys and girls, founded in 1906. It is named King's College.

So, you see, we have been educating our young people for a long time. It originated as a school for the sons of chiefs; but it was soon found extremely useful to include the daughters as well. Another hill is occupied by the Kabaka's palace.

"You must make a tour of the Owen Falls Hydroelectric Scheme when you are in Kampala. The construction is simply amazing and the workings are quite interesting. Well, here we are at the airport. Thank you for joining me today. I hope you enjoyed the tour."

Jon gave the tour guide/taxi driver a big tip. The tour had been even more interesting than Anna said it was, with the added information about Uganda and Kampala.

THE DC3 AWAITING THEM lacked a pressurized cabin, which would be necessary to fly over ten thousand feet; so it flew southeast from Kisangani to Bunia Pass at the southern end of Lake Edward, around the lake, then northeast towards Lake George, and then east to Entebbe, which lies on the equator at four thousand feet.

From the DC3, which is affectionately referred to as a 'tree trimmer', because it flies well at very low altitudes, the seven hills of Kampala were clearly visible as the plane circled on the approach. It was easy to distinguish the mosque with its six minarets from the churches. The college was a sprawling collection of low buildings and treed walkways. Inside the palace walls, the palace itself had a huge central courtyard with stone fountain and gardens. The entire palace was surrounded by exotic formal gardens, each with a central courtyard and statuary fountains, with small gazebos scattered about. While circling for a direct approach to the runway, the vastness of Lake Victoria was visible, for there was no end in sight, just some scattered islands. Not visible from the air was The Owen Falls Hydroelectric Scheme, which harnessed the overflow of Lake Victoria, for Jinja was sixty miles east and a bit north of Kampala.

The Victoria Hotel lobby was almost a carbon copy of the Stanley Hotel. Paula thought: Where do they get all this awful stuff? I wonder if it comes over from England for free...

she smiled at the thought of people in England gladly piling horrible old Victorian furniture on the sidewalk for pickup to Africa... while the concierge told Jon, "There are two trips to the Owen Falls Hydroelectric Scheme. One goes by bus on the main road, but it is fully booked for tomorrow. The other goes on secondary roads through the bush." It took only a moment to decide that through the bush would be fine; with Jon asking, "What method of transportation is used?"

"The bush tour uses modified Land Rovers. They seat six to eight adults comfortably. Both of the back rows have a wide sunroof hatch, where you can stand up through the roof to take pictures. It is the better tour, in my opinion, if you are not in a hurry; it is about two hours longer.

"What time does the tour leave?"

"It leaves at nine a.m. too. It will take two to three hours longer, depending on how often you stop for pictures. In one or two places, you will be able to get out and hike up hills to see the grand vistas. It is a good way to see and to get a feel for Africa. Since the Land Rover takes longer to get to Jinja, the other tour will be gone when you arrive."

Jon and Thomas smiled at each other knowingly. The concierge was so earnest in his descriptions, wanting to make sure they would be happy with the tour; that he noticed not at all.

After settling in their rooms, they went out for a stroll of the tourist shops in Kampala. It was a lovely evening. The direct rays of the sun were dimmed early by the twelve thousand foot Monts Mitumba on the west, which ran from Lake Tanganyika in northern Zambia all the way up to Lake Albert and along the Albert Nile in Uganda; a distance of more than nine hundred miles, with some of the peaks in the chain soaring over seventeen thousand feet high.

The businesses closed at six p.m., but many of the artifacts shops stayed open for the tourist trade until eight p.m. All of the businesses closed from noon to two in the afternoon for manyoya (a nap).

Paula took hold of Thomas' hand while they walked. He was surprised, and then quite pleased, and squeezed her hand gently, which solidified Paula's determination to be alone with him somehow, before she left for Nairobi. She knew that she was going to have to set the pace of the relationship. More than anything, she wanted Thomas to hold her again as he had on their trek back to the cove when she needed his help. As they browsed the shops, her mind conjured up ways to make it happen... then fate lent a hand.

Jon said, "I'm parched. Is anyone else thirsty? Here's a nice pub, I could go for a pint."

Thomas laughed, "What is a pint?"

"Slang expression for a mug of beer." Jon replied.

"I do not know this beer, but I would like a glass of water." They went into the pub and settled at a table near the front window. Jon went to the bar and placed the order: one beer, two waters and one tea. "Do you have a men's room?"

"Yes, in the rear, the door that says: 'kiveo'." Jon was dumbfounded by the facilities, which was a hole in the floor and a can of lime. There was a rusty stained sink with only a cold-water tap–no soap–no paper towels. I think we must drink our drinks and leave here quickly. Jon had seen this primitive type of accommodations before, but never in a restaurant or pub.

When Jon returned to the table, he held his glass up to the light, in the manner of a toast and said, "Drink up me hearties." Actually, he was looking to see if the glass mug looked clean. A group of men had entered the bar while he was in the 'hole-in-the-floor'. They were sitting at the bar. Jon heard a distinctive voice say, "Blast, this isn't ale, it's mead; I hate mead!" Jon tasted his beer, which was ginger beer and laughed, as he looked at the back of the man who hated mead. I think I know that man. He sounds like a dorm-mate, Paul Abbott. He too hated mead. Trying not to stare, Jon kept his eye on the fellow, who finally turned to look at several Ugandans who came in. By Jove, it is Paul Abbott.

Jon stood up and said, "Excuse me, please," to Paula and Thomas and went over to speak with Paul. He stood behind him and whispered in his ear, "Whatever you do, do not use the men's room." Paul turned to face him and he lit up.

"Jon! What are you doing here? Same as the rest of us, I'd wager, the trade fair at Makerere College."

"As a matter-of-fact, no; I know nothing about a trade fair at Makerere College. What is it about?"

"It is an Expo for those that would like a piece of the Ugandan pie. Uganda is rich in cotton, coffee, minerals, wood and wood products, Cola nuts, palm oil and rubber. The Ugandans are looking for modern fixtures and machines. England, France, America and Germany all have representatives here. So, if you're not here for the trade fair, what are you doing in Kampala?"

"I am here with my brother, a friend Paula, and Kybo who is aide to my brother."

"Brother? I thought you only had twin sisters. I never heard you mention a brother."

"It is a long story. Where are you staying for the trade fair?"

"Believe it or not, we are staying in the dorms. It is spring break at the school, and the students go home... taking their personal possessions with them. The cafeteria is serving food for the fair, but if you want a pint, you have to go to town. You should come up and see the trade fair. It is quite interesting."

"I would like that. When would be a good time?"

"Well, we are just heading back. It goes to eight p.m. today. Tomorrow is the last day. It's open from eight a.m. to noon and two p.m. to eight p.m."

"We are going to the Owen Falls Hydroelectric Scheme tomorrow morning; how about late afternoon, say, around four, four-thirty?"

"Just follow the signs to the fair. We'll be there, waiting for you."

Jon returned to his table saying, "That's a fellow from school. We were in the same dorm and several clubs together. The saying, 'The more you travel, the smaller the world gets,' is certainly true. We are going to meet again tomorrow after our tour."

Paula smiled happily saying, "If everyone is finished... it's already after six and I'm desperate for a bath before dinner."

THE RIDE BACK FROM the Owen Falls Hydroelectric Scheme on the improved road was only a little bit better than the road they had taken through the bush. The difference as Paula saw it was that the washes had corrugated metal pipes in them with large stones filling the gaps between metal and bank to make bridges over the gullies. It was still just a dirt road. She actually enjoyed the morning trip out better. It was a roller coaster ride going through the stony watercourses and back up the steep sides of the washes. It had felt good to get back to the savannah and woods. She hadn't realized how much she had enjoyed trekking back to the cove, or how much she now missed it.

At four thousand feet or better, there was no rainforest but what was called woodlands. The trees were not as tall and there was a great deal of brush on the ground; particularly thorn bushes and the ubiquitous wait-a-bit, with its curved, talon-like thorns that caught hold of you and wouldn't let go.

There were patches of tall grassy savannah, then woodlands, back to savannah again. The Land Rovers passed within a thousand feet of a herd of elephants that barely looked at them. Resting in the patchy shade of baobob trees, they saw a pride of lions, with adorable three-month-old cubs playing with their mother's tail and each other. They too ignored the Land Rovers. Zebra abounded, as did Thompson gazelles. These herds moved away from the Land Rovers, maintaining an emotionally safe distance, but they did not flee.

Paula saw several ostriches running with huge strides; they seemed to be the only animals they encountered that were bothered by the Land Rovers... if indeed, it was the Land Rovers that had set them off.

Again the terrain changed and they came upon an area dense with baobab trees and only because they moved, did they see some of the heads of the giraffes.

In a rocky outcropping filled with wild fig bushes, they saw a troop of baboons who raced to nearby trees as the Land

Rovers approached. They sat on the tree limbs and screeched loudly. Thomas said, "It is a good thing we don't speak baboon. I don't think we'd like what they're saying."

Back again in the woodlands, they saw two leopard cubs playing in the scrub while practicing climbing trees. Hearing the Land Rover, they dropped to the ground and hid in the light growth beneath the trees. Nearby, an angry throaty growling hissing snarl got their attention. They looked in the direction of the threatening sound and glimpsed a long leopard tail slipping away through the trees. When they looked back for the cubs, they were gone. The mother leopard had diverted their attention so the cubs could escape unnoticed. During the whole ride, Jon stuck out of the roof taking pictures.

They stopped several times: once, to climb a rocky hill to take pictures of a vast herd of wildebeest. At one point, they watched a cheetah chase down a wildebeest youngster. It was amazing to see the speed and agility of both animals, but the cheetah snagged her meal.

It was a wonderful day. The trip through the bush was the best part of the tour. The hydroelectric plant was interesting, but the wildlife they had seen had been the magnificent highlight of the day. Man might be able to harness waterpower and use the energy, but nature needed no harnessing to exhibit its power and use its energy.

They were back at the hotel before four. Paula asked Kybo to go with Jon to the fair, saying, "We should not go out alone, now that we have once again seen Mr. Hunter and Max on the plane. No sense in taking chances; we have no idea of their intentions." Kybo was delighted to go with Jon. He was very curious about this trade fair.

Paula took a shower and washed her hair. When she was once again dressed, she went to the door dividing the suite. She knocked and Thomas opened the door. She could tell he too had showered and shaved and had put on clean clothes. The hotel was quite efficient. Laundry had been sent out this morning, and it was sitting clean and pressed on the bed when she had returned.

"She smiled and said, "A person could get used to all this service. Did your laundry come back?"

"Yes, and the tea I ordered has just arrived. Would you like a cup now?"

"That would be nice. Have you been out on the balcony yet?"

"No, would you like to have tea out there?"

Paula opened the French doors to the balcony, which was situated to the south and slightly east. She could see over the rooftops to the mountains, and the glowing red orb that was the setting sun, which caused a shimmering reflection on the waters of Lake Victoria, that were visible from the balcony. Thomas handed Paula a cup of tea. She sipped the tea as she gazed at the lowering sun. The Mountains of the Moon were imposing peaks with a ridge fourteen thousand feet high west of Kampala; they would be their horizon tonight.

As she stood gazing at the immense beauty of the mountainous sunset, Thomas came up and stood behind her, slightly off to one side. She could feel the heat of his body he was so close, yet he was not touching her. In a bit, she leaned back just enough and contact was made. It felt wonderful. In a few moments, Thomas increased the pressure. It made her sigh. They were silent, taking pleasure in the touching; the physical closeness was a comfort as well as a thrill. In the sensory silence, Paula set her teacup and saucer on the wide railing, and reached back for his left hand, and brought it up to put around her waist. She covered his arm with her hands and pressed him closer to her. Thomas placed his right hand on her upper arm and barely brushed her bare skin with the tips of his fingers. They stood thus for several minutes, each savoring the tentative moments of their first contact as lovers.

They had fallen deeply in love, but had not had a moment alone, where they could share their feelings physically. These few moments had to be savored, for this was the beginning. Up to now, holding hands had been the extent of their amorous contact. Paula said, "It seems I have waited such a long time to be alone with you again."

"We have both had to wait a long time. I think I fell in love with you the first moment I first saw you coming through the trees. I did not know it then. I just knew I could not let you go away from me. I was thrilled when you asked for my help to return to the cove; and yet, I did not know why. I had never loved anyone before. I loved Nanoka, of course, for she was my mother; I respected Sashono and held Manutu in awe, but I had no strong feelings for others until I saw you. I did not understand my feelings; I just knew I had to be with you for as long as possible. My dearest wish while we were traveling back to the cove was to have you come with me across Africa. I thought of this every night and often through the day too. And here we are, but not exactly as I had imagined."

Paula smiled and said, "It has not been as I imagined it would be either." She chuckled. "Who would have dreamed of all that has happened to us?"

"The past does not matter now. What matters is that we are here together and alone at last." Thomas leaned down and softly kissed the curve of her neck into her shoulder. Paula sighed; he kissed her neck below her ear, like a feather, and then again closer to her ear. When her mind began to swim, and she could no longer resist, she turned in his arms, offering herself to him. Thomas took her face in his hands and lightly kissed her eyes, her cheeks, the tip of her nose, and finally, when she thought she could stand no more evasion, he kissed her lips. Softly, at first and then with a hunger that made her body go limp. She could think of nothing, but the extreme thrill of his kiss, and his touch. Her body was as taut as a fiddle and hummed with excitement. When they needed to breathe again, he wrapped his strong arms gently around her, and held her with exquisite tenderness.

She rested her head against his chest and said, "I never knew I could feel this way. My love for you has crept up on me, day by day, until it has pervaded my entire being. It has enveloped me. I hate to leave you tomorrow. It will be the hardest thing I have ever done. Come to me as soon as you can. I am nothing without you."

"I now regret my decision to meet my parents alone. You

could stay here. You do not have to meet them when I do. It could be later."

"No, the plans have been made. Mr. Latham is expecting us. He has made arrangements for us in Nairobi. It will only be for two days. We can survive apart for that long. Kiss me again–Jon will soon be back for dinner–you know he's never late for a meal." This time Paula was ready for the thrill, the excitement and the passion. It felt just as wonderful as it had before, but now she was able to control the delirious mental fog, which had made her feel so weak moments ago. This time she actively kissed him back and felt his passion rise. All too soon, they heard Jon's key in the door.

"Thomas? Are you here?"

"We're having tea on the balcony. How was the fair?"

23

Reunion

THE DC3 REVVED UP her engines and disappeared down the runway into the morning mist. At four thousand feet above sea level, one could count on morning fog–even low-lying clouds. They stood silent, each lost in thought, as the drone of the engines diminished. Thomas had butterflies in his stomach... angst consumed him. He was worried that his parents would be disappointed in him... and now that Paula had gone to Nairobi, he also felt empty.

Jon hailed a Land Rover taxi outside the Entebbe terminal. He said to Thomas, "We need haircuts and a good barber's shave–driver, take us to the best barber in town, please." Thomas was glad for the diversion. Jon was his effervescent and amusing self, as he directed the cutting of Thomas' curls. It took his mind off the judgment that faced him. The time for emotional preparation was gone; the moment was here; it was now.

Jon saw and understood his apprehension, although he knew it was baseless. His parents were probably more than a bit anxious too; after such a long time, they would find it almost impossible to believe that their long lost son was coming home.

Years ago, they had abandoned all hope, as it fragmented their lives, and got on with living. Jon had quietly watched the process knowing it was essential for them... but inside, deep down in his heart, he somehow knew Thomas was alive; he vowed never to quit until he found him.

BY TWO P.M. THEY had lunched and were showered and dressed

in freshly washed and pressed safari togs. Paula, with Jon's help, when Thomas was off booking the Congo River tour, had purchased a silk ascot in a black, lime green and sapphire blue paisley print to compliment Thomas' kitu-kina. She had given it to him this morning at breakfast. Jon now tied the ascot for him, and Thomas, looking in the mirror said, "I like this decoration and the feel of it next to my skin, but I will wear it another day." Secretly, Jon was relieved as the ascot looked best with dress shirt, jacket or cardigan.

Jon had arranged with his parents, by telegram, to meet in the sitting room of their suite, not at the airport. He felt a private meeting was essential, for he expected emotions would run amok for everyone. The meeting was set for 2:30 p.m. Room service had arrived a few minutes ago. The flowers had arrived before they returned from lunch. Jon fussed about the tea table while Thomas stood on the balcony gazing at a vivid rainbow over Lake Victoria, the result of a short afternoon rain shower. He was remembering yesterday, on this same balcony, and the sensuous moments he had spent with Paula in his arms as a lover for the first time. Her absence made him ache. He felt flat and hollow.

SIR PETER AND LADY Mary had quietly readied themselves for the meeting. Both were absorbed in speculation–what would their son be like? Would they recognize him? Would he remember them? Sir Peter wore gray gabardine slacks and a sky blue Egyptian cotton shirt. Lady Mary wore a pale yellow silk blouse with a purple linen skirt and low yellow pumps. They wanted to look nice and yet be casual enough to make Thomas feel at ease.

At 2:30 p.m., Sir Peter knocked on the door to the sitting room. Jon quickly strode to the door and pulled it wide open, crying out a happy welcome. He immediately stepped to his mother, giving her a kiss and big hug. Jon then moved to his father, who put out his hand and pulled Jon to him in a bear hug. Jon turned, holding out a gesturing hand, and said, "Mom, Dad, this is our Thomas. Beautiful, isn't he?"

Mary stood stunned; the first moment she saw Thomas

standing a few feet behind Jon, she knew it was him. He looked just like he had when he was a boy, only now his features had firmed and defined into classic good looks; now, he was a man. Mary caught her breath and smiled, as the tears of joy welled in her eyes. She lifted her opened arms to him. Thomas needed no urging to step quickly into her embrace. This was the gold and silver hair of his dreams, the smile he never forgot. In her embrace, he remembered her lavender scent and was inundated with long lost memories and strong emotions that made him feel weak. When she whispered into his ear, "My, how I have missed holding you in my arms," the tears came and Thomas no longer cared that Manutu would be disappointed at his loss of control over his emotions.

Over Jon's shoulder, Sir Peter watched with joy as his son cried in his Mother's arms. He had recognized him instantly, and he was as Jon said, beautiful. His heart ached in his chest for it had swelled with elation and euphoria. He was content to watch, for he knew that, at this moment, he would not be able to speak a word, and embraced Jon to cover his turbulent feelings.

When Jon finally stepped out of his grasp, he too had tears rolling down his cheeks. He knew all Thomas' fears were unfounded, for his father had held him with such joy that he knew, he too, had recognized Thomas, and was using all his will power to control his rampaging emotions.

Lady Mary stepped away from Thomas to watch as Sir Peter took his son's extended hand and pulled him to him with such force that he took Thomas' breath away. She hugged Jon again and whispered through her tears, "Thank you Jon, with all my heart I thank you." He whispered back, "I assure you Mother, bringing Thomas home is the very greatest of my pleasures."

She smiled as the tears lined her cheeks and hugged this boy who had been so lonely for so long; and who never, ever gave up the hope of one day finding his lost brother.

When his father finally let him go, and stood patting him on the back, Thomas smiled at Jon, who, in his typical manner, said, "I have a bottle of Champagne in the ice bucket. I think it is time to have a toast to Thomas."

Replies of: "Here! Here!" with chortles agreed, while Jon uncorked the bubbly for them. With glasses in hand, Jon said, "To our long-lost brother and son, welcome home!" Not surprising, but mostly expected and enjoyed was Thomas's reaction to getting Champagne bubbles up his nose. The laughter eased the tension and relaxed them as Jon gestured to everyone to take seats around the tea table as he uncovered the Brie cheese, crackers and strawberries that he had ordered for the occasion. Lady Mary prepared the hors d'oeuvres for each of them, putting a dab of Brie on a wafer-thin rice cracker and a strawberry on each of the small service plates that she passed around.

Jon took advantage of the lull to say, "Well, Mom, Dad, what do you think? Did I do good or what?"

His father was the first to answer saying, "Jon, you have never done better in all your life!"

Lady Mary surprised them by saying, "Jon, you have always been a perfect son, always doing the right thing at the right time. But this time you should have done the right thing a long, long time ago!"

There was a momentary pause, and then Jon laughed and said, "You're absolutely right! Whatever was I thinking?" The laughter was healing. From there, the conversation flowed easily.

Sir Peter said, "Meeting in this suite was a good idea, Jon. But tell me, how did you manage to get ice for the Champagne bucket?"

Jon replied, "With a very large tip! We have had this suite since we arrived. Paula was in your room before she and Kybo left for Nairobi this morning."

"Who is Kybo?" His mother asked.

"Kybo is a Nigerian who has dedicated his life to Tamubu, Medicine Man of the Great Zuri Watu–in other words, to Thomas."

"Are you really a medicine man?" His father asked.

"Yes, I can heal the sick... most of the time." Thomas replied.

"Not only do we get our dearly beloved son back; but he comes back to us hale and hearty and with extraordinary skills. What more could a father ask?"

"He could ask for him to tell us his story." Lady Mary said.

"But, of course! There is nothing we would like better."

Thomas smiled the smile that Paula loved so, with his head tilted to one side, and said, "I have been thinking of this day for a long time. Now that it is here, I find myself wondering what it is that you want to know.

Almost as one, his parents said, "We want to know everything."

"But first, tell us what your life was like living with the Zuri Watu." Lady Mary added.

I was twelve, and mostly recovered from the Malaria, when I asked to go and play with the other boys in the village. It was then that Manutu, the Medicine Chief, took me to his hut and found I had special skills. That day, I received my Kitu-Kina and was told that I must always have it in contact with my body. The next day, Manutu began my education.

Each day, when it was not raining, we went into the bush. Manutu taught me about all the plants, especially the healing plants: how to know them, how to gather them, how to prepare them and what effects they have on the body. He taught me all about nature... about the great bounty God has given us in the plants, trees and animals. Even the insects are a source of help to man, for if you catch flies and let them lay eggs in festering wounds, the maggots will feed on the wounds and clean them. He taught me about the stars and how to use them for travel. He explained the tides, the oceans, and much of the life living there. He taught me to anticipate the weather and to plan accordingly. He taught me how to snare small animals, turtles and game birds.

On rainy days, we prepared the dried plants to be used as medicines. In later years, Manutu took me with him when he tended to the sick, near and far. He taught me how to listen to the problems of a sick person, how to examine the body for the signs of illness and how to question a patient. He taught me about the bones and muscles, how they are connected and how to mend injured ones.

This was the daily fabric of my life. I loved the learning. I eagerly looked forward to each new day. When we traveled to help the sick, Manutu and I would camp on the way. We would catch our meal, usually a fowl of some kind, and roast it over a campfire. We would gather tubers and greens and fruit to go with the meals. Manutu knew all the spices to make food delicious and taught me how to cook. I like to cook and hope to make a special meal for you one day soon.

Some days, when Manutu was in council or away conferring with other Medicine Men, I went into the bush alone. I always had an escort of four warriors, who saw to my safety, but they did not interfere with me. I was able to explore and study nature. Those were special times for me. I loved the freedom. I loved watching nature–undisturbed for hours.

For ten years, I was with Manutu learning from him. Two years ago, he said he had taught me all he knew and that life would have to teach me the rest. During the ten years, we had other gifted children join us to learn. Most stayed only for a few years, some could not tolerate the separation from their families and left early, some did not have the ability to remember so many details...for nothing was written, all was memory.

I traveled alone for two years, not far, but to villages that needed another opinion, which gave Manutu some relief from his unceasing work. Often he tended the sick for days on end without rest. Manutu was strict about cleanliness. He knew about germs and the horror they could bring. If Manutu went to a village that was unclean, he would wait far away, until the villagers had cleaned the huts and burned all the old bedding and flooring and had washed floors and walls and furniture with lye. He would take the sick from these villages to a new shelter built a long way from the village. When there were no new cases of sickness in the village, the patients that survived were allowed to return home. Sometimes, the local witch doctor was not helpful, so the shelters far from the village also protected the patients from the witch doctor's interference.

Manutu is a very special person. He has vast abilities and has the knowledge of the ages. He is in contact with the spirits of long ago. He knows all the ancient secrets, even ones that have been lost. Manutu is known and respected, and often revered, in much of Africa. I am proud to walk in his footsteps and to call myself his mhudumu (acolyte).

This was the way of my life with the Zuri Watu. Nanoka took care of me as a mother, and loved me as a mother. Sashono, her husband, treated me like a son. Sashono is also the Chief of the Zuri Watu and twin brother to Manutu.

In the twelve years that I lived with them, there was never an outbreak of disease in our village. Manutu had rules about cleanliness and inspected the huts every month... a job he gladly gave me when I was fifteen. I took with me warriors who would take old bedding or flooring out to be burned. Some people did not understand this need and did not want to cooperate. Manutu, in order to obtain the cooperation and obedience of all the people, sometimes burned a hut to the ground, if he found wanyama (vermin).

Personal maarifa (hygiene) was very important too. He gave talks to the women about hand washing, cleanliness in the care of children, and in the preparation of food. Manutu would refuse to help their children if the women were not clean. In all my years, I saw this only once, for the people had become used to being clean and now disliked being dirty and smelly.

Each week, two huge pots of water were boiled: one, with a mixture of lye, aloes and soapwort, was used to boil all clothes made of cloth that had been worn during the week. After the clothes were washed, the water was used to wash diapers or sick cloths. Then the diapers and sick cloths were again washed in the second pot of boiling water. Each week, teams of women did the washing supervised by one of Manutu's students. Manutu said, "Cleanliness is the first order for good health."

Once I was cured of the Malaria, I was never again sick. Many people have recurring episodes, but Manutu insisted I drink large quantities of lemon water, which purifies the blood, and repels mosquitoes.

Before Nanoka died, she told me I must go and find my birth family. I was on this mission when I first saw Paula coming through the trees. She had escaped the Ndezi, and was traveling back to the cove alone; but she had become lost. So, when she asked for my help, I gave it gladly.

My life, as an Englishman, began again with Paula. She gave me back my language and often reminded me of things I had forgotten about my past. She was a kind and patient teacher. It was Paula who reminded me that I could write and draw, and she who encouraged me to start a book about the healing plants in the back of her diary.

Then it was Jon who made coming home hakika (a reality). He knew Paula was alone and kupatwa (vulnerable) in the wild rainforest after she had escaped the Ndezi, so Jon went looking for her... against any chance of ever finding her... and found both of us. The End.

There was a brief moment of silence and then cries of 'bravo' and enthusiastic clapping followed. Thomas looked at the shining faces and felt a tightening in his chest. They did love him. Being raised by natives and looking like a native meant nothing to them. He could see the pride and approval in their eyes and smiles. He was home at last and, so far, all was well.

"We will expect many stories of the happenings in your life. The little day-to-day things and experiences you have had." Sir Peter said.

Thomas replied, "It is a custom of many of the tribes for a visiting person to tell stories around the campfire. I will tell you these stories each evening after dinner, if you like. We have been doing that on the trail and have had the great good pleasure of hearing stories from others that we have met while traveling."

Jon arose and said, "Well, I think we must wait a bit for one of your campfire stories. The afternoon has just flown by; it is time to go down to dinner. We can get on with it later." Jon said. "I enjoy hearing those stories myself."

To give Thomas the opportunity to remember the life he had left as a boy, and to learn about the changes, Jon monopolized the conversation in a chatty way during dinner. He talked with his parents about the tea farm, the vineyards, the workers, his old teacher, Kazaii, and of course, the horses. His mother and father quickly caught on to Jon's intent and were careful in their replies, giving answers that left no questions.

Thomas was content to sit and listen, for the lively flow of talk often sparked bits and pieces in his memory. The conversation was a panacea for his trepidation about his acceptance, and fitting-in without embarrassment. He was beginning to look forward to going back to the farm again, and to seeing his old teacher once more.

Jon had ordered coffee, tea and after-dinner liqueurs sent to the suite. After a postprandial stroll in the waning twilight, they returned to sit on the balcony and watch the faint orange-red glow behind the mountains diminish and then vanish. It was an impressive sight; like watching a volcano turning shades of red-gold from the molten lava rising to the rim... but deciding to erupt another day.

Lady Mary asked softly, "Thomas, did you really forget all about us? I mean, did you think of us at all?"

Thomas sagged. This is the part that was hurtful... the part that he feared. He must speak the truth... yet... then he remembered Jon's admonition to 'tell them as it was; that you were happy in your life...' so he said, "Sadly, one of the effects of Malaria is that with the chills and fever, come delusions. I did not forget you, I remembered you as dreams, wonderful dreams that came to me when I was suffering the most.

"But, by the time I was well, I was convinced my visions

were just that, dreams. I had a mother and a father, and my life was one of privilege with days filled with a fascinating education. The dream that persisted longest and came most often, was that of Jon holding my hand, or Jon calling out to me to hurry… or saying, 'Thomas, where are you?' I heard his young voice calling to me at times when I least expected it.

"If I had remembered you to the point where I had questioned Nanoka, she would have sent me back to you. But, a boy does not ask his mother about his dreams. He just accepts them for what they are: bits of recurring happiness that he can enjoy.

"I was sick for two years before the Missionary Doctor came with the quinine. It was a wonder I did not die of the disease… and would have, if it had not been for Manutu and Nanoka.

"So, while they kept me from you, they also saved me for you. I was happy, boy and man. I longed for nothing, except to get well and go outside to play. Later, I was consumed by my interesting life and the learning with Manutu; I was special, I was *chosen*."

"What do you mean, you were *chosen*?" his father asked.

"I told you that Manutu is in contact with the spirits. He found in me the a-ndani (esoteric) ability needed for spirit communication. It is a gift, a gift from God. One day, in the future, we will talk of this, not now. It is the end of the story, not the beginning.

"I would like to tell you a story that will help you understand me and my life away from you. It is the story of myself as a boy, when I was finally strong enough to go out among the villagers. It will tell you who I became and let you know why I was always happy."

"As I gained strength and energy, I wanted to go out and play with the boys while they practiced with their walinkas. Late one night I overheard Nanoka talking to Sashono. She said, 'we must find a boy who is gifted to play with our son. He is lonely and needs friends and companionship.'

'Where are we going to find such a boy? I will ask Manutu if he knows of such a boy, tomorrow.'

"I was weary and gave their conversation little thought... mostly because I didn't understand the meaning behind the words. The next day, I was taken to see Manutu. We sat for a long time over his small fire of coals where he gave me lemon water to drink. After praying for a long time, he gave me the kitu-kina. When we finally left his hut, the day was almost gone. The entire village was seated outside the hut, waiting for us. Manutu raised his arms for silence and said, 'Tamubu na dogo mungu.' I was stunned. What did he mean? I was a little god. Everyone bowed to me including Manutu and Sashono. From that day forward, I had only Manutu for a companion, and later the other acolytes. I was set apart and treated like a king. It was a bit daunting in the beginning, but I soon became used to being special.

"So, you see, my life was one of extreme privilege and we must not mourn for what is lost, but take what is offered and go on in love and be happy with one another. I believe that this is my fate, my destiny, as was my being taken from you. Let us be glad that fate has joined us together again. Let us be thankful for the days we will have together. Let us not darken our days of joy with what is in the past, and can never be again."

SIR PETER AROSE AND said, "Each minute I am with you, I sense more and more your greatness of spirit. We are so proud of you. Be gentle with us. We have had fourteen years of emptiness and longing for our first-born son. It will take a bit of time for us to cast aside the years of our sadness; but with your patience and understanding, we will not darken our days of joy to come."

Lady Mary added, "Your father and I do not understand the life you have lived, but we accept it, and we accept you as you are, and ask for indulgence until we have become accustomed to it."

Jon, never one to be left out, and one who has hindsight mixed in his foresight said, "If you just pay 'never-any-mind' to Thomas, it will be easier. He is definitely different... but he is wonderful in his difference."

24

The Kabaka

Sir Peter snuggled with his wife. Neither one was ready to go to sleep. The events of the afternoon and evening were all consuming. He said, "I feel like I know him... almost as well as I know Jon. Isn't that odd?"

"Yes, it is odd. Why do you say it?"

"Because he is still Thomas, the boy we lost; even his looks are much the same, certainly his smile is unchanged. It is a certain demeanor that he had as a boy that he retains still... do you think it could be as he said... because he is special?"

"I do not know, Peter. I just know that his years with the Zuri Watu were good years for him. Like Jon said, 'he is different to be sure, but he is still Thomas...' I, like Jon, wouldn't change a hair on his head. I am going to try to take Jon's advice to heart, and go on as if the anomalies, whatever they may be, don't exist."

"Yes, that is what we must do. Praise God! I am so happy, I want to dance and sing!"

"Well, that is certainly a first for you. Have you ever danced or sung before?"

"No, but I feel good enough to try it now."

"Maybe you feel good enough to try something else?"

His low chuckle told her he had received the message.

In the morning the four of them were driven to the Kabaka's palace. His highness Mutessa II, who is the thirty-seventh in a direct line to hold the throne of Buganda, met them at the barn. He spoke English proficiently, as he had attended Cambridge University for several years. He liked to embellish his English with British expressions saying to Lady Mary... after he was introduced to Thomas and Jon... "I say, what great chaps you have for sons." And to them, "It's very good of you to come along; could I offer you a spot of tea?"

Jon was amused... tea at ten in the morning was unusual and he replied, "Very kind of you, but we came to see the horses too. Mother is quite pleased that you are showing her horse progeny."

With a delighted air, the thirty-six year old Kabaka led them into the stables and to the stalls of the six and seven year old full brothers sired by her homozygous Dutch Warmblood stallion, out of the Andalusian mare. The stalls were huge with a wide sliding door between them, so the horses could be together if they liked, or separated when necessary. The horses looked identical. Both were light brown bay horses with thick black manes and flowing black tails and four black stockings. Their eyes were rimmed in charcoal gray, as were their muzzles. Each had a white snip that dipped into the gray muzzle, but each snip was of a different shape.

Mary looked the horses over and asked, "What seems to be the problem? They look marvelous." The Kabaka gestured to his barn manager who said, "The problem is both of them want to be the lead horse and do not work well as a team."

"Would it be possible to see them hitched?"

"Of course, dear lady," the manager replied. "It will be a few minutes. Chavo will take you to the lounge for tea."

"I would like to watch the hitching process, if that is possible."

The Kabaka intruded and said, "Whatever pleases you, will please us. The rest of us could use a sniff of fresh air." The Kabaka led Sir Peter, Jon and Thomas, to a covered pavilion at the end of the dressage arena.

Lady Mary watched the grooms lead the horses from the stalls and the grooming and harnessing process. A lovely four wheeled Eagle phaeton was brought to the outside aisle for hitching. Here, Mary saw the first bit of anxiety in Paladin, the six year old that would be hitched to the left, not as lead. Mr. Diembo, the barn manager, stepped up to the driver's seat. Chavo handed him the reins and then climbed to a groom's seat in the rear. The six-year-old Paladin was still worried. When the carriage moved off, the young horse kept stepping into the lead's space. Lady Mary raised a hand and Mr. Diembo reined in. As she went to the head of the pair, Chavo jumped down and ran forward to hold the horses.

Lady Mary talked softly to her former pupils, as she reached up and took hold of the inside blinder of the left horse, Paladin, and turned it back towards his neck. She then took the inside blinder of the lead horse, Galahad, and also turned it back towards his neck. She said to the groom, "Up on your seat with you," and to Mr. Diembo, "Let's see how they go now."

The horses moved down the cedar-lined aisle to the arena in perfect unison. The turn to the arena was first to the right and then to the left after they crossed the arena. Paladin, on the left, moved away perfectly as Galahad, the lead horse, moved towards him. Mary joined the Kabaka and the group on the pavilion. They watched as the team went through their dressage paces, all without a misstep. The Kabaka was ecstatic. "My, they are marvelous together now." Turning to Mary, he clasped her hand while saying, "Lady Mary, you are indeed quite something! You certainly know your horses. We hadn't the foggiest notion what the problem was. How did you know?" he asked.

Lady Mary said, "You must remember, I raised these horses from birth as well as trained them. I could read Paladin's anxiety the moment the bridle was put on–when he could no longer see his brother. When asked to move out, Paladin was just making sure Galahad was still there. It was then logical to remove the inside blinder, for both of them, for Galahad did not seem to mind the pushing."

"My dear lady, you must allow me to entertain you and your family for dinner. How long will you be in Kampala?"

"We are leaving tomorrow for an appointment in Nairobi."

The Kabaka turned to an aide who had been following them silently. "Lester, am I free for lunch today?"

"Yes, your majesty. Her highness and the children will be joining you today. It is Edward, Junior's twelfth birthday."

"Ah, yes, now I remember. We bought him a new saddle to go with his new horse. Will you please join us for the luncheon party? Do not say no. Edward will be thrilled to meet you and your family. It will make the party very special for him. It is now almost eleven. Lester will have time to give you a tour of the palace and gardens before the luncheon party."

Lady Mary looked at her family and saw their desire to be entertained by the Kabaka, Mutessa II... and for a birthday party no less. "Yes, we would be delighted, thank you."

Lady Mary watched as the horses wheeled to the left again as they left the arena at a collected trot. The matched pair had beauty and majesty. Hitched to the elegant black phaeton, which had tufted light brown suede seats with black buttons and piping; light brown burled walnut trim and intricate gold pin striping on the black wheels and body, they were simply stunning. Lady Mary was also pleased that her horses had this caring and pleasant home. They would never be ignored or left to languish here.

Lester spoke up, "Would you please come with me. I will take you to the visitor's parlor, where you can refresh yourselves. The Kabaka will meet us later in the morning room, after the tour."

FAMILY AND FRIENDS WERE gathered in the morning room off the family dining room. Small glasses of sherry and goblets of mint sprigged lemon water were passed among the guests. When Edward, the Kabaka's oldest son appeared, the receiving line was formed in the hall leading to the family dining room. The line was informal in as much as Lester stood casually by the door announcing each guest. Only Edward, his father and his mother were receiving. The line took not ten minutes, as there were only about twenty guests, most of whom were family. When Lady Mary was announced, Edward became visibly excited. He took her hand and leaned forward and air kissed it, and said, "This is the best birthday present of all. I have arranged for you to sit in Mother's seat so we can talk about horses during lunch. Only on my birthday can I arrange the seating; how good of you to come today!"

"Lady Mary replied, "How good it was of your father to invite us to your birthday celebration. I look forward to our conversation."

Peter and Jon then passed, with Thomas bringing up the rear. Lester announced him as Thomas, eldest son of Lady Mary and Sir Peter Caulfield, Medicine Man of the Great Zuri Watu.

Instantly, Edward, Junior was intrigued. "How can you be a medicine man and the eldest son of Sir Peter and Lady Mary?"

Thomas smiled broadly, for he instantly liked this inquisitive and optimistic boy and replied, "The same way you can be heir to the throne and a schoolboy too."

Edward laughed and said, "Yes, our education makes different men of us, doesn't it. I wish I had known you were coming. I would have had you seated in Father's seat.

Hearing his son, the Kabaka said, "It is your birthday today. I will be happy to sit in Thomas' seat so he can sit beside you."

"Oh, thank you Father. You are the best Father a boy could have."

The formality ended at the door to the family dining room. Place cards guided everyone to their seats and the Kabaka gave the blessing from his seat halfway down the table. Then the chatter began. Edward immediately turned to Lady Mary and said; "I heard how quickly you saw the problem in the pair this morning. I told Father that you would know what to do."

"I am glad it was convenient for your Father to receive us this morning... and what a nice surprise to be invited to your birthday luncheon."

"I don't mean to impose, but would you have the time after lunch to watch me with my new horse? He seems to have become afraid of me. I must be doing something wrong. I know he is not one of your horses, but maybe you will see something that we've all missed. He is as sweet and agreeable on the ground as he can be... yet when I mount him, he is tense and balky.'

"I would be happy to watch you ride, but I don't promise anything."

"Nor should you; but it would be a wonderful present to have your opinion."

"And so you shall have it!"

Young Edward turned to Thomas. "I hope you will join us too. I have a feeling that you can divine things that others cannot. Is that something that you learned when you became a Medicine Man?"

Thomas was non-plused. Was this boy gifted? Am I the only one here who senses it? But he replied, "I see that your heart is pure. I will be glad to observe you on your horse, if your parents agree."

"Oh, they must agree, for today is my birthday and I may have anything I want within reason... well, did you?"

Surprised that Edward was not mollified by his answer, he said, "I, like yourself, was born with a gift. We must be wise and keep our special knowledge close to our hearts... and use it only for good."

Edward leaned close and replied, "I am so glad you came. This is by far, my best birthday ever."

Edward, ever the good host, also talked to other guests nearby. He invited them all to come and watch him ride his horse after the party, if it was convenient for them to do so.

The party ran to three o'clock with the opening of presents and then the birthday cake. So, it was almost four before young Edward was dressed in riding togs and ready to ride his almost new horse with the new saddle his Father and Mother had given him. He had asked Lady Mary to be in charge and oversee everything, and had made a small announcement to this effect, which made the guests smile. This boy was already a Kabaka at heart.

LADY MARY DID WATCH everything. The gray horse, a six-year-old Arabian gelding, was tractable and willing on the lunge line. He stood nicely to be tacked up. The horse was neither bored nor wary, even when young Edward came up to him. He put out his ungloved hand and gave the horse a piece of carrot. The horse became tense when he was bridled. When Edward mounted him and took up the reins, the horse stiffened and laid his ears back. Lady Mary knew the horse was going to balk. She went up to Edward and moved his hands forward to the horse's neck, while she gently circled her fingertips down the horse's crest. She felt the horse relax a bit and asked Edward to dismount. She called for a halter and had the horse unbridled. Expertly she opened the horse's mouth and pulling his tongue aside, she felt his teeth on one side and then felt the other side. The teeth were smooth, but he had wolf teeth and these, she found were tender. Asking again for the bridle, which was a medium port Kimberwick bit, she put the bridle on in proper position and then examined the lie of the bit in the horse's mouth. When Edward picked up his reins, the bit made contact with the wolf teeth and had made them sore.

Lady Mary turned to the barn manager and asked, "Do you have a horse dentist on staff?"

"Yes, Lady Mary, but he has looked at the horse's teeth already."

"Did he examine him with a bit in his mouth?"

"No, maam, he did not."

"Well, he must see for himself that these wolf teeth must come out. Most horses loose them naturally, but this fellow has not."

Edward came up asking to see the problem; before he was finished looking in the horse's mouth, a big man arrived with a leather sack of tools.

He quickly opened the horse's mouth and observed the problem. A Kimberwick bit operates by rotating in the horse's mouth, turning the port up to give relief to the tongue, and in so doing, it was bumping into the tender wolf teeth. The man was good at his job and in ten minutes, he had the wolf teeth out, much like removing a splinter, for wolf teeth have very shallow roots.

The horse was bridled again, but before Edward mounted, Lady Mary, standing at his withers, worked the bit. The horse began to stiffen, but feeling no pain, relaxed. Edward mounted and walked his horse around the adjacent courtyard and back. The horse remained relaxed and moved willingly.

"Father, if I may, I will go into the arena now."

"Go, my son, we will watch from the pavilion. Mr. Diembo will walk with you."

Mr. Diembo snapped a lunge line on the noseband ring and walked the boy to the arena saying, "I would like to see the horse work on the lunge line with you up, will that suit your highness?"

"I will be most pleased for your help. *Wind Dancer* and I need to get reacquainted slowly, after his bad experiences."

Wind Dancer was perky now that the pain was gone. He was willing and responsive. His fear had evaporated in Lady Mary's hands. Horses can sense people that care about them and *Wind Dancer* knew his young rider loved him too. He responded instantly to aids. In a few minutes, Edward, who had been riding since he was three years old, was riding free of the lunge and the Arabian was showing off: stopping spot on, with all four feet matched, turning in place and side-passing. The horse had been well trained and enjoyed his work. The audience was thrilled with the small exhibition, for family is always proud of the exploits of their children.

Edward waved Mr. Diembo over and dismounted. He ran up to the pavilion and went directly to Lady Mary. He shook her hand enthusiastically, saying, "Thank you for giving me back my horse. I love him so. He is simply marvelous now, as he was in the beginning. You and your family have made this the very best birthday I have ever had, and you will always be my special friends."

The Kabaka and his wife joined Edward, and other members of the family followed suit, in thanking Lady Mary for helping Edward regain the companionship of his lovely horse.

A DRIVER TOOK THEM back to the hotel in the Rolls Royce Silver Ghost with flags flying. It seemed the entire hotel staff was on hand to greet them. The manager asked if they desired anything. Lady Mary said, "Tea would be nice." Jon said, "Any more bubbly left?"

They were not in their rooms more than ten minutes when the tea tray arrived with a bottle of Champagne in an ice bucket. Jon tipped the boy generously and said, "Tea time, everyone."

Gathered round the tea tray, Jon said, "Well, today was some day; a bit unexpected, but most enjoyable. What a place, the palace... almost like home."

Thomas joined the others when they laughed, saying, "I have had some recurring memories of the farm... and a few of the farmhouse. Do you still have the same farm?"

More delighted laughter with Sir Peter saying, "Yes, it is still the same farm, but it is much improved, although it is nothing like the Kabaka's palace."

Jon continued, "Mom, you were the star of the day. How fortunate for us that the Kabaka called you before you came to Kampala. How doubly fortunate for us, and for the horses and Edward, that you were able to divine the problems so quickly."

"I can't claim all the credit. Edward gave me a big clue when he told me he felt it was something he was doing that made the animal tense. I just watched the signs. He was right. The only thing he did that could make *Wind Dancer* tense up–was to pick up the reins. So, it had to be the bit or his mouth. The boy has good hands."

Thomas sat astonished. He had inherited his gift from his mother. When Jon used the word 'divine', Thomas saw immediately what no one else had ever seen. Lady Mary could divine the subliminal, for she too had the gift. This was one of the reasons why she was so successful in training horses. Thomas had never felt so completely at ease as he did at this moment. He was not an oddity; he was a member of a family of specially gifted people... for Jon was gifted too.

After a light dinner, when they were once again seated in the comfortable sitting room, sipping on a glass of sherry, Jon said, "We were promised a story after dinner. What will it be, Thomas?"

"Let me tell you the story of Fatimi. I was reminded of her today at the palace. Fatimi was the daughter of a Chief. Her father adored her and spoiled her. She was quite pretty, very smart and had a pleasing personality. People wanted to be with her. But Fatimi was selfish. She did not think of others, only of herself. No one faulted her for being selfish, they just accepted it, because no one wanted Fatimi to dislike them... not even her parents.

"When Fatimi became a woman, the chief began to receive offers for her hand in marriage. He had many generous offers from good men, some of whom were highly placed in other villages.

"Fatimi would not hear of being betrothed. "I do not want to leave home. I like it here. Why must I get married?"

"Fatimi had her way and much later her father thought, "Fatimi was fast becoming an old maid, for she was almost eighteen. Who was going to want an old woman for a wife? How could she begin to bear children at such an advanced age? She would more than likely die in childbirth.

"Fatimi's mother had died two years ago... suddenly and unexpectedly. Fatimi had been sick with a fever and her mother was sleeping with her to care for her. Her mother was found dead in the morning while Fatimi was still asleep. The medicine man could find no reason for her death; she had simply stopped breathing. Fatimi now spent all her time with her father. She began to sit with him in his counsel and every now and again offered advice. This was unheard of, but it was not resented, as the men all loved Fatimi. In the evenings, she had long talks with her father and learned all the secrets of the village and the elders. One evening she said to her father, 'Father, who will be chief when you die? You have no son.'

'It will be either Mamnaya, the eldest son of my lieutenant, or Lazima, the eldest son of the medicine man. They are both strong and educated men.'

'But they are both married. Who could succeed you that would be able to marry me?'

"Chief Egemea was astounded. 'There is no one. All those of your age have already married.'

'Could you not name me to succeed you?'

"Chief Egemea did not believe what she asked. 'There has never been a woman chief. The elders would never agree to my request... and if they did, they would not honor it once I was gone.'

"Fatimi persisted. 'Father, if you love me, you will name me as your successor.'

'No Fatimi, I can not do this for you.'

'So be it, Father. You have disinherited me. I disinherit you.'

"Fatimi went to the woman's quarters and was not seen again in public. She refused to see her father and had contact only with her maid. Years went by, her father sickened, and Fatimi still did not come to see him. He was on his deathbed when he called a council of his elders.

'I am not long for this world. Years ago, Fatimi asked me to name her as my successor. I told her you would not accept her and refused her request. These last years have been sad ones for me. I have missed her company and her wisdom. She will never marry and have a family now, but she would make a good aide to the new chief. She would be a big help with woman's matters. If you could see your way to do this for me, I will rest in peace.'

"Two weeks later, the chief died. Fatimi attended the funeral with her maid. Mamnaya was made chief and two days later, he went to talk with Fatimi. He offered her the position of aide, counseling him on woman's matters. Two days later, she accepted the position, as it allowed her to sit in council. Several years went by with Fatimi acting as aide to the chief and council. She was adept and most of the problems were handled fairly and with finesse. Fatimi was now thirty years old. She was still beautiful, and was well loved in the village. The people trusted her and came to her for advice. She helped everyone that asked her and soon she handled more problems than the council of elders.

"A celebration was planned for the new year. A special

dinner was planned. There was singing and dancing and games for the children. At the banquet, the chief and elders along with Fatimi sat on the lanai and were served from a special bowl. That night, all of the elders and Fatimi sickened. By morning the elders were dead but Fatimi was still alive, but she was not expected to survive. Day after day, for two weeks, she hung on and then one day, she was able to hold down a bit of broth. In another month Fatimi was well, although very weak.

"She asked to speak to the people. After dinner, everyone gathered to listen to Fatimi. She said, 'A great misfortune has occurred in this village. We are left with no leaders. I alone was spared. Why? Did the gods spare me, so I could lead you? What other reason could there be? I feel the events in my life have been leading to this day. I feel that fate has cast me, a woman, in the unusual role of leader. Will you accept the will of the gods? Will you have me in this role?' Fatimi stood and said, 'Raise you right hand if you will accept me as your leader.' In a few moments, several women raised their right hands; then, one by one, all the women raised their right hands; then a few men raised their right hands and soon all had raised their right hands. It was unanimous. Fatimi was the leader.

"Alone in her bed that night, Fatimi smiled. It was done. She was the leader. The people had accepted her. Her father was wrong. It was only the elders, men who were jealous of their lofty positions being usurped by a lowly woman, who were against her. Everyone loved her. She had been right to poison the elders. She had not taken enough to kill herself, but she had suffered greatly from the small dose. Her prize was being the leader. Fatimi drank the lemon water she kept near her bed, turned over and went to sleep.

"The next morning, her maid ran out into the street. 'Come quickly, Fatimi is dead.'

"Two days later Lazima was chief. His father, as medicine man was named to the council of elders, as was Mamnaya's oldest son. To this day, the sons of Lazima rule the village."
The End

"WHAT MADE YOU TELL that story, Thomas? What could have possibly happened today to remind you of it?" Jon asked.

"When I heard that the Kabaka was thirty-seventh in a direct line, I thought of the story of Fatimi, the moral of which, is that you can not direct fate. It is a story told so that young people will understand that subversive activities will not change the course of that which is meant to be."

"I find that somewhat puzzling." His father said. "Are you saying that no matter what we do, what will be, will be?"

"I am saying that what we do–is what we are supposed to do. If we go wrong, something will put it right... if putting it right is meant to be. Let's take a page from our own book. Jon and his partner could not free Paula, so Paula escaped. I saw Paula fleeing through the trees and followed her. She injured her ankle and we had to rest for a few days. Then Jon found us and here we are today. If any one of those things had not happened, or happened differently, we would not be here as we are today. Frustration, injury, curiosity, loss and timing all play a part in our lives and make us who and what we are. You can call these things fate, if you like, but it is really destiny."

"All the shauri-ovu (machinations) of Fatimi served for naught. She never profited by her selfishness; she suffered and gave her life for a selfish dream, one that was not meant to be. Who knows what might have happened had she married... her husband might have been a chief who died suddenly, leaving a young son in his place that might have needed her to guide him until he was old enough to take his rightful place. Intelligence is knowing what to do; wisdom is doing it."

WHEN THE EVENING WAS ended, Sir Peter spooned with his wife in bed. The cool evenings at four thousand feet allowed the closeness they enjoyed at home. He said, "I like our boy more and more each day... actually, I am amazed at his sagacity and the enormity of his inner strength."

"Jon was right again when he said, 'You are going to love him so much... he is not the son you would have made of him, but he is just wonderful.' And Peter, do you ever remember seeing Jon so happy?"

"He is like a boy with a new pony... but yet different. Like he knows something that no one else knows."

"Yes, that's it! He knows something important... and he is going to keep it to himself. Now, I'll never get to sleep wondering what it could be!"

"Maybe I should take your mind off Jon and give you something else to think about."

Tonight, it was Mary's turn to chuckle.

25

Nairobi

While they were alone for a few moments, packing up, Jon said, "I say Thomas, things have been going quite well for all of us, don't you think?"

"Yes, they have–better than I expected. I have you to thank for that, Jon."

"My thanks come from seeing Mom and Dad so happy. I can't remember when last they laughed so easily. Joy is in their faces. The dark cloud of lingering grief is gone."

"Lingering?"

"Something still remaining; which reminds me, larding your English with Swahili is clever. It gets you over the rough spots nicely. I can hardly wait for Mom and Dad to meet Paula and Anna Louise tomorrow. I think they will be thrilled for us."

"I will be thrilled for myself to see Paula again. When did you make plans to meet Anna Louise in Nairobi?"

"Paula and Julia planned a get-together when we were in Kisangani, since we are going to be there at the same time"

"Is there a reason why we are going on a tour of the Botanical Gardens at Government House today?"

"Yes, because Mother will enjoy them, she loves gardens. Dad will be talking business with the District Governor, who is interested in obtaining a local supplier of fine wine. We won't be there too long. Our flight is at noon."

Thomas thought of seeing Paula again. He knew his parents would like her; but how long would it be before they could be alone together again? He ached to hold her in his arms once more.

Jon's thoughts ran along similar lines. He was looking forward to seeing Anna Louise in Nairobi. He thought of her quite often these days, and knew his parents would like the Holmesbys. The question that bothered him was: how were he and Anna Louise going to further their acquaintance? Nairobi would be the third time they were together, and then she would be gone.

Jon had never been so deeply attracted to a girl before, except for Paula, and chaffed at the idea of a long separation. The thought of a relationship by letter was not to his liking. Maybe something would take him to England long before the family went, at the end of May, for Hanna's and Sara's graduation from college.

JON SAID, "I SAY old chap, are you planning on getting engaged to Paula? You might not remember it, but English customs are more stringent than native mores about single young ladies traveling with young gentlemen, outside of a dire situation, without a commitment. You must think of her reputation first."

Thomas became concerned and said, "Jon, I expect you to keep me on the right path with Paula. I have no recollection of the English way of doing things properly."

"They are not too dissimilar. You must never be alone with her for more than five or ten minutes, unless you are in a public place, like walking or riding in the park or dining in a restaurant or going to the opera. You must always be in a place where others can come and go, like sitting before the fire in the library at home, until you are wed. You do intend to marry her, right?"

"Yes, if she will have me. But we need time. Our relationship has barely passed friendship."

"I do not think her having you will be a problem. But I do wonder about her snotty mother."

"Paula says she doesn't mean to be snotty. She says her mother just doesn't know she does it."

"Well, maybe so, she was certainly pleasant enough the day we hiked up the foothills north of Mount Cameroon. Paula could be right. Some people, when they are thrust into exotic situations, react poorly. Maybe her mother is one of them?"

"Actually, it is only Paula I care about."

"Boy-o! A happy married life includes a happy extended family. You know that! Love is blind, not stupid."

Thomas laughed. "What did I say that was so funny?" Jon asked.

"You have a peke-yake (unique) way with words."

"I'll take that as a compliment. I'm all packed and I'm starved." Jon went through the sitting room and knocked on the adjoining bedroom door. "We are ready to go down to breakfast, if you are..."

His father opened the door, "Go down and get us a table, we'll be ready in a few minutes."

"Right-o! See you in a bit."

THE DC3 ARRIVED IN Nairobi from Kampala on schedule. Cyril Latham met them in his Land Rover and ferried them to the Mayflower Hotel, for taxis were few and often quite rag-tag. He was delighted to meet Lady Mary and Sir Peter Caulfield, for they were considered leaders in the local business community as well as society, for they were one of the few families that still occupied an original land grant. Most had been sold when the original land grant owners died and their heirs did not want to live in Africa.

JON HAD ASKED THE manager of the Victoria Hotel in Kampala to book a suite at the Mayflower Hotel in Nairobi for them. The manager had made the reservations personally, as he was most happy to assist friends of the Kabaka, especially those who returned to the hotel in his Rolls Royce limousine.

The suite was on the third (top) floor of the Mayflower Hotel. A private elevator served the two Penthouse suites. The suite was entered on the sitting room side of the great room, which included a dining area for ten. The French doors on the far side of the sitting room opened onto a large covered balcony, enclosed on three sides, which was decorated with cushioned wicker furniture, a woven grass rug and potted ferns. The balcony overlooked the walkways and gardens of the hotel compound to the south. The entire hotel and grounds were surrounded by a twelve foot high masonry and mortar-covered wall topped with broken glass.

On one side of the French doors to the balcony, a wet bar was inset with a small stocked refrigerator with icemaker, ice bucket, tongs and shelves of glasses. On the other side of the French doors was a small powder room. On either end of the great room area were the doors to the spacious bedrooms, each with two double beds and a bright roomy bath, with tub and stall shower, lit by a frosted glass skylight. The bedroom windows were also French doors, which opened onto tiny, plant-filled balconies fully enclosed in a decorative wrought iron balloon. The rooms, including the balcony, all had high ceilings with large fans.

Once the bellboy had placed the luggage in the bedrooms as directed, he filled the ice bucket with ice from the refrigerator trays and refilled the trays with water, he was gone. Sir Peter turned to Jon and said, "Why did you arrange for such a grand suite? We would have been just as happy in rooms."

"Dad, this hotel has a small lobby and it is quite public. We are going to be here a few days and need a place to entertain privately. We met some lovely people from England who will be visiting us, and of course, there is Paula and Kybo. We might also be doing some business here as well, for which we will need privacy."

CYRIL LATHAM HAD DISCREETLY gone out on the balcony. The suite was perfect. Obviously, Jon and Thomas had not discussed any of the business about the diary with their parents yet. The negotiations were a 'go' at this point. All of the terms had been met and a preliminary agreement had been reached

"WHAT KIND OF BUSINESS, son?"

"Dad, Mom, come and sit and have a glass of wine; Thomas, Mr. Latham, please join us." Jon gave Mr. Latham a glass of wine and handed Thomas a glass of lemon water. Once everyone was settled, he said, "Thomas, this is really your business. Would you like to tell Mom and Dad about it?"

"No, Jon. You do it. I don't understand most of it; or let Mr. Latham tell them."

"Jon said, "Mr. Latham you have the floor."

Peter and Mary looked at each other with questioning glances.

Cyril Latham stood. It was a habit of his when speaking. "I have had the great good fortune of knowing Paula's Uncle David in Philadelphia. We went through college and law school together. When Paula asked her uncle for advice, he got in touch with me here in Africa. I then met Paula in Yaoundé, where she put me on retainer.

"While Thomas and Paula were traveling back to the cove in the rainforest, Paula, who is a botanist, asked him to draw some of the healing plants, known only to some medicine men, in the back of her diary; for finding this type of plant was the reason for the Expedition of which she was a member.

"Upon reaching the cove, Paula found the Expedition had abandoned her and later she resigned from the Expedition. But not before she allowed Dr. Miles to see the plant drawings in her diary. This, and other problems, caused the cancellation of the Expedition, whereupon Dr. Miles was forced to resign from his position at Penn.

"Paula was again abducted after our meeting in Yaoundé. She had allowed me to take her diary to Nairobi for safekeeping. So, the mercenary hired to obtain the diary was unable to steal it. He let her go unharmed, but it occurred to Paula that the mercenary might then go after the artist, Thomas... and he did. They traveled almost a thousand miles in Africa, trying to escape the mercenary, but he had good intelligence and always managed to find them.

"Finally, in Luanda, they arranged a meeting with the mercenary on Captain Jones' motor yacht. There, they agreed to sell one of the herbal remedies with a ten million dollar binder. My firm has been working on the agreements. At this time, it looks like we have a deal. So, to answer your question: it is an Herbal Medicine business."

"I AM SIMPLY ASTOUNDED! I don't know what to say! Mary, help me out here."

"Peter, I'm speechless too. Such a vast amount of money for one herbal remedy; what does it do?"

At this point Thomas was the expert and he replied, "It is a plant that takes away anxiety and helps you to sleep normally. It has no lingering side effects."

Sir Peter said, "I can see why someone would be willing to pay ten million dollars for the secret to a plant that can do what you say... I, myself, would have given half my fortune for it, at one time." He smiled ruefully.

CYRIL LATHAM CONTINUED. "THERE are other plants in the diary, any one of which could be worth the same amount of money... or more if Thomas and Paula are willing to sell the secrets."

Sir Peter shook his head saying, "Hale, hearty, accomplished, spiritually strong, mentally well-adjusted... and now wealthy. Mary, maybe we should have dropped all of our children out in the bush!"

Sir Peter was not known for his wit, and so caught them all unawares. The laughter continued as Jon quipped, "Well, I for one, always felt a bit 'dropped off'."

As Thomas laughed, he wished Paula were there to enjoy his family's good humor. His father's compliments made his chest ache with pride, and he would have liked for Paula to hear them. She had been so right in her opinion about his parents, and so right about their love for him.

26

Friends

Jon opened the door expecting to see Anna Louise and her parents. "Paula, Kybo, where are the Holmesbys?" He asked.

"They will be along at six thirty." Paula replied."

"Well, come in! You must meet our parents!"

Paula walked into the room with a bright smile and shining eyes, looking for Thomas. There he was, off to the side, looking at her as if no one else existed. She tore her eyes away as Jon said, "Mom, Dad this is Paula Thornton.

Paula held out her hand, first to lady Mary and then to Sir Peter, saying, "I've looked forward to meeting the parents of such illustrious sons, both of whom have literally saved my life. You must be bursting with pride at having such altruistic progeny."

Both Sir Peter and Lady Mary were delighted by Paula. Her intelligence and education were obvious in her speech and friendly manner; she was totally self-confident and assured. Thomas stood aside admiring her. He had never seen her in a dress before with her hair done up. She was lovelier than he remembered.

Jon then introduced Kybo. "Kybo is the newest member of our family, but one who is most important. A distinguished Medicine Man must have an afiza; it is necessary for his status. To this end, Kybo has dedicated his life to Thomas."

Slightly taken aback, Sir Peter held out his hand and said, "We welcome you to our family, Kybo."

Lady Mary, who understood the natives and their mores better than her husband, knew well the depth of such a commitment. She said, "We hope you will be happy with us.

We are pleased that our son has such a worthy person for his aide."

Thomas approached and elaborated: "Kybo's father, Kimbo, works for Max Mason, Jon's trading partner. Kybo is Ibo from Nigeria, a man who sees much with his heart. He is my better half. If I cannot do it, Kybo can."

Kybo smiled his knowing smile and said, "So far, my half has not been needed."

Sir Peter drew Paula into conversation. He had been fascinated by the few details he had heard of Paula's abduction and flight from the Ndezi. He said, "I'm simply amazed by your ability to function under such unbelievable duress."

Paula smiled saying, "I'm sure it was the kimmea that enabled me to function as I did. The natives were giving it to me for days before I realized they had to be drugging me... for I should have been terrified out of my wits... but was only mildly distressed."

Sir Peter looked confused so Thomas explained: "Kimmea is the plant I mentioned earlier. It is a common plant that relieves anxiety, calms the nerves and produces deep restful sleep."

"Who else knows about this plant?" Peter asked, as Jon offered them a beverage while raising an eyebrow at Thomas.

"Just medicine men–but not all medicine men."

A light knock caught their attention. Certain this would be the Holmesbys; Jon handed the tray to Thomas and leaped to the door, yanking it open. His effervescent smile greeted the awaited guests.

Jon said, "Hello! Hello! It's so good of you to come; we are delighted! Come in! Come in! Mom, Dad, these are the Holmesbys; they are our neighbors in England. Harold is a horticulturist and butterfly collector, and Julia, while a school principal, is basically a horseman. Anna Louise graduated at half term from the Croft School. She knows Hanna and Sara quite well."

Conversation soon became animated, for the guests and hosts found many friends and interests in common. As soon as decency allowed, Jon and Anna Louise drifted to the balcony. Thomas saw them go, and smiled wistfully at Paula with a subtle nod of his head. Paula soon disengaged herself from conversation and joined him on the balcony.

In the sitting room, the conversation turned to the horses with Julia being fascinated with Mary's avocation. Harold and Sir Peter were having an in-depth discussion of tea farming and vineyards.

Thomas listened with one ear while his father and Harold talked about the growing of tea and grapes, and wondered about the possibility of growing kimmea plants. If they grew the plants and sold them in a dried and powdered form, he would not be exposing the forests to kuteka (rapacious) people, who might destroy many other plants too, leaving nothing for the natives.

The next hour, until dinner was served in the suite dining area, was very illuminating for Thomas. He was amazed at the change in Paula. She was all light and fluffy. Her thoughtful and quietly reserved demeanor was absent in the chattering conversation. It made him realize how little he really knew Paula and the life she had led before coming to Africa. I must change that.

Cyril Latham and Kybo excused themselves after dinner, when the group set off for an evening stroll.

Thomas held hands with Paula on their walk, which encouraged Jon to do the same with Anna Louise. Thomas questioned the steel fences over the shop windows and doors. Jon explained about the Mau-Mau rebellion and the resultant changes due to the terrorism. Harold and Sir Peter remained deep in tea leaves and grapes. Lady Mary and Julia had migrated to native art and antiques.

Apartheid was rigid in Kenya. Kybo's room fronted the street, outside the compound walls, near the entrance for the tradesmen and kitchen help and housekeeping staff, which was always protected by uniformed and armed guards. The long row of rooms was reserved for the servants of the guests of the Mayflower Hotel. They were Spartan, but clean.

Best of all, Kybo was free to come and go as he chose; he liked that. His free time was an adventure and an education. He saw the misery of the native in Nairobi. He already knew about village misery, but city misery was worse... the quiet dignity of thousands of years of survival was gone, only degradation remained. He was reminded of the street people of Enugu, the ones that had no hope. They lived in a perpetual fog.

Kybo wondered what caused such despair, for you could also find it where natives had a good living. Was it the deep need to belong to a tribe–to function in tribal order? Was it the change in the way the native had to think to associate with the white man? Kybo liked the white man, but he didn't understand his thinking, except for Thomas and Max Mason. He had gotten used to Jon because he liked his happy, easy-going ways.

Thomas and Max understand the black man and how he thinks... that's it! Most white men do not understand how the black man thinks; because the black man reasons differently, the white man thinks he reasons not at all; which leaves the black man in a mental void–not tribal–not white; for few black men, if any, will ever think like a white man. He has not the cultural basis for it, and vice-versa. I must discuss this idea with the kigozi when next we are alone.

CYRIL LATHAM, ESQ., WAS pleased with the events of the afternoon and evening as he drove home. He felt his suggestions to Sir Peter about supplying Government House in Entebbe with table wine, were well received. Cyril had suggested he send sample bottles of various vintages to Government House, requesting full payment with the order, saying, "Once your wine is in Uganda, your bill could be stuck in red tape for years." Sir Peter was accustomed to dealing with people with whom their word was their bond... African governments were indifferent about their word, and had no bond whatsoever.

DURING DINNER, LADY MARY, seconded by Sir Peter, extended an invitation to the Holmesbys to visit the tea farm. Jon, who was overjoyed by the invitation, then suggested, "We can tour a bit of Nairobi in the morning: go to the game park just a few miles away and see the reticulated giraffe, an unusual species; a stop-off to view the great Rift Valley; and then the coffee farm of Karen Blixen, who now writes from her family home in Denmark, under the pen name of Isak Dinesen."

"I have read her work," Julia said, "Anecdotes of Destiny". Oh, I'm so excited. This is such an unexpected pleasure."

"Did you know that 'Mrs. Karen', 'Msabu' to the Kikuyu left Africa in 1931, bankrupt? Her story is one of determination and fortitude in the face of adversity. Her kindness and compassion in dealing with the natives, has over time, made her famous. The natives still hold her in the greatest esteem; and some presently correspond with her. While she owned the farm, she made outright gifts of portions of her land to the squatters, (local term for native farm workers) so they would always have a home. The coffee shamba (farm) of Karen Blixen is on the way home."

Julia and Harold were surprised, but pleased, by the unexpected invitation to Dela-Aden and Jon's tour. Anna Louise glowed with pleasure as she thought. I am so glad I talked Mummy and Daddy out of the bus tour; I was hoping Jon would fill in the gaps. He does so like to plan things.

Paula said, "Thomas and I have a meeting with Cyril Latham tomorrow. We can tour the game park with you, but will have to forego the rest of the tour until another time."

Jon, always quick to adjust, said, "We will return to Nairobi the day after tomorrow. If you are finished your business by then, we can go back to the farm together... if not, I'll just wait until you can leave. Can you spare the Land Rover for a few days Dad?"

"Yes, of course... not a problem."

Thomas saw the teeny smile at the corner of Paula's mouth and the raised eyebrow when she glanced at him, and his heart thumped in his chest. Was he going to achieve his heart's desire soon?

Peter said, "Do we have time for a rubber?"

Harold replied, "We'd be delighted."

While the parents played a game of bridge, the young adults once again retreated to the semi-private seclusion of the balcony, where Thomas had his first exposure to the conversation of young people, who were getting to know one another. He did not know this talking about one's self at all, but he liked hearing it.

The bridge game ended with Harold and Julia winners. As they left, after telling Anna Louise not to make it too late, Thomas had a thought.

"I will be back." He said, and followed Harold and Julia to the elevator.

"Mr. Holmesby, might I have a word with you...?" Thomas asked.

Julia smiled saying, "I'll go on down to our room... might I have the key?"

"Let's sit here on this bench; I have a question for you. As a Medicine Man, I was taught about plants that heal. A common plant, which grows wild in Africa, has some unusual and very helpful effects. My question to you is this: can a plant that grows in the wild, be cultivated?"

"One has only to duplicate the soil and growing needs: light, moisture and temperature, of a plant to cultivate it. Some plants need other plants to grow well, or the manure of certain animals, or the leaf compost of specific trees. A dctailed analysis of the different mediums where the plant presently grows in the wild would be necessary for a successful operation. Does that answer your question?"

"Yes sir, it does. May I call on you again if I need more information?"

"But, of course, dear boy. I'm delighted to be of assistance to you at any time."

"Please don't say anything about our conversation. At this point, I'm just thinking."

Harold put a finger to his lips saying, "Mum's the word," as the elevator door closed.

Paula left Jon and Anna Louise sharing 'getting-to-know-you' stories. She joined Lady Mary and Sir Peter in the sitting room, where they were discussing distance riding, when Thomas returned.

Lady Mary said, “Thomas, do you still ride? I mean, have you ridden these past years?”

“No Mother, I haven’t even seen a horse since I left home.”

“Oh well, it will come back to you easily. You were quite good, you know... a natural rider. My, it has been quite a busy day. I’m ready for bed; coming, Peter?”

THOMAS WATCHED HIS PARENTS shut the door before he seated himself on the settee next to Paula. He took her hand saying, “I have had an idea. What do you think of growing the kimmea ourselves?”

It was an entirely new thought for her, one that stunned her. “That would be a tremendous commitment, Thomas. It isn’t something I can decide without a great deal more information.”

He said, “Yes, I know... but the idea of doing it... what do you think of that?”

Paula looked at him. He did not seem eager, just curious. “Why do you even think of doing this?”

“I am worried about greedy men coming to Africa and destroying the plant life in the forests looking for the kimmea.”

“Yes, I am worried about that too. Maybe you felt my fears. You know the kimmea plant, I do not; but plants in the strawberry family are usually easy to grow.”

“It may not be in the strawberry family; it likes some shade, not full sun. It grows year to year in the same place from its own seed, not the same stalk.”

“Where does it like to grow?”

“It likes to grow in moist places, near moss or ferns; or under oak trees in spotted sunlight. In Africa, you can drop the seeds in a good place and have a grown plant in three moons.”

“Does it make a difference when you drop the seeds?”

"Yes, after a rainy season is better than before. If the ground is too dry, or too wet the seeds do not grow."

"Sounds like a good hothouse plant to me."

"Yes, it likes the same home as the orchids we saw in the flower shop in Kisangani."

"Does the kimmea flower?"

"Yes, it gets tiny white flowers that become the seedpods."

"When is the best time to harvest a plant?"

"After the flowers have all turned to shiny red berries."

"And you say, from start to finish is just three months?"

"Yes, unless it is too dry or too wet, then the growth slows."

"How much kimmea does it take to make a dose?"

"What is a dose?"

Smiling, "A dose is what you put in my broth."

"Oh! One nice bushy plant will make enough kimmea to put in your broth every day for two years." Paula was stunned.

"Two years? Are you sure?"

"Yes, once the plant is dried and powdered, only a few grains are needed. That is why you did not know you were being drugged. Such a small dose has no taste or odor."

"How big do these plants grow?"

"At maturity, before the leaf edges turn brown, it is the size of a squash plant, not taller than your knee, or wider than a melon."

Paula grabbed the bridge score pad and worked the numbers. She shook her head and did the numbers again. Astonished, she looked up at Thomas and said, "A hothouse with planting space that is one hundred feet long by ten feet wide, with artificial light and a sprinkler system, growing on three tiers... has the capability of growing twelve thousand plants a year for a total of seventeen million, five hundred and twenty thousand, doses for an income of eight hundred and seventy six thousand dollars a year at five cents royalty a dose, or 5% of the gross product. I made eighty dollars a week as a 'lab rat' for Dr. Miles."

"I do not understand the money; it sounds like a fantasy. I am concerned only that greedy people will come and ravage

Africa of kimmea plants. Once the plant is harvested and in powder form, they will not know what it looks like. There are two other plants that are similar at harvesting, with the same feel and color. One is poisonous, and will stop you from breathing. The other will give you bowel problems, although neither one gets the red seed pods when the plant has gone past maturity."

Anna Louise came in the sitting room from the balcony and went to the powder room, while Jon came over to join them. "What are you talking about? Did I hear big money mentioned?" Jon asked.

"Yes, you did. But making money is not my desire here." Thomas replied.

"Well, I'm not opposed to making big money... as long as I don't have to do manual labor for it."

Thomas laughed, "You're on Jon; you get the headaches and you can have all the money. You will only have to pay me a small bit for my knowledge."

The smile left Jon's face and he said, "You're serious, aren't you?"

"Yes, but tonight is not the time to talk about it. We have to run all of this by Cyril Latham tomorrow. He may not approve of my idea. It is time to walk the ladies to their rooms or Anna's parents will be annoyed with you.

WHILE THEY WAITED FOR the elevator, Paula realized that she had been so occupied lately that she hadn't had time to think about the mercenary, or wonder why he was on the plane with them. She dreaded that he was hatching another plot. Does he have people watching us? Does he know where we are in Nairobi? Oh, how I hate this feeling. I know I am safe with Thomas and Jon. I must think of something else!

I wonder if Thomas realizes what a big business growing the kimmea would be... and the headaches that would come with such a project. I hate to dump cold water on his ideas... maybe Mr. Latham will do that for me tomorrow.

Outside the door to her room, Thomas said, "What are you worried about?"

"How do you know I'm worried?"

He smiled, "You chew on the inside of your lip when you are worried."

Paula laughed, "Yes, I do. I can't keep secrets with a *tell* like that, can I?"

"Tell?"

"Distinct things that people do, which *tell* others about them, or what they may be thinking, are called, *tells*."

"Do I have any *tells*?"

Paula thought for a moment, then said, "You have a few; nothing distinctive, but someone that knows you might suspect something when you are unusually silent; or that you are frustrated when you press your lips together."

"Yes, you picked up on my silence while we were on the trail. I was not aware of it myself."

"Most of the time, people aren't aware of their own *tells*, but other people notice them."

Thomas smiled and gathered her close as he leaned down and kissed her forehead lightly with little kisses; before lightly kissing her eyelid, her cheek, her ear–where he took her lobe gently in his lips and tugged softly–her neck, her chin and finally, he softly kissed her mouth. Paula had melted in his embrace by the time the little kisses reached her neck, and he had felt her yield to him. Her surrender thrilled him as nothing else in his life ever had. He felt like devouring her, for kissing her deeply inflamed him almost beyond reason.

Paula went with him on his journey into the nether regions of his passion. Her mind floated in a cloud of bliss that enveloped her in its soft undisciplined comfort. A door banged, she heard voices and the cloud vanished. Thomas yielded and let her return to reality. Kissing her lightly on the nose, he said, "One day, we will be alone and the sun, the moon and the stars will be ours."

The hardest thing Paula had ever done was open the door to her room, say goodnight, and close it again... and be all alone. She leaned her head against the door knowing that one day this sensible act of will power would be beyond her. Walking past the bath into the room she gasped, someone had searched through her things again. She ran to the door, opened it and looked down the hall, but Thomas was gone.

SITTING ON THE EDGE of the bed in his pajamas and robe, Harold said to Julia, “Do you like this young man... Jon?”

“Yes, of course; he’s delightful.”

“He has no occupation. He seems the playboy to me.”

“I think he intends to help his father run the tea farm. But his first endeavor was to find his brother... and he did. Now, he is trying to smooth the way for him. It is what he considers most important now.’

“Were you talking to Anna Louise?”

“Yes, she is quite taken with Jon.”

“So I noticed.”

“They are not our class, you know.”

“Yes, but they don’t seem to care about class here in Africa as much as they do at home.”

“I disagree. I think they care more here, but have fewer choices and make the best of what is acceptable.”

“That may be, but we are presentable, and we have much in common. If Jon and Anna Louise get serious, we may be family. Let’s just go on as good guests and friends. What will be; will be.”

“I just don’t want to see Anna Louise hurt.”

“If she gets hurt, it will be her doing, not his.”

A key sounded in the lock, the door opened and Anna Louise stepped in holding the door open. Jon popped his head in and said; “Hope we didn’t keep Anna Louise out too late; the time just flew by. See you at nine for the tour.”

Julia smiled at Harold, who shrugged his shoulders and grimaced.

PETER LOOKED AT MARY and said, “The fat is in the fire now. I suppose your invitation meant that you approved of Anna Louise for Jon.”

“Yes, that’s what it means. Don’t you approve?”

“Of course I do... if you do... I mean... this is your province, not mine; I’m just stunned.”

"Why are you stunned?"

"Jon is so young. He's just out of college. He has no job, just an avocation... he does not know the world..."

"I think you forget yourself. How old were you when you asked me to marry you?"

"That was because of the war."

"Are you saying you didn't love me, didn't want me–it was only because of the war that you married me?"

"Now Mary, don't distort the facts, you know what I mean."

"Do you know what you mean? Jon has a good job with you on the farm. He has always helped when he was home from school, and you didn't have to push him to it. He expects to help you again, once he has Thomas settled, which may disappoint him terribly, for I don't think Thomas will be content on the farm. Without Anna Louise, I think we will lose Jon... to Africa."

Peter sat on the edge of the bed. "That's it! I can sense that Jon will always want to be with Thomas, and Thomas will always want to be with the Zuri Watu."

"It troubles me too. I don't want to lose Thomas again and Jon with him. I love Thomas more now than as a boy. He is the man I dreamed of... when he was a young boy. I can't face the parting." Mary said with anguish in her voice.

"Well, if we let him go, he'll come back; if we try to restrain him, he will go, and never come back. The last few days have been traumatic for us, but they have been wonderful too. Let us dwell only on the joy; there is no sense in experiencing the pain until it comes."

Peter took Mary in his arms saying, "How could you ever think that I didn't love you or want you? Without you, I am nothing."

"Not so Peter, without each other, we are only pillars. Together, we pillars support an arch and the arch is our children and our lives and those that depend on us. I need you just as much as you need me, and that is what makes our love lasting."

"You know, I do like Anna Louise. She is so sweet and gentle."

"I think that is what draws Jon. It would draw any man who is used to having his way. But Jon is also kind and considerate. He will never hurt her and I think that is what draws her to him."

"So, you think it is a good match?"

"I do. The best we could want for Jon. I like Julia and Harold too. They have great self esteem and self confidence, and are quite gracious."

"Yes, Harold is a bit bombastic, but in an enjoyable way. Tomorrow will tell the tale. I'm looking forward to going home."

"Me too; I miss my horses."

Peter kissed Mary on the cheek, thinking: I am the luckiest man in the world... but I think I'm also the most managed man in the world too. He smiled at his erudite deduction... but I wouldn't have it any other way.

27

Surprise

IT TOOK AN HOUR to cover the agreements that Cyril Latham had developed with Corsica Industries, a conglomerate that included transportation, medicine, and foreign development.

"The sticking point is supply." Cyril Latham finished. "I don't have the answers, do you?"

"I might," Thomas replied. "First, let me ask you a question. Do you have confidence in the character of the people you have dealt with so far?"

"Confidence in their character?"

"Yes, do you feel they are worthy people who will keep to their word?"

"It wasn't a consideration on my part. The agreement, when signed, will cover the ethics involved. I have included a fifty million dollar penalty for any breach of contract."

Thomas said to Paula, "Ethics - breach?"

"Ethics: moral requirements; breach: broken promises."

Thomas turned back to Mr. Latham saying, "You told us the one unanswered question was that of supply. Did they offer you any suggestions?"

"No, without the information in Paula's diary, they don't know if the plant can be cultivated. So, that is probably their question of supply."

"The information for growing kimmea is not in the diary; only a drawing of the plant and its use and preparation.

"It is a worry to me that these people are not trustworthy. That once the agreement is signed, they will send hundreds of people into Africa to plunder the bush looking for Kimmea plants. Without the plants going to seed, the kimmea will not grow again.

"I had decided not to sell the kimmea until my father said, 'I would have given half my fortune for such a plant at one time', when he heard of the plant's effects. I would like to help people who suffer, such as my father suffered. For this reason, I have considered growing the plant and supplying it in powdered form, ready to be made into pills. What do you think of that idea?"

Cyril replied, "It is a complex idea–do you want to be tied to growing, harvesting and processing the kimmea? There will be the building of hothouses, the overseeing and the hiring of workers, as well as office staff. For I can tell you, the market for such a remedy is endless."

Cyril leaned back in his executive chair thinking. He has no idea about mass production... a huge can of worms. But he asked, "Do you know if the plant can be cultivated as a crop?"

"Not yet, I must go back to the forest to find kimmea plants. Mr. Holmesby suggested that I test the soil where the kimmea grows well. I have found kimmea in many different places, but some things are always the same. Mr. Holmesby said any plant can be cultivated if you can duplicate its growing needs. I do not want to be tied to a growing process, but Jon might like it. He is a farmer at heart. It might please him."

"I don't suppose you have any preliminary figures for me?"

Paula answered, "Last night I calculated roughly, that a hothouse with a growing area of 100' x 10', using one level, could produce five million, eight hundred and forty doses in a year. If we were able to use growing lights and three tiers, we could triple that number to seventeen million, five hundred and forty thousand doses... at five percent of the gross, that would be eight hundred and seventy six thousand dollars ... if there were ten hothouses–well, you do the math."

"Cyril turned to his calculator. I'm stunned. We are talking billions of dollars here. No wonder they resorted to hiring mercenaries and using multi-million dollar yachts!"

Suddenly Thomas spoke up..."You are right! I do not want

to be tied to growing kimmea. Jon may not want to be tied to it either. I have thought of another option. We could just sell the seed. I have enough seed to start one hot house. In three months, we would have enough seed for thousands of hothouses.

"If we can provide them with an endless supply of seed, there would be no reason for anyone to come to Africa looking for kimmea in the bush."

Paula said, "Oh Thomas, that's a much better idea. What do you think Mr. Latham?"

"Yes, I agree, it's a much better approach; but first, we must find out if the kimmea can be grown in a hothouse. Does kimmea grow locally, or near your parent's farm?" Cyril asked.

"I do not know. I have not yet been to the farm. As a young boy, I did not know about the kimmea."

"Of course, we have ten days. Is that enough time?" Cyril asked.

Paula said, "I can do the soil testing... if we find a place locally where the kimmea grows, so ten days should be enough time to get started. But, until the plants go to seed, in ninety days, we won't know if the cultivation is successful."

"One step at a time, Cyril said. First, we'll see if you can find the kimmea growing locally, so you can test the soil. If we need more time, I'll reset the date. I don't think that will be a problem; what you're doing is taking the time to guarantee a viable product."

Cyril took them to lunch and then back to the hotel. Jon had kept the suite, saying to Paula, "You will be safer in the suite with Thomas, and I will worry less."

The meeting had exhausted Paula. The commitment looming up was a terrible burden to her. She wanted to be free to travel, to go to England, to visit the Holmesbys, to go home to the States and take Thomas with her.

Money? She, like Thomas, felt excess money to be a burden. She wanted enough to do the things she wanted to do... she wanted to be financially secure... but she did not long for great wealth.

PAULA CALLED OUT TO Thomas, "I'm going to unpack, would you ring for tea?" It occurred to Paula that she had not paid for anything since Douala. Jon had picked up all her expenses. She had not planned on any expenses in Africa, short of postage, souvenirs and a few gifts. She checked her traveler's checks. She still had $850.00 of the $1,000.00 dollars she had started out with... without Jon, I wouldn't be here now, for my money would be long gone.

It was a queer feeling. She felt thrust back to the eighteenth century, when people, the upper class and royalty, traveled around the countryside with their personal servants, grooms and horses, living off their hosts, for weeks at a time.

She put on a fresh sundress after washing up, brushed her hair and went out to the sitting room. Thomas was still in his room, so Paula went out on the balcony. It is so pleasant out here, she thought, with this high view of the kidney-shaped gardens that line the walkways. She rested her head in contentment on the lounge chair pillow, closed her eyes, and was soon dozing.

The rattling sound of teacups and silverware awoke her as Thomas placed the tea tray on the table. "How long have I been asleep?"

"Not long, the tea has just arrived."

"This is déjà vu. You and I have been here, and done this before. It must be our fate." Paula said smiling as she accepted a cup of tea from Thomas.

"A fate I have been hoping would happen."

"Yes, it is delightful to be able to talk to you again... like it was on our trek back to the cove."

"Without the lions, the leopards and the gorillas," he said, chuckling, as he sat on the foot cushion of her lounge chair.

She smiled and added, "Without the Ndezi, an injured ankle and a concussion," and they laughed together.

She put her hand on his arm and looked into his eyes, saying, "No matter what the future brings, we must always find time to be alone together, for my happiness is only complete when I am alone with you."

"Yes, everything is different when we are alone together."

A companionable silence filled the air as they sipped their tea. Will this be our last time truly alone together for a long time? Paula thought. No, we must strive to be alone every day, even if it is only for a walk. I need him the way he is when we are alone together.

Thomas was thinking: Is the kimmea going to change everything? No! I will not let it. We must not let it run our lives. I must go back to the Zuri Watu and I want to take Paula with me.

"We might as well get it over with... putting it off only makes me tense." Paula said.

"Yes, let's talk about what we want to do: Kimmea is a good plant to help people. I would like to help people. But I do not want to be tied to growing plants."

"Oh, I'm so glad you said that!" Paula's relief was palpable. "I agree and feel the same way. You mentioned selling the seed to let others do the growing. What about selling the seed you have now, the process for drying and powdering and then asking for a royalty on every pill sold?"

"What is a royalty?"

"An amount paid for each pill sold; I'm sure we'll find a good use for the money, but, most important, Africa would be safe, and the kimmea would be helping people. It would be unnecessary to look for plants in the bush when they can grow all the plants they want in hothouses." Paula sighed, "If it will grow in hothouses, Africa will be safe." A small nagging feeling pulled at her... and then it was gone.

"Jon will be back tomorrow." Thomas continued. "We can go to the farm and explore the forests there. If we find the kimmea, we can get the soil and then we will know. It is a good plan. If we do not find kimmea, we will have to go back to Kampala. I think I saw some plants in the woods where we saw the leopard cubs, but I was too far away to be sure."

Paula was so relieved, that she felt light... like she could float away. The dreadful dilemma that had been looming over her might have a reasonable solution. She had a good idea about the problems of business from helping her Mother at the peak of tax season. Add to that building, growing, harvesting, payroll and staff...and the idea was a nightmare for her.

Paula arose and took her teacup to the table. Thomas took the tray and put it on the bench outside the suite door, while Paula went to get a glass of iced lemon water. "Would you like a lemon water, she asked?"

"Yes, thank you. I feel dry. It must be the altitude."

He came up close and took the drink. Their eyes met as they sipped the cool refreshing liquid... and locked. He looked deeply into her mind and saw she was waiting for him. He leaned closer and closer until he brushed his lips on her forehead, covering her eyes, her cheeks, her chin and her neck with little kisses. He took her drink and his and put them on the bar. Caressing her upper arms with his hands, he continued to cover her neck and ears, and all around her face with soft little kisses. She yearned for him... she wanted more... and then his lips touched hers so softly that she wasn't sure he was kissing her. Paula moaned and felt the slow increased pressure of his lips covering her mouth. His hunger for her was all she could feel. He tightened his hold around her pulling her close against his strong hard body. For long moments, the kiss enveloped them both, body and soul. Needing breath, he covered her cheek and ear with soft slow little kisses, whispering, "I love you. I love you more than life. You are my sun, my moon and my stars. Without you, life would be a dark wilderness for me."

Paula snuggled in his arms, with her head on his chest. She could feel the strong, and somewhat increased, beating of his heart. Never, had she heard such beautiful words, and she nestled closer, basking in the joy of them. His strong fingers caressed her back and neck and riffled through her hair, gently grabbing a handful as he tenderly pulled her head from his chest to kiss her again. The kiss deepened, his hunger exploded and became insistent. She felt her body tingle in places where she had never tingled before. She didn't want him to stop. She wanted to go wherever his passion would take her and urged him on. She was his, she knew that; but now she knew that he was hers too. Now, they could drown together in the fervor of their love.

He drew away just as she thought she would suffocate from the zeal of his passionate kiss. He held her a bit away from him and looked again deeply into her eyes–the windows of her heart and mind. She trusted him. She would willingly go where he would lead. Jon's words came back to him... 'Her future happiness is in your hands'. He pulled her close to his chest and propped his chin on her head. It is enough to know that she would go wherever I would lead her. I can wait to lead her another time... a time that is right for both of us.

Paula knew, by his gentle caress, that he had restrained himself. Her taut body was sad, but her virgin's mind was glad. She now knew that he would always put her first. She could trust him with her heart, her life and her future. They would be safe in his hands.

She whispered. "I love you far beyond what is good for me; because you love me more than you love yourself. No woman could ask, or receive, more than that from a man."

Stepping back, he picked up their lemon drinks, handed her glass to her and said, "Manutu taught me patience in all things, but I doubt if he was thinking of love or lovers at the time."

Paula smiled, "I must one day meet Manutu. I already respect him; but it is difficult to love someone you have never met, yet I think it is so."

Tamubu's heart soared, his chest filled to bursting, an empty buzzing filled his head as a voice said to him. "You have chosen well, my son. I will wait for you."

A KNOCK CAME ON the door. Thomas opened the door to find a hotel porter with a salver with a note upon it. Paula appeared behind him and gave the man a coin as she took the note.

Opening it she read: 'Dear Paula and Thomas, Would it be convenient for you to join me for dinner? I have had the pleasure of a friend from college dropping by, and we would most enjoy your company. Casual dress is fine. I'll call for you at your suite at seven. Please give your reply to the porter. C.L.'

Paula took the proffered pen and scribbled: We accept. P.M.T.

When the porter was gone, Thomas said, "What was all that?"

"We have been invited to dinner with Cyril Latham who has a friend from college visiting him. I accepted, as I knew you would want to go. He will meet us here at seven."

Paula looked at her watch, "It is four-thirty. Would you mind if I took a nap? These long days without our noon rest are catching up to me." Paula kissed Thomas playfully on the cheek saying, "I hate to sleep through our precious moments alone, but if I don't lie down, I'm going to fall down... I'm that tired."

PAULA AGAIN WORE HER white dress, with the black and brown jungle print and the short white jacket. She wore her hair pulled back from the sides and held back with a barrette to show off her earrings. Thomas had showered, shaved and dressed in clean safari clothes and his kitu-kina. Jon had picked up their new clothes, (made by the tailor in Douala) from the shipper yesterday, but Thomas needed Jon to help him dress in those togs. He was now very much at home in his safari clothes.

Thomas had a lemon water drink ready for Paula when she came to the balcony. "Did you have a nice rest?"

"I think I was asleep before my head touched the pillow."

"Do you like this suite?"

"Yes, it is delightful, why do you ask?"

"Is it like your home?

"Yes, a bit. Our home is larger, has more rooms and has several floors."

"Why do you have more than one floor?"

"That is the way the house was built. We have a big family room with a fireplace on the ground floor with the laundry room, powder room, summer porch and Mother's home office. The main floor has the living room, dining room, kitchen and entrance hall. The upper floor has four bedrooms and two baths. One attic was converted to an art studio for Sallee Ann and the other attic is for storage. It is what they call a split-level house."

"I suppose they need extra floors to make the house strong."

"Paula chuckled; the different levels of a house are called floors. There is only one floor on each level."

"I remember many levels on our farm house too. It too, is a big house that wanders through many rooms."

Paula suspected his angst and said, "It will be such fun for you and Jon to explore your old home again. He will take you to all the places you played when you were boys. Do you remember the tree house?"

"Yes and no. I remember a place in the trees, but not a house."

Paula smiled again. "It is only called a house; usually tree houses are just a small, crudely constructed room in a tree where children can play in secret."

"There are so many things I do not know, I need you to teach me to read. On the plane I did not know many of the words in my magazine."

"Thomas, look at me. When she had his full attention, she said, "Has my advice to you been right so far?"

"Yes, it has."

"Then trust me in this. Approach the things that are going to happen to you as a learning time with Manutu, when you did not know everything. It is the same experience. Manutu did not expect you to know everything; he had to teach you. Your family will be exactly like Manutu. They will teach you if you don't know, and will love helping you as Manutu loved helping you. If you do not know something, just ask. No one will think less of you for it, I promise you this.

"You may cause people to smile, as I just did with the floors and levels, but that is like the double meanings of words in the marching songs, they are pleasing and enjoyable. No one will be laughing at you. I would not mislead you in this. They will admire you for wanting to learn and being open about it.

Only a man who is sure of his worth is capable of learning with dignity."

Uncle David

Paula was pouring herself a lemon water, when a tattoo was heard on the door. Curious, for the tattoo was distinctly American, she went to the door and opened it. Paula gasped, tears came to her eyes and she cried, "Uncle David! Oh, my gosh!" Paula rushed to embrace the dignified man standing in the doorway.

Thomas had come in from the balcony to see Cyril Latham standing there with a huge grin on his face, as he said, "I thought Paula might like to see my friend from school."

Paula let go of her Uncle and reached up and gave Mr. Latham a kiss on the cheek, saying, "I'm so glad we were here to receive your note. Come in! Come in! Thomas, this is my Uncle David, my father's brother, my favorite relative."

Uncle David strode forward and held out his hand to Thomas saying, "I'm so glad to meet you. I have letters full of the wonderful Tamubu, I assume you are he?"

"Yes, Tamubu is my tribal name. My birth name is Thomas."

"Well, I'm certainly glad to know this young lady doesn't have a room full of wonderful men!"

Paula laughed, "Uncle David, you are wicked. You have just met Thomas and he doesn't know what a joker you are. He will think I am a loose woman."

"He won't know you very well, if he can think that!"

Thomas said, smiling, "Please, sit. Would you like a glass of wine or some lemon water?"

"Yes Thomas, two wines, two lemon waters, please. Now,

are you going to tell me why you are in Nairobi today, or not?" Paula asked.

"I was in Egypt. My work finished two days early and I decided to come down and see Cyril. I did not know that you were here, too. Cyril said nothing to me on the phone. Just now, he brought me here to introduce me to some important clients saying, 'I might need your help on this one.' I wondered why he gave the college tattoo on the door... but I never, in all my life, expected you to open the door!"

Paula wiped up her tears of joy. Uncle David continued, "I am so happy to see you looking so well. Your jungle adventures had me scared half-to-death. Your last letter was from Angola. I had no idea where you might be. I thought Cyril might help me to get in touch with your Captain Jones and get the scoop from him. Now, I can happily get the scoop from you."

"Let's go out on the balcony. It is so pleasant out there in the evening." Paula and Uncle David headed for the balcony, but Cyril put a hand on Thomas' arm, saying, "I have ordered dinner to be sent up here at eight, do you mind? I thought it would be better than going to the club."

"I think that is a good idea. Right now, we are trying to stay out of public places... Paula is worried about the mercenary again."

"Why? Has something happened?"

"Someone was in her room last night, before she returned from her evening up here. Her things were messed, but nothing was missing. We didn't find out until this morning. Jon had her move up here with me. She doesn't know that I know, let's keep it that way."

"They can't still be looking for the diary."

"Yes, they can. You have made a costly deal. They would probably like to get out of it, if they can still get the information."

"I'll take care of it tomorrow, first thing. You will not be bothered again."

It seemed no time at all before the waiters were at the door with dinner. Dinner was followed by coffee and Amaretto sipped out on the balcony.

"That was a most wonderful dinner, Mr. Latham, thank you. But not as wonderful as the dinner guest you brought with you. That was just the best surprise! We must spend the day together tomorrow. Mr. Latham, can you join us?"

"I think I could play hooky tomorrow after lunch. Isn't Jon due back tomorrow afternoon with the Holmesbys?"

"Yes. Won't he be surprised? Uncle David, where are you staying?"

"I'm putting him up with me in my bachelor's pad." Cyril replied.

"Can you drop him off here in the morning? We can have breakfast together and then pick his brains until you get here for lunch." Paula asked.

"I told you I might need your help on this one... I wasn't kidding, Cyril laughed. She's your niece. You know how persnickety she is... only the best for our lovely Paula."

David Thornton and breakfast arrived together. Over coffee, Thomas outlined his ideas about the forms in which they could sell kimmea. David then said, "I think, off hand, that your best idea is to sell the seed. Let me tell you why:

"One: You would receive the bulk of the money up front and have it to invest.

"Two: You would have no investment in hothouses or crops.

"Three: You would not have to hire workers, or set up the company to pay them, or deal with business expenses.

"Four: You would not be tied down to a day-to-day operation.

"I like Paula's idea of a bulk payment up front, and a royalty on each pill, which would produce perpetual income.

"Take the ten million up front and five million for the next ten years after the seed is provided, plus the royalties of five cents on each pill. After ten years, up the royalty to ten cents a pill. The investors will still make billions, so what you ask is reasonable.

"One other thing: I would suggest that Africa not be included in their distribution area. Only you can grow, harvest, dry, prepare or distribute the kimmea in Africa, as an herbal remedy. This would allow you to set up a corporation to import the manufactured kimmea at net cost and price it for resale. The penalty for breaking any portion of the agreement should be stiff, like one hundred million dollars.

"I will have to run all this by Cyril, of course, but I think it is all possible; any questions?"

Thomas was dazed. He could not fathom the amount of money that David tossed about so easily. But, he liked all of his suggestions, especially keeping the distribution in Africa out of foreign hands.

Paula shook her head, saying, "Not at the moment. I'm sure I will think of something when the shock wears off."

Uncle David smiled, saying, "You have found the golden goose and it will lay golden eggs for a long time."

Paula looked at Thomas, who was puzzled. "It is a fairy tale, a story for children about a giant that had a goose that laid golden eggs."

"Ah, one evening you must tell me this story of the goose that lays golden eggs."

THEY TOOK THEIR LAST cup of coffee to the veranda. The morning sun had cut through the light haze and a soft breeze carried the scent of fragrant flowers. The pleasant atmosphere reminded Paula of Thomas' attentions yesterday. She longed for the time when she would be alone with him, once more.

Paula asked Uncle David about the tax situation. "Cyril told me he has a good investments analyst and taxman in the firm, when I asked him about it. He mentioned that you might want to set up a philanthropic organization and take the income as charitable donations, which would be a plus for the buyer. He told me you might want to set up first aid stations or clinics in Africa, and educational organizations to teach basic first aid. Is this so?"

Thomas smiled at Paula who gave him a questioning look with her head tilted, as if to say, 'Where did he get that idea?'

Thomas had asked Cyril about the hospitals and the schools when Paula was in the lady's room. He had not yet mentioned it to her. "I was thinking about doing that, but I was not yet sure we would sell the kimmea... so I did not mention it to you. Do you dislike the idea?"

"I love the idea, it takes my breath away! Yes! The money from the kimmea will go for the good of Africa. Oh, this idea is so wonderful. It is the right thing to do. It makes selling the kimmea conscionable. Oh, Thomas, it is the perfect solution!"

David Thornton sat quietly, gazing out over the lovely gardens of the compound. He sipped his cold coffee, thinking. She loves him and he loves her. I think they will do great things together. Paula has always been a special person. Over the years, I sensed she had a unique destiny. I'm just glad to be a part of it in some small way.

Thomas was delighted by Paula's enthusiasm at the idea of doing good deeds with the money from the kimmea. She filled not only his heart, but she filled his soul. She was truly a kindred spirit. Manutu was pleased, his parents were pleased and Jon loved her too. Peace filled his being as he thought of their lives together; he was more than happy, he was content.

A KNOCK ON THE door had David out of his seat, saying, "That must be Cyril now. My, the morning has just dashed by."

Cyril came in with a flurry. Behind him, there were several turbaned Indians following an Indian shopkeeper. "I thought we would have Curry for lunch. I stopped on my way over and Farah made up some of my favorites. He's even brought dishes, forks and napkins. And I have dessert. My secretary made a caramel flan for David. You must have enchanted Gloria, David; she has never made a flan for me."

The elevator opened and a kitchen waiter appeared with fresh tea, cups, saucers and dessert plates and a pitcher of minted lemon water and four tall glasses.

The Indian shopkeeper, Farah, set out the lunch so they could serve themselves and took himself and his helpers out when they sat down to eat.

Cyril was expansive and told about each dish and the proper way to build the meal: rice, then the mixture, then sauce, then chutney, then raisins and nuts. The sauce was hot sauce and they could eschew it if they liked. Salt and pepper were to be applied, in lieu of sauce, after the mixture, before the chutney. It was a fun meal and the repartee was delightful. The laughter was hilarious after Thomas said, "This sauce is like eating fire; only a fool would eat fire." Most of the food he had eaten during his life didn't even have salt in it, so the hot sauce was bizarre to him.

Farah returned at two to clear away. He was pleased with the comments about his luncheon. It made the extra effort worthwhile.

Ensconced, once again, on the delightful veranda, Cyril listened to the summation of the morning's discussion. David had given them good advice. His entire office was humming as everyone was working on the phases that were his or her particular bailiwick in this deal. That is the strength of a law firm; many minds fine tuning every phase of a transaction.

THE CONVERSATION FINALLY LANDED on the establishment of a charitable organization and the pros and cons of doing it.

"You will only be able to draw salaries, of course, but they will be in ratio to the contributions received and will be subject to income taxes. Development expenses will be paid by the organization, and you will have to have a board of directors. I suggest that Thomas be Chairman; Paula, vice chairman; and Sir Peter, Lady Mary, Jon, myself and David be directors with Dr. Albert Schweitzer as director, at large... if he will accept the post. But with the stipend we will be offering, I don't think he will refuse. He is very private, but he always needs money. His work at Lambaréné is funded by religious charity, which is never enough."

Paula spoke up. "Dr. Schweitzer might be more agreeable than you think; he seemed quite interested in my findings about healing plants when we visited him. He asked me to keep him informed by letter. With all of our problems, I haven't had the opportunity to write to him."

Thomas frowned, "I don't think I should be the leader. I think Jon should be the Chairman. I do not have the experience needed for such a position."

There was silence for a few moments as everyone considered Thomas' suggestion.

Cyril replied, "Why don't we let Jon decide?"

David said, "Yes, It will be a big commitment, and only he will know if he wants the job. Another person to consider as a director is Paula's father, my brother Charles. He could bring a great deal of expertise to the development of the schools for the organization."

Paula said, "I think Dad would like that very much. Is anyone, besides me, ready for some exercise? I would love to take a walk."

Four o'clock is a lovely time of day in Nairobi. The heat of the sun has diminished, which often brings cooling showers. All of the shops are still open. The traffic noise and congestion is less than it will be after five o'clock, when the offices close. They walked to the city park, and wandered the various paths, surrounding the monument to Lord Delamere, Hugh Cholmondeley, 3rd Baron Delamere, who began the white settlement in Kenya; and was its leader for thirty years until his death in 1931. The shade trees along the walkways and the soft smell of flowers made for a pleasant stroll.

Arriving back at the suite, they found Jon had arrived with Julia and Harold and Anna Louise. Introductions were made and Jon was thrilled to meet the legendary Uncle David, saying. "It seemed as if every other sentence was, Uncle David this and Uncle David that..." which made David smile at Paula, who said, "You must know that Jon can't make a statement without exaggerating, but, for once, he doesn't."

"Where's Kybo?" she asked.

"He wanted to stay at the farm, rather than ride back and forth." Jon replied. When Dad found out Kybo used to be a teamster in Enugu, he asked him to drive a wagon so they could get the tea harvest in before the evening rain. Kybo was thrilled."

Thomas spoke up, "I didn't know Kybo was a teamster. Why did he stop?"

"Seems the owner abused the mules; loads too heavy and not enough feed. He was fired for reducing loads." Jon said.

"His father then took him on safari with him, but Kybo hated the shooting of animals for sport. Kybo joined up when Max was recruiting in his village, and his father joined with him. Kybo was the only family Kimbo had after his wife died."

"How did you learn all this? Kybo hardly ever talks."

"Unless you are playing a game of stones with him; then he talks all the time to distract you, so he can win!"

Paula and Thomas laughed. That Kybo had beaten Jon so often and so easily at the game of stones, was a sore point with him.

THE LATE AFTERNOON PASSED pleasantly while Paula, Thomas, David and Cyril listened to a description of their visit to the tea farm. Julia gushed about the horses. Harold remarked on the excellence of the crops and Anna Louise filled in the gaps. Jon just sat bemused with it all, smiling at Anna Louise.

WHEN THE HOLMESBYS LEFT to get freshened up for dinner, the group moved to the balcony with a libation. Here, Cyril told Jon what had transpired that day and asked if he would consider the position of Chairman of the Board for the charitable organization. He listed his duties and responsibilities saying, "It will be a big important job; one that will keep you busy and leave little time for the tea farm. You will be running the show with the board to advise you at meetings."

Jon said, "When would I start?"

"Not until after the sale of the kimmea is finalized, and the charity is set up; several months at least."

"I will need many more details, but at this time, I would consider the position. Do I have to live in Africa?"

"Surprised, Cyril said, "It would be best to be close to where the money is being invested. Why?"

"Well, I might want to go to England for a while. If I can't go to England, I don't want the job."

"Do you mean to stay in England?"

"Not permanently, but possibly for weeks at a time."

David spoke up, "You do know you will have a staff. There will be many people working for you, as well as a President, who would oversee the day-to-day operations... and he too, will have a staff. We are talking about a corporation here, a lean one to be sure, but one person cannot do all the work that will have to be done. Your job, as Chairman, will be to see that the decisions of the board are carried out.

"I need some time to think about this. I'm not sure I'm ready for such a big responsibility."

"It won't start out big, but it will get bigger as time goes by. The job comes with a very nice salary," Cyril said.

"How nice?"

"No way to be sure just yet, but I'd guess low six figures."

"Dollars or pounds?"

"Dollars."

"JON, THE DAY BEFORE yesterday you were interested in running a farming operation that would keep you busy from dawn to dusk. Now you are reluctant to sit in the big seat, why?" Thomas asked.

Jon, never one to prevaricate, said, "Anna Louise told me this morning that she did not want to have her children born in Africa."

This was the big bug-a-boo for English women in Africa. Most, if not all, of the women went home when they were six or seven months pregnant. Even Thomas, Jon and the twins had been born in England.

There was nothing more to say. Only time would tell, but the group knew, without a doubt, that Jon had set his heart on Anna Louise. He was not going to do anything that would jeopardize his chances with her.

Cyril said, "We have plenty of time. Nothing needs to be

decided today or even next month. Let's just see what the breeze blows by."

AT SIX THE HOLMESBYS came back for cocktails. Everyone had freshened up, with Cyril and David using the powder room to shave.

At seven they left for the Club and dinner. Cyril and David had on the old school tie and shook hands with the likewise members that Cyril knew. The meal was English: roast beef, Yorkshire pudding, salad, asparagus hollandaise, bread and butter and spotted dick for desert.

All too soon the bell tolled ten, and the dining room was closed. The group made their way back to the hotel where Julia and Harold excused themselves, and Cyril took David home with him. Paula and Thomas, Jon and Anna Louise played a game of hearts. Thomas got stuck with the queen of spades only once and then blitzed them all. "You said you've never played cards. Was that a fib?" Paula asked?

With his head tilted and eyebrow up? Paula said, "A small lie."

Thomas laughed, "You sound like Jonas when Kybo beat him at stones." Paula laughed. "I guess then, it was just beginners luck."

Anna Louise said, "If you don't mind, I think I'll turn in. It has been a long and busy day. We have another early day tomorrow."

JON LEFT TO ESCORT Anna Louise to her room, but they sat in the hall for a bit before calling for the elevator.

"Jon, I've never known a man that I've cared for as much as you. I so enjoyed going to see your home and traveling around Kenya with you. It has been the highlight of the trip for me. We are leaving tomorrow and I wonder if I will ever see you again."

"We will be in England for your formal graduation in May and to see Hanna and Sara graduate. You will see me then."

"And then what?"

"I do not know. I have been offered a very good, high paying job as Chairman of the Board of a charitable organization here in Kenya. But I would have to spend a good bit of my time here to do the job properly."

"What type of charitable organization?"

"An organization to set up medical centers and schools to teach first aid."

"Oh, Jon! That is such a worthy job. That is why I am afraid to live in Africa. They are so backward in medicine and education.'

"Yes, it is a very worthy job, but it would not be a good job for me, without you. I don't know if it will make any difference to the way you feel about Africa, but you would be able to go to England for several months each year if you like. I would be able to fly back and forth to visit you while you were away. But, I would have to spend the bulk of my time here in Africa."

"I will have to think about it Jon. Are you sure you would have enough money to do that Jon? Travel is so expensive now."

"They are talking 50,000 pounds or more a year plus travel expenses. You tell me."

"Take me down, Jon. I have to think. It is so hard to think wisely sitting next to you, for my heart gets in the way, and then I can't think sensibly at all."

The elevator came and Anna Louise stood inside thinking. She had been stunned by the enormous sum Jon had just so casually mentioned. Her father and mother made about 15,000 pounds a year between them. The Caulfields were truly wealthy. She could go home to have her children and spend each summer visiting in England. Maybe they could live on the tea plantation; she felt safe there. Oh, I don't know... I love Jon, but I'm afraid of Africa.

The elevator stopped; Jon pushed the 'close door' button and took Anna Louise in his arms. He had ached to hold her and this was his last chance for months. She came to him easily, slipping into his arms as if she belonged there. She tilted up her face and smiled, saying, "Jon, I am going to kiss you." Anna stood on tiptoes and put her soft lips on his. The shock was electrifying. The thrill went from his mouth, through his chest, to his toes. He pulled her tight against him and kissed her back hungrily. She melted in his arms. His kiss became more insistent and a soft moan escaped her throat. Jon went livid with desire and caressed her back and neck with longing. The elevator bell rang and the elevator started to the lower floor. The door opened and the kitchen waiter started to step on with a tray. "So sorry bwana; not see you. I go later."

Jon pushed the button for the first floor and took Anna in his arms again. He kissed her lightly and said, "I love you Anna. I am going to miss you terribly."

Anna was delighted by his avowal and replied. I love you too, Jon, it is Africa that I don't love." Jon walked Anna up the stairs to the room she shared with her parents, asking, "Will I see you in the morning before you leave?"

"We have to be at the airport early. Our flight leaves at ten."

"I can take you in the Land Rover. What time are you leaving?" "Daddy said we must leave at 8:30 a.m. Is that too early?"

"No, I will have the Land Rover out front at 8:15 a.m."

Anna kissed him briefly before she opened the door.

Anna's parents were sitting in the upholstered chairs, sharing the lamp between them reading. It is what they liked to do in the evenings, wherever they were.

"I'm glad you made it an early night, dear. We have to be up with the sun in the morning. Are you packed?"

Yes, except for a few things. Jon has offered to take us to the airport in the morning. He said he would have the Land Rover outside at 8:15 a.m."

"How nice, her father said. I'm afraid they are spoiling us, though."

THOMAS AND PAULA SAT talking when Jon returned to the balcony and said, "I am taking Anna and her parents to the airport at 8:15 tomorrow morning. Want to come with me?"

"I don't think so," Paula replied. "But we might sit together in the dining room for breakfast; that would be nice."

"Well, Anna said her father wanted to breakfast when the

dining room opens, which will be at seven. Does that suit you?"

"I thought the dining room opened at six, Thomas said."

"Yes, but only for a Continental breakfast, coffee, tea, juice and scones. I think Harold will want a full breakfast for the flight."

"Where are they going?"

"Madagascar. I say, Thomas, you don't think me a quitter do you?"

Thomas knew that his probing question had nettled Jon, but they needed to know his reasoning. "No, Jon; of course not. We will just be patient and see what time brings us. Until you say no, I have you down for a yes."

"Thanks, old man. I knew I could count on you to understand. I'm going to bed. I'll set the alarm for six-thirty."

Jon turned and left them. Paula said, "I love it out here on the balcony. I think I'll get in my jammies, grab a pillow and blanket and sleep out here."

"Might I join you?"

She smiled knowingly, "Of course, it will be like it was when we were traveling together. Will you tell me a story?"

"What story do you want to hear?"

"I like the learning stories. They help me to understand how the African thinks."

"I think you might like the story of the Rich Poor Man."

29

The Story of the Rich Poor Man

"Long ago, in a very poor village, there was a man for whom life had been hard. His wife, the mother of his five children had died, two of his infant children had died and his three sons had left the poverty of the village to seek better fortunes. He was alone except for the old crone who cooked for him. Everyone thought her to be a witch and had cast her out. But, the man needed someone to cook for him. It took him all day to find enough food to eat, and then he was too tired to cook it.

"One rainy night when they sat inside with their meager meal, the old crone said to him. 'You could be a rich man, if you wanted.'

'What nonsense is it that you speak?'

'I speak the truth, it is not nonsense.'

'You are so old, your mind has died.' He told her.

'Listen to me. I know where there are great riches to be had just for the taking.'

'If this is true, old woman, why have you not taken the riches?'

'Because one needs to commune with the spirits to go there, and when one is a spirit, one can carry nothing.'

'Bah, your mind is not only dead, it is mafuu.'

"The old woman thought, I must show him that what I say is true, but he will be so frightened he might chase me from my home. The old woman then had a thought. I will cast a spell over him and while he is in the spell, I will guide him to the riches and he will gather them.

"The next rainy night, the old crone made a treat of rabbit

stew and put in a powder, which would put the man in a trance.

"When he was in the trance, she used the last of her powders for spirit travel to leave her body and commune with the spirits. To get to the riches, they had to pass through a vast curtain of mist, where the spirits will get a man lost forever, but the crone guided him safely through the mist. They had to cross a river on a fallen tree, where a man would slip, if he stepped on the moss and fall into the crocodile infested waters. The crone guided the old man safely across the water to a cave that had many tunnels, which so confused a man that he could never leave once he was inside.

"She guided him deftly to a spot and watched as he dug in the sand for the bright gold coins. The old man picked up the coins and filled a pouch at his waist; he then turned to leave. She walked him through tunnel after tunnel and began to worry that she was lost: when finally, she saw the opening and directed the man out of the cave. She again found the fallen tree over the river and crossed safely. They passed through the mist after walking what seemed like miles. It was morning when they arrived back at their small hut.

"The witch was very tired, but restored herself to her body and went to take the pouch from the old man's girdle. He was still in a trance, so she laid him down on his pallet and closed his eyes before she took the pouch. He would be so astonished when she showed him the gold, for he would remember nothing of the time he was in the trance. She sprinkled the coins on a cloth and gazed at them, imagining fresh meat and garden vegetables in her cooking pot. After a while, the old crone wrapped the coins in the cloth and hid them in the chungu (chamber pot) and went to sleep.

"When she awoke, the old man was gone. The old crone made herself some broth and ate a fig. Before she left to gather fruit and look for tubers, she wanted to once again see the coins and went to the chungu. It was gone! She searched the hut, but the chungu was missing. She went out looking for the old man and saw him sitting with the chungu, talking to a friend.

"She went up to him and said, 'Bring the chungu back now; I need it.' She then went back to the hut.

"The old man returned and apologized for stopping to talk to his friend, but he said, 'I wanted to clean the chungu for you. That rabbit stew gave me loose bowels so I washed the chungu out for you.'

"The old crone grabbed the chamber pot from his hands and lifted the lid. The chungu was clean. She sat down and began to cry.

'What is wrong?' he asked.

'Did you go to the endless hole to empty the chungu?'

'Yes, I did.'

'We had a fortune last night. Today, you threw it down the endless hole. I had put our gold in the chamber pot to keep it safe, thinking: no one will think a chungu is full of gold... and I was right. This is one time when I would rather that I was wrong.'"

"The moral of the story is that: A man can plot and scheme, and spend all his time thinking of ways to become rich and end up with nothing. He is better off with honest work for honest wages."

"I LOVE YOUR STORIES; that one has much to make a person think."

"Stories with a moral are supposed to make you think; that is the purpose of them."

Paula laughed: "Of course, silly me!"

Thomas chuckled and said, "Is there room on that long chair for me to snuggle beside you, so I can hold you?"

Paula's heart fluttered and anticipation made her tingle; but her reply was cautious. "There is room, but do you think it is wise?"

"I just want to hold you. It will be a long time before we have this opportunity again."

Paula skooched over and Thomas spread his length against her back with his left arm under his head; he draped his right arm over her waist. Paula sighed and shared her blanket.

She could feel all the contours of his body through her thin nightshirt. He still had all his clothes on, but her senses were so attuned that she could feel him breathe. Happy, as she had ever been, she closed her eyes and was soon asleep.

Thomas was awake for a long time, thinking about his future with Paula. She never talked of going home. It was as if Africa was her home now. In the business of the kimmea, he felt she was as involved as he was, and shared his goals.

He longed to cement the words they had spoken in the Wahutu courting lanai. He had felt her to be his partner in life since that day.

We have been together almost constantly for two moons, more time than if I had courted her for three years in the usual fashion. She has told me she loves me and I love her. I will ask her tomorrow... here on this very balcony that she enjoys so much.

While Jon is gone, we can talk about going to America. We could take Jon and Kybo with us. Then go to England for Hanna and Sara's graduation.

With a plan that pleased him, he fell asleep to pleasant dreams.

The Holmesbys were surprised when Jon, Thomas and Paula joined them for breakfast the next morning. Paula hoped things would work out for Jon and Anna Louise. She was really the perfect girl for Jon. She was shy and quiet, but she had backbone, and Jon needed to be held in check. I wonder if she told him she did not want to have her children born in Africa as a test, to see if Jon was amenable to her wishes. Jon is an extremely caring and considerate man, but he can be a bit headstrong and dogmatic. It seemed no time at all before the Holmesbys were leaving to continue their African tour.

Paula liked to walk in the mornings when the day was still cool before the sun rose to heat the day. In Nairobi, at fifty four hundred feet, the effects of the sun were felt even more, for there were few trees to shade the streets, which seemed to hold the heat. They window-shopped as they strolled; in a jeweler's window, a ring of diamonds and sapphires caught Paula's eye. Beside her, Thomas admired a wristwatch; but they both kept their thoughts close.

BACK IN THE SUITE, Thomas called down for fresh lemon water, while Paula packed up her things, for on Jon's return they would leave for the tea farm.

The room service waiter came promptly and Thomas took the tray to the balcony. It had rained during the night and now the morning sun was making the mist rise from the gardens below; soon the wispy mist would be gone.

Paula joined him in looking down from the railing, saying, "I love this balcony. It is so private, so secluded, and the view is lovely."

Thomas took her hands, looked into her eyes, smiled and said, "I will never be able to forget being on this pleasant veranda with you, because it is the place where I asked you to be my wife." Her face lit up and Thomas saw the delight in her eyes. It emboldened him to continue: "Paula, I love you. I want to love you for the rest of my life. Will you marry me?"

Paula threw herself into his arms and hugged him with all her might (which was considerable) and said in his ear, "Yes, yes, a thousand times, yes."

Thomas gently pushed her arms away so he could look, once again, into her eyes; he saw the tears of joy gathering as she blinked to stop them from escaping. With a thumb, he caressed away the wayward tears, and *little kissed* her forehead, her cheeks, her eyes and the corners of her mouth.

Paula turned her lips to join his and kissed him deeply. She loved the way he courted her with little kisses. They were more erotic than anything she had ever imagined.

Thomas felt her passion and deepened the kiss, allowing his passion free rein. She gave what she received, and for long moments they were as one, savoring the thrill of wanting and being wanted. Their bodies hummed with mounting desire, while their hands caressed one another as they pressed tightly together.

Too soon, they heard the door to the suite open, and Jon called out: "Anybody home?"

"We're on the balcony, Jon. Would you like a lemon water?" Thomas replied as he smiled at Paula. "We have news for you."

Jon popped out to the secluded little haven, accepted the drink and said, "What news?" It did not escape him that they were holding hands and that Paula was flushed.

Thomas looked at Paula, she smiled and shook her head yes, and Thomas turned to Jon, saying, "I asked Paula to marry me a few minutes ago, and she said, yes!"

Jon jumped up hooting, "I say, old chap, jolly good show! Can I still be the duenna? May I kiss the beautiful fiancée?"

Thomas, smiling ear to ear, said, "Yes... you may."

Jon bussed Paula and gave her a big hug, saying, "I am so happy for the both of you. You are perfect together."

He shook Thomas' hand and pulled him in for a hug and whispered in his ear, "What about the ring?"

Thomas looked him in the face and said, "All we need are your Traveler's Checks. I think Paula saw a ring she fancied on our walk this morning."

"Well, what are we waiting for?" And Jon was gone to get his checkbook.

"What's that?" Thomas asked.

"It's a checkbook. One check does the work of many Traveler's Checks."

The ring was exquisite. A raised center sapphire surrounded by diamonds set in filigreed platinum. Paula bought the wristwatch for Thomas. It was an Omega Sea Master in 14 karat gold, with an expandable gold-filled wristband. Once back on the balcony, Thomas placed the ring on her finger and she placed the watch on his wrist. Jon poured the champagne. The pledge was sealed.

30

Dela-Aden

Jon, with his enthusiasm and knowledge, was a great tour guide. At Karen Blixen's coffee farm, he was in full stride saying, "This farm is a page out of the story of the early white settlers in Africa. Until 1931, when Lord Delamere died and Karen Blixen left Africa, colonial Africa thrived. Karen Dinesen arrived in Africa in 1913 to marry her Swedish cousin, Baron Bror von Blixen-Fienecke, who was a white hunter. She was nineteen when they were wed. In the first year of her marriage, Bror infected her with syphilis. After that, he was rarely home and therefore, of no help in running the coffee shamba. It fell to her alone, to clear the scrubland to plant coffee bushes, and to build the large coffee-processing shed, where the sorting, processing and packing were done. She suffered from severe bouts of her illness, and had to go back to Denmark for treatment.

Then came a year, in 1930, when the rains did not come. The crop withered on the bush, the coffee bushes died and without her annual income from the crop, she was bankrupt. After eighteen years of effort–all was lost. At the mid-life age of thirty-seven, she returned to her native Denmark, dependent on her family, for she had divorced Bror after seven years of the disastrous marriage.

Still, her story is one of courage in the face of disaster. Were it not for her mountainous debt and lack of credit, one thinks Karen would have struggled to overcome her adversity, and triumphed over her devastating loss; for she loved Africa and the native peoples deeply... and they loved her, some of whom still write to her today. Karen has since become a successful author under the pen name of Isak Dinesen."

"I must get some of her books when I get home. What are they about–do you know?"

"Julia said she had read 'Anecdotes of Destiny', which was published in London–about her African experience, I imagine."

Thomas was surprised by her casual remark. She had referred to America as home, which of course it was and is, but she said it like it was her final destiny. Maybe he had read too much into her lack of talking about home. But his anxiety lessened as he reasoned: she knows I could not possibly live in America. She has agreed to be my wife; maybe, I'm reading things into her words that are not there, after all, what else would she call the place where she grew up... but home.

THE ROAD FROM NAIROBI to *Dela-Aden*, as the tea farm was named, was a dirt road, badly rutted and full of potholes so progress was slow.

"Why are so many people walking alongside the road?" Paula asked, for it seemed most of native Africa was to-ing and fro-ing on either side of the road where wide paths existed. Some had bicycles, which were used to carry huge baskets. One woman on a bicycle had a basket fastened to the handlebars, a huge basket on the rear fender and one on her head. Considering the condition of the road, it was a tremendous feat of agility. The women were garbed in bright patterned pambishas, but most of the men wore shirts and short trousers. Most significant though, was the silence of the travelers.

Jon answered, "There are several flea markets along the road where the natives barter or sell food, clothing and all manner of handmade items. It is like this every day. On Sunday, the flea markets are closed, but the natives are still out walking the roads, going to church, visiting family or conducting personal business."

"There are many bicycles."

"Yes, the bicycle is the black man's automobile in Africa. I have seen them transport a casket, with a dead person inside on side-by-side bicycles. I have seen a father, with a mother riding on the frame, holding a babe with three children on an elongated rear fender."

When they left the main road, there were few people walking on the secondary roads. An occasional man with a mule or a pushcart was all they saw. It made Paula wonder how all the people got out to the main road.

Mary had said to Peter, "Try to be back for tea, dear. Jon said he thought they would be here by then. After tea, we can all go for a ride. You can finish your inspection then, and also give us a guided tour. I asked Suffo to clean up the old pony trap in case Thomas didn't want to ride. He and Jon can drive like they used to do when they were boys. I think Thomas might like that."

After the flurry of arrival, Mary showed Paula to the second floor guest room, the upstairs sitting room with a small library of novels, and the bath across the hall, chatting all the while about towels, lights, the generator and the cold nights. Jon took Thomas to their old digs on the third floor.

Paula asked, "How did you come to live in Africa?"

"My grandmother inherited the ancestral Hall in Berkshire, but my grandfather had a strong desire to go to Africa to Lord Delamere. In 1907, they left the Hall in the care of my aunt, Dame Rebecca, my Mother's sister and her husband, and with my newlywed parents, Edith & Phillip Woleston came to Kenya to Lord Delamere.

"My older brother, John, died in World War II, in 1943. At the beginning of the war, John's wife, Jane, who is an American, took their three children to America, to the Nelson grandparents for safety.

"When my mother died, I inherited this farm. The Hall passed to John's oldest child, my niece Emily. Her mother, Jane, did not want to live in England, so forfeited the Hall, and it too came to me.

"My younger sister, Margaret, and her children had been

living in the Hall with me and our four children during the war, for Peter was a Captain in the RAF and James, Margaret's husband, was an Intelligence Officer.

"Since we could not live in two places after the war, we decided to live in Africa. Margaret and her family stayed at the Hall, while Peter and I came to Africa in 1946; for Peter has always been a frustrated farmer. This house was built in 1908 and restored and remodeled in 1948. We usually go back to England during the rainy season here, when it is summer in England.

"We are going for a ride after tea. Did you bring riding clothes?"

"I have half-chaps; I can wear them with tights."

"Good, come down and join us as soon as you're ready."

PAULA LOVED HEARING ABOUT the ancestors. It made her feel a part of the family already... and this room was lovely... welcoming, and friendly. It told her a great deal about her mother-in-law to be.

The predominately yellow flowers with red stamens, on the white chintz curtains matched the bed flounce and the seat cushion on the vanity stool. The big bed was covered with a yellow down quilt, with a white-painted wicker headboard. It reminded her a bit of the guest room at home, with the question-mark clothes tree, the beveled pier glass between the windows and the potted plants on the sills in their white wicker cachepots. The upholstered gooseneck rocking chair with matching stool and the hand-cut shade on the reading lamp in the corner by the window made a cozy retreat. The clothes chest and end tables were white wicker with beveled glass tops like the vanity. The mostly red with white, yellow and black-outlined patterns in the Oriental rug set off the décor perfectly. The pale yellow walls were covered with gaily matted and red-framed pictures, which she found, were all drawings done by Thomas as a boy. She felt happy and completely at home as she wandered down to the library where tea was being served.

On the altered third floor, Jon said, "After you were lost, I slept in the guest room downstairs until Dad gave me Kazaii as a tutor. Then our nanny went to a neighboring family and I moved into her room. I loved that little room on the front of the house, with its walls of closet drawers, its tiny roofed porch and French doors. Mother said it used to be the linen room. She made it a sitting room when they remodeled the third floor. The playroom/schoolroom was converted into two guest rooms and a shower bath was added. The old guest house became the farm manager's cottage. So, you will be quite comfortable up here now. Don't dawdle. I'm dying to hear you tell the *Nobles* your news." Thomas startled and laughed, "I forgot we used to call them that. It is good to be home Jon. I'll be down soon."

Thomas was glad his parents had done the third floor over. He was dreading the melancholy he might feel for his lost years as a boy here. He could remember only some of it and that was good enough.

The house had a terra cotta tile roof, which funneled hot air up and out the ridge vent, making the third floor rooms pleasant even in the heat of the day. Thomas was by now, accustomed to beds with linens, and carpets on the floor. It occurred to him that all the unexpected events that had happened to him on his trek home, had prepared him well. If he had just trekked home alone as originally planned, he would have felt so very awkward here.

Paula was the last to arrive for tea. "I'm sorry to be tardy, but I was looking at the pictures on the guest room walls. Thomas, even as a boy you were immensely talented. I'm impressed."

Not knowing that his mother had framed some of his old pictures, Thomas said, "I must stop by your room and see these pictures that you think I drew."

Mary said, "They are from your pastels sketch book: pictures of the gardens, flowers, horses and the barn cats."

"I hate to say it, but I don't remember them."

"After our ride you can go and look at them, Peter said."

He did want to inspect some fields before it got too late. While the dusk was long and pleasant, the visibility for an inspection decreased in the lengthening shadows.

"Well, father, before you bundle us off, Paula and I want to tell you our good news." Paula and Thomas were sitting on the leather settee, with Peter in a leather club chair and Mary in its mate. Jon was preparing another plate from the assorted delights on the tea tray, and turned to observe the *Nobles* reaction when they heard the news.

"Yes, well don't keep us on pins and needles, what is it?" His father asked.

"This morning I asked Paula to marry me. This morning she accepted."

Big smiles, exclamations of congratulations, happiness, hugs, kisses, hand shakes and delight with Paula's ring and Thomas' watch filled the room.

All at once, inspecting the fields seemed of no consequence. Our eldest boy has come home: strong, wise, a man of worth and a healer. Now, he has chosen a lovely woman for his bride. Thank you God; forgive me for all those years when I questioned your wisdom.

Mary said, "Well, what's it to be? Are we going out to see the fields before it gets too late or not?"

A chorus of voices wanted to go out and tour the farm. It was an unusual day for April. It had been sunny between the clouds and the late afternoon was filled with shafts of golden beams, tinged with salmon-pink and silver, a delightful time for a ride.

Suffo and Abumi and Kybo had the horses groomed and ready for the ride. Mary showed Paula and Thomas the horses suitable for riding saying, "There are three horses that have finished their training. Two will be used for Dressage, but *Sunshine* here doesn't like working in the arena. She prefers the trails and will go all day long if asked. Paula was immediately taken with the Palomino mare. She had kind and intelligent eyes and a low swirl below her eyes; unusual because swirls were usually between or just above the eyes.

She was a nice size at 15.2hh, not too tall, but a good size for Paula's height.

Jon was delighted to see the pony trap out and he and Thomas reminisced a bit about childhood escapades. Mary had one of her driving pair of Haflingers hitched to the trap. Paula was soon mounted on *Sunshine*, while Peter and Mary rode their usual mounts. Kybo had eschewed the junket, saying, "I do not know horses except to drive mules and I did that all day today. I will see you tomorrow."

"Where are you going, Kybo?"

"I am to help Mr. Hanley."

As Kybo walked away, Mary said, "I think Kybo has a paramour. Mr. Hanley thinks so too."

The pony trap brought up the rear of the little cavalcade, and Thomas said to Jon, "Paramour?"

"Lover: one that is secret."

In two hours, they covered about six miles with the pony trap and about eight miles on the horses, which could go down some of the rows where the pony trap was unable to negotiate turns. They saw the orderly acres of tea bushes spread in a panorama across the hillsides.

On a wide and level hilltop, the vineyard lay in neat rows of posts and wire with large deep green leaves shielding the hard bright green grapes. Because birds were a problem with the ripening crop, the vineyard was staked on tall posts, which were topped with fine wire mesh. These same posts supported a watering system for the roots in the dry seasons. Soft net drapes hung on the ends of the aisles. A lovely adobe building with a terra cotta roof had been built to process the grapes, and house the aging wines. The wine master and his wife lived in a spacious apartment on the second floor.

But, best of all, were the wide trails through the woods. Here was the forest she loved; where she and Thomas would spend the day tomorrow looking for kimmea plants.

About thirty percent of the land was under cultivation. About half was woods and fields for hay and grazing of domestic livestock, with the rest homes and gardens for the workers. The land grant here had been the same as for Lord Delamere, one thousand acres.

The farm was a world unto itself and self-sufficient. It included a dairy, a slaughterhouse and a smokehouse way off beyond the fields. Closer to the house there was a large vegetable garden and a lovely flower garden. Woven throughout the tapestry of buildings were stands of woods, trails and the manager's cottage.

Thomas was amazed. He did not remember anything about the farming end of the plantation. They saw Kazaii and Thomas remembered him instantly. When Thomas asked him to guide them tomorrow, Kazaii was hard pressed to keep the tears from his eyes. He had mourned the loss of this boy more than the other natives, for he had seen in him the makings of a great man. Now, with his lost hopes for the future of his bright pupil standing before him fulfilled, he was almost speechless.

Kazaii was old and had been retired when he was given charge of Thomas' nature learning as a boy. Now, with added years, he seemed unchanged except for the staff he used when he walked. His smile had fewer teeth, but his eyes were bright with knowledge and his voice was strong.

Thomas looked at the neat and tidy worker's village. Oh, if Manutu could see this, he would die a happy man. His father had incorporated all of the things that Manutu wanted to see in the villages. There were shade trees in front of the huts, with benches for sitting out or socializing. Each room in the hut had a window to let in the light to kill the molds and fungi that liked the dark. Each abode was built in the style of a native hut with long eaves, but larger; each had a great room for sitting, cooking and eating and three bedrooms: one for boys, one for girls and one for the parents. Most had a loft too. The "cottages" as Dad called them, were built in native fashion, but plaster replaced the dung and straw of the bush huts. The floors were tongue and groove wood planks so they could be kept clean and vermin kept out. Braziers outside replaced the ground fires of the forest villages. Small woodstoves inside, for cooking in inclement weather, produced a bit of heat for the cold nights at 5800 feet.

His father had retained all the feeling of a native village, but their lot was greatly improved, for they each had personal gardens, milk and cheese from the dairy and a meat ration from the slaughterhouse, as well as a salary.

AMONG THE BUSH NATIVES, the richest man lives in the same manner as the poorest man; his wealth is in his children and his livestock. Here, at Dela-Aden, the worker's values had changed slightly. Now, affluence was gauged not only by their children, but by who was able to send their children to formal school in Nairobi when they were twelve. Primary schooling was provided to the children on the estate... and there were evening classes twice a week for adults wanting to increase their knowledge.

The workers' village had a headman; usually the oldest and wisest man and he had two assistants, usually men of stature to maintain order and to settle disputes. Any man that caused trouble, or beat his wife or children was fired and evicted from the estate, so there were few problems.

ROUNDING A HUGE FIELD, Paula asked Mary if they could go for a trot. Mary was only too glad to oblige. *The Wizard* took off at a nice collected trot and when Mary realized that Paula was keeping up with her easily, let him out a bit. They came to a crossroad and took a left, heading into the woods. Mary called back, "How about a canter?"

Paula called out, "That would be wonderful."

Lady Mary kept *The Wizard* in a collected canter, and even so he covered huge amounts of ground at a stride. But the Palomino mare, *Sunshine,* had a marvelous coordinated canter with fluid lead changes on the curves and seemed only to flick her hooves at the ground to keep up with the big, 16.2hh, gelding.

When *The Wizard* started to sweat, *Sunshine* was still cool and dry. After a few miles of delightful forest paths, they came back to the huge hayfield and saw Peter with Jon and Thomas coming towards them.

Mary said, "How are you doing back there?"

"I'm doing just great." Paula had fallen in love with the Palomino mare. She was smooth, solid and sure; wasted no effort and responded instantly to aids.

"We'll walk back to cool them out. How do you like *Sunshine*?"

Paula moved up beside Mary saying, "*Sunshine* is terrific! I think I'm in love."

Mary smiled. At last, there was someone else in the house that loved horses as she did. Peter cared for and respected horses, but he did not love them. It was the difference, in Mary's opinion, of being a rider or being a horseman. Jon could take riding or leave it. The twins enjoyed the pony trap, but didn't like getting dirty, preferring reading, writing and the arts to horses.

"I'm teaching *Sunshine* to drive to a Meadowbrook cart. She seems to like it, and has even done well in Dressage Driving with the fiacre, if I work her on trails before and after the test. She just doesn't like working only in the arena. But she loves the trails.

"My kind of horse... I don't like working in an arena either!" and she smiled at her hostess.

They came up to the men and Peter asked with a sparkle in his eyes, "Well, did you have a nice little jaunt?"

Lady Mary and Paula just smiled knowingly at one another.

DINNER WAS AT EIGHT. Thomas was subdued, for he remembered other dinners, birthday parties and family celebrations. He looked at the shining and happy faces around him and thought: I have missed a great many of these meals, but I am still glad for the Zuri Watu. What would I have become if I had been raised here? Would I still have become a healer? Somehow, I doubt it. What I loved was nature, and Manutu turned my love into knowledge, which turned into healing.

Thomas thought about Paula meeting Manutu and of the wonders he would find in her. I wonder if Paula will like staying with the Zuri Watu. She might, but I know she would be happy if she could stay here.

This was the first time Thomas had pictured Paula living with the Zuri Watu. He realized that there would be almost no use for her talents there... no call for all the things she did so well. Unexpectedly, the idea of Paula living in a native village made him feel anxious... it would be like me living in America.

"THOMAS, WHEN YOU HAVE filled in the memory gaps, would you please pass the salt and pepper?" Paula asked.

Thomas, who was sitting across the table from her, smiled and said, "You know me too well for my own good."

This brought a chuckle from his father, who said, "It's a wife's trick, to know the husband too well–Paula is just getting an early start."

Sitting in front of the fire in the library, Jon said, "It is time for a story Thomas... remember, you promised."

"Yes, I did. What story would you hear?"

Mary spoke up and said, "Would anyone, besides me, like to hear about your early life in the village?"

Thomas looked at the smiling nodding heads and began.

"Once I was well and Manutu had announced that I was ***chosen****, I had complete freedom of the village. If I left the village, four warriors followed me to keep me safe, but they never tried to stop me from doing anything or going anywhere.*

"Each day that Manutu was not with me, I had an assignment from him: 'go and find six eagle feathers', or 'find two tadpoles not yet frogs', or 'bring a new egg from a guinea fowl's nest'.

"In my wanderings and my searches, I found many other things. I found stones of unusual colors; I found bones I could not identify; I found small skulls with teeth from an unknown critter; I found snakeskins and their owners; I found beetles that had caught other bugs so big, they died trying to eat them.

"I took all of these things back to Manutu, who taught me what the animal was, how old it was and how it had died. The

teeth of each animal are unique and each jinsi (genus) can be identified from their teeth or bite marks. We powdered the bones to find out if the animal had died from poison, a lack of food or water, or was killed by another animal and its flesh eaten.

"Each day, with or without Manutu, was an adventure. At first, I was a bit lonely; but then we had another lad come for training. He was haughty and made fun of my delight in the wonders of nature. Manutu sent him home after a few days, saying, 'His mind is tarnished by his ego. He will never be a useful person.' I was then glad to go out by myself once more and never again was I lonely. I realized what a gift it was to be able to explore alone, but in complete safety.

"There were days when we had more excitement than was desired. One day I was following the trail of a sow and her piglets in the tall grass. I was sure I could snag one of the piglets with my slingshot. I was better with this weapon than I was with the walinka. I had a nice pouch of smooth rounded stones. I had killed a rabbit and two squirrels and a giant rat with my slingshot. I was sure I could kill a piglet. My guards waited at the edge of the tall grass, so as not to give me away to my prey. When last I parted the grass hoping to see the sow and her piglets, I came face to face with a female lion. She was as surprised to see me as I was to see her, for she too was tracking the sow and her piglets. I recovered from my amazement before she did, [I later realized she was a very young cat and still liked to play at stalking], and let go with a stone, which hit her on the nose. She raised her head so suddenly from the sharp pain on her nose, that she was seen by my guards who immediately ran towards her making all sorts of loud noises. The young lion took one last look at me and turned and ran away.

"When I stood up, I saw that she had not been far from her pride, which was resting in the shade of the tall grass. With the noise from my guards, the pride went on guard and the adults all dropped their shoulders to assume an attack posture. The one thing I had been told, over and over, was never, ever run from a big cat; it only inflames their minds

to the kill. My guards also knew this and had taken up a protective stance on either side of me, but low, leaving the cats wondering where we had gone. I took a stone from my pouch and without raising my head above the top of the tall grass I managed to hit the front lion, a female, in the nose. She turned and ran back a few steps before she turned to face us again; but her sudden retreat had a devastating effect on the others, who now were standing tall to find the threat. I again loaded my slingshot and fired at the closest lion, a young male. The stone bounced off the tip of his nose and hit him in the eye. With a huge grunt, he turned and ran for the boulders behind him. I fired once again and hit another female on the lip. She growled and then turned and loped away. It was too much for the pride. They needed to see their antagonist, and staying low in the grass hid us as well as it hid them when they were on the prowl.

As a group, they turned and retreated to the boulders, which I now know, were dens for the females. We stayed low, in a crouch, and made our way to a stand of fig trees. After we were certain that they were not trying to sneak up on us, we took a path that led from tree to brush to snag and back to the village. I was thirteen. For a few days, I stayed away from the tall grass. Lions are not fools, and the first time I scared them off with my slingshot was just a learning experience for them.

Manutu heard the story from my guards and chastised me for being so careless in my hunt, saying, "The easiest prey is the one who is hunting." It was a good learning experience for me too. It made me realize that fear is the lion's weapon, his biggest weapon. He is not prepared for a prey that is not afraid of him and one that is willing to face him down or use tricks to escape. Since that day, I have faced the lion several times and as you can see, I am still here."

THOMAS SMILED AT HIS rapt audience. With cries of approval, they clapped, not only for the story, but also for his courage as a boy.

The parents retired and Jon took a book from the shelf,

saying, "I started this book a year ago, I wonder if I'll remember any of it." He turned and left for the third floor guest rooms.

Thomas took a half-turn to face Paula on the small settee. "I was put in mind of a serious question today, when you said you would order Karen books when you got home. What do you perceive our future together will be?"

"Yes, I saw your reaction to my comment."

"I had no reaction to your comment!"

"Yes, you did. Remember when we talked about tells. Well, when something displeases you or is unexpected, you flatten your lips into a small grimace."

Thomas was amazed. "Do I really do that?"

"Yes, and you will never be able to stop doing it. It is part of you, like the color of your eyes."

Thomas laughed. "Father was right, you know me too well; but I need an answer to my question."

"I thought we would go to America to tell my parents we are engaged. I thought we would take Jon and Kybo with us. I even thought of asking Captain Jones and Jonas to go with us. I would like to be married in America, while we are there.

"From there, I thought we would all go to England for your sisters' graduation from Croft School, and if you like, we can have a marriage ceremony again in England after the graduation, for your family there, before we return to Africa.

"If all the agreements are finished and signed, before we leave for America, we will return to Kenya to begin the process of finding land, building buildings and hiring staff for the first aid clinics. Once that is set in motion, we will visit the Zuri Watu. I have not thought of things much further than that."

"You say, 'visit the Zuri Watu'. What if I want to stay with them longer than just a visit?"

"Then you have serious decisions to make. You must decide if you want to get the clinics going or stay with the Zuri Watu. I cannot see how it is possible to do both."

She is right... again. The clinics in themselves would be a major effort to get started. Cyril would take care of the details, but I would still have to be available to make decisions until the program was fully established.

"How long do you think it might take to get the clinics to the point where I do not have to be in Kenya all the time?"

"I really don't know. That is a good question for Cyril. But I would think at least a year. What I see is that you will travel a good bit of the time. You will want to go and see where they suggest that the clinics be set up. You will want to go to the Zuri Watu often. You will want to be with me in America when our children are born."

The stunned look and surprise grimace told Paula he had not even thought of this; so she continued. "An English woman wants her children born in England; an American woman wants her children born in America."

"Why is Africa not good enough for our children to be born here? Hundreds of healthy children are born here every day."

"It is called citizenship. I want our children to be American and English, if possible; but Americans first. If you were an American, it would make no difference where our children were born, they would still be Americans. With mixed citizenship, they are neither fish nor fowl; if they are born in Africa, they will be Africans."

"I see I have much to think about." Thomas arose and held out his hand to Paula. She took his hand and stood up close to him, saying:

"We both have much to think about, but I would not have agreed to marry you if I didn't feel we could find a middle road that would satisfy both of us."

Thomas pulled her close and lightly kissed her forehead, thankful for her intelligent thoughts. His ardor at the feel of her in his arms pushed past his reasoning as he softly kissed her eyelids, thankful that she saw so much. He little-kissed her cheeks and nose, thankful that they were so pretty. When he kissed her lips, he thought only of his deep, deep love for this woman who was to be his wife. His anxieties disappeared in his consuming desire to possess this woman... now. She was with him, her heat urged him on, and he felt powerless to stop his hunger.

THEY HEARD AN 'AHEM' behind them and Thomas lifted his head and saw Jon standing there with a silly smile on his face, saying, "I hate to intrude, but this book is a dreadful bore. I need to choose another."

The moment was gone. Thomas had his senses back and replied, "We were just saying goodnight. We are on our way up now."

31

Kimmea Plants

It was Wednesday and a workday, so Peter and Mary had their usual breakfast at six and were gone before the others came down. Helen set up a buffet of sausages, bacon, pancakes and scrambled eggs with English muffins, lemon curd and jam.

The smell of freshly brewing coffee awoke Jon. Thomas used the shower in the new bath, while Jon shaved at the sink. Thomas stepped out and said, "This is simply wonderful. I feel so clean and refreshed, like bathing in a waterfall."

They traded places, with Jon saying: "I haven't slept so well in ages; how about you?"

"I am getting used to beds... and yes, I also slept well."

Together they went down to Paula's room to find the door open, her bed made and Paula gone. Following their noses they found her sipping a cup of Earl Grey tea while she waited for them in the breakfast room.

"Good morning: I was hoping you would be down soon. Everything smells so good–I feel ravenous." Thomas leaned down to kiss her on the cheek asking, "How did you sleep?"

"I've never slept better! My bed felt just like my bed at home. Did you have a good night?"

Thomas had been awake a long time before he slept, but he had come to a decision; one that he liked and one that he hoped would also please Paula. "I slept just fine. I listened to the rain, as I had when I was a boy. It comforted me, as it did then. With the windows open on three sides, it was better than sleeping out in the forest. You could hear all the night sounds, but you were warm and dry and safe... and there was no fire to tend all night."

Paula and Jon looked at Thomas and chuckled, not for what he had said, but for what he had left out: the crawling bugs, the slithering snakes, the biting mosquitoes, the leaks in the leaf roofs and the mini-streams running through the shelters, all with the roars of carnivores nearby.

Paula smiled at Jon, saying: "You look chipper today, is something afoot?"

Jon had asked Thomas if he could go with them and Kazaii to look for the kimmea, and he readily assented. Jon, with his cheerful disrespect, was always a pleasant companion.

"I am going with you to look for kimmea plants today, if you don't mind."

"Not at all, it will be nice to have your help with the manual labor."

"Manual labor! What manual labor? I thought you were looking for plants."

"We are... but if we find them, we will be taking soil samples; we are pleased that you want to help."

The look on Jon's face was stricken and priceless. Both Paula and Thomas had to use all of their self control not to burst out in laughter.

At nine, after the morning haze had burned off, they presented themselves to Kazaii. He was ready to go, for his granddaughter had wrapped his lower legs first in old tail wraps and then in long strips of hide as protection from the thorns. Thomas, Paula and Jon wore their half chaps, which Kazaii admired. Thomas told him that Paula had had them made for them. Kazaii looked at her anew in the morning sunlight, and liked what he saw.

Thomas told Kazaii about the kind of places where he had often found kimmea. "I know such places," he replied, "And I think I know the plant you describe. It is not yet mature."

"We want to take samples of the soil and dung and tree leaves."

"Why do you want to do that?"

"We want to see if we can make the plant grow in a hothouse, not in the forest."

"If it is the plant of which I think, it is fussy about light and water. It does not grow in many places."

In an hour's walk, Kazaii led them to a bed of kimmea. The plants were young, but sufficiently grown to withstand the rains. Jon took notes for Thomas, on a pie chart, as he identified the trees and plants growing nearby. Thomas found scat from the Black-and-White Colobus monkey. The Colobus monkey, in several variations, is found in a broad band through central Africa from the Nigerian coast and Cameroon to Lake Victoria and Kenya. He also found the desiccated peels of bananas and other fruit rinds. Samples were taken of everything. Paula took samples of the soil around the plants and meter tested the moisture of the soil recording the readings on a chart. She took samples of the soils every five feet in three directions to ascertain the differences, if any, for the plants might have grown all over the area if the seeds had been dropped there.

Lady Mary gave them the use of the potting shed for the tests. It suited their needs perfectly with a large central work table with long growing tables down each side of the attached greenhouse, which had roll-up shades to diffuse the sun. A waterfall generator, which ran at night to fill the water tower, also supplied power for the farm buildings including the gardening shed and greenhouse. The workers' cottages had no power, and their water was obtained from communal hand pumps to retain the style of life they were accustomed to in the native villages.

"Use whatever equipment or supplies you need, and if you want anything, tell Samuel. He is our head gardener and obtains all the gardening supplies." Both Peter and Mary were excited about the experiments.

The next two days Paula worked on the soil testing. Thomas, Jon and Kazaii looked for other patches of kimmea and gathered soil to grow the seed.

Paula had never been happier. She loved her surroundings, the people and the farm. She could see herself here permanently. Lady Mary and Sir Peter were so accommodating that Paula wondered if it was a form of implied invitation... not to live in the main house, but maybe a small place built nearby. Would Thomas like that? If Jon and Anna Louise lived here too, it would be perfect.

The only thing missing was the Zuri Watu for Thomas... but, if the kimmea deal went through, they could fly to Yaoundé, hire a helicopter and visit the Zuri Watu often.

JON HAD BEEN WATCHING Paula working in the shed. She seemed so happy and content. He wondered why she was happy here and Anna Louise was not... "I say, Paula, you are wrapped tight in your work. I've been lolling here in the portal for ten minutes."

Paula turned and smiled at Jon, he was so little boyish. (I am here, why didn't you notice me?) "I was writing down some of the test results and was totally absorbed by the findings."

"Good news?"

"I'd say yes, very good news."

"Neato; I'd like to ask you a personal question, do you mind?"

"Of course not; how can I mind anything someone does or asks if he has saved my life?"

Jon's face flushed and he said, "I didn't save your life!"

Paula turned and faced him, "Jon, only you believed I was alive after I escaped the Ndezi. Only you came looking for me. Only you found me. In my book, that adds up to saving my life. What did you want to ask me?"

Somewhat taken aback, Jon blurted out, "Why are you so happy here and Anna was not?"

"I see... you are in love with Anna, but she is afraid of Africa and you don't know what to do about it. Am I right?"

"Spot on."

"She liked being here on the farm, did she not?'

"Yes, but the children thing?"

"She is not alone Jon. I want to go back to America to have our children."

Jon just gaped, speechless, and finally blurted out, "Why?"

"It is as I told Thomas, mostly citizenship. If our children are born here, they will be Africans, not English, not Americans. If Thomas were American, our children would be American. Both you and Anna are English citizens, so your children born here would be English. But I agree with Anna that medicine is still primitive here and while the natives manage to have many healthy babies... you don't hear about the ones that died or the women that died and you rarely see the ones who have birth defects because they die from neglect.

"Thomas is also a midwife and has brought many babies into the world. But the strict rule in medicine is that you never practice on your family, except for minor things, or emergencies."

Jon didn't know what to say. She was right about the citizenship, she was probably right about the natives too, and most damning of all, she was right about the state of medicine in Africa.

"If I were you Jon, I would ask your parents if there would be room in the house for you and Anna, if Anna agrees to marry you. Later, when children come, you could build a house close by. Anna might prefer her own domicile anyway. She is a lovely girl, but she has led a sheltered life. It is so peaceful here at Dela-Aden that I think she would soon get used to Africa, especially with all the family support. I think she has the backbone to do it; she just has to find the courage.

"My advice to you is that you do not compare Anna to me. She has to do what makes her comfortable and happy. She cannot live in fear, so you must deal with that. Expect her to go to England in the summer, and plan to go with her. I understand that the Hall in the Cotswolds belongs to your mother. Who will inherit it, do you know?"

"Thomas will inherit everything unless Mother sets up this estate for Thomas and the Hall for me. That's what Grandmother did."

"Could you be happy at the Hall?"

"It is a beautiful Tudor manor with large rooms and many leaded glass windows. It is set on a hundred acres of woods, fields and lawns. I have always been happy visiting there, but I would miss Africa terribly.

"What about the twins?"

"They will have a good dowry when they marry."

"Where would you rather be, Jon?"

"I love Africa. I love this farm. England is fine for a bit, but then I long for Africa."

"Thomas loves Africa too. He would never want to live in England or America. But I think he might be happy here if he could spend part of his time with the Zuri Watu. He would still have natives to tend, for he loves his work. He could travel around the district if there wasn't enough to keep him busy here on the farm. He will have the first aid clinics to supervise too.

"Might I suggest that you ask your parents if you could invite Anna Louise to come out and stay for a few months, to see if she could be happy living here. If not, Jon, you are only looking at heartaches if you try to change her or yourself."

"Would you be happy living with the Zuri Watu?" Jon asked.

"I don't know; I have not yet met them. But I suspect that I'm too worldly to live a permanent native life in the bush. I would miss my books, the horses, my work and people with whom I share an interest. For me, it will have to be visits, I think.

"Thomas and I have a lot of things to talk over. The kimmea deal, if it goes through, will force us to certain decisions, but I do not want it to take over my life and Thomas feels the same way. We will have to find a suitable middle road. Now that your parents have agreed to be board members, I am gaining confidence in the Organization.

"One good thing about the kimmea deal is that it will give us all an income on which we can do just about anything we please. You could have a home in England as well as here. You will have the money to fly anywhere at any time for any reason, if you accept the position as Chairman. You will be able to find a larger place for Anna's parents in England, where they can keep horses, instead of boarding them out, if they like; a place large enough to house all of you when you are in England visiting.

"But I digress. I am happy here because I have come to love Africa and this is the best place that I have been in Africa. It lives up to its name of 'Eden'.

"Anna is afraid of the Kikuyu, because of the Mau Mau rebellion. It was a terrible predicament for both black and white, and it changed many things so they will never again be the same. But, your parents survived because they treat fairly with the natives. They do not expect them to change those things that make no difference to integrity, honesty and cleanliness. The natives here are content for they can be who they are, and be liked for themselves.

"It takes a wise man to understand that the natives have been thinking the way they do for thousands of years, and to take the one thing that the natives all respect and make the most of it. They like to admire an important leader. To be associated with a distinctive person gives them status in their own minds. To be noticed by this exalted personage, they will work for him and themselves; they will be honest and God-fearing; they will go to school to learn and improve themselves. Your father was wise to set himself up as a Chief/ King and to make the inspections of their work himself and to notice any extra effort and praise it.

"Another thing that kept this farm out of the Mau Mau problem is that the natives have a village here and do not leave each night to go to a village that is exposed to rabid external forces, which forced many loyal workers to do the things they did. Here, they are in the center of the compound and, I understand, there are trip wires that will set off alarms at night for their protection.

"With all these good things about the farm, Anna should be put at ease about what happened out there, for it never happened here."

"How did you know about the trip-wires?"

"Kazaii told us about them when we were looking for plants."

"I can see why Thomas loves you so much; you are such

a sensible person. Kybo holds you in awe, and today Kazaii said to me 'the golden lady is mbali na taz', which means: the golden lady is different and special.' And he hasn't even seen you walk on your hands yet!"

They laughed together and Thomas arrived with more soil. "Do you think we have enough soil yet?"

"I think we have enough soil to try setting out flats of peat pots. If the seeds grow well, we can move them into beds later. If they do grow, we have to work on reproducing the soil they prefer... but it makes me wonder about selling only the seed. Without the Colobus dung and rind compost, the seeds might sprout, but the plants might not thrive.

"I had an idea. If we separate the piglets from the main sty, and feed them a monkey diet of fruits, tree beans and flower pods, we might be able to duplicate the monkey dung, and then compost it with peels and rinds. If all the villagers save their fruit refuse and green refuse from their gardens and cooking parings, we will have enough to feed the piglets and make the compost. With a compost drum, we can have usable soil in a week."

Thomas just stared at her. "I think you are enjoying all of this."

"Yes, I am. It is what I studied in school. Part of studying a plant is learning what makes it grow–where, why and how."

Thomas asked, "Why just the piglets?"

"Several reasons: they are smaller and have different digestive systems from the adults; they will be easier to work around when gathering the dung and they will require less to eat than an adult pig.

"I did not know that a biologist knew as much about animals as they do of plants, Thomas said.

"Paula smiled and said, "I did not know that an African Medicine Man could work miracles with plants either."

Jon stood smiling at the exchange. Would Anna ever be so casual and open about learning about Africa and him?

After a late tea, with the day's work at an end for Paula and Thomas, she suggested they go for a walk in the forest. They walked in silence for a while and then Thomas asked, "When will we know if the kimmea can be cultivated or not?"

"I don't know, but probably not until the plant has gone to seed. If the seeds we planted today sprout, it will be encouraging; but not until we have a grown plant ready for harvesting will we be sure."

"What about the contract?"

"We should ask Cyril for his input; but my opinion is to push everything off until the end of July. If the plants are to grow, they will be grown by then. You will have had time to dry and powder some of the hothouse-grown plants and see if the are still efficacious, (that which produces the desired effect). We don't want to sell a 'pig-in-a-poke' to someone who will hunt us down to extract vengeance."

"I wonder if I will ever be able to follow everything you say... what is a 'pig-in-a-poke'? What is: extract vengeance?"

Paula smiled, "Literally? It is the head of a pig sticking out of a sack of sawdust and stones. It's an expression that means 'to fool somebody'. Extract vengeance is to 'seek revenge'."

"Yes, I agree. We don't want to have vengeful enemies."

"Between Samuel and Kazaii, I think they can manage here. We expect a viable (sufficiently developed to live on its own or workable) product here. But, if we can't sell the seed because the substitute soil with pig dung doesn't nourish the plants, we will have to consider selling the powder, which means a growing operation.

"So, before we get our knickers in a knot (upset), we should have a long talk with Cyril."

Thomas tilted his head and gave her his wry smile saying, "Did you do that on purpose, or can't you help yourself?"

Paula laughed, "I can't help myself. You have such an adorable look on your face when I use expressions."

THOMAS TOOK HER IN his arms and whispered in her ear, "And you drive me to distraction with your 'expressions', so now it is my turn. He began his dance of little kisses over her face, ears and neck and when he finally kissed her lips, she was longing for the soft warm sensuous contact. Together they sunk into a world of emotional bliss. Long pleasurable moments passed while they were pressed tightly together, each wanting the other to make the first move to go further, each held back because the path was a public place. He took her face in his hands, little kissing her cheeks and nuzzling her neck and breathed in her ear, “Soon... but not now.”

He fluffed her hair, kissed her again softly on the lips and took her hand. “We need to get back. Mother has invited neighbors for dinner. I was thinking we could fly to the States after we have settled things with Cyril tomorrow. What do you think?”

Paula stopped, turned to face him and said, “Are you serious? I would love that! We could stay until we have to be back for Hanna and Sara’s graduation. Is it what you want to do?”

“I want to marry you as soon as possible. You could wire your parents that we are coming, so it won’t be too much of a surprise for them...”

Paula looked at him with dismay and panic. He asked, “What’s wrong?”

“You don’t have a passport!”

“What’s a passport?”

“It’s identification that says who you are and it states your nationality, English, and home, Africa. You can’t travel out of Africa without it. You can’t get into England or America without it either.”

“We’ll go back and talk with Father. He will know what to do.”

They found Sir Peter at the barn putting Midnight Rider up. Suffo was getting ready to sponge the horse down.

“Dad, we have a question for you. How do I get a passport? We were thinking of going to the States to tell Paula’s parents our news when she said I had to have a passport.”

Peter smiled at his son. Each day he liked the man his son had become more and more: so direct, so uncomplicated and so open. “When we returned home from Kampala, your mother dug out your old passport from when you were ten. She sent it and a picture of you she had taken with your Polaroid

Camera gift to be renewed. It might be ready to be picked up now. You have to sign it at the Immigration Office, in front of a Notary, before you can have it. Do you remember that your given name is Peter Thomas Caulfield, II? That is the name you must sign on your passport."

"Yes, Jon told me my 'proper' name when we were in the forest on our way home." He looked at Paula and said, "I told you Father would know what to do."

She smiled at Thomas and at Sir Peter, who was beaming from the scant praise. "Are you finished here?" She asked. "We were just going up to the house."

"I always clean up down here. I'll be up soon." Sir Peter replied.

Thomas and Paula left holding hands, and Sir Peter watched them go. He had great hopes that they would settle on the farm for part of the year, for he couldn't see Paula living in a native hut for very long. Mary had the same high hopes, for finally there was someone in the house besides her that loved horses.

Now, if Jon and Anna were to live in Africa for part of the year, all would be well. But, I'm getting ahead of myself; Peter sighed, wishing and planning would not make it so; but enjoying the present fortified the future.

32

Travel Plans

Jon helped Thomas dress for dinner. He was to wear his new clothes for the first time: black tassel loafers, navy hose, medium blue gabardine slacks, a pale pink shirt, navy sports jacket and the ascot Paula had given him. Jon said, "You look terrific! You are going to set the tongues wagging when they get a look at you and your kitu-kina. Let's practice a bit. I'll be a male guest, you be me."

"Jon, how are you? How did you like being a Trader?" (as he shook Thomas' hand)

(Thomas replied as Jon) "I found it to be a lot of traveling in the forest, but I also found my brother."

(Jon said as himself) "You don't need practice, you're better at this than I am. But, if anyone asks you a question that you'd rather not answer, just say, "Why do you ask?" I don't think anyone will be rude enough to say, "Because I want to know, or never ask a question to which you don't want an answer."

Paula had gone down early to give Lady Mary a hand with place cards and the flowers. She wore the one dressy dress she had brought with her to Africa: the indispensable black sheath, with a black and white zebra patterned silk and Angora wrap and black patent leather pumps. She had on a string of pearls and pearl earrings, borrowed from Lady Mary, and her engagement ring. Her simplicity was beguiling. Lady Mary could not have asked for a more charming daughter-in-law to be.

They both turned as Jon and Thomas came into view at the bottom of the staircase in the hall. Both stopped as if frozen in time. Mary did not recognize Thomas until he turned his head and smiled at her. Then her hand flew to her chest and with a great uptake of breath, she said, "Thomas, you look simply marvelous. For a moment, I thought you were your father. Jon, I see your hand in this. Our guests are going to be quite surprised!" She laughed at the thought of her guest's consternation as she approached them.

While Paula, on the other hand had such flutters that she could hardly breathe. How could he get to be more handsome and stunning than he already was? Her feelings of pride in the man who had asked her to be his wife knew no bounds; he turned his smile on her and she smiled back. He held out his hand as she walked towards him saying, "You look like the King of England, but better, taller and more handsome."

Thomas smiled his mocking smile with his head tilted and said, "I am not the one who is wrapped up like a beautiful Egyptian queen, in shades of black and white and gold. With the side of his index finger, he tipped her head back and kissed her on the cheek, saying softly, "This little kiss is taking all my will power; I want to devour you."

Paula chuckled and stepped back, taking his hand, she said to his mother, "Are we finished here?"

Mary said, "Go. I have just a few things to do here."

Jon said, "What about me? Don't I look wonderful too?"

Amid the amused smiles, Mary complimented Jon on his outstanding good looks and Paula remarked on his talent for high fashion.

THOMAS GENTLY TUGGED PAULA away, leading her to the open porch, which surrounded the front half of the house. They sat on the porch swing in the box end of the side porch. "We only have a little time before the guests arrive. I wanted to tell you that Kybo isn't going to the States with us, since he doesn't have a passport, but you probably knew that. I also think Mr. Hanley is right and Kybo has a girlfriend; I'm glad he has settled in here so well. But, Jon wants to go. Is that all right with you? He wants to send a wire to Captain Jones telling him when we will be in Philadelphia, and ask that he and Jonas join us there."

"Oh, Thomas, that would be wonderful, but what about your passport?"

"I asked Mother about it. She said she gave my old passport and the new photo to Mr. Latham. He told her it would only take a few days. It may be ready now. We could head into Nairobi tomorrow, give Mr. Latham a report on the kimmea, and see if the passport is ready."

"Good, I'd like that; just a day trip; right?"

"That's how Jon sees it, down and back the same day if we get an early start."

Cocktails set the tone for the evening. Each arriving guest was like an aunt or uncle that was seeing a lost nephew once again. Thomas handled the hugs, kisses and lusty handshakes with aplomb. I don't remember any of these people, he thought, but they certainly remember me. I seem to have forgotten more than I realized.

Jon was protective and easily fobbed off invasive questions with the "Why do you ask" routine. Once Thomas saw the effectiveness of the rhetorical question, he was able to use it with confidence. None of the guests wanted to embarrass Thomas, but some were a bit obtuse. All in all, it was a most pleasant evening and most of the guests were impressed that Thomas was a medicine man of some renown.

The evening ended at ten, as it was Wednesday and Thursday was a workday. The guests, who were mostly neighbors, were gentlemen farmers too.

Jon, Thomas and Paula took a late walk on the paths through the gardens and planned their day trip to Nairobi.

On the road from the farm, about a half mile before the main road to Nairobi, there was a large mailbox. One side was a large box for outgoing mail and parcels. Each farmer took a day of the week to go to Nairobi for supplies, picking up the outgoing mail and returning with incoming mail. Yesterday, Jon had put a letter in the box for Cyril Latham, to let him know of their impending arrival. This morning, the letter was gone.

Cyril had received Jon's letter and had stopped at the Immigration Office to see if Thomas' passport was ready.

"You have an appointment to pick up your passport just before noon, which will give us time to update your affairs. You go first."

Paula brought Cyril up to speed on the kimmea and the possible problems. "We need to put off finalizing the agreement until the end of July; until we know if the plants will grow and be efficacious."

"What you are doing now, is making sure that the product and information you are selling will be usable to them. I cannot see how they can object to the delay. But, if your efforts look promising, I would like to have a preliminary meeting early in June. I've had a letter from APCO; they want to bid on any herb remedy we want to sell. This is good; but we still need to clarify our position and satisfy the acquisition angst of Corsica Industries; how's Monday, the 13th of June, let's say one in the afternoon?"

"That should be fine," Paula replied, "we plan to arrive back in Nairobi late on the 9th. We will have to go to the farm to see how the plants are doing, which will give us a few days to recover from jet lag. Don't expect all the answers by the 13th, but we can give a progress report and a projection of the possibilities."

"That will have to do, then. I would like you to join me at my club for lunch when you are finished at the Immigration Office. By coincidence, I am having lunch with an eminent herbalist, who may be able to give us some pointers. He is responsible for several European plants being transplanted and grown here in Africa. Maybe he has information that goes the other way. At any rate, it should be interesting talking to him. His name is Miles Cavendish."

Paula drew in a sharp breath, "**The** Miles Cavendish? The author? His books were required reading in college."

Cyril smiled. "I thought you might know him. Yes, **The** Miles Cavendish!"

Conversation at lunch was gratifying. Paula and Miles found kindred souls in one another. "You are doing all the right things with your tests, but you must go one step further. You must see if the seed from the propagated plants will grow and be viable."

Cyril said, "That would mean another three months or a bit more."

"Yes, possibly so; but it is a drop-in-the-bucket-of-time where science is concerned." Miles replied.

Thomas asked, "Why is this second step so important?"

"Because, you have changed the place, nutrients and habitat of the plant; not by much, but enough for a mutation to occur. If all else remains the same, it would show the mutation in the seed."

Jon, who was interested in growing things, asked, "What type of mutation are we talking about here?" as he imagined giant man-eating plants.

Miles smiled and said, "The seed of the plant may no longer retain the special properties that the plant now possesses if it mutates.

"Let me explain," he continued. "When a corm or tuber is brought to Africa, and if the corm or tuber grows here, and if it flowers, you must let the bloom go to seed in order to propagate the species. For, most likely the imported corm or tuber will never blossom–or even grow another year. In the one growing season, the mutation or change needed for the plant to survive in Africa is stored in its seed.

"Now you are dealing with a plant that is already native to Africa, but it is a plant that has special properties. Changing the habitat could produce a change in the seed. So, you see, you must go the extra step: harvest the seed from your hothouse plants and grow viable plants from the hothouse seed. If you can do that, then your test results will be conclusive."

The time passed all too quickly when Cyril said, "I have a one-thirty appointment, so I must go."

"I, too, have another engagement," Miles replied, rising.

"It has been an extraordinary pleasure to meet you, sir. Thank you for your advice. We will definitely do as you say, and grow the seed from the hothouse plants." Paula smiled as she shook his hand.

"My pleasure too, sir" Jon added, as he clasped Miles Cavendish's hand with both of his. Thomas said, "Thank you for sharing your knowledge with us."

Cyril lagged a bit, giving Miles Cavendish time to get out of earshot before he said, "I think it would be best to wait for the 13th before we impart this news to Corsica Industries, if we impart it at all. In the meantime, I'm going to send your diary to another firm for safe-keeping. I feel apprehensive about this unexpected delay."

They left Cyril and went to the Travel Agent, where they found that there was a flight on Saturday at 11am for London, via Cairo. On Sunday, there was a flight for New York at 8am, which arrived at 11am D.S.T. "But there are only first class seats available," said the agent. Jon booked three seats on the spot saying, "If we are going to do this... let's just do it!"

They stopped at the telegraph office and Paula sent a wire to her parents, announcing their arrival in New York on Sunday; while Jon composed a message to Captain Jones, saying they were going to the States... and there was a wedding in the offing, more to follow.

Then Jon took Thomas shopping for casual clothes while Paula bought gifts for her family and friends back home.

Paula was very concerned about her mounting debt to Jon, and on the way back to Dela-Aden, she said, "Jon, I have not paid my way in Africa. You have paid for everything, except for Thomas' watch. I would like for you to figure up how much I owe you so I can pay you when we get to the States."

"Fiddle-de-dee! Why do you want to do that? We are soon

to be family. What's mine is yours–even so, talking about money is a frightful bore."

"But you have put out a good deal of money in my behalf."

"Paula, the money is not even a consideration. I will be insulted if you insist; I refuse to allow you to pay me a farthing."

In the long uncomfortable silence that followed, Paula sulked. She felt a loss of her independence and resented Jon for not allowing her to pay her way. She wasn't family yet!

Jon sighed; he realized he couldn't bully her... whatever made him think he could? It was worth a try though. He had suspected, and rightly, that Paula was not prepared for the expense of independent travel in Africa–and seeing her thin book of traveler's checks, when she paid for Thomas' watch confirmed his suspicions. Even if she had had enough money with her, it would have been a severe trial for Jon to watch her pay her way.

He sighed again and said, "You must promise me two things: one, that you will never, ever tell a living soul, except possibly Mother, what I am about to tell you; and two, after you hear what I say, you will forget about repaying me. Do you both promise?"

Thomas looked at Paula; he knew she was angry, but she was also curious. He smiled his adorable questioning smile at her as he said to Jon, "Yes, I promise."

"If Thomas thinks it proper, then I too, give you my word."

"Well then, let me put your minds at ease. I have a great deal of money, my own money... not Fathers or Mothers. My great aunt, Rebecca Alice Clarke Cecil, who died after her husband, and without issue, left her entire fortune to me. Her husband was a second son who had married her for her money, which was substantial. She wasn't married long when she realized that Alfred had not been in love with her as he had professed. Rebecca was a true romantic and was crushed by his deception. She remained a disappointed woman all of her life. She decided to make sure that I, as a second son, would be able to marry for love.

"I have never told anyone about the money. I have always wanted everyone to think I was spending my parent's money. Only Mother knows the true extent of the inheritance; Father just thinks I have a nice little personal income. Now only three people know, and I want to keep it that way!"

PAULA WAS SITTING IN the second seat alone, for Thomas was up front learning to drive by watching. Now, things make some sense–why Jon was willing to give up his trading venture to go looking for me, when it could have been a big financial loss for him. How he was able to hire special tutors for his African studies while in college. Why he always paid my hotel bills and why he always reserved the best suites. Why he took Thomas to a tailor and had his clothes custom made. Why he bought expensive gifts for Captain Jones and his parents. Why anything Thomas wanted to buy was okay with him. Why his Father did not chastise him for reserving the Penthouse suite in the Mayflower Hotel. Why he never seemed to worry about the future or having a job.

The tea farm I'm sure is prosperous, but a great deal of money was put back into the farm via the vineyard and winery. Profligate spending was nowhere to be seen. Even the horses paid for themselves. Jon's confiding in us, makes me realize that he wants to be thought of as the son of wealthy parents, soon to be a working stiff, like the rest of the world; but he is hardly that.

THEY ARRIVED BACK AT the farm in time for cocktails at seven. It had been a long day, but an exciting one. Peter and Mary were dumfounded when they heard that they were leaving on Saturday for the States.

Thomas followed his Mother into the pantry for more crackers, as Jon was making up for his missed tea. "Mother, I want to tell you that I am planning to marry Paula while we are in the States. We are hoping you and Dad will be able to come to America for the ceremony. Paula thinks you might like to have a marriage ceremony or reception in England too, after Hanna and Sara's graduation, for the family and close friends there. If that is something that would please you and Dad, would you take care of the arrangements? Jon wants us to do this, and to invite the Holmesbys, so he has offered to pay the bill.

Mary looked her son in the eyes and love flooded her as it had when she first saw him again in Kampala, and said, "I would be delighted to do that for you and Paula. As soon as you know the date of your marriage in America, send us a telegram. I don't want to wait for the invitation to arrive by mail. I am going to miss you terribly, but I am happy for your plans." Mary put the crackers and more cheese on a plate and handed Thomas a fresh pitcher of lemon water.

Jon looked relieved when they arrived back in the library saying, "I was getting ready to go and find you. How long can it take to put cheese and crackers on a plate?"

Mary smiled at her always-ravenous son. "How you can eat so much... and stay so slim... is the eighth wonder of the world. You must have worms!"

Friday was a flurry of activity. Paula showed Samuel and Kazaii how to tend the young plants and make the compost. Kazaii had the best garden amongst the natives. His vegetable garden always had extras that he sold to make a bit of spending money. He had asked if he could help with the project as had Samuel, who felt he needed to be in charge, since both the garden shed and greenhouse were his domain.

They were good workers and knew instinctively the right things to do for the seeds planted in the peat pots. Paula explained the making of the compost in an unused wine barrel, which had a galvanized pole through the center and out each end; these ends were supported on a frame eighteen inches off the ground. The piglet manure and fruit rinds with garden and leaf debris, water, and some of the soil dug up from the forest were put in the barrel through a chamfered door on the barrel, which was held in place by clips and wing nuts. Then the barrel was turned a few turns every hour during the workday. At the end of the day, Paula checked on the compost. Samuel and Kazaii were amazed. Most of the leaf and vegetable leavings were gone. Only bits of the rinds and fruit skins were still recognizable. The next morning, the worms had proliferated. More vegetable matter, manure and water were added, for the bulk had been reduced by more than half. Kazaii named the compost barrel: ule matumbo kangi–the garbage eater.

That evening, as she and Thomas sat swinging on the porch before dinner, they saw Kazaii going towards the potting shed–followed by a line of adults and children. He was going to show them the newest wonder on the farm: ule matumbo kangi.

JON HELPED THOMAS LAY out his new clothes in outfits: underwear, socks, shirt and slacks. He had eight changes, two cardigan sweaters, two sport jackets, two neckties and his ascot. The navy blue sport jacket could be worn with the navy blue slacks to make a suit, if needed. And the seersucker sports jacket could be worn with the white duck slacks for casual affairs. His mother and father had given him onyx cuff links, an onyx pinky ring with the family crest and an onyx necktie stud, also with the family crest. Jon had bought him riding breeches and jodhpur boots, which could be worn with the half chaps. His safari clothes would be good summer clothes with his new docksiders. Jon showed him how to pack his new canvas and leather suitcase, and his travel case. His pouches were now in a matching overnight bag with his shaving kit. He had a new wallet, with identification and money and a leather sleeve for his passport.

Then Thomas helped Jon pack and was surprised that Jon packed for himself just as he had packed for Thomas. "Saves having to think about what goes with what? I always pack this way."

WHILE THOMAS WATCHED JON pack his bag, he thought of fishing with Kazaii that morning; and smiled when he remembered Kazaii saying they had to ask permission to fish in the waterfall lake on the farm. Thomas had reasoned with him. "If I am to inherit this land, who is better qualified to fish there than me?" Thomas carried his fishing reel, which was his own invention, with his pouches; so Kazaii got a pail and led him to the lake. His fishing apparatus was an eight inch piece of hollow leg bone about two inches in diameter around which he had wound his fishing line. He had a fat tapered stick that he slid into the hollowed out bone; by pushing the stick into the hollowed out bone, he was able to cast the line out and slow or stop the line feeding out. To bring the line in, he just alternated turning the bone with his hands.

Soon, he had six nice size carp for the special family dinner he was going to cook tonight. He gave a fish to Kazaii, but Kazaii gave the fish back to him saying, "I would like it better cooked."

Once Jon was packed up, they went down to the patio where Thomas had started his fire in the brick barbeque pit. The coals were ready. He went into the kitchen and prepared the fish. Helen assisted when needed. While the fish baked in the coals, (wrapped in aluminum foil, for they had no papyrus on the farm) they joined the others in the Library for cocktails.

"Thomas, I have been meaning to ask you if you need some money." His father asked.

"I've got that covered, Dad," Jon said. "Everything has been taken care of... and when you make your plane reservations to go the States; that too has been paid."

"A bit generous, Jon; are you sure you won't find it a burden?"

"Not at all, Dad; consider it an anniversary present from Thomas and me."

Lady Mary said, "Thank you, Jon. You are quite thoughtful."

The first course of soup was skipped, so that the fish could be served as soon as it came off the grill. Thomas, flanked by Helen, the cook, put the platters and bowls on the table to be served family style. After the first cries of delight from the diners, there was mostly silence. Thomas was worried. His fish tasted like the Pymtu fish, why were they so silent. He looked at Jon, who saw his consternation and said, "We are much too busy eating to talk. This fish is as good, or possibly better, than the Pymtu fish."

Lady Mary said, "I have never, and I do mean never, eaten fish that was so delicious. We must have the recipe."

Peter said, "I'm glad you asked dear, I wasn't sure if Thomas would take me seriously, if I asked for the recipe."

Jon exploded with laughter. "I don't know about Thomas, Father, but the rest of us would have thought it a marvelous joke!" His Father couldn't make toast.

"With Thomas as the cook, we ate food as good as this every night while we were on the trail." Paula said.

Jon said, "Yes, we did, it was amazing."

Peter said, "Surely, you are joshing me."

Kybo, who had earlier taken a cooked fish to Kazaii, and had shared it with him, had returned to bring Kazaii's praise for his one-time pupil. He heard Peter's remark and could not help adding, "The Kigozi is a masterful cook. Captain Jones' cook, Jonas, wanted his recipes. Even Motozo, cook for Max Mason, said he was the best cook of all men who did not cook for a living. Kazaii sends his thanks for your fish and he too, wants the recipe."

Elizabeth gave Kybo some custard for Kazaii when he was leaving, for he had a tryst arranged and did not want to linger.

Thomas smiled, for he had often wondered how a virile young man like Kybo could make do with only being his afisa.

Back in the library for coffee and liqueurs, Jon said, "Well, Thomas, this could be our last story for awhile; what will it be?"

Thomas looked around at his audience. The smiles and anticipation were a boon to his soul. He felt love, as he had from Nanoka and Manutu and he said. "Something happened the other day that reminded me of an old story. It is a story for children who have lost their fathers."

"The Shadow Husband"

"Once there was a place called a beautiful village. All the people in the beautiful village were happy and good workers. There were few disputes, for no one envied his neighbor.

"One day a lone woman arrived at a place called, The Beautiful Village. She was young, she was pregnant and not far from her time. She did not speak the dialect of the village, but an old woman called Soffo knew her words, for she had lived in the stranger's village before she was married. The lone woman told a very sad tale about the people in her village–they had all been taken as slaves. The old ones and the babes had been slaughtered.

"'My husband and I escaped only because we had gone into the wilderness to see the Old Crone, who was thought to be a witch, for a potion to ease my labor.

"'When we returned and saw the carnage, we left to come here to The Beautiful Village, for we knew of it and of Soffo.

"'Along the way, we stopped and saw the old crone again to tell her what had happened. She said to my husband, 'You will have more trouble. If your child is to be born safely, you must hide your wife and take this potion when you come to the danger.'

"'After two days, when we were halfway here, two lions stalked us. My husband put me up a tree and then he took the potion, for he could not kill two lions with just his spear. I listened, but I never heard the lions confront my husband. The lions came and sat under the tree and tried to climb it to reach me, but could not. My husband never came. The lions tired of waiting for me and went away. I came down from the tree and looked for my husband's body, thinking he must be dead, but I never found him.

"'I do not know how I came to be here. I did not know the way. I did not know where there was water or food, but each day I heard a voice in my head, which told me where to find water and food; and each day the same voice told me which

trail to take to get here. I never again saw any beasts, and each evening I found a safe place to sleep.

"'I have a trade that I learned from my mother. I can make rope. She showed the listeners her rope bag, and from it she took other ropes, some made of sisal threads and hair, some of frond stems, but all were beautiful. If you will give me a place to stay, I will pay my way by making ropes for you.'

"The elders did not talk long before they announced. 'Lilith, you will live in the cottage of Soffo, because she can teach you to speak our words; and because she is alone in her cottage, since her husband died a moon ago. She will treat with our people for your services and set a fair price for your wares.'

"Lilith was happy in her new home. For some reason, she did not miss her husband like she thought she would, for he still felt close to her. By the next moon, Lilith had made many rope bags and was more than paying for her keep. Her hands were supple and dexterous and she worked so fast, it was hard to see what she was doing. Soffo liked Lilith for she was quiet and docile.

"In the night, Soffo heard Lilith moan. Thinking, it is her time, she got up and put more wood on the fire and fresh water in a clean pot. She washed her hands and went behind the drape to attend to Lilith.

"She was surprised to see a man sitting beside Lilith holding her hand. "'Who are you? What are you doing here?'

"'I am Lilith's husband.'

"'Where have you been all this time?'

"'I do not know.'

"'What do you mean, you do not know. How can that be?'

"Lilith smiled up at Danii, for that was her husband's name, and he continued. 'I put Lilith up a tree to protect her from the lions and took the potion the old crone had given me to save our child. The next thing I remember is sitting here beside Lilith, and her time has come.'

"'Bah,' said Soffo. What a lot of nonsense.' But she thought: how did he get in here? How did he get past the sentries and my closed door without anyone hearing him? Through the night, they attended the birthing. Early, just before sunlight, a son was born. He was strong and healthy. Lilith was tired but all had gone well. Soffo swaddled the child and laid him in his mother's arms and they both slept. Soffo went off to sleep until the child awoke, for she was old and needed her rest.

"She laid her head down thinking, I am glad Danii was here. He was a big help and his presence calmed Lilith greatly. He did not seem to mind helping with the birth, using his strong hands to help her push. I wish more husbands would be involved in the birth of their children, but maybe Danii is special for he was so calm and encouraging during her agony. It was unusual. Soffo fell to sleep and awoke when the babe cried.

"When she arrived, Lilith was already feeding her son. 'Where did Danii go?' she asked.

"'I told you when I came here. I do not know what happened to Danii.'

"'No, no, I mean, where did he go this morning after he helped you birth your son?'

"Lilith looked at the old woman, who seemed rational enough saying, 'Only you helped me birth my babe in the night. There was no one else.'

"Soffo looked at Lilith. She is speaking the truth, as she knows it, for she is looking at me like I am seeing things. I must keep this to myself. Maybe I dreamed it when I fell asleep... but Soffo knew Danii had been here. There were the footprints of a man's sandals in the rushes beside the bed and they were new rushes yesterday."

The moral of the story is: A father's love will always find a way.

Peter sat bemused. These stories were marvelous. It was an aspect of village life that he had never experienced. He did not think the Kikuyu told stories like this, if they did, he had never heard them. "Was it a custom of the Zuri Watu to tell stories like this? I have not heard our Kikuyu tell such stories."

"I am sure they do, but they would not tell such stories in front of you. They would think it like telling children's stories at a celebration, for most of the stories are learning stories for children."

"That story did not seem like a story you would tell a child."

"Actually, it is a story that is told to a child to let them know that even when their fathers are gone, they still care deeply for their children. I thought of it yesterday when Kazaii was helping his little granddaughter to plant some seeds, and he told me her father had died young."

Paula loved the stories, especially near bedtime. "I am tired, I am going to bed; breakfast at seven–right?"

Sir Peter cleared his throat and arose, "Before you go, we, Mary and I, want you to know that we are hoping you will plan on spending time here with us after you are married. We hope you will consider Dela-Aden your home in Africa until you need to make other plans. Nothing would please us more."

Paula went to Mary and then Peter and gave them hugs, saying, "Nothing would please us more, either. We love it here and we love you for welcoming us."

Thomas followed Paula, giving his father a handshake and a hug and his mother a kiss on her cheek with a big hug, saying, "I feel like I have never been away–and leaving you again is very hard to do."

Jon sat watching the familial moments hoping that one day he and Anna would be the recipients of the same invitation. He had mentioned to his mother that he was thinking of asking Anna to come for an extended visit after graduation, and she had said, "We'd be delighted, dear."

Peter followed Mary up to the master bedroom: a big, bright room with southern exposure over the breakfast room. He took off his cuff links and said, "I'm going to miss them. This house will seem like a mausoleum without them. Did you mind me asking them to live here, when they come back to Kenya?"

I'm one step ahead of you. I think we should encourage them to build a cottage of their own here. Thomas told me that he intends to marry Paula while they are in the States, and he asked us to be there. I accepted. Also, he said, if we would like it, we could have a ceremony in England too, after the girl's graduation, for our family and friends, making sure to invite the Holmesbys."

"He is most considerate, isn't he? We are so blessed!" Peter came out of his dressing room in his pajamas and sat in a club chair by the window. "Did he say when he expected to marry Paula?"

"I asked him to send us notice of the date they plan to marry by telegram. I am looking forward to being there, how about you?"

"Yes, of course. Wouldn't miss it for anything; never been to America; think it would be a jolly good show."

Mary came out of her dressing room in a negligee and matching nightgown, and floated about the room, moving decorative pillows to the chaise longue and turning down the coverlet. She loved fancy lingerie and her figure did justice to the diaphanous drapery. "How nice it would be if both Thomas and Jon decided to settle here for most of each year. We know the girls will get married and go off, but it would be wonderful to have the boys settle here."

"Yes, it would be wonderful," she replied, "but I'm not counting on it until it happens, although I'm not beyond taking out a little insurance."

"What do you mean, Mary... insurance... insurance for what?"

Mary kissed him on the cheek saying, "I have decided to give Paula *Sunshine* for a wedding present, and you are going to offer to build them a cottage in a place of their choosing on the estate."

Peter's eyes widened and his lips formed a smirky smile.

"I never thought of you as devious, Mary... but apparently I'm devious too, for I think those are marvelous ideas."

"Yes, if they have a reason to come back to Dela-Aden... I think they will come and then possibly stay. Nice to daydream about it, isn't it?"

"Yes, but I don't want to set myself up for a disappointment." He reached out and caught her hand and gently tugged her down on his lap.

He kissed her deeply and then nestled his head on her chest, saying, "I'm not as tired as I thought I was."

And Mary smiled.

33

Leaving Africa

PAULA SAT QUIETLY IN the Land Rover, watching the rolling savannah of the Kikuyu Escarpment, with its patches of woods and bush, roll by. She felt dejected. Am I ever going to see this bewitching land again? I've been so content lately. I feel like I've found my niche in life... the place I want to be forever. I'm euphoric that Thomas is going home with me as my betrothed. I already love his family, and I'm so glad they're coming to our wedding in America. So, why do I feel so sad?

THOMAS WATCHED PAULA IN surreptitious glances. Her face was set in lines of stillness, which reflected her thoughts. She is sad that we are leaving Africa; that is good, for it means she will want to come back. I am sad to leave Africa too, and sad to leave Kybo; I am sad to leave my birth family and sadder still that I will not see Manutu for a long time.

They were passing the Ngong Hills and the play of light and shadow cast a purple aura over the trees of the woods spreading into the dales, where a light mist was suspended here and there. I wonder if there will be such mystic beauty in America.

JON, WHO SAT IN the back, back seat of the Land Rover with Kybo listened to the pleasant chatter of his parents, who were still discussing the oddity of the natives lining up to see them off, saying: "They have never done that before, I wonder what it means?"

Kybo, who was usually reticent, said: "Bibi Mzazi, (great

lady) it is done so you will remember each one of them and remember too, they will wait for you to come back."

"Thank you, Kybo, what a lovely sentiment."

Jon became lost in his own thoughts, for in a few weeks, he would be faced with unavoidable decisions. How had he arrived so suddenly at these crossroads? Jon opined sometimes, but never worried, he had always found a way out of tight spots without even thinking about them... but now... he was faced with decisions that would affect not only his heart, but the rest of his life.

Kybo was conflicted about the Kigozi going to the States without him, but the idea of flying such a long way over water had panicked him, for he could not swim and always avoided deep water. He worried too, about going to a land where nothing would be as he knew it... where he would not know what was expected of him... where he could err and not even know it? His guilt had been assuaged by a twist of fate when the kigozi told him he could not go to America with them, for he did not have a passport. The kigozi had said it could take months to get the proper papers and have them processed. Still, the guilt did not completely go away, and Thomas' leaving without him left him feeling forlorn.

Mary was quite excited about going to America for the wedding. She told Peter they could book the seats today on their way home from the airport. She and Paula had meshed calendars and Mary had set Monday the 16th of May as the day to leave Africa, for the wedding on the 22nd. Like Peter, Mary had never been to the States and was thrilled with the reason to go... and by going. She hummed softly to herself as they passed the throngs of natives too-ing and fro-ing beside the Nairobi Road. She was surprised and pleased that Peter had agreed so readily to leave the farm for three weeks; I suppose he feels it will be our usual summer hiatus moved to the spring. She would turn the horses out while they were gone; it would be a vacation for man and beast... and it would give the boys time to whitewash the inside of the barn.

PETER THOUGHT OF ALL those years of gray days, when he had mourned the loss of his son. Now, he was determined not to miss a moment that he could share with him. There was nothing so important that he would miss the wedding of his son in America. From now on, if he was invited into Thomas' life, he would go and thank God for giving him the opportunity.

His attention was needed to avoid the potholes and endless deep ruts in the road, but with his new outlook on life, he felt younger and stronger than he had in years, and he and Mary had never been closer. He had good people on the farm. It would be their chance to show him how well they could manage for him while he was gone. It was a win-win situation and the prospect pleased him.

ONCE SETTLED IN THE Boeing 707, with Thomas in the window seat next to her and Jon in the aisle seat across from her, Paula folded the New York Times to the Thursday puzzle. (It took two days for the newspapers to reach Nairobi.) Thomas was reading a pictorial history of America, which his father had loaned him from his library. Jon was busy with his date book/planner, making notes and reading the mail he had picked up in Nairobi when they had stopped at the Post Office.

Paula's thoughts turned to the travel plans they had made. Jon had insisted they take a commuter plane to Philadelphia from New York, saving her parents two hundred miles of driving.

For a few days, while recovering from jet lag, they could go riding at Fair Hill in the mornings and tend to wedding preparations in the afternoons. Thomas would enjoy the wooded paths and open fields of the bridle trails. Mary had already had Thomas up, and in just one day his body had remembered his seat, leg and foot positions. Like his mother had said, "... he was a born horseman."

She could let him ride Goldie, her Palomino gelding, for

he had gentle hands; Goldie could be more than a handful if kept on the bit.

They had five weeks before the wedding, and could spend three of them traveling across the country. First though, a few day trips or some overnight trips: I want to take them up Hawk Mountain; that would be a good weekend trip for the whole family. We could go to Cape May, at the southern tip of New Jersey and take the Lewes Ferry to Delaware and go to Cape Henlopen, a nice overnight trip. Then we could go to Scott's farm in Fort Valley, Virginia, which backs up to the National Forest, and has great trails for hiking and riding. From Virginia, we could take I64 west, which is a gorgeous drive. I'm sure Mom will let us use the motorhome that she takes to overnight competitions, as she has written that her office work has used up her time to condition for long distance rides this year. That way we won't have to stop at motels and Thomas can cook the food he likes. I'm sure one American cheeseburger will be more than he'll ever want.

We have friends and relatives all the way to California, so we can stop and visit too... but California is just too much driving and too little sightseeing... besides, we can spend a day or two in San Francisco when we fly to California to go to Hawaii for our honeymoon. Thomas has to see the fantastic Redwood forest of Muir Woods and the charming bay town of Sausalito.

I hope Mom is able to get the entries for the competitive ride at Fair Hill the Saturday before our wedding. For Mary and Peter, it will be their first distance ride. Jon and Thomas are not physically conditioned to enjoy it, so they can pit crew for us instead; feeding us, getting water and holding our horses if we have to use the potty. It will be so much fun. Taking pen and paper, she started to organize the daily events.

THOMAS PRETENDED TO BE reading his book, but he was really thinking about the incredible changes in his life since he began his walk to Kenya. But foremost in his mind were his Mother and Father. In just a few days he had felt completely at home, like he had never been gone; but he hadn't remembered his parent's personalities: he had forgotten how quiet and thoughtful his Father could be... he only remembered his bedtime stories and his occasional displeasure. He didn't remember his Mother being so active or so lively at all. He did remember that she had smiled at him often, and she still smiled much of the time. He remembered some of the places on the farm where he and Jon had played, once he saw them again. Kazaii was a strong link for him in bridging the distance between the Zuri Watu and being heir to Dela-Aden. Kazaii's quiet acceptance of him as both Medicine Man and jitu-nundu (big boss) gave him the strength of mind he needed to continue in good spirits through the difficult moments.

He tried to recall more of Paula's parents when they had been on the beach together, but at the time, he had had other things to occupy his attention and he only remembered Charles as being well spoken and witty. He remembered Lisa as haughty and narrow-minded. Well, I'm not going to lose any sleep over her. I will see her for a few days only, and after that, not often. I can handle that. He looked over and saw that Jon was asleep with his headphones on. Jon loved classical music and was making the most of his time to listen to it once again.

Jon, dear Jon; no wonder I never forgot his voice. He is like my inner self. I'm so glad he wanted to come with us. I am even happier that Paula does not mind. She accepts Jon, as a part of me, for that is what he is, the mirror image of my soul. I thought he might want to go to England to see Anna Louise, but I sense his reluctance to face her issues with living in Africa.

It was a surprise to learn that he did not need the job as Chairman of the Board to afford homes in England and Africa. According to Mother, he is wealthier than all of their family put together. She said to me, "Even your Father isn't aware of his vast wealth. He just thinks he is comfortably well off. I'm surprised that he told you. He had sworn me to complete secrecy."

He remembered how his answer had astounded his Mother. "I think he had to tell us, for his wedding gift to us was to pay all of the expenses for our wedding, including transportation for you and Dad to America, our traveling expenses and our honeymoon. Paula said she wouldn't hear of it, so that is when he had to tell us. Even so, she was reluctant, but Jon was so downhearted and disappointed that she finally gave in... and accepted his generous gift."

Only yesterday, Jon told me that he intends to fly to England after our wedding to spend the time with Anna Louise; intending to base himself at the Hall with Aunt Margaret and Uncle George until the Croft School graduation.

PLEASED WITH HIS IMMEDIATE future, Thomas put his head back and let his thoughts drift to being completely alone with Paula in Hawaii, and with a smile on his lips, he daydreamed... remembering tender moments.

34

America

Paula sat on a big rock with her arms hugging her bent knees. It was the first pull-off on the Skyline Drive from the entrance in Front Royal, Virginia. "Yesterday, when we were riding on the mountain ridge behind Scott's farm, you asked me, 'How far is that ridge over there?' and I replied, about twenty-five miles. Well, you are now looking at the ridge we were riding yesterday, when we were looking at this one."

Jon was taken with the spectacular view across the valley that wound down between the mountain ridges. Yesterday, after they had passed through Little Crease on the trail, they had been able to see the mountains that lined the Shenandoah Valley to the west, which going north ended in Strasburg at Signal Knob, which was the high bluff ending of the ridge and used as a message relay point in the Civil War; going south the ridge continued into North Carolina. Today, the ridge of the mountain chain they were traveling continued south into Western North Carolina, but the destination today was Luray and the Luray Caverns.

Thomas said, "I was wondering if I would ever see anything as beautiful as Africa when we were here... but the scenery here is just as beautiful as Africa... it is just very different. I liked sitting on the high porch last night waiting for the deer and the black bears to come and eat the corn. It was like waiting for the elephants in the trees."

Paula smiled. She remembered how astonished and dismayed Thomas had been when they landed in New York and later Philadelphia. Nairobi is the equivalent of a sprawling Appalachian town compared to either New York or Philadelphia. She could see him gather his resolve and determination to be of good cheer and take it all in stride... for it was only going to be for a short time.

Jon, ever the world traveler, enjoyed everything and was able to explain many facts to Thomas, some of which, Paula didn't even know. I am so glad he came with us. Everything is so much nicer when Jon is around. He is so urbane and yet so simplistic, I am going to miss him in Hawaii... and she smiled at the inane thought.

Paula had called AAA when they had arrived and AAA had sent a complete itinerary, triptick, and tourbooks listing interesting stops along the way. Tomorrow they planned to take the Interstate south and then west to Louisville, Kentucky, traveling on back roads to Cairo, Illinois, and on secondary roads to St. Joseph, Missouri, where they could pick up the Interstate System to Omaha, Nebraska, going through Kansas to Colorado. Paula wanted them to see the Rocky Mountains and Breakheart Pass as well as Independence Pass through Mount Massive into Leadville from Aspen. Out to Las Vegas and then take the northern route to come back home. It was a lovely time to be traveling: the flowering trees and the bright yellow forsythia would be blooming, along with the daffodils and jonquils, which grew in mass profusion in the road divides.

Jon and Paula took turns driving the Motorhome. Paula liked to drive in the morning and rest on the sofa after lunch, for she had gotten used to napping at mid-day in Africa. Jon rested, but rarely napped, as he felt it spoiled his sleep at night. Thomas kept up a constant flow of chatter while they drove for he enjoyed being a perpetual passenger, gazing out the windows to his heart's content. Jon was a marvel at translating maps to roads, and once he had the route in his mind, he needed no help in navigating.

Paula lay with her eyes closed and, to the muted sounds of soft conversation, reminisced about the family dinner on Sunday evening, when they had arrived at her home. The evening had been an incredible success. The whole family had turned out for the event including Uncle David and his wife Aunt Isabel (Bela) and their two sons, Dave and Chuck. Sallee Ann and Mother had made a turkey, Thanksgiving style, with all the trimmings. Thomas and Jon delighted in experiencing the American tradition and the festive meal.

Mother made her one special meal: baked ham and a macaroni and cheese casserole with Brussels sprouts saying, "With all the busy plans, we won't have time to cook... and this makes great leftovers."

Sallee Ann had cleaned up her studio so Jon and Thomas could use the old trundle bed up there, with Peter and Mary in the guest room. She would stay in her room with Sallee Ann; Scott and Eric would be in their old room; a full house, but lots of fun.

Uncle David had enlightened the family about Thomas and Jon while they waited for us to arrive, so Thomas and Jon were the ones who had to get to know the others. Jon with his urbane British wit was an instant hit, while Thomas charmed them with his incredible presence and polite dignity. I think Thomas was taken aback when Dad asked him to tell a story after dinner, "What I remember most about Africa," he said, "was the story telling. Would you share a story with us tonight?"

Thomas hesitated, so I asked him to tell us the story of Shawna. "You said that story was one of your favorites, and it is a wonderful verbal picture of the people of Africa." The story about the wayward boy was a hit. You could see it in the eyes and the attention of the listeners. Most had never been to Africa, but the story made them feel as if they knew Africans. I think it was the moment when Thomas began to feel at ease in America. He had been on tenterhooks and hadn't even known it.

I think he and Jon are truly enjoying themselves now, especially after last weekend when we all hiked up Hawk Mountain. Jon had refused to try rappelling, but Thomas had made a short drop to a ledge, before climbing back up again. Everyone had cheered for him and Scott and Eric had slapped him on the back in a manly fashion, which was a new experience for Thomas. Both the Africans and British are stuffy about men touching men. He has been smiling a lot and that is good. She smiled too, once again anticipating Hawaii, before she dozed off.

35

The Excitement

THE WEATHER WAS A delight. It was a sunny day, but cool, which was perfect for horse and rider. Lady Mary was riding Sallee Ann's half Arabian Pinto gelding, with Sir Peter on Charles's big gray Arabian gelding; Lisa rode her half Arabian, half Saddlebred Palomino mare and Paula rode Goldie.

Lisa had asked that their group be allowed to go off last. The other riders had drawn starting positions, but it was not a problem... usually no one wanted to go last anyway. Stallions were allowed to go off first, for it kept them from being downwind of mares that might be in season. Paula led the little group, for Goldie was not one to trail after his barn buddies, with Lisa bringing up the rear. Paula knew the pace to set, a mile every 9 minutes, to accomplish a 6.5 mph average. She set her watch to noon and pushed the stem in when she passed the starting line.

The average horse walks slowly at 2 mph, normally at 3 mph and briskly at 4 mph. Lisa had ponied her young horses off Paula's Missouri Fox Trotter, Goldie, whose flat walk was 5 mph uphill or down, and whose running walk went from 6 mph to 10 mph. This ability of their horses to walk out made it easier for the horses to keep up the pace, so they only had to trot the good level stretches with an occasional fun canter up short hills or in the open fields. A horse trots from 6 mph, which is slow, to 10 mph, which is normal, and from 12 mph to 18 mph, which is fast, except for the racing breeds, which are faster still. The trails are marked for mileage every 5 miles and every mile for the last 5 miles to the finish, which translates into doing 5 miles every 45 minutes, which still includes a good bit of trotting given the terrain; but the strategy of where and when to trot is important.

In a Competitive Trail Ride, you can finish last and still be Grand Champion, for you are riding against yourself. You must bring your horse back as near as possible to the condition in which he was vetted before he went out. Any change is noted and a deduction is made for the degree of change. So, if your *hydration skin pinch* was a *one* before you went out, and it is a *one* when you come back, there is no deduction; and if you can do that for every section of the score sheet, you win. Each horse starts out at 100, and points are deducted for the changes. The horse with the *least* deductions, wins.

Lisa won her division, taking a first in middleweight. Lady Mary won her division, taking a first in lightweight division. I placed third, middleweight. Peter took a fifth in the heavyweight division. To get the divisions, all riders are weighed with tack. Then, the riders are listed in order of weight: the first one-third of the list becomes the lightweight division; the second one-third becomes the middleweight division; and the last one-third becomes the heavyweight division. [No advantage is gained or lost by weight division; the heaviest rider must bring back his horse in as good a condition as the lightest rider.]

You think this unfair? Well, consider this. If a horse is conditioned with a heavyweight rider up, he will be in better condition than a horse that was conditioned with a lightweight rider up, that did exactly the same work. [To have a horse *conditioned* by a heavyweight rider, and then *competed* by a lightweight rider, will most definitely increase the horse's ability in competition.] Grand Champion went to the first place heavyweight rider, a long-time friend, Mary Coleman, who had bred, raised and trained her horse herself.

An incredible surprise was seeing Captain Jones and Jonas at the finish line. They had arrived in Philadelphia on Thursday and had called and talked to Sallee Ann. She had concocted the surprise at the finish line... knowing distractions were not good before a ride. Paula was thrilled to see them; happy that they had been able to come to America for their special day.

But, for Captain Jones, attending the wedding was a special treat, for without children of his own, he thought of Paula as the daughter he would have liked to have had, and felt his 'cup runeth over' with pride and joy.

The more he knew of this young woman, the more he admired her. Thomas and Jon had caught them up on the news while they were waiting for the riders at the finish line. After vetting, they had Italian hoagies, chips and sodas for the rider's meal with homemade brownies for dessert. Sallee Ann had called the ride manager and ordered extras for guests from Africa. To everyone's surprise, Jon was asked to tell a story about their adventures in Africa. The normally routine Awards Ceremony became a huge hit. Jonas was disappointed that Kybo was still in Africa, but Eric, Paula's twin brother, had come over after his half-day at the Vet Clinic, and had played a game of stones with him; Jonas won... but not easily.

Tired, but elated, they went home, cared for the horses, then showered and gathered in pajamas and robes for a nightcap. Sir Peter was full of excitement from the competition, saying: "I wish we had those rides in Africa. We certainly have the land for it."

Lady Mary asked Lisa. "Is there a lot to do to set up a ride?"

"Yes and no," she replied, "for a first ride I would say yes, but the succeeding rides would be less work. Once you have a good trail set up and accurately measured, it comes down to keeping it cleared." The paper work is pretty much the same each time. Getting workers and Vets could be a problem. The Vets are required to take a course on judging, so are the lay judges; but I would imagine you don't have a sanctioning body in Africa. You could probably import someone who could get you started."

Paula added. "When we get back to Kenya, I'll look into it for you, if you like."

Both Peter and Mary were happy to hear her volunteer. It was what they were hoping for... and had tossed out running rides as another enticement.

Sir Peter added. "We imagined that America would be like London... but it is more like the English countryside, except that your villages are new instead of hundreds of years old; and instead of being clustered together, they are spread out over the whole area. We are looking forward to Philadelphia and Washington next week. It makes me wish we had more time to spend here. You have been simply grand hosts. We hope you will come to Africa some day and let us return the hospitality."

Lady Mary added her compliments and then said. "Twenty five miles doesn't sound like much... until you do it. I'm ready for bed." She rose, and was accompanied by Sir Peter, who was saying; "We have a big day tomorrow."

The next day, after church services, Paula Mahree Thornton would marry Peter Thomas Caulfield, II, at 2 p.m. Thomas would wear his white dinner jacket, black tux slacks and cummerbund, as would Jon, his Best Man. Paula had purchased a white silk shantung dress with a balloon overskirt and a small pillbox hat with veil and white patent leather pumps. Sallee Ann, the Maid of Honor wore her long black taffeta skirt with the full-sleeved white silk blouse that she wore for concerts.

The reception, for about a hundred people, was held at the Red Rose Inn in Jennersville, where the couple would spend their honeymoon night. Monday morning, they would leave for Hawaii, and Jon would leave for England. Captain Jones, on Sallee Anne's advice, had rented a station wagon, so they could drop Jon and the honeymooners off at the airport in the morning on their way back to Rittenhouse Square, where Jonas would continue his visit with his mother. On Tuesday, Captain Jones planned to fly to Florida to visit his brother and his family. Jonas would join him there later in the week for the flight back to Africa.

Paula was in a state of bliss as she leaned her head against Thomas' shoulder in the first class seats aboard the Boeing 707. It had been an early morning after a short night and while tired, Paula had never been happier. She was glad they had arranged a suite at the Fairmont Hotel in San Francisco. She would never have been able to tolerate another six-hour flight from San Francisco to Hawaii on the same day. Life kept on getting better for her. She had never imagined such rapture, or that loving another person as she loved Thomas could bring so much joy.

Thomas felt Paula nestle her head on his shoulder, not an easy thing to do in these wide first class seats, but he had skooched over to be closer to her. Soon, she let her seat back and was sound asleep. He was not far behind her, but his thoughts wouldn't let go of his memories of last night. He had never imagined such passion could exist, for he had been exalted to a plane far above any previous experience. He had felt insatiable, only to be met by a similar desire.

She was his... and he was hers... forever. Life was good!

THE END

Glossary

Acolyte	Follower – Helper
Afisa	Aide
Afrikaner	Person of South Africa (white)
Afrikaans	Language of South Africa
Asante	Thanks!
Assagi	Zulu spear
Bahariki	Sea Goddess or Sea Witch
Belgian Horses	Goldie & Sunny (for landaulet in Douala)
Bibi	Lady
Boma	Thorn bush fence
Bwana	Master – Sir
Chief Egemea	Story of Fatimi
Chukikibeti	Hairy Ones (malicious dwarfs)
Chungu	Earthen pot – chamber pot
Conchos	Silver or ivory bases for harness fittings
Corsica Industries	Conglomerate bidding on the herbal remedies
Croft School	Private College in England for young ladies
Dawamtu	Medicine man
Dela-Aden	Name of Caulfield farm in Kenya
Déjà Vu	Memory distortion – event has happened before

Fatimi	Story of selfish, egocentric woman
Gojani	Large edible leaves (like Swiss Chard)
Grande Hotel	Yaoundé, Cameroon, West Africa
Hakika	Reality
Haliiki	Goddess of Nature
Hippo Grooves	Channels made by hippos from the river to land
Jambo	Hello or Goodbye (casual like: hi or bye)
Jambo-nataz	Goodbye or Goodnight
Jitu-nundu	Big boss
Joined	Mental connection
Just Cause	Expedition yacht for biological research
Jumbe	Chief
Kabaka	King (in Uganda, Africa)
Kakabara	Tribal lands
Kali-taz	Unfriendly warriors (Dzem)
Kiazitaz	Potato pancakes
Kijiko	Pygmy eating spoon-stick (teak)
Kimmea	Plant to relieve anxiety; a sleep aid
Kisha	Assistant to the Leader
Kitamba(s)	Light cloaks worn toga-like by men
Kitu-Kina	Cape from the Spirits
Kiveo	Toilet/rest room
Kowanya	Nut, bacon & liver fried treats
Kupatwa	Vulnerable
Kuteka	Rapacious
Kwa heri	Goodbye – Godspeed
Lanai	Roofed platform (attached to a hut)

Landaulet	Four wheel carriage with seats facing each other
Maarifa	Hygiene
Mafuu	Crazy
Manyoya	Nap
Marahaba	Many thanks
Mbogo	Large spinach-like leaves for roll-ups
Mhudumu	Acolyte
Mitiriki	Tree Goddess
Mjeni	Visitors
Mkuu	Chef - Cook
Monts Mitumba	Mountains of the Moon – to 17,000 feet
Mshenzi	Boor
Mtu	Man
Mtumishi	Manservant
Muhogo	Large edible tuber (like a rutabaga)
Na	And
Ndugui	Brother
Nyelamosi	Hairy Ones: (the Chukikibeti)
Ongokea	Be well
Peke-yake	Unusual
Piataz	Top caretaker
Roam	Tamubu traveling as a spirit
Safi-Mitiriki	White Tree Goddess
Saying-Paula's Gymnastic Coach	"Go lightly; never show off... and you'll always be a winner."

Segued (seg'way)	To change or pass without a break
Shamba	Farm
Shauri Ovu	Machinations
Shuka	Loincloths for women (Pygmy)
Shukrani	I am grateful to you (Thank you)
Shukuru	I thank you
Siasa	Careful
Sudd	Thick floating river/pond vegetation
Tamutunda	Cakes made of dates, coconut, honey and farina
Tupashindo	Slingshot
Ule matumbo kangi	The garbage eater (a compost barrel)
Uumenea	Penis covers (Pygmy)
Uzingizi	Rest
Walinka	Throwing club
Wanyama	Vermin

Characters & Names

Ahidjo, President	New President of Cameroon: Jan. 1, 1960
Arthur	Caretaker & cook for The Just Cause
Athos, Mr.	Owner of the luxury yacht, The Gallant Lady
Caulfield ancestral estate	Woleston Hall – foot of the Cotswold Hills near Lyford in Berkshire, England (S.W.)
Caulfield, Jonathan (Jon)	Younger brother of Thomas Caulfield, a.k.a. Tamubu

Caulfield, Lady Mary	Mother of Thomas, Jon and twins: Hanna & Sara
Caulfield, Sir Peter	Father of Thomas (Tamubu), Jon and twins: Hanna & Sara
Caulfield, Thomas	(a.k.a. Tamubu) Older brother of Jon, Hanna & Sara
Cavendish, Miles	African herbalist and author
Chumley, Mrs. Anna	Owner, Port-Gentil Guest House; friend of Captain Jones
Comtesse DuVries	Deceased employer of Ben and his mother, Maybella
Croft School, The	Private Ladies College at Bath in Somerset, England
Elizabeth	Housekeeper at Dela-Aden, Kenya
Expedition yacht	The Just Cause
Farah	Indian restaurateur in Nairobi, Kenya
Gallant Lady	Name of Mr. Athos' 167' ocean going luxury yacht
George	Office manager and Sir Peter's Secretary
Gloria	Secretary to Cyril Latham, Esq.
Hanley	Overseer of farm workers at Dela-Aden, Kenya
Helen	Cook at Dela-Aden, Kenya
Holmesby Family	Harold (Mr.), Julia (Mrs.), Anna Louise (daughter); from Swindon in Wiltshire, England (S.W.)
Hunter, Mr.	Mercenary hired to steal Paula's diary
Just Cause	62' sailing yacht with laboratory for biological Expedition
Jones, Captain Hannibal	Skipper of the Wind Drift (deceased wife, Beth)

Jones, M.D., Edwin	Captain Jones' brother in St. Augustine, Florida
Kybo bin Kimbo	(Kybo, son of Kimbo) Afisa (aide) to Tamubu
Landaulet	Ben's horse drawn carriage
Latham, Cyril Esq.	Attorney, Rue de la Maison, Nairobi, Kenya
Mason, Max	African Trader and partner to Jon Caulfield
Miles, Ph.D., George	Leader of the 'plant finding' expedition to Africa
Safi-Mitiriki	White Tree Goddess – Tamubu's name for Paula
Schweitzer, Dr. Albert	Founder of the Leper Colony and hospital at Lambaréné in Gabon, West Africa
Shoby, Mr.	Grande Hotel manager in Yaoundé, Cameroon, West Africa
Simmons	Caulfield Estate Manager of Dela-Aden, Kenya. East Africa
Smith, Max	Henchman for the mercenary: Mr. Hunter
Tamubu, a.k.a. Thomas	Medicine Man of the Great Zuri Watu – Tribal name of Thomas Caulfield, son of Lady Mary and Sir Peter Caulfield of Kenya, Africa
Thornton, Charles Scott	Paula's father; College Professor, Inventor
Thornton, Charles Scott, Jr.	Paula's eldest brother, U.S. Air Force Pilot
Thornton, Esq., David	Paula's Uncle – Patent attorney; wife Isabel (Bela); sons: Dave and Chuck
Thornton, Eric Arlen	Paula's twin brother, Veterinarian

Thornton, Lisa Wagner	Paula's mother; tax accountant, horseman
Thornton, Paula Mahree	Protagonist; gymnast, cliff-face climber, biologist
Thornton, Sallee Anne	Paula's older sister; artist, pianist, fashion designer
Wind Drift III	95' luxury motor yacht of Captain Hannibal Jones

Horses' Names

Belgian Horses	Goldie and Sunny (for landaulet in Douala, Cameroon)
Diablo-Aire (Wind Devil)	Light Bay Dutch Warmblood stallion: 17.3hh
Galahad*	7 year-old Dutch Warmblood & Andalusian gelding**
Golden Boy	Paula's Palomino gelding at home in Oxford, PA
Midnight Rider	Sir Peter's 15.3hh black Arabian gelding
Paladin*	6 year-old Dutch Warmblood & Andalusian gelding**
Sunshine	Palomino pleasure horse at Dela-Aden
The Wizard	Lady Mary's 17hh gelding (Dutch Warmblood & Thoroughbred) Sport Horse – 3 day eventer
Wind Dancer	6 year-old gray Arabian gelding belonging to Edward, the Kabaka's eldest son who is twelve

*Matched Pair (Bred and trained by Lady Mary – sold to the Kabaka in Kampala, Uganda, Africa.

** Full brothers

Native Characters

Bahati	Djoumani – Kutoto's Lieutenant
Ben	Carriage driver (called Baba by his son, Gomojo)
Ben's Mother	Maybella
Bolbonga	Chief of the Ndezi
Bonomo	Wahutu scout
Bubé	Cab driver in Yaoundé – friend of Gangis
Chandi	Sick 8yr-old daughter of Pymtu Chief, Mzutu
Chavo	Groom for the Kabaka in Kampala
Chief Agnozo	Duibo Tribe/daughter m. Chief Chabo's son
Chief Chabo	Djoumani Tribe/son m. Chief Agnozo's daughter
Chief Kuteka	Wahutu Tribe
Chief Mzutu	Pymtu Tribe on River Kom
Countess DuVries	Employer of Ben and Maybella
Dalitta	Kybo's girlfriend at Dela-Aden
Danaii	Character – Story of Shadow Husband
Diembo, Mr.	Barn manager for the Kabaka in Kampala
Djoumani Scouts	Dodi/lead scout & Efo
Elizabeth	Cook at Dela-Aden
Farah	Indian Restaurateur in Nairobi
Fatimi	Story Character who wanted to be Chief

Fulani	Tribe of lads: Kabanza, Kasuku, Mguru& Nashutu
Gangis	Mule cart taxi driver in Yaoundé
George	Secretary to Sir Peter Caulfield
Gloria	Secretary to Cyril Latham, Esq.
Gomojo	Carriage groom, Son of Ben & Tirini
Gretchen	Maid at Grand Hotel in Yaoundé
Gubo	Wahutu scout sent to fetch Tamubu back
Hanley	Overseer at Dela-Aden
Helen	Cook at Dela-Aden
Hemeti	Beggar in Lomie
Homoso	Scout Leader/Djoumani
Jordan, Mr.	Bank Manager in Luanda, Angola
Kaaka Lands	North of Lomie, Cameroon
Kira	First wife of Bolbonga, Chief of the Ndezi
Kutoto	Djoumani Captain who died on the trail
Kybo	Nigerian (Ibo) aide (afisa) to Tamubu 6'6" 250#
Lester	Secretary to the Kabaka in Kampala
Lilith	Character – Story of the Shadow Husband
Manutu	Medicine Chief of the Zuri Watu
Maybella	Ben's Mother; Caretaker of the cemetery cottage
Mbili	Shy boy in Wahutu village
Motozo	Cook for Traders Max & Jon
Muklu	Gielli Pygmy "Keeper of Legends"

Nanoka	Zuri Watu adopted mother of Tamubu
Nashini	Kybo's cousin m. Wahutu warrior
Norunda	Bube's (taxi driver in Yaoundé) wife
Odouri	Medicine Man in Pymtu village
Ovidio, Mme. Rosata	Translator in Wahutu village
Pandi, Mr.	Douala Hotel Manager
Pimio	Wahutu Scout
Pygmy Guides	Asu, Ocha of Gielli Clan
Robergo	Yaoundé policeman
Rubio	Cab driver in Luanda – knows Kybo
Ruffo	Duibo – Kybo's host in Lomie
Sabuno	Bully boy in Wahutu village
Samuel	Head gardener at Dela-Aden
Sashono	Zuri Watu Chief, adopted father of Tamubu
Shoby, Mr.	Grand Hotel Manager in Yaoundé, Cameroon
Simmons	Estate Manager at Dela-Aden, Kenya
Suffo	Character – Story of The Shadow Husband
Tirini	Ben's wife – Gomojo's mother
Troli	Wife of Gangis – cab driver in Yaoundé
Tundee	Umpiti Medicine Man
Umpopo	Hall steward at Lomie Lodge, Cameroon

Native Tribes

In Order Of Appearance

Ndezi	The tribe that abducted Paula from the cove
Zuri Watu	The tribe that found and raised Tamubu
Wahutu	Tribe near Douala of Kybo's cousin, Nishani
Umpiti	Yaoundé tribe – helped to elude mercenary
Machozi	First village stop on trek to Kenya
Gamboula	Tribe between Yaoundé and Lomie
Duibo	Hosts to Kybo at Lomie – helped with escape
Kaaka	Tribe north of Lomie
Dzem	Tribe east of Lomie (unfriendly)
Gielli Pygmies	Evening hosts – Story of "Fire"
Djoumani	Tribe of warriors – provide bearers & canoes – River Kom
Chukikibeti	Hairy dwarfs – tree dwellers – flesh eaters
Pymtu	Tribe on River Kom – provide bearers & supplies

Breinigsville, PA USA
17 February 2010

232706BV00001B/1/P